Dear Reader,

Good news! Prince Cha[...] the pages of the Silhou[...] fact, in this collection of three [...] of royal romance, you'll find no less than *three* [...] hearts and souls are as loyal to the women they love as they are to the crowns they serve.

The collection begins with "Night of Love," a classic novel by international bestselling author Diana Palmer. In this breathtaking book, you'll meet Steven Ryker, a mesmerizing man who is duty bound to protect a mysterious Middle Eastern sheik—and determined to take one more night of passion from the woman he has always loved.

Next, Joan Elliott Pickart pairs up one of her beloved MacAllister brood with a prince in "A Wish and a Prince." Look for more books in the MacAllister family saga coming to Silhouette Special Edition in 2002. You also won't want to miss Silhouette's continuity, CROWN AND GLORY, beginning in Silhouette Special Edition in April 2002.

In Linda Turner's "Royally Pregnant," you'll become intimately acquainted with the royal family of Montebello as a gardener's daughter falls in love with a royal duke— and finds herself carrying his secret child. You won't want to miss this story, as it kicks off ROMANCING THE CROWN, a brand-new, twelve-book continuity featuring the royal family of Montebello, starting in January 2002 in Silhouette Intimate Moments.

We hope you enjoy this collection, as well as all the wonderful stories of royal romance coming to Silhouette Books in 2002.

Happy reading!

The Editors at Silhouette Books

DIANA PALMER

has a gift for telling the most sensual tales with charm and humor. With over 40 million copies of her books in print, Diana Palmer is one of North America's most beloved authors and is considered one of the top ten romance authors in America. Diana's hobbies include gardening, archaeology, anthropology, iguanas, astronomy and music. She has been married to James Kyle for over twenty-five years, and they have one son.

JOAN ELLIOTT PICKART

is the author of over eighty-five novels. She is a two-time Romance Writers of America RITA Award finalist. Her highly successful books in the MacAllister family saga continue in 2002 in Silhouette Special Edition and Desire. When she isn't writing, she has tea parties, reads stories, plays dress up—and the list goes on—with her young daughter, Autumn. Joan also has three grown daughters and three wonderful little grandchildren. Joan and Autumn live in a small town in the high pine country of Arizona.

LINDA TURNER

began reading romances in high school and began writing them one night when she had nothing else to read. She's been writing ever since. Single and living in Texas, she travels every chance she gets, scouting locales for her books. This bestselling author's next book, The Man Who Would Be King, will lead off the ROMANCING THE CROWN continuity for Silhouette Intimate Moments in January 2002.

DIANA PALMER

JOAN ELLIOTT PICKART
LINDA TURNER

CROWNED HEARTS

WITHDRAWN

Silhouette Books

Published by Silhouette Books

America's Publisher of Contemporary Romance

Special thanks and acknolwedgment are given to Linda Turner for her contribution to the ROMANCING THE CROWN series.

SILHOUETTE BOOKS

CROWNED HEARTS

Copyright © 2001 by Harlequin Books S.A.

ISBN 0-373-48452-6

The publisher acknowledges the copyright holders of the individual works as follows:

NIGHT OF LOVE
Copyright © 1993 by Diana Palmer

A WISH AND A PRINCE
Copyright © 2001 by Joan Elliott Pickart

ROYALLY PREGNANT
Copyright © 2001 by Harlequin Books, S.A.

Visit Silhouette at www.eHarlequin.com

Printed in U.S.A. PAP
ROMANCE
6/17

CONTENTS

NIGHT OF LOVE
Diana Palmer

For Judy

Dear Reader,

It is a pleasure to share a book with Linda Turner and Joan Elliott Pickart in this *Crowned Hearts* anthology. My contribution is "Night of Love," which features not only a mysterious and very important politician from a Middle Eastern nation, but also the goofiest secret agent I ever created. Both the politician and the agent later ended up in books of their own, but this is the one that started the trilogy.

In it, Steven Ryker owns an aircraft corporation in Wichita, Kansas, which makes fighter jets. His client is a mysterious diplomat who is being pursued by enemies who want to overthrow his country's government. This puts not only Steven but also his ex-fiancée, Meg Shannon, right into the line of fire. She is "rescued" by Lang, the secret agent, who manages to make enemies of just about everybody else in the book with his antics. The end of the book features an unmasking of several characters, and the suspense is just part of the fun.

I adored all these characters, and I love seeing them in print once more. I hope you enjoy this collection of "regal" Silhouette stories!

Your biggest fan,

Diana Palmer

Prologue

Steven Ryker paced his office at Ryker Air with characteristic energy, smoking a cigarette that he hated while he turned the air blue in quiet muttering. A chapter of his life that he'd closed the door on four years past had reopened, leaving his emotional wounds bare and bleeding.

Meg was back.

He didn't recognize his own fear. It wasn't a condition he'd ever associated with himself. But things had changed. He'd gone through a period of mourning when Meg had walked out on him to begin a balletic career in New York. He'd consoled himself with woman after willing woman. But in the end, he'd been alone with the painful memories. They hurt, and because they still hurt, he blamed Meg. He wanted her to suffer as he had. He wanted to see her beautiful blue eyes fill with tears, he wanted to see pain on that exquisite face framed by soft blond hair. He wanted consolation for the hell she'd put him through by leaving without a word when she'd promised to be his wife.

He put out the cigarette. It was a habit, like loving Meg. He hated both: cigarettes and the blond memory from his past. He'd never had a woman jilt him. Of course, he'd never asked a woman to marry him, either. He'd been content to live alone, until Meg had kissed him in gratitude for the present he'd given her when she turned eighteen. His life had turned over then.

Their fathers, hers and his, had become business partners when Meg was fourteen and her brother, David, just a little older. The families had developed a closeness that tied their lives together. Meg had been a sweet nuisance that Steven had tolerated when he and David had become best friends. But the nuisance grew up into a beautiful, regal woman who'd melted the ice around his hard heart. He'd given everything he was, everything he had, to Meg. And it hadn't been enough.

He couldn't forgive her for not wanting him. He couldn't admit that his obsession with her had all but cost him his sanity when she left. He wanted vengeance. He wanted Meg.

There would be a way to make her pay, he vowed. She'd hurt her leg and couldn't dance temporarily. But that ballet company she worked for was in real financial straits. If he played his cards right, he might yet have that one magical night in Meg's arms that he'd dreamed of for years. But this time, it wouldn't be out of love and need. It would be out of vengeance. Meg was back. And he was going to make her pay for what she'd made of him.

Chapter 1

Meg was already out of humor when she went to answer the phone. She'd been in the middle of her exercises at the bar, and she hated interruptions that diverted her concentration. An injury had forced her into this temporary hiatus at her family home in Wichita, Kansas. It was hard enough to do the exercises in the first place with a damaged ligament in her ankle. It didn't help her mood when she picked up the receiver and found one of Steven Ryker's women on the other end of the line.

Steven, the president of Ryker Air, had been playing tennis all afternoon with Meg's brother, David. He'd obviously forwarded his calls here. It irritated Meg to have to talk to his women friends at all. But then, she'd always been possessive about Steven Ryker; long before she left Wichita for New York to study ballet.

"Is Steve there?" a feminine voice demanded.

Another in a long line of Steve's corporate lovers, no doubt, Meg thought angrily. Well, this one was going to become a lost cause. Right now.

"Who's calling, please?" Meg drawled.

There was a pause. "This is Jane. Who are you?"

"I'm Meg," she replied pertly, trying not to laugh.

"Oh." The voice hesitated. "Well, I'd like to speak to Steve, please."

Meg twirled the cord around her finger and lowered her voice an octave. "Darling?" she purred, her lips close to the receiver. "Oh, darling, do wake up. It's Jane, and she wants to speak to you."

There was a harsh intake of breath on the other end of the line. Meg stifled a giggle, because she could almost read the woman's mind. Her blue eyes twinkled in her soft oval face, framed by pale blond hair drawn into a disheveled bun atop her head.

"I have *never...!*" An outraged voice exploded in her ear.

"Oh, you really should, you know," Meg interrupted, sighing theatrically. "He's so *marvelous* in bed! Steven, darling...?"

The phone was slammed in her ear loud enough to break an eardrum. Meg put a slender hand over her mouth as she replaced the receiver in its cradle. Take that, Steven, she thought.

She turned and walked gingerly back into the room David had converted from the old ballroom into a practice room for his sister. It didn't get a lot of use, since she was in New York most of the year now, but it was a wonderfully thoughtful extravagance on her brother's part. David, like Meg, had shares in Ryker Air. David was a vice president of the company as well. But the old family fortune had been sacrificed by their late father in an attempt to take over the company, just before his death. He'd lost, and the company had very nearly folded. Except for the uncanny business acumen of Steven Ryker, it would have. Steve pulled the irons out of the fire and made the company solvent. He owned most of it now. And he should, Meg thought charitably. Heaven knew, he'd worked hard enough for it all these years.

As she exercised, Meg felt wicked. She shouldn't have caused Steve problems with his current love. They hadn't been engaged for four years, and she'd long ago relinquished the right to feel possessive about him.

Pensively she picked up her towel and wrapped it around her long, graceful neck, over the pink leotard she wore with her leg warmers and her pitiful-looking toe shoes. She stared down at them ruefully. They were so expensive that she had to wear her old ones for practice, and anyone seeing her in them would be convinced that she was penniless. That was almost the truth. Because despite the shares of stock she held in Ryker Air—the company that Steven's father and Meg and David's father had founded jointly—Meg *was* practically destitute. She was only a minor dancer in the New York ballet company she'd joined just a year ago, after three years of study with a former prima ballerina who had a studio in New York. She had yet to perform her first solo role. Presumably when she passed that landmark, she'd be higher paid, more in demand. Unless she missed a jump, that was, as she had a week ago. The memory was painful, like her ankle. That sort of clumsiness wasn't going to get her any starring roles. And now she had the added worry of getting her damaged tendon back in shape.

The exercise, recommended and outlined by a physical therapist, was helping. But it was torturously slow, and very painful, to exercise those muscles. It had to be done carefully, too, so that she wouldn't damage them even further.

She went back into her disciplined exercises with a determined smile still on her face. She tried to concentrate on fluidity of movement and not the inevitable confrontation when Steve found out what she'd said to his girlfriend. Her whole life seemed to have been colored by him, since she was fourteen and their fathers had become business partners. Her father had worshiped Steven from the beginning. So had David. But Meg had hated him on sight.

For the first few years, she'd fought him tooth and nail, not bothering to hide her animosity. But on the eve of her eighteenth birthday, things had changed between them quite suddenly. He'd given her a delicate pearl necklace and she'd kissed him for it, a little shyly. Except that she'd missed his lean cheek and found his hard, rough mouth instead.

In all fairness, he'd been every bit as shocked as Meg. But instead of pulling away and making a joke of it, there had quite suddenly been a second kiss; one that couldn't be mistaken for anything but a passionate, almost desperate exchange. When it ended, neither of them had spoken. Steven's silver eyes had flashed dangerously and he'd left the room abruptly, without saying a single word.

But that kiss had changed the way they looked at each other. Their relationship had changed, too. Reluctantly, almost helplessly, Steven had started taking her out on dates and within a month, he proposed marriage. She'd wanted ballet so much by that time that despite her raging desire and love for Steve, she was torn between marriage and dancing. Steven, apparently sensing that, had turned up the heat. A long bout of lovemaking had almost ended in intimacy. Steven had lost control and his unbounded ardor had frightened Meg. An argument had ensued, and he'd said some cruel things to her.

That same evening, after their argument, Steven had taken his former mistress, Daphne, out on the town very publicly, and an incriminating photo of the couple had appeared in the society column of the daily newspaper the next day.

Meg had been devastated. She'd cried herself to sleep. Rather than face Steven and fight for a relationship with him, she'd opted to leave and go to New York to study ballet.

Like a coward, Meg had run. But what she'd seen spoke for itself and her heart was broken. If Steven could go to another woman that quickly, he certainly wasn't the type to stay faithful after he was married. Steven had been so ardent that it was miraculous she was still a virgin, anyway.

All of those facts raised doubts, the biggest one being that Steven had probably only wanted to marry her to keep all the stock from the partnership in the family. It had seemed quite logical at the time. Everyone knew how ambitious Steven was, and he and his father hadn't been too happy at some of the changes Meg's father had wanted to make at the time of the engagement.

Meg had gone to New York on the first plane out of Wichita, to be met by one of her mother's friends and set up in a small apartment near the retired prima ballerina with whom she would begin her studies.

Nicole, meanwhile, met Steve for coffee and explained that Meg had left town. Afterward, Meg heard later, Steven had gotten roaring drunk for the first, last and only time in his life. An odd reaction for a man who only wanted to marry her for her shares of stock, and who'd thrown her out of his life. But Steven hadn't called or written, and he never alluded to the brief time they'd spent as a couple. His behavior these days was as cold as he'd become himself.

Steve hadn't touched her since their engagement. But his eyes had, in a way that made her knees weak. It was a good thing that she spent most of her time in New York. Otherwise, if she'd been around Steven very much, she might have fallen headlong into an affair with him. She wouldn't have been able to resist him, and he was experienced enough to know that. He'd made sure that she kept her distance and he kept his. But the lingering passion she felt for him hadn't dimmed over the years. It was simply buried, so that it wouldn't interfere with her dreams of becoming a prima ballerina. She'd forced herself to settle; she'd chosen not to fight for his love. Her life since had hardly been a happy one, but she told herself that she was content.

Steve still came to the Shannon house to see David, and the families got together at the annual company picnics and benefits. These days, the family meant Steven and his mother and Meg and her brother David, because the older Shannons were dead now.

Mason Ryker, Steven's father, and John and Nicole Shannon had died in the years since Meg went to New York; Mason of a heart attack, and John and Nicole in a private plane crash the very year Meg had left Wichita. Amy Ryker was as protective of Meg as if she'd been her mother instead of Steve's, but she lived in West Palm Beach now and only came home when she had to. She and Steven had never really been able to bear each others' company.

Steven had women hanging from the chandeliers, from what Amy told Meg on the occasions when she came to New York to watch Meg dance. He was serious about none of them, and there had never been a whisper of a serious commitment since his brief engagement to Meg.

Meg herself had become buried in her work. All she lived and breathed was the dance. The hours every day of grueling practice, the dieting and rigid life-style she lived made relationships difficult if not impossible. She often thought she was a little cold as a woman. Since Steven, she'd never felt her innocence threatened. Men had dated her, of course, but she was too conscious of the dangers to risk the easy life-styles some of the older dancers had once indulged in. These days, a one-night stand could be life-threatening. Besides, Meg thought sadly, only Steven had ever made her want intimacy. Her memories of him were devastating sometimes, despite the violent passion he'd shown her the last time they'd been together.

She stretched her aching muscles, and her mind wandered back to the mysterious Jane who'd telephoned. Who the hell was Jane? she wondered, and what did Steven want with someone who could speak that haughtily over the phone? She pictured a milky little blonde with a voluptuous figure and stretched even harder.

It was time to take off the lean roast and cottage

potatoes she was cooking for supper by the time David walked in the door, still in his tennis outfit, looking as pleasant and jovial as ever. He had the same coloring his sister had, but he was shorter and a little broader than she.

He grinned at her. "Just thought I might mention that you're in it up to your neck. Steve got a call while we were at his house, and your goose is about to be cooked."

She stopped dead in the hall as Steven Ryker walked in behind her brother. Steve was a little over six feet tall, very dark and intimidating. He reminded her of actors who played mobsters, because he had the same threatening look about him, and even a deep scar down one cheek. It had probably been put there by some jealous woman in his checkered past, she thought venomously, but it gave him a rakish look. Even his eyes were unusual. They were a cross between ice blue and watered gray, and they could almost cut the skin when they looked as they did at the moment. The white shorts he was wearing left the muscular length of his tanned, powerful legs bare. A white knit shirt did the same for his arms. He was incredibly fit for a man on the wrong side of thirty-five who sat at a desk all day.

Right now he looked very casual, dressed in his tennis outfit, and that was the most deceptive thing about him. He was never casual. He always played to win, even at sports. He was also the most sensuous, sexy man she'd ever known. Or ever would. Just looking at him made her weak-kneed. She hid her reaction to him as she always had, in humor.

"Ah, Steven." Meg sighed, batting her long eyelashes at him. "How lovely to see you. Did one of your women die, or is there some simpler reason that we're being honored by your presence?''

"Pardon me while I go out back and skin a rock," David mumbled with a grin, diving quickly past his sister in a most ungentlemanly way to get out of the line of fire.

"Coward!" she yelled after him as the door slammed.

"You wouldn't need protection if you could learn to keep your mouth shut, Mary Margaret," Steven said with a cool smile. "I'd had my calls forwarded here while I was playing tennis. Jane couldn't believe what she'd heard, so she telephoned my home again and got me. It so happened David and I had stopped back by the house to look at a new painting I'd bought. I canceled the call forwarding just in time— or I might have been left in blissful ignorance."

She glared at him. "It was your own fault. You don't have to have your women telephone you here!"

The glitter in his eyes got worse. "Jealous, Meg?" he taunted.

"Of you? God forbid," she said as casually as she could, and with a forced smile. "Of course I do remember vividly the wonderful things you can do with your hands and those hard lips, darling, but I'm quite urbane these days and less easily impressed."

"Careful," he warned softly. "You may be more vulnerable than you realize."

She backed down. "Anyway," she muttered, "why don't you just take Jane Thingamabob out for a steak and warm her back up again?"

"Jane Dray is my mother's maiden aunt," he said after a minute, watching her reaction with amusement.

"You might remember her from the last company picnic?"

Meg did, with horror. The old dowager was a people-eater of the first order, who probably still wore corsets and cursed modern transportation. "Oh, dear," she began.

"She is now horrified that her favorite great-nephew is sleeping with little Meggie Shannon, who used to be such a sweet, innocent child."

"Oh, my God," Meg groaned, leaning against the wall.

"Yes. And she'll more than likely rush to tell *your* great-aunt Henrietta, who will feel obliged to write to my mother in West Palm Beach and tell her the scandalous news that you are now a scarlet woman. And my mother, who always has preferred you to me, will naturally assume that I seduced you, not the reverse."

"Damn!" she moaned. "This is all your fault!"

He folded his arms over his broad chest. "You brought it on yourself. Don't blame me. I'm sure my mother will be utterly shocked at your behavior, nevertheless, especially since she's taken great pains to try to make up for the loss of your own mother years ago."

"I'll kill myself!" she said dramatically.

"Could you fix supper first?" David asked, sticking his head around the kitchen door. "I'm starved. So is Steve."

"Then why don't the two of you go out to a restaurant?" she asked, still reeling from her horrid mistake.

"Heartless woman." David sighed. "And I was so looking forward to the potatoes and roast I can smell cooking on the stove."

He managed to look pitiful and thin, all at the same time. She glared at him. "Well, I suppose I can manage supper. As if you need feeding up! Look at you!"

"I'm a walking monument of your culinary skills," David argued. "If I could cook, I'd look healthy between your vacations."

"It isn't exactly a vacation," Meg murmured worriedly. "The ballet company I work for is between engagements, and when there's no money to pay the light bill, we can't keep the theater open. Our manager is looking for more financing even now."

"He'll find it," David consoled her. "It's an established ballet company, and he's a good finance man. Stop brooding."

"Okay," she said.

"Do we have time to shower and change?" David asked.

"Sure," she told him. "I need to do that myself. I've been working out all afternoon."

"You push yourself too hard," Steve remarked coolly. "Is it really worth it?"

"Of course!" she said. She smiled outrageously. "Don't you know that ballerinas are the ideal ornament for rich gentlemen?" she added, lying through her teeth. "I actually had a patron offer to keep me." She didn't add that the man had adoption, not seduction, in mind, and that he was the caretaker at her apartment house.

Incredibly Steve's eyes began to glitter. "What did you tell him?"

"That I pay my own way, of course." She laughed. She held on to the railing of the long staircase and leaned forward. "Tell you what, Steve. If you play your cards right, when I get to the top of the ladder and start earning what I'm really worth, I'll keep *you*."

He tried not to smile, but telltale lines rippled around his firm, sculptured mouth.

"You're impossible." David chuckled.

"I make your taciturn friend smile, though," she added, watching Steve with twinkling eyes. "I don't think he knew how until I came along. I keep his temper honed, too."

"Be careful that I don't hone it on you," he cautioned quietly. There was something smoldering in his eyes, something tightly leashed. There always had been, but when he was around her, just lately, it threatened to escape.

She laughed, because the look in those gunmetal-gray eyes made her nervous. "I won't provoke you, Steven," she said. "I'm not quite that brave." He scowled and she changed the subject. "I'm sorry about Aunt Jane," she added with sincere apology. "I'll call her and explain, if you like."

"There's no need," he said absently, his gaze intent on her flushed face. "I've already taken care of it."

As usual. She could have said it, but she didn't. Steven didn't let grass grow under his feet. He was an accomplished mover and shaker, which was why his company was still solvent when others had gone bankrupt. She made a slight movement with her shoulders and proceeded up the staircase. She felt his eyes on her, but she didn't look back.

When Meg had showered and changed into a lacy white pantsuit, she went back downstairs. She'd left her long blond hair in a knot, because she knew how much Steven disliked it up. Her blue eyes twinkled with mischief.

Steve had changed, too, and returned from his house, which was barely two blocks away. He was wearing white slacks with a soft blue knit shirt, and he looked elegant and unapproachable. His back was broad, his shoulders straining against the expensive material of his shirt. Meg remembered without wanting to how it had felt all those years ago to run her hands up and down that expanse of muscle while he kissed her. There was a thick pelt of hair over his chest and stomach. During their brief interlude, she'd learned the hard contours of his body with delight. He could have had her anytime during that one exquisite month of togetherness, but he'd always drawn back in time. She wondered sometimes if he'd ever regretted it. Secretly she did. There would never be anyone else that she'd want as she had wanted Steve. The memories would have been bittersweet if they'd been lovers, but at least they might fill the emptiness she felt now. Her life was dedicated to ballet and as lonely as death. No man touched her, except her ballet partners, and none of them excited her.

She'd always been excited by Steven. That hadn't faded. The past two times she'd come home to visit David, the hunger she felt for her ex-fiancé had grown unexpectedly, until it actually frightened her. *He* frightened her, with his vast experience of women and his intent way of looking at her.

He turned when he heard her enter the room, with a cigarette in his hand. He quit smoking periodically, sometimes with more success than others. He was restless and high-strung, and the cigarette seemed to calm him. Fortunately, the house was air-conditioned and David had, at Meg's insistence, added a huge filtering system to it. There was no smell of smoke.

"Nasty habit," she muttered, glaring at him.

He inclined his head toward her with a mocking smile. "Doesn't your great-aunt Henrietta dip snuff…?"

She sighed. "Yes, she does. You look very much as your father used to," she murmured.

He shook his head. "He was shorter."

"But just as somber. You don't smile, Steve," she said quietly, and moved gracefully into the big front room with its modern black and white and chrome furniture and soft honey-colored carpet.

"Smiling doesn't fit my image," he returned.

"Some image," she mused. "I saw one of your vice presidents hide in a hangar when he spotted you on the tarmac. That lazy walk of yours lets everyone know when you're about to lose your temper. So slow and easy—so deadly."

"It gets results," he replied, indicating that he was aware of the stance and probably used it to advantage with his people. "Have you seen a balance sheet lately? Aren't you interested in what I'm doing with your stock?"

"Finance doesn't mean much to me," she confessed. "I'm much more interested in the ballet company I'm working with. It really is in trouble."

"Join another company," he said.

"I've spent a year working my way up in this one," she returned. "I can't start all over again. Ballerinas don't have that long, as a rule. I'm going on twenty-three."

"So old?" His eyes held hers. "You look very much as you did at eighteen. More sophisticated, of course. The girl I used to know would have died before she'd have insinuated to a perfect stranger that she was sharing my bed.''

"I thought she was one of your women," Meg muttered. "God knows, you've got enough of them. I'll bet you have to keep a computer file so you won't forget their names. No wonder Jane believed I was one of them without question!"

"You could have been, once," he reminded her bluntly. "But I got noble and pushed you away in the nick of time." He laughed without humor. "I thought we'd have plenty of time for intimate discoveries after we were married. More fool me." He lifted the cigarette to his mouth, and his eyes were ice-cold.

"I was grass green back then," she reminded him with what she hoped was a sophisticated smile. "You'd have been disappointed."

He blew out a soft cloud of smoke and his eyes searched hers. "No. But you probably would have been. I wanted you too badly that last night we were together. I'd have hurt you."

It was the night they'd argued. But before that, they'd lain on his black leather sofa and made love until she'd begged him to finish it. She hadn't been afraid, then. But he hadn't. Even now, the sensations he'd kindled in her body made her flush.

"I don't think you would have, really," she said absently, her body tingling with forbidden memories as she looked at him. "Even so, I wanted you enough that I wouldn't have cared if you hurt me. I was wild to have you. I forgot all my fears."

He didn't notice the implication. He averted his eyes. "Not wild enough to marry me, of course."

"I was eighteen. You were thirty and you had a mistress."

His back stiffened. He turned, his eyes narrow, scowling. "What?"

"You know all this," she said uncomfortably. "My mother explained it to you the morning I left."

He moved closer, his lean face hard, unreadable. "Explain it to me yourself."

"Your father told me about Daphne," she faltered. "The night we argued, she was the one you took out, the one you were photographed with. Your father told me that you were only marrying me for the stock. He and your mother cared about me—perhaps more than my own did. When he said that you always went back to Daphne, no matter what, I got cold feet."

His high cheekbones flushed. He looked...stunned. "He told you that?" he asked harshly.

"Yes. Well, my mother knew about Daphne, too," she said heavily.

"Oh, God." He turned away. He leaned over to crush out his cigarette, his eyes bleak, hopeless.

"I knew you weren't celibate, but finding that you had a mistress was something of a shock, especially when we'd been seeing each other for a month."

"Yes. I expect it was a shock." He was staring down into the ashtray, unmoving. "I knew your mother was against the engagement. She had her heart set on helping you become a ballerina. She'd failed at it, but she was determined to see that you succeeded."

"She loved me..."

He turned, his dark eyes riveting to hers. "You ran, damn you."

She took a steadying breath. "I was eighteen. I had

reasons for running that you don't know about.'' She dropped her eyes to his broad chest. ''But I think I understand the way you were with me. You had Daphne. No wonder it was so easy for you to draw back when we made love.''

His eyes closed. He almost shuddered with reaction. He shook with the force of his rage at his father and Meg's mother.

''It's all water under the bridge now, though,'' she said then, studying his rigid posture with faint surprise. ''Steve?''

He took a long, deep breath and lit another cigarette. ''Why didn't you say something? Why didn't you wait and talk to me?''

''There was no point,'' she said simply. ''You'd already told me to get out of your life,'' she added with painful satisfaction.

''At the time, I probably meant it,'' he replied heavily. ''But that didn't last long. Two days later, I was more then willing to start over, to try again. I came to tell you so. But you were gone.''

''Yes.'' She stared at her slender hands, ringless, while her mind fought down the flood of misery she'd felt when she left Wichita. The fear had finally defeated her. And he didn't know...

''If you'd waited, I could have explained,'' he said tautly.

She looked at him sadly. ''Steve, what could you have said? It was perfectly obvious that you weren't ready to make a real commitment to me, even if you were willing to marry me for your own reasons. And I had some terrors that I couldn't face.''

''Did you?'' he asked dully. He lifted the cigarette to his chiseled mouth and stared into space. ''Your

father and mine were involved in a subtle proxy fight
about that time, did anyone tell you?''

"No. Why would they have needed to?''

"No reason,'' he said bitterly. "None at all.''

She hated the way he looked. Surely what had happened in the past didn't still bother him. His pride
had suffered, though, that might explain it.

She moved closer, smiling gently. "Steve, it was
forever ago,'' she said. "We're different people now,
and all I did really was to spare us both a little embarrassment when we broke up. If you'd wanted me
that badly, you'd have come after me.''

He winced. His dark silver eyes caught hers and
searched them with anguish. "You're sure of that.''

"Of course. It was no big thing,'' she said softly.
"You've had dozens of women since, and your
mother says you don't take any of them any more
seriously than you took me. You enjoy being a bach-
elor. If I wasn't ready for marriage, neither were
you.''

His face tautened. He smiled, but it was no smile
at all. "You're right,'' he said coldly, "it was no big
thing. One or two nights together would have cured
both of us. You were a novelty, you with your innocent body and big eyes. I wanted you, all right.''

She searched his face, looking for any trace of soft-
ening. She didn't find it. She hated seeing him that
way, so somber and remote. Impishly she wiggled her
eyebrows. "Do you still? Feel like experimenting?
Your bed or mine?''

He didn't smile. His eyes flashed, and one of them
narrowed a little. That meant trouble.

He lifted the cigarette to his lips one more time,
drawing out the silence until she felt like an idiot for

what she'd suggested. He bent his tall frame to put it out in the ashtray, and she watched. He had beautiful hands: dark and graceful and long-fingered. On a woman's body, they were tender magic...

"No, thanks," he said finally. "I don't like being one in a queue."

Her eyebrows arched. "I beg your pardon?"

He straightened and stuck his hands deep into his pockets, emphasizing the powerful muscles in his thighs, his narrow hips and flat stomach. "Shouldn't you be looking after your roast? Or do you imagine that David and I don't have enough charcoal in our diets already?"

She moved toward him gracefully. "Steve, I dislike very much what you've just insinuated." She stared up at him fearlessly, her eyes wide and quiet. "There hasn't been a man. Not one. There isn't time in my life for the sort of emotional turmoil that comes from involvement. Emotional upsets influence the way I dance. I've worked too hard, too long, to go looking for complications."

She started to turn away, but his lean, strong hands were on her waist, stilling her, exciting her.

"Your honesty, Mary Margaret, is going to land you in hot water one day."

"Why lie?" she asked, peering over her shoulder at him.

"Why, indeed?" he asked huskily.

He drew her closer, resting his chin on the top of her blond head, and her heart raced wildly as his fingers slid slowly up and down from her waist to her rib cage.

"What if I give in to that last bit of provocation?" he whispered roughly.

"What provocation?"

His teeth closed softly on her earlobe, his warm breath brushing her cheek. "Your bed or mine, Meg?" he whispered.

Chapter 2

Meg wondered if she was still breathing. She'd been joking, but Steve didn't look or sound as if he were.

"Steve…" she whispered.

His eyes fell to her mouth as her head lay back against his broad chest. His face changed at the sound of his name on her lips. His hands on her waist contracted until they bruised and his face went rigid. "Mouth like a pink rose petal," he said in an oddly rough tone. "I almost took you once, Meg."

She felt herself vibrating, like drawn cord. "You pushed me away," she whispered.

"I had to!" There was anger in the silvery depths of his eyes. "You blind little fool." He bit off the words. "Don't you know why even now?"

She didn't. She simply stared at him, her blue eyes wide and clear and curious.

He groaned. "Meg!" He let out a long, rough breath and forcibly eased the grip of his lean hands and pushed her away. He shoved his hands into his pockets and stared for a long time into her wide, guileless eyes. "No, you don't understand, do you?" he said heavily. "I thought you might mature in New York." His eyes narrowed and he frowned. "What was that talk about some man wanting to keep you, then?"

She smiled sheepishly. "He's the caretaker of my apartment house. He wanted to adopt me."

"Good God!"

She rested her fingers on his arms, feeling their strength, loving them. She leaned against him gently with subdued delight that heightened when his hands came out of his pockets and smoothed over her shoulders. "There really isn't room in my life for complications," she said sadly. "Even with you. It wouldn't be wise." She forced a laugh from her tight throat. "Besides, I'm sure you have all the women you need already."

"Of course," he agreed with maddening carelessness and a curious watchfulness. "But I've wanted you for a very long time. We started something that we never finished. I want to get you out of my system, Meg, once and for all."

"Have you considered hiring an exorcist?" she asked, resorting to humor. She pushed playfully at his chest, feeling his heartbeat under her hands. "How about plastering a photo of me on one of your women…?"

He shook her gently. "Stop that."

"Besides," she said sighing and looping her arms around his neck, "I'd probably get pregnant and there'd be a scandal in the aircraft community. My career would be shot, your reputation would be ruined and we'd have a baby that neither of us wanted." Odd that the threat of pregnancy no longer terrified her, she thought idly.

"Mary Margaret, this is the twentieth century," he murmured on a laugh. "Women don't get pregnant these days unless they want to."

She turned her head slightly as she looked up at him, wide-eyed. "Why, Mr. Ryker, you sound so sophisticated. I suppose you keep a closetful of supplies?"

He burst out laughing. "Hell."

She smiled up at him. "Stop baiting me," she said. "I don't want to sleep with you and ruin a beautiful friendship. We've been friends for a long time, Steve, even if cautious ones."

"Friend, enemy, sparring partner," he agreed. The smile turned to a blank-faced stare with emotion suddenly glittering dangerously in his silver eyes. His chest rose and fell roughly and he moved a hand into the thick hair knotted at her nape and grasped it suddenly. He held her head firmly while he started to bend toward her.

"Steve..." she protested uncertainly.

"One kiss," he whispered back gruffly. "Is that so much to ask?"

"We shouldn't," she whispered at his lips.

"I know..." His hard mouth brushed over hers slowly, suggestively. His powerful body went very still and his free hand moved to her throat, stroking it tenderly. His thumb tugged at the lower lip that held stubbornly to its mate and broke the taut line.

Her hands pressed at his shirtfront, fascinated by warm, hard muscle and a heavy heartbeat. She couldn't quite manage to push him away.

"Mary Margaret," he breathed jerkily, and then he took her mouth.

"Oh, glory...!" she moaned, shivering. It was a jolt like diving into ice water. It burned through her body and through her veins and made her go rigid with helpless pleasure. He was far more expert than he'd been even four years ago. His tongue gently probed its way into the warm darkness of her mouth and she gasped at the darting, hungry pressure of its invasion. He tasted of smoke and mint, and his mouth was rough, as if he'd gone hungry for kisses.

While she was gathering up willpower to resist him, he reached down and lifted her in his hard arms, crushing her into the wall of his chest while his devouring kisses made her oblivious to everything except desire. At the center of the world was Steve and his hunger, and she was suddenly, shockingly, doing her very best to satisfy it, to satisfy him, with her arms clinging helplessly around his neck.

He lifted his mouth to draw in a ragged breath, and she hung there with swollen lips, wide-eyed, breathing like a distance runner.

"If you don't stop," she whispered unsteadily, "I'll tear your clothes off and ravish you right here on the carpet!"

Despite his staggering hunger, the humor broke through, as it always had with her, only with her. There had never been another woman who could make him laugh, could make him feel so alive.

"Oh, God, why can't you shut up for five minutes?" he managed through reluctant laughter.

"Self-defense," she said, laughing, too, her own voice breathless with traces of passion. "Oh, Steve, can you kiss!" she moaned.

He shook his head, defeated. He let her slide down his body to the floor, close enough to feel what had happened to him.

"Sorry," she murmured impishly.

"Only with you, honey," he said heavily, the endearment coming easily when he never used them. He held her arms firmly for a minute before he let her go with a rueful smile and turned away to light another cigarette. "Odd, that reaction. I need a little time with most women. It was never that way with you."

She hadn't thought about it in four years. Now she had to, and he was right. The minute he'd touched her, he'd been capable. She'd convinced herself that he never wanted her, but her memory hadn't dimmed enough to forget the size and power of him in arousal. She'd been a little afraid of him the first time it had happened, in fact, although he'd assured her that they were compatible in every way, especially in that one. She didn't like remembering how intimate they'd been, because it was still painful to remember how it had all ended. Looking back, it seemed impossible that he could have gone to Daphne after they argued, unless...

She stiffened as she remembered how desperately he'd wanted her. Had he been so desperate that he'd needed to spend his desire with someone else?

"Steve," she began.

He glanced at her. "What?"

"What you said, earlier. Was it difficult for you," she said slowly. "Holding back?"

"Yes." His face changed. "Apparently that didn't occur to you four years ago," he said sarcastically.

"A lot of things didn't occur to me four years

ago,'' she said. She felt a dawning fear that she didn't
want to explore.

"Don't strain your memory," he said with a mocking smile. "God forbid that you might have to recon-
sider your position. It's too damned late, even if you
did.''

"I know that. I wouldn't...I have my career.''

"Your career." He nodded, but there was something disconcerting in the way he said it, in the way
he looked at her.

"I'd better see about the roast," she murmured,
retreating.

He studied her face with a purely masculine appreciation. "Better fix your lipstick, unless you want David making embarrassing remarks.''

"David is terrified of me," she informed him. "I
once beat him up in full view of half our classmates.''

"So he told me, but he's grown.''

"Not too much." She touched her mouth. It was
faintly sore from the pressure of his hard kisses. She
wouldn't have expected so much passion from him
after four years.

"Did I hurt?" he asked quietly. "I didn't mean
to.''

"You always were a little rough when we made
love," she recalled with a wistful smile. "I never
minded.''

His eyes kindled and before he could make the
move his expression telegraphed, she beat a hasty re-
treat into the kitchen. He was overwhelming at close
range, and she couldn't handle an affair with him. She
didn't dare try. Having lived through losing him once,
she knew she'd never survive having to go through it
again. He still wanted her, but that was all. She was

filed under unfinished business, and there was something a little disturbing about his attitude toward her. It wasn't quite unsatisfied passion on his part, she thought nervously. It was more like a deeply buried, long-nurtured vendetta.

It was probably a good thing that she was going back to New York soon, she thought dimly. And not a minute *too* soon. Her knees were so wobbly she could barely walk, and just from one kiss. If he turned up the heat, as he had during their time together, she would never be able to resist him. The needs she felt were overpowering now. She was a woman and she reacted like one. It was her bad luck that the only man who aroused her was the one man she daren't succumb to. If Steve really was holding a grudge against her for breaking off their engagement, giving in to him would be a recipe for disaster.

Supper was a rather quiet affair, with Meg introspective and Steven taciturn while David tried to carry the conversation alone.

"Can't you two say something? Just a word now and again while I try to enjoy this perfectly cooked pot roast?" David groaned, glancing from one set face to the other. "Have you had another fight?"

"We haven't been fighting," Meg said innocently. "Have we, Steve?"

Steven looked down at his plate, deliberately cutting a piece of meat without replying.

David threw up his hands. "I'll never understand you two!" he muttered. "I'll just go see about dessert, shall I? I shall," he said, but he was talking to himself as he left the room.

"I don't want any," she called after him.

"Yes, she does," Steve said immediately, catching her eyes. "You're too thin. If you lose another two or three pounds, you'll be able to walk through a harp."

"I'm a dancer," she said. "I can't dance with a fat body."

He smiled gently. "That's right. Fight me." Something alien glittered in his eyes and his breathing quickened.

"Somebody needs to," she said with forced humor. "All that feminine fawning has ruined you. Your mother said that lines of women form everywhere you go these days."

His eyes contemplated his coffee cup intensely and his brow furrowed. "Did she?" he asked absently.

"But that you never take any of them seriously." She laughed, but without much humor. "Haven't you even thought about marrying?"

He looked up, his expression briefly hostile. "Sure. Once."

She felt uncomfortable. "It wouldn't have worked," she said stiffly. "I wouldn't have shared you, even when I was eighteen and naive."

His eyes narrowed. "You think I'm modern enough in my outlook to keep a wife and a mistress at the same time?"

The question disturbed her. "Daphne was beautiful and sophisticated," she replied. "I was green behind the ears. Totally uninhibited. I used to embarrass you…"

"Never!"

There was muted violence in the explosive word. She glanced up at him curiously. "But I did! Your father said that's why you never liked to take me out in public..."

"My father. What a champion." He lifted the cold coffee to his lips and sipped it. It felt as cold as he did inside. He looked at Meg and ached. "Between them, your mother and my father did a pretty damned good job, didn't they?"

"Daphne was a fact," she replied stubbornly.

He drew in a long, weary breath. "Yes. She was, wasn't she? You saw that for yourself in the newspaper."

"I certainly did." She sounded bitter. She hated having given her feelings away. She forced a smile. "But, as they say, no harm done. I have a bright career ahead of me and you're a millionaire several times over."

"I'm that, all right. I look in the mirror twice a day and say, 'lucky me.'"

"Don't tease."

He turned his wrist and glanced at the face of the thin gold watch. "I have to go," he said, pushing back his chair.

"Are you off to a business meeting?" she probed gently.

He stared at her without speaking for a few seconds, just long enough to give him a psychological advantage. "No," he said. "I have a date. As my mother told you," he added with a cold smile, "I don't have any problem getting women these days."

Meg didn't know how she managed to smile, but she did. "The lucky girl," she murmured on a prolonged sigh.

Steve glowered at her. "You never stop, do you?"

"Can I help it if you're devastating?" she replied.

"I don't blame women for falling all over you. I used to."

"Not for long."

She searched his hard face curiously. "I should have talked to you about Daphne, instead of running away."

"Let the past lie," he said harshly. "We're not the same people we were."

"One of us certainly isn't," she mused dryly. "You never used to kiss me like that!"

He cocked an eyebrow. "Did you expect me to remain celibate when you defected?"

"Of course not," she replied, averting her eyes. "That would have been asking the impossible."

"Fidelity belongs to a committed relationship," he said.

She was looking at her hands, not at him. Life seemed so empty lately. Even dancing didn't fill the great hollow space in her heart. "Being in a committed relationship wouldn't have mattered," she murmured. "I doubt if you'd have been capable of staying faithful to just one woman, what with your track record and all. And I'm hardly a raving beauty like Daphne."

He stiffened slightly, but no reaction showed in his face. He watched her and glowered. "Nice try, but it doesn't work."

She glanced up, surprised. "What doesn't?"

"The wounded, downcast look," he said. He stretched, and muscles rippled under his knit shirt. "I know you too well, Meg," he added. "You always were theatrical."

She stared at him without blinking. "Would you have liked it if I'd gone raging to the door of your apartment after I saw you and Daphne pictured in that newspaper?''

His face hardened to stone. "No," he admitted, "I loathe scenes. All the same, there's no reason to lie about the reason you wanted to break our engagement. You told your mother that dancing was more important than me, that you got cold feet and ran for it. That's all she told me."

Meg was puzzled, but perhaps Nicole had decided against mentioning Daphne's place in Steven's life. "I suppose she decided that the best course all around was to make you believe my career was the reason I left."

"That's right. Your *mother* decided," he corrected, and his eyes glittered coldly. "She yelled frog, and you jumped. You always were afraid of her."

"Who wasn't?" she muttered. "She was a world-beater, and I was a sheltered babe in the woods. I didn't know beans about men until you came along."

"You still don't," he said flatly. "I'm surprised that living in New York hasn't changed you."

"What you are is what you are, despite where you live," she reminded him. She looked down again, infuriated with him. "I dance. That's what I do. That's all I do. I've worked hard all my life at ballet, and now I'm beginning to reap the rewards for it. I like my life. So it was probably a good thing that I found out how you felt about me in time, wasn't it? I had a lucky escape, Steve," she added bitterly.

He moved close, just close enough to make her feel threatened, to make her aware of him so that she'd look up.

He smiled with faint cruelty. "Does your good fortune compensate?" he asked with soft sarcasm.

"For what?"

"For knowing how much other women enjoy lying in my arms in the darkness."

She felt her composure shatter, and knew by the smile that he'd seen it in her eyes.

"Damn you!" she choked.

He turned away, laughing. "That's what I thought." He paused at the doorway. "Tell your brother I'll call him tomorrow." His eyes narrowed. "I hated you when your mother handed me the ring you'd left with her. You were the biggest mistake of my life. And, as you said, it was a lucky escape. For both of us."

He turned and left, his steady footsteps echoing down the hall before the door opened and closed with firm control behind him. Meg stood where he'd left her, aching from head to toe with renewed misery. He said he'd hated her in the past, but it was still there, in his eyes, when he looked at her. He hadn't stopped resenting her for what she'd done, despite the fact that he'd been unfaithful to her. He was in the wrong, so why was he blaming Meg?

"Where's Steve?" her brother asked when he reappeared.

"He had to go. He had a hot date," she said through her teeth.

"Good old Steve. He sure can draw 'em. I wish I had half his... Where are you going?"

"To bed," Meg said from the staircase, and her voice didn't encourage any more questions.

Meg only wished that she had someplace to go, but she was stuck in Wichita for the time being. Stuck with Steven always around, throwing his new conquests in her face. She limped because of the accident, and the tendons were mending, but not as quickly as she'd hoped. The doctor had been uncertain as to whether the damage would eventually right itself, and the physical therapist whom Meg saw three times a week was uncommunicative. Talk to the doctor, she told Meg. But Meg wouldn't, because she knew she wasn't making much progress and she was afraid to know why.

Besides her injury, there was no work in New York for her just now. Her ballet company couldn't perform without funds, and unless they raised some soon, she wouldn't have a job. It was a pity to waste so many years of her life on such a gamble. She loved ballet. If only she were wealthy enough to finance the company herself, but her small dividends from her stock in Ryker Air wouldn't be nearly enough.

David didn't have the money, either, but Steve did. She grimaced at just the thought. Steve would throw the money away or even burn it before he'd lend any to Meg. Not that she'd ever ask him, she promised herself. She had too much pride.

She'd tried not to panic at the thought of never dancing again. She consoled herself with a small dream of her own; of opening a ballet school here in Wichita. It would be nice to teach little girls how to dance. After all, Meg had studied ballet since her fourth birthday. She certainly had the knowledge, and she loved children. It was an option that she'd never seriously considered before, but now, with her injury, it became a security blanket. It was there to keep her going. If she failed in one area, she still had prospects in another. Yes, she had prospects.

* * *

The next morning, it was raining. Meg looked out the front window and smiled wistfully, because the rain pounding down on the sprouting grass and leafing trees suited her mood. It was late spring. There were flowers blooming and, thank God, no tornadoes looming with this shower. The rain was nice, if unexpected.

She did her exercises, glowering at the ankle that was still stiff and painful after weeks of patient work. David was at the office and no doubt so was Steve—if he wasn't too worn out from the night before, she thought furiously. How dare he rub his latest conquest in her face and make sarcastic and painful remarks about it?

He wasn't the person she'd known at eighteen. That Steve had been a quiet man without the cruelty of this new man who used women and tossed them aside. Or perhaps he'd always been like this, except that Meg had been looking at him through loving eyes and missed all his flaws.

She didn't expect to see him again after his harshness the night before, but David telephoned just before he left the office with an invitation to dinner from Steve.

"We've just signed a new contract with a Middle-Eastern potentate. We're taking his representative out for dinner and Steve wants you to come with us."

"Why me?" she asked with faint bitterness. "Am I being offered as a treat to his client or is he thinking of selling me into slavery on the Barbary Coast? I understand blondes are still much in demand there."

David didn't catch the bitterness in her voice. He laughed uproariously, covered the mouthpiece and mumbled something. "Steve says that's not a bad idea, and for you to wear a harem outfit."

"Tell him fat chance," she mumbled. "I don't know if I want to go. Surely Steven has plenty of women who could help him entertain his business friends."

"Don't be difficult," David chided. "A night out would do you good."

"All right. I'll be ready when you get home."

"Good."

She hung up, wondering why she'd given in. Steven had probably invited one of his women and was going to rub Meg's face in his latest conquest. She herself would no doubt be tossed to the Arab for dessert. Well, he was due for a surprise if he thought she'd go along with his plotting!

By the time David opened the front door, Meg was dressed in an outfit she'd bought for a Halloween party in New York: a black dress that covered her from just under her ears to her ankles, set off by a wide silver belt and silver-sprayed flat shoes. It was impossible to wear high heels just yet, and even though her limp wasn't pronounced, walking was difficult enough in flats. Her hair was in its neat bun and she wore no makeup. She didn't realize that her fair beauty made makeup superfluous anyway. She had an exquisitely creamy complexion with a natural blush all its own.

"Wow!" David whistled.

She glowered at him. "You aren't supposed to approve. I'm rebelling. This is a revolutionary outfit, not debutante dressing."

"I know that, and so will Steve. But—" he grinned as he took her arm and herded her out the door "—believe me, he'll approve."

Chapter 3

David's remark made sense until he escorted Meg into the restaurant where Steve—surprisingly without a woman in tow—and a tall, very dark Arab in an expensive European suit were seated. The men stood up as Meg and David approached. The Arab's gaze was approving. The puzzle pieces as to why Steve would be happy with her outfit fell into place.

"Remember that the Middle East isn't exactly liberated territory," David whispered. "You're dressed very correctly for this evening."

"Oh, boy," she muttered angrily. If she'd thought about it, she'd have worn her backless yellow gown....

"*Enchanté, mademoiselle,*" the foreigner said with lazy delight as he was introduced to her. He smiled and his black mustache twitched. He was incredibly handsome, with eyes that were large and almost a liquid black. He was charming without being condescending or offensive. "You are a dancer, I believe? A ballerina?"

"Yes," Meg murmured demurely. She smiled at him. "And you are the representative of your country?"

He quirked an eyebrow and glanced at Steve. "Indeed, I am."

"Do tell me about your part of the world," she said with genuine interest, totally ignoring Steve and her brother.

He did, to the exclusion of business, until Steve sat glowering at her over dessert and coffee. She shifted a little uncomfortably under that cold look, and Ahmed suddenly noticed his business colleague.

He chuckled softly. "Steven, my friend, I digress. Forgive me. But *mademoiselle* is such charming company that she chases all thought of business from my poor mind."

"No harm done," Steve replied quietly.

"I'm sorry," Meg said genuinely. "I didn't mean to distract you, but I do find your culture fascinating. You're very well educated," Meg said.

He smiled. "Oxford, class of '82."

She sighed. "Perhaps I should have gone to college instead of trying to study ballet."

"What a sad loss to the world of the arts if that had been so, *mademoiselle*. Historians are many. Good dancers, alas, are like diamonds."

Her cheeks flushed with flattery and excitement.

Steven's fingers closed around his fork and he stared at it. "About these new jets we're selling you, Ahmed," he persisted.

"Yes, we must discuss them. I have been led astray by a lovely face and a kind heart." He smiled at Meg.

"But my duty will not allow me to divert my interests too radically from my purpose in coming here. You will forgive us if we turn our minds to the matter at hand, *mademoiselle?*"

"Of course," she replied softly.

"Kind of you," Steven murmured, his dagger glance saying much more than the polite words.

"For you, Steven, anything," she replied in kind.

The evening was both long and short. All too soon, David found himself accompanying the tall Arab back to his suite at the hotel while Steven appropriated Meg and eased her into the passenger seat of his Jaguar.

"Why is it always a Jaguar?" she asked curiously when he was inside and the engine was running.

"I like Jaguars."

"You would."

He pulled the sleek car out into traffic. "Leave Ahmed alone," he said without preamble.

"Ah. I'm being warned off." She nodded. "It's perfectly obvious that you consider me a woman of international intrigue, out to filch top-secret information and sell it to enemy agents." She frowned. "Who is the enemy these days, anyway?"

"Mata Hari, you aren't."

"Don't insult me. I have potential." She struck a pose, with her hand suspended behind her nape and her perfect facial profile toward him. "With a little careful tutoring, I could be devastating."

"With a little careful tutoring, you could be concealed in an oil drum and floated down the river to Oklahoma."

"You have no sense of humor."

He shrugged. "Not much to laugh about these days. Not in my life."

She leaned her cheek against the soft seat and watched him as he controlled the powerful car. It was odd that she always felt safe with him. Safe, and excited beyond words. Just looking at him made her tremble.

"What are you thinking?" he asked.

"That I'm sorry you never made love to me," she said without thinking.

The car swerved and his face tautened. He never looked at her. "Don't do that."

She drew in a slow breath, tracing patterns in the upholstery. "Aren't you, really?"

"You might have been addictive. I don't like addiction."

"That's why you smoke," she agreed, staring pointedly at the glowing cigarette in his lean, dark hand.

He did glance at her then, to glare. "I'm not addicted to nicotine. I can quit anytime I feel like it."

"What's wrong with right now?"

His dark eyes narrowed.

"What's wrong? Are you afraid you can't do without it?" she coaxed.

He pressed the power window switch, then threw the cigarette out when there was an opening. The window went back up again.

Meg grinned at him. "You'll be shaking in seconds," she predicted. "Combing the floor for old cigarette butts with a speck of tobacco left in them. Begging stubs from strangers."

"Unwise, Meg."

"What is? Taunting you?"

"I might decide to find another way to occupy my hands," he said suggestively.

She threw her arms out to the side and closed her eyes. "Go ahead!" she invited theatrically. "Ravish me!"

The car slammed to a halt and Meg's eyes opened as wide as cups. She stared at him, horrified.

He lifted an eyebrow as her arms clutched her breasts and a blush flamed on her face.

"Why, Meg, is anything wrong?" he asked pleasantly. "I just stopped to let the ambulance by."

"What amb—"

Sirens and flashing red lights swept past them and vanished quickly into the distance. Meg felt like sinking through the floorboard with embarrassment.

Steven's eyes narrowed just a little. He looped one long arm over the back of her seat and studied her in the darkened car.

"All bluff, aren't you?" he chided. "Didn't I warn you that playing games with me would get you into trouble?"

"Yes," she said. "But you've done nicely without me for four years."

He didn't answer. His hand lowered to her throat and he toyed with a wisp of her hair that had come loose from her bun, teasing her skin until her pulse began to race and her body grew hot in the tense silence.

"Steven, don't," she whispered huskily, staying his hand.

"Let me excite you, Meg," he replied quietly. He moved closer, easing her hand aside. His mouth poised over hers and he began all over again, teasing, touching, just at her throat while his coffee-scented

breath came into her mouth and made her body ache.
"It was like this the first night I took you out. Do
you remember?" His voice was a deep, soft caress,
and his hand made her shiver with its tender tracing.
"I parked the car in your own driveway after we'd
had dinner. I touched you, just like this, while we
talked. You were more impulsive then, much less uninhibited. Do you remember what you did, Meg?"

She was finding it difficult to talk and breathe at
the same time. "I was very...young," she said, de-
fending herself.

"You were hungry." His lips parted and brushed
her mouth open, softly nibbling at it until he heard
the sound she made deep in her throat. "You unbut-
toned my shirt and slid your hand inside it, right down
to my waist."

She shivered, remembering what that had triggered.
His mouth had hit hers like a tidal wave, with a groan
that echoed in the silence of the car. He'd lifted her,
turned her, and his hand had gone down inside the
low bodice of her black dress to cup her naked breast.
She'd come to her senses all too soon, fighting the
intimacy. He'd stopped at once, and he'd smiled
down at her as she lay panting in his arms, on fire
with the first total desire she'd ever felt in her life.
He'd known. Then, and now...

"You were so innocent," he said quietly, remembering. "You had no idea why I reacted so violently
to such a little caress. It was like the first time I let
you feel me against you when I was fully aroused.
You were shocked and frightened."

"My parents never told me anything, and my girl-
friends were just as stupid as I was, they made sure
of it," she said hesitantly. "All the reading in the

world doesn't prepare you for what happens, for what you feel when a man touches you intimately.''

His hand smoothed over the shoulder of her black dress, back to the zipper. Slowly, gently, he eased it down, controlling her panicked movement with careless ease.

"It's been four years and you want it,'' he said. "You want me.''

She couldn't believe that she was allowing him to do this! She felt like a zombie as he eased the fabric below the soft, lacy cup of her strapless bra and looked at her. His big, lean hand, darkly tanned, stroked her collarbone and down, smoothing over the swell of her breasts while he looked at her in the semidarkness.

His mouth touched her forehead. His breath was a little unsteady. So was hers.

"Let me unhook it, Meg. I want you in my mouth.''

This had always been his sharpest weapon, this way of talking to her that made her body burn with dark, wicked desires. Her forehead rested against his chin while his fingers quickly disposed of three small hooks. She felt the cool air on her body even as he moved her back and looked down, his posture suddenly stiff and poised, controlled.

"My God.'' It was reverent, the way he spoke, the way he looked at her. His hands contracted on her shoulders as if he were afraid that she might vanish.

"I let you look at me...that last night,'' she whispered unsteadily. "And you went to her!''

"No. No,'' he whispered, bending his head. "No, Meg!''

His mouth fastened on her taut nipple and he

groaned as he lifted her, turned her, suckling her in a silence that blazed with tension and promise.

Her fingers gripped his thick hair and held on while his mouth gave her the most intense pleasure she'd ever known. He'd tried to kiss her this way that long-ago night and she'd fought him. It had been too much for her already overloaded senses and, coupled with his raging arousal and the sudden determination of his weight on her body, she'd panicked. But she was older now, with four years of abstinence to heighten her need, strip her nerves raw. She was starved for him.

His mouth fed on her while his fingers traced around the firm softness he was enjoying. She felt his tongue, his teeth, the slow suction that seemed to draw the heart right out of her body. She shuddered, helpless, anguished, as the ardent pressure of his mouth only made the hunger grow.

He felt her tremble and slowly lifted his head.

"*Noo…!*" She choked, clutching at him, trying to draw his mouth back to her body. "Steve…please… please!"

He drew her face into his throat and held her, his arms punishing, his breath as ragged as her own.

"Please!" she sobbed, clinging.

"Here…!" He fought the buttons of his shirt open and dragged her inside it, pressing her close to him, so that her bare breasts were rubbing against the thick hair on his chest, teasing his tense muscles. "Meg," he breathed tenderly. "Oh, Meg, Meg…!" His hands found their way around her, sweeping down her bare back in long, hungry caresses that made the intimacy even more dangerous, more threatening.

Her mouth pressed soft kisses into his throat, his neck, his collarbone, and she felt the need like a knife.

He turned her head and kissed her again, a long, slow, deep kiss that never seemed to end while around them the night darkened and the wind blew.

Somewhere in the middle of it, she began to cry; great, broken sobs of guilt and grief and unappeased hunger. He held her, cradled her against him, his eyes as anguished as his unsatisfied body. But slowly, finally, the desire in both of them began to relax.

"Don't cry," he whispered, kissing the tears from her eyes. "It was inevitable."

She turned her face so that he could kiss the other side of it, her eyes closed while she savored the rare, exquisite tenderness.

When she felt his lips reluctantly draw away, she opened her eyes and looked into his. They were soft, just for her, just for the moment. Soft and hungry, and somehow violent.

"You're untouched," he said huskily, his face setting into hard, familiar lines. "Even here." His hand smoothed over her bare, swollen breast and as if the feel of it drove him mad, he bent his head and tenderly drew his lips over it, breathing in the scent of her body. "Totally, absolutely untouched."

"I...can't feel like this with any other man," she confessed, shaken to her soul by what they were sharing. "I can't bear another man's eyes to touch me, much less his hands."

His breath drew in raggedly. "Why in God's name did you leave, damn you?"

"I was afraid!"

"Of this?" His mouth opened over her nipple and

she cried out at the flash of pleasure it gave her to feel it so intimately.

"I was a virgin," she gasped.

"You still are." He drew her across him, one big hand gathering her hips blatantly into the hard thrust of his, holding her there while he searched her eyes. "And you're still afraid," he said finally, watching the shocked apprehension grow on her face. "Terrified of intimacy with me."

She swallowed, then swallowed again. Her eyes dropped to his bare chest. "Not...of that."

"Then what?"

His body throbbed. She could feel the heat and power of it and she felt faint with the knowledge of how desperately he wanted her. "Steven, my sister died in childbirth."

"Yes, I know. Your father told me. It was such a private thing, I didn't feel it was my place to ask questions. I just know she was twelve years older than you."

She looked up at him. "She was...like me," she whispered slowly. "Thin and slender, not very big in the hips at all. They lived up north. It snowed six feet the winter she was ready to deliver and her husband couldn't get her to a hospital in time. She died. So did the baby." Meg hesitated, nibbling her lower lip. "Childbirth is difficult for the women in my family. My mother had to have a cesarean section when I was born. I was very sheltered and after my sister died, mother made it sound as if pregnancy would be a death sentence for me, too. She made me terrified of getting pregnant," she added miserably, hiding her face from him.

He eased his intimate hold on her, stunned. His

hand guided her cheek to his broad, hair-roughened chest and he held her there, letting her feel the heat of his body, the heavy slam of his heart under her ear.

"We never discussed this."

"I was very young, as you said," she replied, closing her eyes. "I couldn't tell you. It was so intimate a thing to say, and I was already overwhelmed by you physically. Every time you touched me, I went lightheaded and hot and shaky all over." Her eyes closed. "I still do."

His fingers tangled gently in her hair, comforting now instead of arousing. "I could have reassured you, if you'd only told me."

"Perhaps." She nuzzled her cheek against him. "But I had terrors of getting pregnant, and you came on very strong that night. The argument...seemed like a reprieve at the time. You told me to get out, and then you took Daphne to a public place so that it would be in all the papers. I told myself that choosing dancing made more sense than choosing you. It made it easier to go away."

He lifted his head, staring out the darkened window. Seconds later, he looked down at her, his eyes lingering on her breasts.

She smiled sadly. "You don't believe me, do you? You're still bitter, Steven."

"You don't think I'm entitled to be?"

She shifted against him, her eyes adoring his hard face, totally at peace with him even in this intimacy now. "I didn't think you cared enough to be hurt."

"I didn't," he agreed readily. "But my pride took a few blows."

"Nicole said you got drunk..."

He smiled cruelly. "Did she add that I was with Daphne at the time?"

She stiffened, hating him.

His warm hand covered her breast blatantly, feeling her heartbeat race even through her anger. He searched her eyes. "I still want you," he said flatly. "More than ever."

She knew it. His face was alive with desire. "It wouldn't be wise," she said quietly. "As you once said, Steven, addictions are best avoided."

"You flatter yourself if you think I'm crazy enough to become addicted to you again," he said with a faintly mocking smile as all the anguish of those four years sat on him.

Meg was arrested by his expression. The mention of the past seemed to have brought all the bitterness back, all the anger. She didn't know what to say. "Steven..."

His hand pressed closer, warm against her bare skin in the faint chill of the car. "Your ballet company needs money. All right, Meg," he said softly. "I'll get you out of the hole."

"You will!" she exclaimed.

"Oh, yes. I'll be your company angel. But there's a price."

His voice was too silky. She felt the apprehension as if it were tangible. "What is the price?" she asked.

"Can't you figure it out?" he asked with faint hauteur in his smile. "Then I'll tell you. Sleep with me. Give me one night, Meg, to get you out of my system. And in return, I'll give you back your precious dancing."

Chapter 4

Meg spent a long, sleepless night agonizing over Steven's proposal. She couldn't really believe that he'd said such a thing, or that he'd actually expected her to agree. How could his feverish ardor have turned to contempt in so short a time? It must be as she thought: he wanted nothing more than revenge because she'd run out on him. Even her explanation had fallen on deaf ears. Or perhaps he hadn't wanted to believe it. And hadn't he been just as much at fault, after all? He was the one who'd sent her away. He'd told her to get out of his life.

She wished now that she'd reminded him of that fact more forcibly. But his slowly drawled insult had made her forget everything. She'd torn out of his arms, putting her clothes to rights with trembling hands while he laughed harshly at her efforts.

"That was cruel, Steven," she'd said hoarsely, glaring at him when she was finally presentable again.

"Really? In fact, I meant it," he added. "And the offer still stands. Sleep with me and I'll drag your precious company back from the brink. You won't have to worry about pregnancy, either," he added as he started the car. "I'll protect you from it with my last breath. You see, Meg, the last thing in the world I want now is to be tied to you by a child." His eyes had punctuated the insult, going slowly over her body as if he could see under her clothes. "All I want is for this madness to be over, once and for all."

As if it ever would be, she thought suddenly, when he'd left her at her door without a word and drove off. The madness, as he called it, was going to be permanent, because she'd taken the easy way out four years ago. She hadn't confessed her fears and misgivings about intimacy with him, or challenged him about Daphne. She'd been afraid to say what she thought, even more afraid to fight for his love. Instead, she'd listened to others—his father and her own mother, who'd wanted Meg to have a career in ballet and never risk pregnancy at all.

But Steven's motives were even less clear. She'd often thought secretly that Steven was rather cold in any emotional way, that perhaps he'd been relieved when their engagement ended. His very courtship of her had been reluctant, forced, as if it was totally against his better judgment. Meg had thought at the time that love was something he would never understand completely. He had so little of it in his own life. His father had wanted a puppet that he could control. His mother had withdrawn from him when he was still a child, unable to understand his tempestuous nature much less cope with his hardheaded determination in all things.

Steven had grown up a loner. He still was. He might use a woman to ease his masculine hungers, but he avoided emotional closeness. Meg had sensed that, even at the age of eighteen. In a way, it was Steven's very detachment that she'd run from. She had the wisdom to know that her love for him and his desire for her would never make a relationship. And at the back of her mind, always in those days, was her unrealistic fear of childbirth. She wondered now if her mother hadn't deliberately cultivated that fear, to force Meg into line. Her mother had been a major manipulator. Just like Steven's father.

Meg had gone quickly upstairs the night before, calling a cheerful good-night to her brother, who was watching a late movie in the living room. She held up very well until she got into her own room, and then the angry tears washed down from her eyes.

A night of love in return for financing. Did he really think she held herself so cheaply? Well, Steven could hold his breath until she asked him for financial help, she thought furiously! The ballet company would manage somehow. She wouldn't meet his unreasonable terms, not even to save her career.

By the time Meg was up and moving around the next morning, David had already gone to the office. She had a headache and a very sore ankle from just the small amount of walking she'd done the night before. She couldn't quite meet her own eyes in the mirror, though, remembering how easily she'd surrendered to Steven's hot ardor. She had no resistance when she got within a foot of him.

She washed her face, brushed her teeth and ate

breakfast. She went to the hospital for her physical
therapy and then came back home and did stretches
for several minutes. All the while, she thought of
Steven and how explosive their passion had been. It
didn't help her mood.

David came home looking disturbed.

"Why so glum?" Meg teased gently.

He glanced at her. "What? Oh, there's nothing,"
he said quickly, and smiled. "If you haven't cooked
anything, suppose we go out for a nice steak supper?"

Her eyebrows arched. "Steak?"

"Steak. I feel like chewing something."

"Ouch. Bad day?" she murmured.

"Vicious!" He shrugged. "By the way, Ahmed
said that he'd like to join us, if you don't mind."

"Certainly not!" she said, smiling. "I like him."

"So do I. But don't get too attached to him," he
cautioned. "There are some things going on that you
don't know about, that you're safer not knowing
about. But Ahmed isn't quite what he seems."

"Really?" She was intrigued. "Tell me more."

"You'll have to take my word for it," he said.
"I'm not risking any more scathing comments from
the boss. He was out for blood today. One of the
secretaries threw a desk lamp at him and walked out
of the building without severance pay!"

Meg's eyebrows arched. "Steven's secretary?"

"As a matter of fact, yes." He chuckled. "Everybody else ran for cover. Not Daphne. I suppose she'd
known him for so long that she can handle him."

Meg's heart stopped beating. "Daphne—*the*
Daphne he was sleeping with when he and I got engaged?"

David's eyes narrowed. "I don't think they were

that intimate, and certainly not after he asked you to marry him. But, yes, they've known each other for years.''

''I see.''

''She was the reason you argued with him. The reason you left, as I remember.''

She took a deep breath. ''Part of it,'' she replied, correcting him. She forced a smile. ''Actually she did a good turn. I'd never have had the opportunity to continue my training in New York if I'd married Steven, would I?''

''You haven't let a man near you since you left Wichita,'' David said sagely. ''And don't tell me it's due to lack of time for a social life.''

She lifted her chin. ''Maybe Steve's an impossible act to follow,'' she said with an enigmatic smile. ''Or maybe he taught me a bitter lesson about male loyalty.''

''Steven's not what he seems,'' he said suddenly. ''He's got a soft center, despite all that turmoil he creates. He was deeply hurt when you left. I don't think he ever got over you, Meg.''

''His pride didn't, he even admitted it,'' she agreed. ''But he never loved me. If he had, how could he have gone to Daphne?''

''Men do strange things when they feel threatened.''

''I never threatened him,'' she muttered.

''No?'' He stuck his hands into his pockets and studied her averted face. ''Meg, in all the years we've known the Rykers, Steve never took a woman around for more than two weeks. He avoided any talk of involvement or marriage. Then he took you out one time and started talking about engagement rings.''

"I was a novelty." She bit off the words.

"You were, indeed. You melted right through that wall of ice around him and made him laugh, made him young. Meg, if you'd ever really looked at him, you'd have seen how much he changed when he was with you. Steven Ryker would have thrown himself under a bus if you'd asked him to. He would have done anything for you. Anything," he added quietly. "His father didn't want Steven to marry you because he thought Steve was besotted enough to side with you in a proxy fight." He smiled at her shocked expression. "Don't you see that everyone was manipulating you for their own gain? You and Steven never had a chance, Meg. You fell right into line and did exactly what you were meant to do. And the one who really paid the price was poor old Steven, in love for the first time in his life."

"He didn't love me," she choked.

"That's true. He worshiped you. He couldn't take his eyes off you. Everything he did for that one long month you were engaged was designed solely to please you, every thought he had was for your comfort, your happiness." He shook his head. "You were too young to realize it, weren't you?"

She felt as if her legs wouldn't hold her. She sat down, heavily. "He never said a word."

"What could he have said? He isn't the type to beg. You left. He assumed you considered him expendable. He got drunk. Roaring drunk. He stayed that way for three days. Then he went back to work with a vengeance and started making money hand over fist. That's when the women started showing up, one after another. They numbed the ache, but he was still hurting. There was nothing anyone could do for him, except watch him suffer and pretend not to notice that he flinched whenever your name was mentioned.''

She covered her face with her hands.

He laid a comforting hand on her shoulder. "Don't torture yourself. He did, finally, get over you, Meg. It took him a year and when he got through it, he was a better man. But he's not the same man. He's lost and gained something in the process. It's hardened him to emotion.''

"I was an idiot," she said heavily, pushing back her loosened hair. "I loved him so much, but I was afraid of him. He seemed so distant sometimes, as if he couldn't bear to talk to me about anything personal.''

"You were the same way," he prompted.

She smiled wistfully. "Of course I was. I was hopelessly repressed and introverted, and I couldn't believe that a man who was such a man wanted to marry me. I stood in awe of him then. I still do, a little. But now I understand him so much better...now that it's too late.''

"Are you sure that it is?"

She thought about the night before, about his exquisite ardor and then the pain and grief of hearing him proposition her. She nodded slowly. "Yes, David," she said, lifting pain-filled blue eyes to his. "I'm afraid so.''

"I'm sorry."

She got to her feet. "Don't they say that things always work out for the best?" She smoothed her skirt. "Where are we going to eat?"

"Castello's. And I'm sorry to have to tell you that so is Steve.''

She hated the thought of facing him, but she was no coward. She only shrugged fatalistically. "I'll get dressed, then."

He told her what time they needed to leave and went off to make a last-minute phone call.

Meg went upstairs. "I think I'll wear something red," she murmured angrily to herself. "With a V-neck, cut to the ankles in front, and with slits up both sides..."

She didn't have anything quite that revealing, but the red dress she pulled out of its neat wrapper had spaghetti straps and fringe. It was close-fitting, seductive. She left her blond hair down around her shoulders and used much more makeup than she normally did. She had some jewelry left over from the old days, with diamonds. She got it out of the safe and wore it, too. The song about going out in a blaze of glory revolved in her mind. She was going to give Steven Ryker hell.

As David had said, he was, indeed, in the restaurant. But he wasn't alone. And Meg's poor heart took a dive when she saw who was with him: a slinky, sultry platinum blonde with a smooth tan, wearing a black dress that probably cost twice what Meg's had. It was Daphne, of course, draped against Steve's arm as if she were an expensive piece of lint. Meg forced a brilliant smile as Ahmed rose from the table, in a distinguished dark suit, and smiled with pure appreciation as she and David approached.

"Mademoiselle prompts me to indiscretion," he said, taking her hand and bowing over it before he kissed the knuckles in a very continental way. "I will bite my tongue and subdue the words that tease my mouth.''

Meg laughed with delight. ''If you intend asking me to join your harem,'' she returned impishly, ''you'll have to wait until I'm too old to dance, I'm afraid.''

''I am devastated,'' he said heavily.

Steven was staring at her, his silver eyes dangerous. ''What an interesting choice of color, Meg,'' he murmured.

She curtsied, grimacing as she made her injured ankle throb with the action. ''It's my favorite. Don't you think it suits me?'' she asked with a challenge in her eyes.

He averted his gaze as if the words had shamed him. ''No, I don't,'' he said stiffly. ''Sit down, David.''

David helped Meg into the chair next to Ahmed and greeted Daphne.

''How did you manage this?'' David asked the other woman.

''He likes having things thrown at him, don't you, Steven, darling?'' Daphne laughed. ''I got rehired at a higher salary. You should try it yourself.''

''No, thanks.'' David sighed. ''I'd be frog-marched to the elevator shaft for my pains.''

''I don't suppose Meg is the type to throw things, are you, dear?'' Daphne asked.

''Shall we find out?'' Meg replied, lifting her water glass with a meaningful glance in Daphne's direction.

David put a hand on her wrist, shocked by her reaction.

''Forgive me if I've offended you,'' Daphne said quickly. She looked more than a little surprised herself. "Heavens, I just open my mouth and words fall out, I suppose," she added with a nervous, apologetic glance toward Steven.

Steven was frowning and his eyes never left Meg's.

"No need to apologize," Meg said stiffly. "I rarely take offense, even when people blatantly insult me."

Steven looked uncomfortable and the atmosphere at the table grew tense.

Ahmed stood up, holding his hand out to Meg. "I would be honored to have you dance with me," he offered.

"I would be honored to accept." Meg avoided Steven's eyes as she stood up and let Ahmed lead her onto the dance floor.

He held her very correctly. She liked the clean scent of him and the handsome face with liquid black eyes that smiled down at her. But there was no spark when he touched her, no throbbing ache to possess and be possessed.

"Thank you," she said quietly. "I think you saved the evening."

"Daphne has no malice in her, despite what you may think," he said gently. "It is quite obvious what Steven feels for you."

Meg flushed, letting her eyes fall to his white shirt. "Is it?"

"This dancing…it hurts you?" he asked suddenly when she was less than graceful and fell heavily against him.

She swallowed. "My ankle is still painful," she said honestly. "And not mending as I had hoped." Her eyes lifted with panic in their depths. "It was a bad sprain…"

"And dancing is your life."

She gnawed on her lower lip, wincing as she moved again with him to the bluesy music. "It has had to be," she said oddly.

"May I cut in?"

The voice was deep and cutting and not the kind to ignore unless a brawl was desirable.

"But of course," Ahmed said, smiling at Steven. *"Merci, mademoiselle,"* he added softly and moved back.

Steven drew Meg to him, much too closely, and riveted her in place with one long, powerful arm as he moved her to the music.

"My ankle hurts," she said icily, "and I don't want to dance with you."

"I know." He tilted her face up to his and studied the dark circles under her eyes, the wan complexion. "I know why you wore the red dress, too. It was to rub my nose in what I said to you last night, wasn't it?"

"Bingo," she said with a cold smile.

He drew in a long breath. His silver eyes slid over the length of her waving hair, down to her bare shoulders. They fell to her breasts where the soft V at the neckline revealed their exquisite swell, and his jaw clenched. The arm of her back went rigid.

"You have the softest skin I've ever touched," he said gruffly. "Silky and warm and fragrant. I don't need this dress to remind me that I can't think sanely when you're within reach."

"Then stay out of reach," she shot back. "Why don't you take Daphne home with you and seduce her? If you didn't on the way here," she added with hauteur.

She missed a step and he caught her, easily, holding her upright.

"That ankle is hurting you. You shouldn't be dancing," he said firmly.

"The therapist said to exercise it," she said through her teeth. "And she said that it would hurt."

He didn't say what he was thinking. If the ankle was painful after five long weeks, how would she be able to dance on it? Would it hold her weight? It certainly didn't seem as if it would.

She saw the expression on his face. "I'll dance again," she told him. "I will!"

He touched her face with lean, careful fingers, traced her cheek and her chin and around her full, bow mouth. "For yourself, Meg, or because it was what your mother always wanted?"

"It was the only thing I ever did in my life that pleased her," she said without thinking.

"Yes. I think perhaps it was." His finger traced her lower lip. Odd how tremulous that finger seemed, especially when it teased between her lips and felt them part, felt her breath catch. "Are you still afraid of making a baby?" he whispered unsteadily.

"Steven!" she exclaimed. She jerked her face back and it flushed red.

"You made me think about what happened that last night we were together before we fought," he said, as if she hadn't reacted to the question at all. "I remember when you started fighting me. I remember what I said to you."

"This isn't necessary…!" she broke in frantically.

"I said that if we went all the way, it wouldn't really matter," he whispered deeply, holding her eyes. "Because I'd love making you pregnant."

She actually shivered and her body trembled as it sought the strength and comfort of his.

He cradled her in his arms, barely moving to the music, his mouth at her ear. "You didn't think I was going to stop. And you were afraid of a baby."

"Yes."

His fingers threaded into her soft, silky hair and he drew her even closer. His legs trembled against her own as the incredible chemistry they shared made him weak. And all at once, instantly, he was fully capable and she could feel it.

"Don't pull away from me," he said roughly. "I know it repulses you, but, my God, it isn't as if I can help it…!"

She stilled instantly. "Oh, no, it isn't that," she whispered, lifting her eyes. "I don't want to hurt you! You used to tell me not to move when it happened, remember?"

He stopped dancing and his eyes searched hers so hungrily that she could hardly bear the intensity of the look they were sharing.

His lips parted as he tried to breathe, enmeshed by his hunger for her, by the beauty of her uplifted face, the temptation of her perfect, innocent body against his. "I remember everything," he said tautly. "You haunt me, Meg. Night after empty night."

She saw the strain in his dark face and felt guilty that she should be the cause of it. Her hand pressed flat against his shirtfront, feeling the strength and heat and under it the feverish throb of his pulse.

"I'm sorry," she said tenderly. "I'm so sorry…"

He fought for control, his eyes lifting finally to stare over her head.

Meg moved away a little, and began talking quite

calmly about the state of the world, the weather, dancing lazily while he recovered.

"I have to stop now, Steven," she said finally. "My ankle really hurts."

He stopped dancing. His eyes searched over her face. "I'm sorry about what I said to you last night, when I asked you," he said curtly. "I wanted you to the point of madness." He laughed bitterly. "That, at least, has never changed."

Her eyes adored him. She couldn't help it. He was more perfect to her than anything in the world, and when he was close to her, she had everything. But what he wanted would destroy her.

"I can't sleep with you and just...just go on with my life," she said softly. "It would be another night, another body, to you. But it would be devastating to me. Not only my first time, but with someone whom I..." She averted her eyes. "Someone for whom I once cared very much."

"Look at me."

She forced her eyes up to his, curious about their sudden intent scrutiny.

"Meg," he said, as the music began again, "it wouldn't be just another night and another body."

"It would be for revenge," she argued. "And you know it, Steven. It isn't about lovemaking, it's about getting even. I walked out of your life and hurt you. Now you want to pay me back, and what better way than to sleep with me and walk away yourself?"

"Do you think I could?" he asked with a bitter laugh.

"Neither of us would really know until it happened." She stared at his chest. "I know you'd try to protect me, but you aren't quite in control when we make love. You certainly weren't last night." She raised her face. "Then what would we do if I really did get pregnant?"

His lips parted. He studied her slowly. "You could marry me," he said softly. "We could raise our child together."

The thought thrilled, uplifted, frightened. "And my career?"

The pleasure washed out of him. His face lost its softness and his eyes grew cold. "That, of course, would be history. And you couldn't stand that. After all, you've worked all your life for it, haven't you?" He let her go. "We'd better go back to the table. We don't want to put that ankle at risk."

They did go back to the table. He took Daphne's hand and kept it in his for the rest of the evening. And every time he looked at Meg, his eyes were hostile and full of bitterness and contempt.

Chapter 5

David and Meg, who'd taken a cab to the restaurant, rode back to their house with Ahmed in his chauffeured limousine. Steven, Meg noticed, hadn't even offered them a ride; he probably had other plans, ones that included Daphne.

"It's been a great evening," David remarked. "How much longer are you going to stay in Wichita, Ahmed?"

"Until the last of the authorizations are signed," the other man replied. He glanced at Meg with slow, bold appraisal in his liquid black eyes. "Alas, then duty forces me back to my own land. Are you certain that you would not consider coming with me, *ma chou?*" he teased. "You could wear that dress and enchant me as you dance."

Meg forced a smile, but she was having some misgivings about her future. Her ankle was no stronger than when it was first damaged. Her concern grew by the day.

"I'm very flattered," she began.

"We are allowing our women more freedom," he mused. "At least they are no longer required to wear veiling from head to toe and cover their faces in public."

"Are you married?" she asked curiously. "Aren't Moslems allowed four wives?"

The laughter went out of his eyes. "No, I am not married. It is true that a Moslem may have up to four wives, but while I accept many of the teachings of the Prophet, I am not Moslem, *mademoiselle*. I was raised a Christian, which precludes me from polygamy."

"That's the road, just up ahead," David said quickly, gesturing toward their street. "You haven't seen our home, have you, Ahmed?" he added, smiling at the other man.

"No."

"Do come in," Meg asked. "We can offer you coffee. Your chauffeur as well."

"Another time, perhaps," Ahmed said gently, glancing behind them at a dark car in the near distance. "I have an appointment this evening at my hotel."

"Certainly," Meg replied.

"Thanks for the ride. I'll see you tomorrow, then," David said as they pulled up in the driveway.

Ahmed nodded. "Friday will see the conclusion of our business," he remarked. "I should enjoy escorting the two of you and our friend Steven to a performance at the theater. I have obtained tickets in anticipation of your acceptance."

Meg was thrilled. "I'd love to! David…?"

"Certainly," her brother said readily. He smiled. "Thank you."

"I will send the car for you at six, then. We will enjoy a leisurely meal before the curtain rises." He didn't offer to get out of the car, but he smiled and waved at Meg as David closed the door behind her. The limousine sped off, with the dark car close behind it.

"Is he being followed?" she asked David carefully.

"Yes, he is," David said, but he avoided looking at her. "He has his own security people."

"I like him," she said as they walked toward the front door.

David glanced at her. "You've been very quiet since you danced with Steve," he observed. "More trouble?"

She sighed wistfully. "Not really. Steven's only shoving Daphne down my throat. Why should that bother me?"

"Maybe he's trying to make you jealous."

"That will be the day, when Steven Ryker stoops to that sort of tactic."

David started to speak and decided against it. He only smiled as he unlocked the door and let her in.

"Ahmed is very mysterious," she said abruptly. "It's as if he's not really what he seems at all. He's a very gentle man, isn't he?" she added thoughtfully.

He gave her a blank stare. "Ahmed? Uh, well, yes. Certainly. I mean, of course he is." He looked as if he had to bite his tongue. "But, despite the fact that Ahmed is Christian, he's still very much an Arab in his customs and beliefs. And his country is a hotbed of intrigue and danger right now." He studied her closely. "You don't watch much television, do you, Meg? Not the national news programs, I mean."

"They're much too upsetting for me," she confessed. "No, I don't watch the news or read newspapers unless I can't avoid them. I know," she said before he could taunt her about it, "I'm hiding my head in the sand. But honestly, David, what could I do to change any of that? We elect politicians and trust them to have our best interests at heart. It isn't the best system going, but I can hardly rush overseas and tell people to do what I think they should, now can I?"

"It doesn't hurt to stay informed," he said. "Although right now, maybe it's just as well that you aren't," he added under his breath. "See you in the morning."

"Yes." She stared after him, frowning. David could be pretty mysterious himself at times.

David didn't invite Steve to the house that week, because he could see how any mention of the man cut Meg. But although Wichita was a big city, it was still possible to run into people when you traveled in the same social circles.

Meg found it out the hard way when she went to a men's department store that her family had always frequented to buy a birthday present for David. She ran almost literally into Steve there.

If she was shocked and displeased to meet him, the reverse was also true. He looked instantly hostile.

Her eyes slid away from his tall, fit body in the pale tan suit he was wearing. It hurt to look at him too much.

"Shopping for a suit?" he asked sarcastically. "You'll have a hard time finding anything to fit you here."

"I'm shopping for David's birthday next week," she said tightly.

"By an odd coincidence, so am I."

"Doesn't your *secretary,*" she stressed the word, "perform that sort of menial chore for you?"

"I pick out gifts for my friends myself," he said with cold hauteur. "Besides," he added, watching her face, "I have other uses for Daphne. I wouldn't want to tire her too much in the daytime."

Insinuating that he wanted her rested at night. Meg had to fight down anger and distaste. She kept her eyes on the ties. "Certainly not," she said with forced humor.

"My father was right in the first place," he said shortly, angered at her lack of reaction. "She would have made the perfect wife. I don't know why it took me four years to realize it."

Her heart died. *Died!* She swallowed. "Sometimes we don't realize the value of things until it's too late."

His breath caught, not quite audibly. "Don't we?"

She looked up, her eyes full of blue malice. "I didn't realize how much ballet meant to me until I got engaged to you," she said with a cold smile.

His fists clenched. He fought for control and smiled. "As we said once before, we had a lucky escape." He cocked his head and studied her. "How's the financing going for the ballet company?" he added pointedly.

She drew in a sharp breath. "Just fine, thanks," she said venomously. "I won't need any...help."

"Pity," he said, letting his eyes punctuate the word.

"Is it? I'm sure Daphne wouldn't agree!"

"Oh, she doesn't expect me to be faithful at this stage of the game," he replied lazily. "Not until the engagement's official, at least."

Meg felt faint. She knew the color was draining slowly out of her face, but she stood firm and didn't grab for support. "I see."

"I still have your ring," he said conversationally. "Locked up tight in my safe."

She remembered giving it to her mother to hand back to him. The memory was vivid, violent. Daphne. Daphne!

"I kept it to remind me what a fool I was to think I could make a wife of you," he continued. "I won't make the same mistake again. Daphne doesn't want just a career. She wants my babies," he added flatly, cruelly.

She dropped her eyes, exhausted, almost ill with the pain of what he was saying. Her hand trembled as she fingered a silk tie. "Ahmed invited us to dinner and the theater Friday night." Her voice only wobbled a little, thank God.

"I know," he said, and sounded unhappy about it.

She forced her eyes up. "You don't have to be deliberately insulting, do you, Steven?" she asked quietly. "I know you hate me. There's no need for all this—" She stopped, almost choking on the word that almost escaped.

"Isn't there? But, then, you don't know how I feel, do you, Meg? You never did. You never gave a damn, either." He shoved his hands deep into his pockets and glowered at her. She looked fragile somehow in the pale green knit suit she was wearing. "Ahmed is leaving soon," he told her. "Don't get attached to him."

"He's a friend. That's all."

His silver eyes slid over her bowed head with faint hunger and then moved away quickly. "How are the exercises coming?"

"Fine, thanks."

He hesitated, bristling with bad temper. "When do you leave?" he asked bluntly.

She didn't react. "At the end of the month."

He let out a breath. "Well, thank God for that!"

Her eyes closed briefly. She'd had enough. She pulled the tie she'd been examining off the rack and moved away, refusing to look at him, to speak to him. Her throat felt swollen, raw.

"I'll have this one, please," she told the smiling clerk and produced her credit card. Her voice sounded odd.

Steven was standing just behind her, trying desperately to work up to an apology. It was becoming a habit to savage her. All he could think about was how much he'd loved her, and how easily she'd discarded him. He didn't trust her, but, God, he still wanted her. She colored his dreams. Without her, everything was flat. Even now, looking at her fed his heart, uplifted him. She was so lovely. Fair and sweet and gentle, and all she wanted was a pair of toe shoes and a stage.

He groaned inwardly. How was he going to survive when she left again? He never should have touched her. Now it was going to be just as bad as before. He was going to watch her walk away a second time and part of him was going to die.

Daphne was coming with him tonight or he didn't think he could survive Meg's company. Thank God for Daphne. She was a friend, and quite content to be that, but she was his co-conspirator as well now, part of this dangerous business that revolved around Ahmed. She was privileged to know things that no one else in his organization knew. But meanwhile she was also his camouflage. Daphne had a man of her own, one of the two government agents who were helping keep a careful eye on Ahmed. But fortunately, Meg didn't know that.

Steven was in some danger. Almost as much as Ahmed. He couldn't tell Meg that without having to give some top-secret answers. Daphne knew, of course. She was as protected as he was, as Ahmed was. But despite his bitterness toward Meg, he didn't want her in the line of fire. Loving her was a disease, he sometimes thought, and there was no cure, not even a temporary respite. She was the very blood in his veins. And to her, he was expendable. He was of no importance to her, because all she needed from life was to dance. The knowledge cut deep into his heart. It made him cruel. But hurting her gave him no pleasure. He watched her with possessive eyes, aching to hold her and apologize for his latest cruelty.

Her purchase completed, Meg left the counter and turned away without looking up. Steven, impelled by forces too strong to control, gently took her arm and pulled her with him to a secluded spot behind some suits.

He looked down into her surprised, wounded eyes until his body began to throb. "I keep hurting you, don't I?" he said roughly. "I don't mean to. Honest to God, I don't mean to, Meg!"

"Don't you?" she asked with a sad, weary smile. "It's all right, Steve," she said quietly, averting her eyes. "Heaven knows, you're entitled, after what I did to you!"

She pulled away from him and walked quickly out of the store, the cars and people blurring in front of her eyes.

Steve cursed himself while he watched her until she was completely out of view. He'd never felt quite so bad in his whole life.

Meg spent the rest of the week trying to practice her exercises and not think about Steve and Daphne. David didn't say much, but he spoke to Steve one evening just after she'd met him in the store, and Meg overheard enough to realize that Steve was taking Daphne out for the evening. It made her heart ache.

She telephoned the manager of her ballet company, Tolbert Morse, on Thursday.

"Glad you called," he said. "I think I may be on the way to meeting our bills. Can you be back in New York for rehearsals next week?"

She went rigid. In that length of time, only a miracle would mend her ankle. But she hesitated. She didn't want to admit the slow progress she was making. Deep inside she knew she'd never be able to dance that soon. She couldn't force the words out. Dance was all she had. Steve had made his rejection of Meg very blatant. Any hope in that area was gone forever.

Her dream of a school of ballet for little girls was slowly growing, but it would have to be opened in Wichita. Could she really bear having to see Steven all the time? His friendship with David would mean having him at the house constantly. No. She had to get her ankle well. She had to dance. It was the only escape she had now! Steven's latest cruelty only punctuated the fact that she had no place in his life anymore.

Fighting down panic, she forced herself to laugh. "Can I ever be ready in a week!" she exclaimed. "I'll be there with my toe shoes on!"

"Good girl! I'll tell Henrietta you'll want your old room back. Ankle doing okay?"

"Just fine," she lied.

"Then I'll see you next week."

He hung up. So did Meg. Then she stood looking down at the receiver for a long time before she could bring herself to move. One lie led to another, but how could she lie when she was up on toe shoes trying to interpret ballet?

She pushed the pessimistic thought out of her mind and went back to the practice bar. If she concentrated, there was every hope that she could accomplish what she had to.

David paused in the doorway to watch her Friday afternoon when he came home from work. He was frowning, and when she stopped to rest, she couldn't help but notice the concern in his eyes, quickly concealed.

"How's it going?" he asked.

She grinned at him, determined not to show her own misgivings. "Slow but steady," she told him.

He pursed his lips. "What does the physical therapist say?"

Her eyes became shuttered and she avoided looking directly at him. "Oh, that it will take time."

"You're supposed to start rehearsing in a month," he persisted. "Will you actually be ready by then?"

"It's in a week, actually," she said tautly, and told him about the telephone call. He protested violently. "David, for heaven's sake, I'll be fine!" she burst out, exasperated to hear her own fears coming from his lips.

He stuck his hands into his pockets with a long sigh. "Okay. I'll stop. Ahmed's going to be here at six."

"Yes, I remember. And you don't have to look so worried. I know that he invited Steve and Daphne, too."

His shoulders rose and fell heavily. He knew what was going on, but he couldn't tell Meg. She looked haunted and he felt terrible. "I'm sorry."

She forced down the memories of her last meeting with Steven, the painful things he'd said. "Why?" she asked with studied nonchalance. She dabbed at her face with the towel around her neck. "I don't mind."

"Right."

She lifted her eyes to his. "What if I did mind, David, what good would it do? I ran, four years ago," she said quietly. "I could have stayed here and faced him, faced her. I let myself be manipulated and I threw it all away, don't you understand? I never realized how much it would hurt him...." She turned, trying to control her tears. "Anyway, he's made his choice now, and I wish him well. I'm sure Daphne will do her best to make him happy. She's cared about him for a long time."

"She's cared about him, yes," he agreed. "But he

doesn't love her. He never did. If he had, he'd have married her like a shot.''

"Maybe so. But he might have changed his feelings toward her.''

He gave her a wry glance. "If you could see the way he treats her at the office, you wouldn't believe that. It's strictly business. Not even a flirtatious glance between them.''

"Yes, but you said that it all came to a head when she quit.''

He grimaced. "So it did.''

Her heart felt as heavy as lead. She turned away toward the staircase. "Anyway, I'm going back to New York soon.''

"Sis,'' he said softly. She paused with her back to him. "Can I help?''

She shook her head. "But, thanks.'' She choked. "Thanks a lot, David.''

"I thought you might get over him, in time.''

She studied her hand on the banister. "I've tried, you know,'' she said a little unsteadily. She drew in a small breath. "I do have my dancing, David. It will compensate.''

He watched her go up the staircase with a terrible certainty that ballet wouldn't compensate for a life without Steve. Her very posture was pained. Her ankle wasn't getting any better. She had to know it. But she must know, too, that Steve wasn't going to give in to whatever he felt for her; not when he'd been hurt so badly before. David shook his head and went upstairs to his own room to dress.

The limousine was prompt. Meg didn't have many dressy things, but once she'd bought a special dress for a banquet. She wore it this evening. It was a strappy black crepe cocktail dress with a full skirt and a laced-up bodice. David gave her an odd look when she came downstairs wearing it.

"Ahmed will faint," he remarked.

She laughed, touching the high coiffure that had taken half an hour to put up. Little blond wisps of hair trailed around her elegant long neck. "Not right away, I hope," she murmured. "It isn't really revealing," she added, to placate him. "It just looks like it. It was a big hit when I wore it in New York City."

"This isn't New York City, and Steven's going to go through the roof."

The sound of his name made her heart leap. Her eyes flickered. "Steven can do so with my blessing."

He gave up trying to reason with her. But he did persuade her to add a lacy black mantilla to the outfit by convincing her that Steven might take his rage out on David instead of Meg.

The limousine was very comfortable, but Meg had the oddest feeling that she was being watched. She glanced out the back window and not one but two cars were following along behind.

"Who's in that second car, I wonder?" she murmured.

"Don't ask." David chuckled. "Maybe it's the mob," he mused, leaning close and speaking in a rough accent.

"You're hopeless, David."

"You're related to me," he replied smugly. "So what does that make you?"

She threw up her hands and laid her head back against the seat.

It was an evening she wasn't looking forward to. All week, she'd dreaded this. But once Ahmed was gone, she wouldn't need to see Steve again socially. She could avoid him until she left to go back to New York. Meanwhile, if the sight of him with Daphne cut her heart out, there was nobody to know it except herself.

Chapter 6

Steven's reaction to the black dress was almost the same as it had been to the red one she'd worn before, only worse. Meg remembered too late that the dress she'd had on the night she and Steven had parted had been black, too.

After a rather strained but delicious meal, Meg headed for the entrance lobby while the men paid the bill.

An uncomfortable-looking Daphne excused herself. Meg only nodded with forced politeness and stayed where she was. She had no intention of sharing even a huge ladies room with her rival. Unfortunately that left her unexpectedly alone with Steve, when Ahmed and David also excused themselves. Steve was fuming.

"Was that deliberate?" he asked Meg, nodding toward her dress.

She didn't pretend ignorance. She pulled the man-

tilla closer around her shoulders. "No," she replied
after a pause. "Not at all."

He leaned against the wall and stared down at her,
oblivious to the comings and goings of other patrons.
The buzz of conversation was loud, but neither of
them noticed.

"You wore black the night we argued," he said
tautly. He caught her gaze and held it hungrily. "You
let me undress you and touch you." His face hardened. "My God, you do enjoy torturing me, don't
you, Meg?"

"I didn't do it on purpose," she said miserably.
"Why do you always think the worst of me?"

"I'm conditioned to it, because I'm usually right,"
he said through his teeth. He dragged his eyes away,
looking toward where the others had disappeared.
"Damn them for deserting us!"

His violent anger was telling. She moved closer,
unable to resist the power and strength of him. His
cologne was the same he'd worn then. She got drunk
on the scent as she looked up into silver eyes that
began to glitter.

His eyes darkened as she approached, stopping her
in her tracks. She hadn't realized quite what she was
doing.

"Feeling adventurous?" he asked with a cold
smile. "Don't risk it."

She clutched her purse. "I'm not risking anything.
I was just getting out of the way of the crowd."

"Really?" He caught her hand in his and jerked.
Under the cover of his jacket, he pressed the backs
of her fingers deliberately against the hard muscle of
his upper thigh, holding it there. "Look at me."

She panicked and pulled back, but he wouldn't let

go. His strength was a little frightening. "Steven, please!" she whispered.

"There was a time when you couldn't wait to be alone with me," he said under his breath. "When your hands trembled after you fumbled my shirt open. Does dancing give you that incredible high, Meg?" he asked. "Does it make you sob with the need for a man's body to bury itself deep in yours?"

She moaned at the mental pictures he was producing, shocking herself. She dragged her hand away and all but ran to escape him, blindly finding her way to her brother. She found him in the hall, on his way back to where he left her.

"There you are," he said. "Ready to go, sis?"

"Where's Ahmed?" she asked, flustered and unable to hide it.

"He'll be right here."

As he spoke, Ahmed came through another door, looking for a moment as if he were someone Meg had never met. Another man was with him, a smaller and very nervous man with uplifted hands, who was grimacing as Ahmed spoke in a cutting soft tone to him in a language Meg couldn't translate.

The smaller man sounded placating. He made a gesture of subservience and abruptly departed as if his pants were on fire.

Ahmed muttered something under his breath, his black eyes cruel for an instant as he turned to the Americans. He saw the apprehension in Meg's face and the expression abruptly vanished. He was the man she knew again, smiling, charming, unruffled.

He strode to meet her, bending to kiss her knuckles. "Ah, my dancing girl. Are you ready to sample the theater?"

"Yes, indeed," she said, smiling back.

"I will have the driver bring the car around."

"I'll, uh, help you," David said nervously, with an incomprehensible glance over Meg's head at Steven.

"What's going on?" Meg asked curiously.

"A problem with the car," Steven said suavely, smiling down at Daphne as he linked her hand in his arm. "Shall we go, ladies?"

They were on the sidewalk, when the world shifted ten degrees and changed lives. As Steven left the women to follow Ahmed and David across the street to where the limousine had just pulled up, a car shot past them and sounds like firecrackers burst onto the silence of the night.

It seemed to happen in slow motion. The car sped away. Steve fell to the pavement. Ahmed quickly knelt beside him and motioned the others back toward the restaurant.

Daphne screamed. David caught her arm and rushed her toward the building yelling for Meg to follow. But Meg was made of sterner stuff and terror gave her strength she didn't know she had. She ran toward Steve, not away from him, deaf to the warnings, the curses Steve was raining on her as she reached him.

"Get back inside, you little fool!" he raged, his eyes furious. "Meg, for the love of God...!"

She didn't register the terror that mingled with anger in his face. "You've been hit," she sobbed. Her hands touched him, where blood came through his torn jacket sleeve. "Steven!"

"Oh, my God, get her out of here!" he groaned to Ahmed. "Get under cover, both of you! Run!"

But Ahmed wouldn't go and Meg clung. She

wouldn't be moved. "No!" she whispered feverishly. "If they come back, they'll have to get both of us…!" she blurted out, shaking with fear for him.

Sirens drowned out any reply he might have made. His stunned eyes held hers while Ahmed got to his feet in one smooth movement, and his gaze searched the area around them. Satisfied that no other would-be assassins were lurking nearby, Ahmed murmured something to Steven and moved away toward two men—a dark one and a fair one—with drawn pistols who made a dive for him, through the crowd that was gathering just as the police and paramedics rushed forward. Meg's heart stopped, but Ahmed apparently knew the men and allowed himself to be surrounded by them and escorted to safety.

Meg sat on the pavement next to Steve, holding his hand, while the paramedics quickly checked his arm and bandaged what turned out to be only a flesh wound. Her white face and huge eyes told him things she never would have. His fingers entwined in hers and he watched her with fascination while stinging medicine and antiseptic was applied to the firm muscle of his upper arm.

"I'm all right," he told her softly, his tone reassuring, comforting, but full of wonder.

"I know." She was fighting tears, not very successfully.

"We'd better get him out of here," the officer in charge said grimly, staring around. "Don't spare the horses. We'll be right behind you with your friends," he told Steve. "Young lady, you can come with me," he added to Meg.

"No." She shook her head adamantly. "Where he goes, I go!"

The policeman smiled faintly and moved away.

"Don't get possessive, Miss Shannon," Steve remarked without smiling. "I don't belong to you."

Meg began to realize just how possessive she was acting and she felt embarrassed and a little guilty. "I'm sorry," she said, falteringly. "I forgot about Daphne..."

His face closed up completely. He averted his eyes. "You were upset. It's all right." He got to his feet a little unsteadily. "Go with the others," he told her. He turned when she hesitated, his eyes flashing. "Will you send Daphne here, please?"

"Of course," she said through numb lips. "Of course, I will."

So much for feeling protective. She'd given herself away and he didn't care. He didn't give a damn. He was still bearing grudges for old wounds. Why hadn't she known that?

He started to speak, but she was already walking away, her carriage proud despite the faint limp. He wondered if his heart might burst at the feelings that exploded into it. He couldn't tell her what was going on; she'd be safer that way.

"Steven wants you to go with him," Meg told Daphne, refusing to meet her shocked eyes. "He's at the ambulance."

"But, shouldn't you...?" Daphne asked uncertainly.

Meg looked at her. "He asked for you," she said unsteadily. "Please go."

Daphne grimaced and went, but there was something new in her face, and it wasn't delight. She passed one of the two men who had guarded Ahmed, the blond one, and smiled at him rather secretively.

He gave her a speaking glance before a terse comment from his tall, dark partner captured his attention.

Meg watched curiously until her brother interrupted her thoughts. "Are you all right?" David asked.

"Yes," she said slowly. She moved toward the Arab while his companions were momentarily diverted by policemen. "Ahmed, are you okay?" she asked the tall man gently. "In the confusion, I suppose I acted like an idiot."

"No. Only like a woman deeply in love," he said gently, and he smiled. "I am fine. I seem to invite Allah's protection, do I not? I have not a scratch. But I would not have had my friend Steven shot on my account."

"He'll be fine. Steve's like old leather," David said, chuckling with relief. "They're waiting for us."

"I don't suppose anyone would like to explain what's going on to me?" she asked the men when they were situated in the back of the police car heading toward the hospital.

David thought carefully before he replied. "We're selling some pretty sophisticated hardware to Ahmed's country. He has a hostile neighbor, a little less affluent, and they've made some veiled threats. We've had our security people and some government people keeping an eye on them. Tonight, they came out in the open with a bang. They're making their protests known in a pretty solid way."

"You mean they tried to kill Steve because you bought a plane?" she gasped, turning to Ahmed.

Ahmed grimaced. He exchanged a complicated glance with David and then shrugged. "Ah, that is so. Simplified, of course, but fairly accurate."

"They tried to kill Steven. Oh, my gosh!" she burst out.

"Equally simplified and fairly accurate," David added grimly. It wasn't the truth, but he couldn't tell her what was.

"Steve does have government protection?" she asked.

"Of a certainty." Ahmed gestured over his shoulder, and Meg saw a big black car following them and the police car ahead of them that carried Steven and Daphne.

"Who are they?" she asked nervously.

"CIA," David said. "They had us under surveillance, but nobody really expected this to happen. Now, of course, we'll be on video if we sneeze."

"You're kidding!" Her voice sounded high-pitched and uncertain.

There was a tiny noise and she jumped as "Gesundheit," came in an amused drawl from the police car's radio.

Steven was patched up, given a tetanus shot and released with an uneasy Daphne at his side. Ahmed and David kept Meg too busy talking to suffer too much at the sight.

Then they were all taken to police headquarters where two tall, tough-looking men—the same two who'd surrounded Ahmed after the shooting—sat down with the group and began to ask questions of everyone except Ahmed. That gentleman had been met by a small group of very respectful Arabs who surrounded him and preceded him into another room. It didn't occur to Meg just then to wonder why, if

Steve was the target, these government agents had rushed to protect Ahmed.

As he spoke with his people, Ahmed, again, looked like someone considerably more important than a minor cabinet minister of a Middle Eastern nation. His very bearing changed when he was approached, and he seemed not only more elegant, but almost frighteningly implacable. The liquid black eyes, which for Meg had always been smiling, were now icy cold and threatening. He spoke to the men in short, succinct phrases, which the other Arabs received with grimaces and something oddly like fear.

Meg frowned at the byplay, drawn back into the conversation by the CIA.

"Are you a permanent resident of Wichita?" the blond one asked.

She shook her head. "No. I live and work in New York most of the time. I've had a small injury…"

"Left ankle, torn ligaments, physical therapy and rest for one more week," the big, dark-headed agent finished for her. Her mouth fell open and he leaned forward. "Gesundheit," he said, grinning wickedly.

David laughed. "Meg, I hope you don't have any skeletons in your closet."

Meg suddenly remembered the night in Steve's car and flushed. She didn't dare look at him, but the big, dark agent pursed his lips and deliberately turned his head away. She could have gone through the floor.

There were a few more questions and some instructions, but it was soon over and they were allowed to leave.

Ahmed was in the hall with the other Arabs. The government agents greeted him with quiet respect and a brief conversation ensued. He nodded, said some-

thing in Arabic to his companions and moved forward
to say goodbye to his friends.

Meg came last. He took her hand in both of his,
and the dark authority in his face made her start. This
was not the charming, pleasant, lazily friendly man
she thought she knew. Ahmed was quite suddenly
something out of her experience.

"I hope that the evening has not been too strained
for you, *mademoiselle*. I hope to see you again soon,
and under kinder circumstances. *Au revoir.*"

He kissed her hand, very lightly. With a nod to
Steve and David, he strode back toward his men.
They surrounded him quickly, flinging hurried, respectful questions after him, and followed him out
into the night with the big dark government man a
step behind.

Meg had the oddest feeling about Ahmed. She had
to bite her tongue to keep the words from tumbling
out. But her concern now was only for Steve. Her
eyes slid around to where he was standing close to
Daphne and the tall blond agent. "They'll catch the
men who tried to kill him, won't they?" she asked
David worriedly.

"Sure they will. Don't worry, now, it's nothing to
do with you." He held up a restraining hand when
she opened her mouth to ask some more questions.
"Steve was barely scratched, despite the amount of
bleeding. He'll be carefully looked after. Everything's
fine."

"What is Steve selling to Ahmed?" she asked ag-
itatedly.

"A fighter plane. Very advanced. All the latest
technology. The government approves, because we're
allies of Ahmed's strategically placed little nation."

"But if they're trying to stop the sale, why shoot at Steve?"

Meg was too quick. "Probably, they were shooting at both of them but Steve got the bullet," he said.

"Oh." She relaxed a little. "But what if they try again?"

"I told you, they're going to be surrounded by government people."

"Won't they try to get Ahmed out of the country now?"

David grimaced. "I don't know. Calm down now, Meg. Try not to worry so much. It's all under control, believe me."

Meg finally gave in. David did look less concerned now, and she had to accept that Steve would be protected from further attacks.

David, meanwhile, was shaking inside. What he and Steven had learned from the CIA agents and Ahmed was enough to terrify anyone. Ahmed couldn't go home just now, and while he was in Wichita, he was in mortal danger. It was far more serious than a protest over an arms sale. A coup was in progress in Ahmed's nation and Ahmed had been targeted by its leaders.

Ahmed's position was top secret, so Meg couldn't be told. Only Daphne knew, because of her engagement to Wayne Hicks, the blond CIA agent. She was an unofficial liaison between the government men and Ahmed. There were secrets within secrets here. It was a tricky situation, made more so by Steven's apparent relationship with Daphne while Meg stood by helplessly and fumed.

Meg glanced at Steven. "Are you going to be all right?" she asked without meeting his eyes.

"I'm indestructible," he said tautly. "I only needed a bandage, believe it or not. I'd better get Daphne home," he added.

"Thanks, Steve," Daphne said gently, smiling up at him.

Meg looked away, so she didn't see Daphne's expression or Steve's. Her heart was breaking. She smiled dully and took David's arm. "In that case, I'll take my brother and go home. Good night, then."

David got them a cab right outside the door. Presumably Daphne was going to drive Steven's Jaguar.

Meg sat quietly in the corner of the cab, still trying to focus on the shocking, violent events of the night. The shots, Steve's wound, Ahmed's incredible transformation from indulgent friendliness to menacing authority, the police, the government men, the hospital…it all merged into a frightening blur. Meg closed her eyes on the memories. Daphne had won and the only course of action Meg had was to concede the field to the other woman once more. If Steve loved her, she'd stay and fight. But he didn't. Hadn't he made it abundantly clear that he preferred Daphne?

Always before, she'd had the sanctuary of her New York apartment to run to. But now, with her ankle in this shape, she knew for certain that it would be a very long time before she was fit enough to dance again. A very, very long time. She had to consider a new career. If she couldn't dance, she had to find a way to support herself. A ballet school was the ideal way. She'd studied ballet all her life. She knew she could teach it. All she required was a small loan, a studio and the will to succeed.

The fly in the ointment was that it would have to be here in Wichita. New York City was full of ballet schools, and rental property cost a fortune. She'd never be able to afford to do it there. Here in Wichita, she was known in local circles, even if the family was no longer wealthy. Her roots went back four generations here. The downside was that she'd have to see Steven occasionally, but perhaps she could harden her heart.

Meanwhile, Steven and David would be fine now, surely, with the CIA watching. And of course, they'd get Ahmed out of the country.

But, would *she* be fine, she wondered? It was like losing Steven all over again. She didn't know how she could bear it.

Meg went to bed and didn't sleep. Steve had taken Daphne home. She was tormented by images of Daphne in Steven's arms, being thrilled and delighted by his kisses. She couldn't bear it.

She couldn't sleep on Friday night, and was listless all day Saturday and Sunday. She worked on her exercises, but her lack of progress just made her more depressed. She went to sleep on Sunday night, but again couldn't rest easily. She got out of bed and decided to go down for a cup of hot chocolate. Maybe it would help her sleep.

She opened her door and heard movement downstairs. Her first thought was that it might be a burglar, but the lights were all on.

She went to the banister and leaned over. David was in the hall putting on a raincoat.

"David?" she called, surprised.

He glanced up at her. He held a briefcase under his arm. "I thought you were asleep."

"I can't sleep."

"I know. Well, I've got to run this stuff over to Ahmed…"

"It's midnight!"

He glowered at her. "Ahmed doesn't recognize little things like the hour of the night. And before you start worrying, I've got an escort waiting outside. Try to get some sleep, will you?"

She sighed. "Okay. Be careful."

"Sure thing."

She wandered back into her bedroom. She heard a door slam twice and David's car pulling away. Odd, two slams, but she was sleepy. Perhaps she'd counted wrong.

She looked at herself in the mirror, in the sexy little lavender night slip that stopped at her upper thighs. She looked very alluring, she decided, with her hair down her back and those spaghetti straps threatening to loosen the low bodice that didn't quite cover the firm swell of her creamy breasts. She sighed.

"Too bad your hair's not platinum," she told her reflection. "And your legs are too long." She made a face at herself before she opened the bedroom door and wandered slowly downstairs, careful not to let her weak ankle make her fall as she negotiated her way down. A cup of hot chocolate might just do the trick.

She yawned as she ambled into the kitchen. But she stopped dead at the sight of the man standing there, staring at her with eyes that didn't quite believe what he was seeing.

"Steven!" she gasped.

He was fully dressed, a light blue sports jacket paired with navy slacks, a white shirt and a blue striped tie. But there was no bulge high up on his left arm, no bandage.

"Why are you here?" she asked bluntly, getting her breath back. She refused to try to cover herself. Let him look, she thought bitterly. "And do try to remember not to sneeze," she added, glancing around paranoidly. "They're probably got video cameras everywhere. Oh, Lord!" she added suddenly, glancing down at her state of undress and remembering that dark-haired agent with the wicked smile.

"There are no hidden cameras here," he returned. "Why would there be?" His silver eyes narrowed. "Which is just as well, because I don't want anyone else to see you like this."

"For your eyes only?" she taunted. "Well, save it all for Daphne, Steve, darling. What do you want here? David just left."

"I know. I'm here to keep an eye on you while he's gone." He shouldered away from the door facing. "You aren't planning to cut your visit short and go back to New York, are you?" he asked bluntly.

She didn't want to answer that. Her ankle was killing her this morning, from the slight exercise it had been put through the night before. She could hardly walk on it. The thought of dancing on it made her nauseous.

"Am I being asked to leave town?" she hedged.

"No. Quite the contrary." He stuck his hands into his pockets and studied her through narrowed eyes. "I think it might be better if you stay in Wichita. But don't go out without David, will you?"

"They shot at you, not me," she reminded him, and had to choke down the fear the words brought back. He could have been killed. She didn't dare think about it too much. "You're really all right, aren't you?" she added reluctantly.

"I'm really all right." He saw the concern she couldn't hide, but he knew better than to read too much into it. She'd loved him once, or thought she had, before she decided that dancing was of prime importance. He stared at her with growing need. Dressed that way, she aroused him almost beyond bearing. He didn't know if he could keep his hunger for her under control. That gown...!

She stared down at her bare feet. "I'm glad you weren't hurt."

He didn't reply. When she looked up again, it was to find his silver eyes riveted to her breasts, to the pink swell of them over her bodice. The look was intimate. Hungry. She could almost see his heartbeat increasing.

"Don't, Steve," she said quietly.

"If not me, who, then?" he asked roughly, moving slowly toward her. "You won't give yourself to anyone else. You're twenty-three and still a virgin."

She gnawed her lower lip. "I like it that way," she said unsteadily, because he was close now, towering over her. She could feel the heat of his body, smell the spicy cologne he wore. It was a fragrance that she'd always connected with him. It aroused her.

"The hell you do. You waited for me. You're still waiting." His silver eyes dropped to her bodice and found the evidence of her arousal. "You can't even hide it," he taunted huskily. "All I have to do is look at you, or stand close to you, and your body begins to swell with wanting me."

She swallowed. "Don't humiliate me!" she whispered tightly.

"That isn't what I have in mind. Not at all." His hands came out of his pockets. They moved slowly to the smooth curve of her shoulders and caressed away the tiny spaghetti straps. His breath was at her temple, on her nose, her mouth. She ached for him in every cell of her body.

"Steve." She choked. "Steve, what about Daphne…?"

"Daphne who?" he breathed, and his mouth settled on hers as his hands moved abruptly, sending the gown careening recklessly down her body to land in a silken lavender pool at her feet.

Chapter 7

Right and wrong no longer existed separately in Steve's tormented mind. Meg wanted him and he wanted her. All the pain and anguish of the past four years fused in that one thought as he felt her mouth soften and open under his. He kissed her until she went limp in his arms, until his own body went rigid with insistent desire. And only then did he lift his head to look at what his hands had uncovered.

Meg felt the impact of Steven's eyes on her bare breasts like a hot caress on her skin. She stood before him in only a pair of lacy, high-cut pink briefs, insecure in her nudity. But when her hands lifted automatically, he caught her wrists and drew her hands to his chest. His steely eyes held hers while he pressed them there.

"Don't hide from me," he said quietly. His eyes fell to her body and sketched its pink and mauve contours with slow, exquisite appreciation. "You're more beautiful than a Boticelli nude, Mary Margaret."

"You're forgetting Daphne." She choked out the words, beyond protest. "She has a hold on you."

He was still staring at her, unblinking. "You might say that."

"Steve…"

"Don't talk, Meg," he replied, his voice deep and soft, almost lazy as his dark head started to bend toward her. "Talking doesn't accomplish a damned thing."

"Steven, you mustn't…!"

"Oh, but I must," he breathed as his mouth opened just above her taut nipple. "I must…!"

She felt the soft tracing of his tongue just before the faint suction that took her breast right into the dark warmth of his mouth.

Steve heard her gasp, felt her whole body go rigid in his grasp. But he didn't stop. He nuzzled her gently and increased the warm pressure. A little sound passed her lips and then she began to push toward him, not away from him. He groaned against her as his hands slid up the silky softness of her back and drew her into the aroused curve of his body.

Meg had stopped thinking altogether. The insistent hunger of his mouth made her body throb in the most incredible way. She cradled his dark head against her, leaning back in his embrace. She felt as if she were floating, drifting.

Steve was kneeling, easing her down to the floor, his mouth against her. He pulled her over him, parting her smooth legs so that they were hip to hip. His mouth moved to her other breast, then to her throat and finally up to her parted lips. He kissed her with slow, aching passion, all the while exploring her body with deft, sure hands. He whispered things she couldn't even hear for the roar in her ears. And then he shifted her, just a little, and she felt the aroused thrust of him as his body began to rock sensually against hers.

She gasped and stiffened, because even their most intimate time hadn't been quite this intimate.

He lifted his head. His silver eyes were misty with desire as he searched hers. He moved, deliberately, so that she felt him intimately, and a wave of pleasure rippled up her body. She couldn't hide the shocked delight in her eyes. He smiled, slowly, and moved again. This time her hands gripped his shoulders and she relaxed, shyly bringing him into even greater intimacy with her.

His lean hand slid up her thigh, tracing its inner curve. She saw his mouth just before it settled on hers again. He touched her as he never had. Waves of pleasure jolted her. She tried to protest, but it was far too late. She began to whimper.

His tongue tangled with hers, thrust deep into her mouth. She felt tears in her eyes as he held her in thrall. Her body arched helplessly toward him. She felt his mouth sliding down to her breasts, possessing her. He stroked her until she was weeping with helpless desire, her voice breaking as she whispered, pleaded, begged.

The husky pleas, combined with the sensual movement of her body over his, removed him sufficiently from reality so that it was impossible for him to pull back in time. He kissed her. His mouth bit into hers and she felt him move, felt the soft tearing of her briefs, felt the air on her body. She heard the rasp of a zipper, the metallic sound of a belt.

He pulled her up so that she was sitting with her legs on either side of him. She heard his breathing, rough and unsteady at her ear, as his lean hands suddenly gripped her bare thighs deliberately and he lifted her.

"Easy," he whispered as he brought her to him and slowly pulled her down.

She had a second to wonder about the faint threat of his hold on her, and then his mouth opened on hers and she felt the first insistent thrust of him against the veil of her innocence.

Her eyes flew open. She cried out at the flash of hot pain. He held her still, breathing roughly. His face was rigid, his teeth clenched, his breathing audible through his nose. He looked into her wide, frightened eyes and held them as he pulled her slowly down on him again.

"Don't be afraid, Meg," he whispered deeply. "It's only going to hurt for a few seconds."

"But...Steve..." She gasped, trying to find the words to protest what was happening.

"Let me love you," he said unsteadily. His hands tugged her over him and he shivered. His face was tormented, his eyes like silver fires. "God, baby...let me. Let me!" He ground out the words.

She knew that it would be impossible for him to stop. She loved him. That was all that really mattered now. She gave in, yielding to the pain, her hands taut on his shoulders. Her hold on him tightened and she flinched.

"Just a...little further. Oh, Meg," he growled, shivering as he completed the motion and felt her all around him. His eyes closed and he shivered. Then they opened again and searched hers as he repeated the slow, deliberate movement of his hips until his possession of her was complete and the lines of strain left her face. Then he rested, his body intimately joined to hers, and gently pushed her disheveled hair back from her face.

She swallowed. There was awe in her eyes now, along with lingering pain and doubt and shock.

"I've waited so long, Meg," he said unsteadily. "I've waited all my life for this. For you."

Her fingers trembled on his shirtfront. "Steve, you're…part of me," she burst out.

Color burned along his high cheekbones. "Yes." He moved, as if to emphasize it, and she blushed. "Unfasten my shirt, Meg. Let me feel your breasts against my skin while we love."

While we love. She must be insane, she thought. But she was too involved to stop, to pull back. She was in thrall to him. Her hands fumbled with his tie, his jacket, his shirt. She fumbled, but finally she stripped it all off him.

Her hands speared through the thick mat of hair that covered him from collarbone to below his lean waist. She looked down and stared helplessly, her body trembling. His powerful hands lifted her up just a little, smiling even through his need at the expression on her face.

"Steve…"

He tilted her face and brought his mouth down on her lips with exquisite tenderness as he began to guide her hips again. This time there was no pain at all. There was a faint pleasure that began to grow, to swell, to encompass her. She gasped and her nails bit into his shoulders.

"Like this?" he whispered, and moved again.

She sobbed into his shoulder, her mouth open against his neck, clinging to him as he increased the rhythm and pressure of his body. His hand clenched in the hair at her nape and he caught his breath, shivering.

"Relax, now," he said, sliding a hand under her thigh to pull her to him roughly. "Yes…!"

His image began to blur in her open, startled eyes as the pleasure became suddenly violent, insistent. She felt herself tense as he lifted to her as they knelt so intimately together, shivering with every movement, reaching for something she couldn't quite grasp. Her strength gave out, but his was unfailing, endless.

"Help me," she whispered brokenly.

"Tell me how it feels, Meg," he whispered back, his voice rough, deep as he pushed up insistently. "Tell me!"

"It's so sweet…I can't…bear…it!" She wept.

"Neither can I." His hands tightened on her thighs almost to bruising pain and he lost control. "Meg…. Meg….!"

She felt him go rigid just before her mind was submerged in a heated rush of pleasure. It was a kind of pain, she thought blindly. A kind of sweet, unbearable pain that hit her like a lightning bolt, lifting her in his arms, making her cry out with the anguish it kindled. She didn't know if she could bear it and stay alive.

Steven's heart was beating. She felt the heavy, hard beat against her breasts, felt the blood pulsating through him as he eased her down on her back, still

a part of him. He relaxed, his arms catching the bulk
of his weight while he struggled to breathe normally.
The intimacy of their position was beyond her wildest
dreams. She closed her eyes, experiencing it through
every cell of her body.

He could hardly believe what he'd done. The rush
of pleasure had almost knocked him out. He'd been
so desperate for her that he hadn't even removed all
his clothing. He'd fought them both out of their garments and taken her sitting up on the carpet, when
her first time should have been in a bed with their
wedding night before them and everything legal and
neatly tied up. And worst of all, he hadn't had the
foresight to use any sort of protection. He groaned
aloud as sanity came back in a cold rush. "Oh, hell!"
He ground out the words.

He levered himself away from her and got to his
feet a little shakily. He zipped his trousers with a
vicious motion of his hands before he fumbled a cigarette out of the pocket of his discarded shirt and lit
it. He put on his shirt. He didn't look at Meg, who
finally managed with trembling hands to slide her
gown back on. The briefs were beyond wearing at all.

Steve smoked half the cigarette before he crushed
it out in an ashtray on the table, one that David kept
for him. He buttoned his shirt and replaced his tie and
jacket before he spoke.

By then, Meg was sitting on the very edge of the
sofa, feeling uncomfortable and very ashamed.

He stood over her, searching for the right words.
Impossible, really. There weren't any for what he'd
done.

"You'll be sore for a while," he said stiffly. "I'm
sorry I couldn't spare you the pain."

She wrapped her arms around herself and shivered.

He knelt just in front of her, his hand on the sofa beside her as he searched her wan, drawn face.

"Meg," he said roughly, "it's all right. You don't have anything to be ashamed of."

"Don't I?" Tears rolled down her cheeks.

"Oh, baby," he groaned. He pulled her down into his arms and sat on the carpet, cradling her against him. His lips found her throat and pressed there gently. "Meg, don't cry."

"I'm easy, I'm cheap…!"

"You are not." He lifted his head and held her eyes. "We made love to each other. Is that so terrible? If I hadn't gone crazy and chased you away, it would have happened four years ago, and you know it!"

She couldn't really argue with that. He was telling the truth. "Will you tell Daphne?" she asked.

"No, I won't tell Daphne," he replied quietly. "It's none of her business. It's no one's, except ours."

She still felt miserable, but some of the pain eased away as he smoothed her against him. Her eyes closed and she wished that she never had to move away again. He was warm and strong and it felt right to be lying with him this way. What had happened felt right.

His lean hand smoothed over her flat belly. He drew back a little and stared down at it, his face troubled.

She knew what he was thinking. It had just occurred to her, too.

"You didn't use anything," she whispered.

"I know. Damn me for a fool, I was too far gone

to care." He lifted his eyes to hers and grimaced. "I'm sorry. It was irresponsible. Unforgivable."

Her blue eyes sketched his dark face, down to his stubborn chin and the breadth of his shoulders.

"What are you thinking?" he asked curiously.

"You were an only child," she said. "Did your father have any sisters?"

He shook his head. His brows curved together and then a smile tugged at his firm mouth as he searched her eyes. "Boys run in my family, Meg. Is that what you wanted to know?"

She nodded, smiling shyly.

His big hand pressed slowly against her belly. "A baby would cost you your career," he said slowly.

She looked up at him. "You don't think my ankle won't?"

The expression drained out of his face, leaving it blank. "What do you mean?"

She threw caution to the wind. It was time for honesty. Total honesty, despite the cost. She'd truly burned all her bridges.

"It hurts just from walking. It's swollen. It's been weeks, and it's no better." She traced a pearly button on his shirt with her fingernail as she forced herself to face the fear she'd been avoiding. "Rehearsals begin at the end of next week, but it might as well be yesterday. Steve, I won't be able to dance. Not for a long time. Maybe not ever."

He didn't move. His eyes searched her face, but he didn't speak, either.

She looked up at him miserably. "What will happen to you and Daphne if I get pregnant? It would ruin everything for you." She sighed wearily, closing her eyes as she laid her cheek on his chest. "Oh, Steve, why is life so complicated?"

"It isn't, usually."

"It is right now." She bit her lower lip. "Would you...want a baby?"

His body began to throb. Light burst inside him. A child. A little boy, perhaps, since they ran in his family. A bond with Meg that nothing could break. The thought delighted him.

But he didn't answer immediately, and Meg thought the worst. She had to fight tears. "I see," she said brokenly. "I guess you'd want me to go to a clinic and—"

"No!"

"You wouldn't?"

"Of course I wouldn't!" he said curtly. He held her face up to his. "Don't you even think about it! I swear to God, Meg, if you do anything...!"

"But, I wouldn't!" she said quickly. "That's what I was going to tell you. I couldn't!"

He relaxed. His hand moved to her cheek and brushed back the disheveled hair around its flushed contours. "Okay. Make sure you don't. People who don't want babies should think before they make them."

"Like we just did," she agreed with a flicker of her dry humor.

He lifted an eyebrow. "Right."

She relaxed a little more. He did look marginally less rigid and austere. "I could have said something."

"Of course. Exactly when did you think of saying something?"

She flushed and dropped her eyes.

"That's when I thought of saying something. It was

a bit late, of course." He frowned slightly and his silver eyes twinkled. "It was very intense, wasn't it? Even for you."

"I'd wanted you for a long time," she confessed quietly.

"And I, you." He drew in a long, slow breath. "Well, it's done. Now we have to live with it. I'll get your ring out of the safe and bring it over. We are now officially reengaged."

"But Steve, what about Daphne?" she exclaimed.

"If you mention Daphne one more time today, I'll—!" he muttered. He let her go and got to his feet, pulling her up beside him. "She'll understand."

"You haven't asked if I want to be engaged again," she protested, trying to keep some control over her own destiny.

He pulled her to him and his hand curved around her flat stomach. "If you've got a baby in here, you don't have much choice. My mother would bring the shotgun all the way from West Palm Beach and point it at both of us before she'd see her first grandchild born out of wedlock."

She smiled, picturing his mother staggering under the weight of one of Steven's hunting rifles. "I guess she would at that." She glanced at him wryly. "And I'd already be sitting on your doorstep wearing a sign —*and* maternity clothes—so that everyone would know who got me pregnant in the first place."

He felt the world spin around him. He mustn't read too much into that beaming smile on her face, he told himself. After all, with her ankle in this condition, she had no career left. He was still second best in her life. At least she would want a child, if they'd made one.

She looked up and encountered the cold anger in his face and knew instantly that despite his hunger for her, all the bitterness was still there.

He shrugged. Bending, he pushed back her tousled hair. "I want you. You want me. Whatever else there is, we'll have that." He sighed gently. "Besides, if the attraction we feel is still strong enough four years after the fact to send us making love on the carpet, it isn't likely to weaken, is it?"

"For heaven's sake, Steve!" she exclaimed, outraged.

"Meg, you're repressed." He shook his head. "What am I going to do with you?"

"You might stop embarrassing me," she muttered.

His eyebrow jerked as he stared at her. "My beautiful Mary Margaret," he said softly. "When I wake up in the morning, I'll be sure that I was only dreaming again."

"Did you dream of me?" she asked involuntarily.

"Oh, yes. For most of my life, I think." He searched her soft eyes. "'There be none of Beauty's daughters with a magic like thee…'" he quoted tenderly, and watched the heat rise in her cheeks. "Do you like Lord Byron, Meg?"

"You never read poetry to me," she said with a sad little smile.

"I wanted to. But you were very young," he recalled, his face going hard. "And I was afraid to trust my heart too far." He laughed suddenly as all the bitterness came sweeping back. "Good thing I didn't. You walked out on me."

"You made me," she shot right back. "You know you did." The anger eased as she saw the pained look on his face. "You haven't had a lot of love, Steven," she said. "I don't think you trusted anyone enough to let them close to you—not Daphne, and certainly not me. You like my body, but you don't want my heart."

He was shocked. He stared at her, searching for words. He couldn't even manage an answer.

"I'd love you, if you'd let me," she said gently, her blue eyes smiling at him.

His jaw clenched. "You already did, on the floor," he said coldly. All sorts of impossible things were forming in his mind. He felt vulnerable and he didn't like it. He glared at her. "You didn't even try to stop me. Since you can't dance anymore, what a hell of a meal ticket I'll make!"

She stared at him and suddenly saw right through the angry words. She knew with a flash of intuition that he was still fighting her. He cared. Perhaps he didn't know it. Perhaps he'd even convinced himself that he really loved Daphne. But he didn't. Even though she was innocent, Meg knew that men didn't lose control as Steve had tonight unless there were some powerful emotions underlying the desire. He was fighting her. It had been that all along, his need to keep emotional entanglements at bay. He was afraid to risk his heart on her. Why hadn't she seen that years ago?

"No comeback?" he taunted furiously.

She smiled again, feeling faintly mischievous. "Are you going to bring my ring back tonight?"

He hesitated. "Meg..."

"I know. It's way after midnight and David will be home soon, I suppose," she added. "But you could come to supper tomorrow night. And bring my ring back," she emphasized. "I hope you haven't lost it."

He glared at her. "No, I haven't lost it. I can't bring it tomorrow night. I have a dinner meeting with Ahmed. Daphne's coming along," he reminded her.

She felt a little uncertain of her ground, but something kept her going, prodded her on.

She moved toward him, watching his expressions change, watching his eyes glitter. She caught him by the lapels and went on tiptoe, softly brushing her body against his as she reached up and drew her mouth tantalizingly over his parted lips. She could feel his heartbeat slamming at his ribs, hear his breathing. He was acting. It was a sham. She bit his lower lip, gently, and let go of him, moving away.

"What was that all about?" he asked gruffly.

"Didn't you like it?" she asked softly.

His jaw clenched. "I have to go."

"To dinner, perhaps. But not to Daphne's bed. Not now."

"What makes you so sure that I won't?" he demanded with a mocking smile.

She searched his eyes. "Because it would be sacrilege to do with anyone else what we just did with each other."

He would have denied it. He wanted to. But he couldn't force the words out. He turned and went to the door, pausing just to make sure the lock was on before he glanced back.

"Buy a wedding gown," he said curtly. "And if you try to run away from me this time, I'll follow you straight to hell if I have to!"

He closed the door behind him, and Meg stared at

it with a jumble of emotions, the foremost of which was utter joy.

Steve was feeling less than pleased. He had Meg, but it was a hollow victory. Despite the exquisite pleasure she'd given him, he was no closer to capturing her heart. He wanted it more than he'd ever realized.

She cared about him. She must, to give herself so generously. For Meg, physical need alone would never have caused such a sacrifice. But he had to remember that her career was no longer a point of contention between them. Her career was history. Even if she cared about him, ballet would have come first if it had been an option. He knew it. And that was what made him so bitter.

Chapter 8

Later that same night, after a refreshing shower, Meg went to bed, feeling tired. But she barely slept at all, wondering at the way things had changed in her life.

David gave her curious looks at the breakfast table. "You look like you haven't slept at all," he remarked.

"I haven't," she confessed, smiling at him. "Steven and I got engaged again last night."

He caught his breath. The delight in his eyes said everything. "So he finally gave in."

"Not noticeably," she murmured dryly.

"He's taken the first step," he replied. "You can't expect a fine fighting fish to just swallow a hook, you know."

"This fighting fish is a piranha. He's very bitter, David," she said quietly. She sipped coffee, her brows knitted. "He's never really forgiven me for leaving—even though he drove me away."

He smiled at her, his eyes kind and full of warmth. "I gather that he'll be over tonight?"

"Probably not. I doubt if Daphne can spare him," she muttered. "He's having dinner with her."

He grimaced at the expression on her face. He knew what was going on, and that Steve couldn't tell her. Neither could he.

"Things aren't always what they seem," he began.

"It doesn't matter, you know," she replied with resignation. "I love him. I never stopped. The past four years have been so empty, David. I'm tired of running from it. At least he still wants me, you know. I may not win entirely, but I'll give Daphne a run for her money," she added with a tiny smile.

"That's the spirit. You might consider, too, that if he didn't care, why would he want to marry you?"

She couldn't tell him that. She changed the subject and led him on a discussion of local politics.

But she did go around in a daze for the rest of the day. She wouldn't have believed what had happened if it hadn't been for the potent evidence of it in her untried body. Her memories were sweet. She couldn't even be bothered to worry about Daphne anymore. She did worry about Steven. If a crazed terrorist was after him, how would the authorities be able to stop him? And what about Ahmed?

The questions worried her, so she found solace in her exercises. Even so, she only did them halfheartedly. Ballet had been her life for years, but now she thought about loving Steven and having a baby of her own. Suddenly her fear of childbirth seemed to diminish, and her disappointment over her injury faded. Ballet was a hobby. It was nothing more than a hobby. She was daydreaming now, of little baby clothes and bassinets and toys scattered around a room that contained Steven and herself as well as a miniature version of one of them. Anything seemed possible; life was sweet.

Steven tossed and turned until dawn and went into the office in a cold, red-eyed daze. His life had shifted without warning. He'd made love to Meg and nothing would ever be the same again. If he was besotted with her before, it was nothing to what he was now that he'd known her intimately. He wasn't certain that he could even work.

Daphne brought in the mail. She saw his worried expression and paused in front of the desk.

"Something's wrong, isn't it?" she asked with the ease of friendship. "Can I help?"

"Sure," he agreed, leaning back in his big desk chair. "Tell me how to explain to Meg, to whom I've just become reengaged, why I'm going out with you tonight."

She whistled. "That's a good one."

"Isn't it?"

"Can't you get permission to tell her the truth?"

He shook his head. "Your own fiancé told me not to tell. He thinks too many people are in the know already." He closed his eyes with a long sigh. His body was pleasantly tired and still faintly throbbing from its exquisite knowledge of Meg.

"Isn't she going back to New York temporarily?" Daphne asked.

"I'm afraid to let her," he said wearily. "At least here she can be protected along with David. But I can't tell her what's going on. I'm going to have to ask her to trust me, when I never trusted her."

"If she loves you enough, she will," Daphne said with certainty. "And anyway, surely it will all be over soon."

"God, I hope so!"

"How's the arm?"

"Is wasn't exactly a major wound," he mused, chuckling. "The bullet broke a small vein. I've got a bandage over it. Funny, I didn't even notice—" He broke off, feeling uncomfortable as he remembered the night before, when he and Meg had both forgotten it. He changed the subject, quickly. "Have we heard from Ahmed today?"

She grimaced. "Indeed we have. He came in surrounded by bodyguards and government agents, and eventually chewed up one of the girls in the typing pool, who stopped bawling long enough to take a leaf out of my very own book. She threw a paperweight at him on his way out."

"What?"

"Calm down, it was a very small paperweight— not in the same league as the lamp I threw at you— and she missed on purpose, too," Daphne said quickly, with a grin. "He was surprised, to say the least. In his country, women don't react like that."

"I don't guess they do. Certainly not with Ahmed!"

"But, then, Brianna our typist didn't know who he was," Daphne reminded him. "And she still doesn't. She told me that if he sets foot in the building again, she's quitting," she added. "She is a very angry young lady, indeed."

"I need to have a word with your fiancé," Steve said. "Just to see what else needs doing so we can wind up this mess."

"Ahmed's under twenty-four-hour guard. He's used to it, of course. I understand he had a slight altercation with his bodyguard when they didn't see the assassins coming last night."

"I noticed the bruises," Steven mentioned.

"I'm sorry about Meg," Daphne said, grimacing. "I seem to keep complicating things for her."

"Not your fault this time," he said. "Or last time, either. It was my pride that sent her running. I hope I'll have better luck now."

"So do I," Daphne told him sincerely. "We're good friends, Steve. We always have been. I'm so happy. I hope you're going to be, too, you and Meg."

He only nodded. "We'd better get to work."

"Yes, sir," she said with a grin. "I'll send Wayne in."

Daphne's fiancé was blond and blue-eyed, a screaming contrast to his partner, who was tall and very dark and had a sense of humor that had already sent Steven up the wall.

The dark one looked around very carefully, even peering under Steve's desk.

"Looking for bugs?" Steve asked with a twinkle in his eyes.

"No," he replied. "Paperweights and blue-eyed brunettes." He grinned. "She's a dish."

"Yes, she is, but you're on duty," Wayne told his partner.

"So I am." He straightened, wiped the smile off his face and stared grimly at Steven. "Sir, have you noticed any bombs or enemy missiles in your office—oof!"

Wayne calmly removed his elbow from his friend's

ribs. "I'm going to feed you to a shark on our next assignment."

The taller man lifted both bushy eyebrows. "Copycat. James Bond did that to an enemy agent in one of his films."

"Are you sure you're suited to this line of work, Lang?" Wayne asked somberly.

"Plenty of people with badges have a sense of humor." Lang glared at his friend. "Plenty more don't, of course."

"To the matter at hand," Wayne interrupted, glancing at Steve. "We need your itinerary for the rest of the week, right down to the minute. And if you plan any more impromptu evening outings..."

"Not me," Steven said with a slow grin, indicating his arm. "I've gone right off night life without adequate protection."

"Fair enough. We're now in the process of bugging everything you own, from cars to houses to aircraft, as well as Mr. Shannon's home," Wayne continued, noticing Steve's faint color with absent curiosity. "We would have done it sooner, but until this morning we hadn't quite decided about how much surveillance was required. It would be pretty stupid to overlook protection for your chief executive, Mr. Shannon, and his sister, especially since they were seen in the company of Ahmed. These people will use whatever bargaining tools they can get, and Ahmed's fondness for Miss Shannon was pretty obvious."

Steve didn't like remembering that. He was jealous of Ahmed now—jealous of any man who looked at Meg.

"Isn't it dangerous politically to let Ahmed stay here, in the States?" Steve asked suddenly.

"Certainly," Lang told him. "Suicidal, in fact." He grinned and his dark eyes twinkled. "But we're responsible for him. So if we send him home and somebody blows him away, guess who gets the blame?"

"We're in between a rock and a hard place," Wayne agreed. "That's why we're going to keep Ahmed here and see if we can draw the other agents out into the open again."

"They were in the open last night."

"Ah," Lang replied, "but it was just a routine surveillance until then. We didn't have any advanced warning of an assassination try until the coup attempt was made in Ahmed's home country. And by then the terrorists were already in position here and making their move. Now that we know what's afoot, we're ready, too."

"We're on it. We'll handle this. How about Miss Shannon?" Wayne asked Steven. "Can you get her out of town?"

"I can," Steven agreed. "But what if they find out that she and I are engaged again and make a grab for her, where she's totally unprotected?"

The smile vanished from Lang's face. "You're engaged again?"

Steven nodded.

Lang exchanged a long glance with Wayne. "That changes things. We'd better keep her in town. But she can't know why," he emphasized.

Steven just nodded, because Wayne had already told him that. He could break their confidence, of course, but now that the house and his car and God knew what else was bugged, he couldn't tell Meg anyplace that they wouldn't overhear. He was going to have to watch what he said altogether. And the complication was that he not only couldn't tell Meg that, but he wouldn't be able to touch her without being overheard. He could have groaned out loud.

Meg was home alone that afternoon. David was still at work.

Steven drove up to the Shannon house just a few minutes after quitting time, casually dressed in jeans and a knit shirt, topped off with a suede jacket.

He smiled at Meg when she opened the door, approving the pretty blue sundress that complemented her fairness. She'd left her hair down, and he ached to get his hands in its silky length.

"Give me your hand," he said without preamble.

She lifted the left one, and he slid the sapphire and diamond engagement ring he'd given her four years ago smoothly on to her ring finger. It was a perfect fit.

He lifted the hand to his lips and kissed it very gently.

"Oh, Steve," she whispered, reaching up to him.

He caught her wrists and stepped back, painfully aware of surveillance techniques that could pick up heavy breathing a mile away. He laughed a little shortly, trying to ignore Meg's shocked, embarrassed expression.

"How about some coffee?" he asked.

She faltered a little. "Of course," she said. "I'll, uh, I'll just make some." She was near tears. They'd made love, they'd just gotten reengaged, and suddenly Steven couldn't bear her to touch him!

He followed her into the kitchen, grimacing at her expression. He couldn't tell her everything, but he had to tell her this, at least.

As she turned on the faucet to fill the drip coffee maker, Steve reached over her shoulder and took the coffeepot away, leaving the water running just briefly.

He bent to kiss her, whispering under his breath, ''We're on Candid Camera.''

She let him kiss her, but her wide eyes stayed open. He drew back, shutting off the faucet.

She was suddenly very alert. She looked around the room. ''Achoo?'' she whispered.

''Gesundheit!'' came the deep, chuckled reply.

Meg went every shade of scarlet under the sun as she looked at Steven. She gasped in horror.

''It's all right,'' he said quickly. ''They've only just done it!''

She chewed the ends of her fingers as the flat statement finally began to make sense and she relaxed. ''Oh, thank goodness!''

The back door opened and the big, dark agent entered, a finger to his lips.

He whipped out a pad and pencil and wrote something on it, showing it to Meg and Steve. He'd written: *Our team wasn't the only one wrangling bugs around here this afternoon. Watch what you say.*

Do they have cameras? Steve scribbled on the paper.

The agent shook his head, grinning. He made a sign with two forked fingers like someone poking eyes out.

Steve gave him a thumbs-up sign. The agent put away his pad and pencil and looked at the coffeepot longingly.

Meg held up five fingers. He grinned and started

back out. Then he glanced at the two of them and
made a kissing motion followed by a firm shaking of
his head. Meg stuck her tongue out at him. He smothered a laugh as he let himself back out the door.

Meg busied herself with the coffeepot, worried
about living in a goldfish bowl. It would be like this
from now on, she was sure, until they caught the people who were responsible for the attack at the restaurant.

"Cream?" Steven asked when she poured coffee
into two cups.

"I'll get it."

She handed it to him, carrying a cup of black coffee
to the back door. A huge hand came out and accepted
it. She peered around the door, eyebrows raised. The
agent made a sign with his thumb and forefinger and
eased back around the side of the house with his cup.

Meg closed the door gently and followed Steve
back into the living room.

"I can't stay long. I have a date," he told Meg.

She glared at him. "Of course. With Daphne."

"And Ahmed," he replied. "At the Sheraton.
More business discussions."

It didn't occur to her right then why Steve had
given away his movements, when he knew the house
was bugged. "I don't suppose I could come along?"
she asked.

"No."

"I like Ahmed. He likes me, too."

"Of course he likes you. You're blond."

She glared at him.

"And pretty."

The glare softened.

"And very, very sweet."

She smiled.

He sipped his coffee. "Where are we going to live when we're married?"

"I like Alaska..."

He glowered at her. "In Wichita, Meg. I don't work in Alaska."

"What's wrong with your house?" she asked.

"It doesn't have much of a yard," he replied. "We'll need a place for a swing set and some outdoor playthings for the kids."

She flushed, averting her eyes. "So we will."

He stared at her until she lifted her face, and he smiled. He slid his arm over the back of the couch and his eyes narrowed. His head made a coaxing motion.

She put her coffee cup down, her blood throbbing in her veins, and went across to join him on the sofa.

He put his thumb over her mouth and pulled her down into his arms. As his hand lifted, his lips parted on her mouth, and he kissed her with long, slow passion. His hand found her breast, teasing the nipple to hardness while he kissed her as if he could never get enough.

When he lifted his head, her eyes were misty and dazed, her body draped over his lap.

He looked at her for a long, long time.

"I have to go," he said quietly.

She started to protest, but she knew that it would do no good at all.

"Will I see you tomorrow?" she asked miserably as he helped her up.

"Probably." He stood close to her, his eyes troubled. "Lock the doors. David will be home soon."

"My brother is a poor substitute for my fiancé," she muttered.

"It won't always be like this," he said solemnly. His silver eyes searched hers for a long time. "I promise you it won't."

She nodded. "Do be careful. The way you drive…" She stopped when he frowned. "Well, I'd like to think you could get all the way home in one piece."

He lifted an eyebrow. "Do you worry about me?"

"All the time," she said honestly, her blue eyes wide and soft.

His heart raced as he looked down at her. If she was putting on an act, it was a good one.

Gently he brought her against him and bent to brush his open mouth softly over her own. She moved closer. His arms enfolded her, cherished her. She wrapped herself around him and gave way to the need to be held.

But things got out of hand almost immediately. He caught her hips and pushed her away, his face set in deep, harsh lines as he fought to control his passion for her.

"Go back inside," he said huskily. "I'll phone you in the morning."

"Why did you bother to get engaged to me when you plan to spend your nights with another woman?" she asked miserably.

"You know why," he said, his voice deep, his eyes glittering. "Don't you?"

Because they'd stepped over the line and she might be pregnant. How could she have forgotten? She moved back from him, averting her eyes.

"Yes," she replied, freezing up. She'd tried to forget, but he wasn't going to let her. She was weaving daydreams. The reality was that he'd lost his head and now he was going to do the honorable thing. "Of course I know why, Steven. Silly of me to forget, wasn't it?"

He scowled and his face tautened. She had the wrong end of the stick again. But he couldn't, didn't dare, say anything. "David should be here any minute," he added. "Don't go outside, and lock the door after me."

"I'll do that."

He glanced around. Nothing and nobody was in sight, but he was certain that one of the agents guarding Meg was nearby. He'd arranged that before he left the office.

"I'll phone you tomorrow. Maybe we can go out."

"What a thrill," she said.

He glared at her. "Keep it up."

"I'm trying."

He made an exasperated sound, stuck his hands into his pockets and moved toward his Jaguar.

After he drove away, Meg closed the door and locked it, and went back into the living room.

David came home long enough to change and went right back out again, apologizing to Meg. He had to go along with Steve and Daphne to hobnob with Ahmed.

"Is everybody going except me?" Meg groaned, exasperated.

David grinned at her. "Probably. Have a nice evening, now."

She glared at him. He left and she busied herself watering her house plants. The house was unusually quiet, and she kept imagining noises. They made her uneasy, especially under the circumstances. She heard movement in the living room and slowly stuck her head around the door to see what it was, her heart pounding madly.

But it was only the big dark agent standing there, grinning at her. He put a finger to his lips, pushed a button on some small electronic device in his hand, and chuckled as it emitted a jarring noise.

"There'll be plenty of headaches tonight," he murmured dryly.

"What did you do?" she asked, and then clapped a hand over her mouth.

"It's okay. I jammed them." He studied her through narrowed eyes. "I need to talk to you."

"What about?" she asked, and waited almost without breathing for the answer.

He was serious then, the twinkle gone from his dark eyes. He towered over her, almost as tall as Steve and just about as intimidating. He pushed the button on the jamming device with a calculating look on his face, shutting off the interference.

"I'm going to get you out of here, right now. Tonight. I want you to come with me, no arguments."

She hesitated. "Shouldn't we call Steve or your partner?"

"No one is to know. Not even my partner."

She didn't like the sound of that. She liked this man, but she didn't completely trust him.

"Why isn't your partner to know?" she asked curiously.

He muttered something under his breath. Then he calmly pulled out his automatic pistol and leveled it at her stomach. He seemed to raise his voice a little. "Because he would try to stop me, of course," he replied. "I plan to turn you over to Ahmed's buddies outside. You'll be a hell of a bargaining tool for them."

"You can't do this!" she exclaimed, thinking of ways to escape, but unable to come up with anything. There was an automatic pistol pointed at her stomach. She'd heard it said that even a karate black belt would hesitate to fight off an armed man.

"But I can," he assured her. "In fact, I'm doing it. Let's go."

Chapter 9

Meg felt her breath catch in her chest as she stared down numbly at the muzzle of the pistol. Dozens of wild thoughts passed through her mind, none of which lingered long enough to register except one: she was never going to see Steve again.

Her blue eyes lifted to Lang's dark ones. He didn't look as if he meant to kill her.

He jerked his head toward the front door and indicated that he wanted her to go out it. "I said let's go," he said. "Now."

She hesitated. "Can't we...?"

He took her arm firmly and propelled her forward. She felt the presence of the gun, even if she didn't feel it stuck in her back. She noticed that he looked around from side to side as if he was expecting company.

Perhaps the enemy agents would shoot him. But that wasn't likely. If they'd overheard what he said, and that jammer had seemed to be turned off at the last, they'd be waiting out here for him to turn her over to them. Would they pay him? Of course they would. They'd keep her hostage and use her to trade to Steve for Ahmed. She felt sick.

"Hey!" he called as they got to the front porch. "Let's make a deal, boys. I'm cutting myself in on the action!"

"You turncoat," Meg cried furiously.

"Stop struggling," he said calmly. "How about it!"

"We have already heard you," came a distinctly accented reply. "How much do you want for the woman?"

Lang turned toward the voice. "Let me come over there and we'll talk about it. No shooting."

"Very well!"

A shadowy figure appeared. Lang measured the distance from where the car was to where the man was and began to walk down the middle of it with Meg.

"Keep your nerve," he said unexpectedly. "For God's sake, don't go to pieces now."

"I'm not the screaming type," she muttered. "But I am not going to let you give me to those people without a fight!"

"Good. Uh, don't start fighting until I tell you, okay? I breathe better without extra holes in my chest." He lifted his head and marched her quickly forward, beginning to veer almost imperceptibly when the car was in running distance.

"Wait! Stop there!" the voice called.

Lang broke into a run, dragging Meg with him. The

sudden movement startled the two men who were in
view now. Guns were raised and Lang groaned.

"Stop!" the accented voice warned harshly. "Do
not attempt to enter the car!"

Lang stopped at his dark blue car with the hand
holding the pistol on the door handle and lifted his
head. The wind whipped his dark hair around his face.
"Why not?" he called back. "It's a great night for a
ride!"

"What are you doing?!"

"I thought it was obvious," he replied. "I'm leaving."

"You agreed to bargain! Let the girl go and you
may go free!"

"Make me."

He pushed Meg into his car and locked the door
from the passenger side. He jumped in on the other
side and started the car. After a glance in the rearview
mirror, he dropped it in gear, and shot off as two men
came into view. Shots were fired into the air, but he
didn't even slow down.

Meg felt sick. She huddled against her door, wondering frantically if it would kill her to force the handle and jump out at the speed they were going. Lang's
actions were more puzzling by the minute. Was he
holding out for a better price?

"Don't be a fool," Lang said curtly. He didn't look
at her, but he obviously knew what she was considering. "You'd be killed by inches."

"Why?" She groaned. "Why?"

"You'll find out. Be a good girl and sit still. You
won't come to any harm. I promise."

"Steve will kill you," she said icily.

His eyebrow jerked. "Probably," he murmured.

"He'll have to wait in line. It was all I could think of on the spur-of-the-moment." He glanced in the rearview mirror and mumbled something about a force the size of NATO coming up behind, in a jumble of international agents.

"They're chasing you?" She smiled gleefully. "I hope they shoot your tires out and kidnap you and sell you into slavery!"

He chuckled with pure delight, glancing at her. "Are you sure you want to be engaged to Ryker? I'm two years younger than he is and I've got an aunt who'd pamper you like a baby."

"She'll be very ashamed of you when you end up in prison, you traitor!" she accused.

He shook his head. "Oh, well. Duck, honey."

"Wha…?"

He pushed her down and dodged as a bullet came careening through the windshield, leaving shattered glass all over the front seat, including Meg's lap.

"Oh, my God!" she screamed.

"Keep your head," he said curtly. "Don't panic."

Another bullet whizzed past. She kept her head down, mentally consigning him to the nether reaches.

"Exciting, isn't it?" he shouted above the gunfire and the roar of the engine. His dark eyes glittered as he weaved along the highway just ahead of his pursuers. "God, I love being a secret agent!"

She stared at him from her hiding place on the floorboard as if he were a madman.

He was singing the theme song from an old spy TV show, zigzagging the car on the deserted highway as more bullets whizzed past.

"Hold on, now, here we go!"

He hit the wheel hard. Tires spun on the pavement,

squealing like banshees, and they were suddenly going in the opposite direction across the median. Blue
lights flashed and sirens sounded.

"The police!" she gasped. "Oh, boy! I hope they
fill you full of lead! I hope they mount your head on
a shortwave antenna and throw the rest of you to the
buzzards! I hope…!"

He grabbed for the mike on his two-way radio.
"Did you get the signal? Here they are, boys. Go get
'em!" he said into it.

He stopped the car and as Meg peered over the
broken dash, three assorted colors and divisions of
police car went flying across the median and after the
horrified occupants of the two cars that had been in
hot pursuit of Meg and Lang.

"Now, admit it," he said, breathing heavily as he
turned to her, grinning. "Wasn't this more exciting
than watching some stupid game show on TV? The
thrills, the chills, the excitement!"

She felt sick all over. She started to speak and suddenly wrenched the door handle. He pushed the un-
lock button on the driver's armrest just in the nick of
time. Meg lost everything she'd eaten earlier in the
day.

Lang passed her a handkerchief and managed to
look slightly repentant when she was leaning back
against the seat of the police car that had picked them
up when one carful of enemy agents was in custody.

"They ought to put you in solitary and throw away
the key," the young police lieutenant told Lang when
Meg had finished sipping the thermos cup of strong
black coffee he'd fetched for her. "You poor kid,"
he told Meg.

"I told you, it was all I could think of," Land replied, lounging nonchalantly against the rear fender of the police car. "I overheard them talking. They were going to snatch her. So I jammed their signal into the house to get their attention, then let them hear me selling her down the river. I beeped you guys once we were in the car to let you know something was going down. I didn't have time to do any more than that. They were headed toward the house when I decided to get her out."

"You didn't have to hold a gun on her!" the policeman raged.

"Sure I did," he replied. "She's a fighter. She was going to argue or maybe start a brawl with me. But when I pointed the pistol at her, she went with me without a single argument. And because they thought I was going to hand her over to them, they didn't shoot at me until it was too late."

"I still say…"

With a long suffering sigh, Lang pulled out his automatic and slapped it into the policeman's palm.

The officer stared at him, puzzled.

"Well, look at it," Lang muttered.

The policeman turned it over and sighed, shaking his head.

Lang held his hand out. When the weapon was returned to it, he pulled the missing clip out of his pocket, slammed it into the handle slot and cocked it, before putting on the safety. Then he slid it back into his underarm holster and snapped it in place.

"It wasn't loaded?" Meg asked, aghast.

"That's right," Lang told her. He glowered at her. "And you thought I was selling you out. She called me everything but a worm," he told the policeman.

"A traitor, a turncoat. She said she hoped they hung my head on a radio antenna!"

The policeman was trying not to laugh.

"I didn't know you were trying to protect me," Meg said self-consciously.

"Next time, I'll let them have you," he said irately. "They can throw you into somebody's harem and I hope they dress you in see-through plastic wrap!"

The policeman couldn't hold it back any longer. He left, quickly, chuckling helplessly.

"I like that," Meg said haughtily. "At least I'd look better in it than you would!"

"I have legs that make women swoon," he informed her. "*Playgirl begs* me for photo sessions."

"With or without your gun?" she countered.

He grinned. "Jealous because you don't have one? Pistol envy?"

She burst out laughing. Lang was incorrigible. "All right, I apologize for thinking you sold me out," she told him. "But you were pretty convincing. I had no idea you had on a mask, figuratively speaking."

"You'd be amazed at how much company I have," he said dryly. He glanced up as a car approached. "Oh, boy."

She looked where he was staring. It was a big black limousine. Her heart leaped when it stopped and a white-faced, shaken Steven jumped out, making a beeline toward Meg.

He didn't break stride except to throw a heated punch at Lang, which the younger man deflected.

"She's okay," Lang said, moving back. "I'll explain when you cool off."

"You'd better do your explaining from someplace

where I can't reach you," Steve replied, and he looked murderous.

"I told you!" Wayne raged, moving into view behind Steve. "You idiot, I told you not to do things on your own!"

"If I hadn't they'd have carried her off!" Lang shot back, exasperated. "What was I supposed to do, call for reinforcements from the trunk of their damned car on the way to the river?"

"They wouldn't throw you in any river, you'd pollute it and kill the fish!"

Lang's voice became heated as the two men moved out of earshot. Steven paused just in front of Meg and looked down at her from a strained face.

"Are you all right?" he asked tersely.

"Yes, thanks to Lang," she replied. "Although I wasn't exactly thanking him at the time," she added, nodding toward the remains of the car Lang had rescued her in.

Steve didn't look at it very long. It made him sick. He reached for Meg and pulled her hungrily into his arms. He held her bruisingly close, rocking her, while his mind ran rampant over all the horrific possibilities that had kept him raging all the way to the scene after Wayne had gotten the news from the city police about the chase.

"I guess your evening with Daphne was spoiled?" she asked a little unsteadily.

"If anything had happened to you, I don't know what I'd have done," he groaned.

She eased her arms under his jacket and around him, holding on. It was so sweet to stand close to him this way while around them blue and red lights still flashed and voices murmured in the distance.

"You'd better get her home, sir," the police officer said gently. "Everything's all right, now."

"I'll do that. Thanks."

He led her back to the limousine. "What about Lang?" she asked Steve. "And didn't his friend... Wayne...ride with you?"

"They can go with the police or hitchhike," Steve said. "Especially Lang!"

"What about Daphne...?"

"I'm taking you home, Meg," he said. "Nobody else matters right now."

"Is David there?"

He nodded. "He doesn't know about any of this. I didn't want to worry him."

She crawled into his lap when the chauffeur started the car, to Steve's amazement.

"Your seat belt," he began.

"I've had my close call for tonight," she told his chest. "Let me stay."

His arms curved around her, pulling her closer. They rode home like that, without a word, cradled together.

David turned white when he learned what had happened. "But how did they know?" he groaned.

"The house is bugged," Meg said, sitting down heavily on the couch. "Lang had some sort of jamming device..."

"He blew up the bugs," David explained. "Scrambled their circuits. One of the agents explained that device to me, but I hadn't seen one until I got home. When I saw it lying here, and you were gone, I knew something had happened. But I couldn't find out anything."

"Sorry," Steven said. "I took off out the door the minute I heard what had happened, with Wayne two steps behind me. I didn't want to worry you." He grimaced. "I have to phone Daphne and tell her where we are."

Meg didn't look at him as he lifted the receiver on the telephone and dialed.

"I'll go up and change my things," she told David. She had pieces of glass on her skirt and in her hair. "It's been a pretty rough night."

"I can imagine. You're limping!"

"I always limp," she said dully. "It's worse because I've walked on it." She laughed mirthlessly. "I don't think it's going to get any better, David. Not ever."

He watched her go with quiet concern. Steve hung up the phone after he'd explained things to Daphne and turned to David.

"This whole thing is getting out of hand," he said tersely. "I can't take much more of it. She looks like a ghost, and that damned fool agent could have killed her driving like that!"

"What if he hadn't gotten her out of the house, Steve?" David asked, trying to reason with his friend. "What then?"

It didn't bear thinking about. Steve stuck his hands into his pockets. "My God."

"How about some coffee?" David asked. "I was about to make a pot."

"I could drink one. They'll have Ahmed under guard like Fort Knox by now. I'll go up and see about Meg. She was sick."

"That doesn't surprise me. Her ankle is bothering

her, too." He turned to Steve. "She's not going to be able to dance. You know that, don't you?"

Steve nodded. "Yes, I know it. Why else do you think she's willing to marry me?" he added cynically. "We both know that if she really had a choice, her damned career would win hands down."

"Try to remember that neither your father nor our mother wanted Meg to marry you."

"I know that."

"And Meg was very young. Afraid, too." He studied Steve. "Has she explained why?"

Steve looked hunted. "She gave me some song and dance about being afraid of pregnancy."

"She wasn't afraid of it, she was terrified. Steve," he added quietly, "she was with our sister when she died in childbirth. She was visiting during that snowstorm that locked them in. She watched it happen and couldn't do a thing to help."

Steven turned around, his face contorted. "Meg was there? She never said anything about that!"

"She won't talk about it still. It affected her badly. All this happened while you were away at college. Meg was only ten years old. It was, is, a painful subject. It was never discussed."

"I see." Poor Meg. No wonder she'd been afraid. He hadn't known, her father had told him, but at the time he had not felt comfortable asking questions. He felt guilty. He wondered if she was still that afraid, and hiding it.

"Go on up and get Meg. I'll fix that coffee," David said, clapping his friend on the shoulder.

Meg was just climbing out of the shower when Steve opened the bathroom door and walked in.

She gasped, clutching the towel to her.

"You blush nicely," he mused, smiling gently. "But I know what you look like, Meg. We made love."

"I know, but…"

He took the towel from her hands and looked down at her, his silver eyes kindling with delight. "Pretty little thing," he mused. "I could get drunk on you."

"David is just downstairs," she reminded him, grabbing at her towel. "And spies have bugged the whole house. They're probably watching us right now!"

"They wouldn't bug the bathroom," he murmured dryly.

"Oh, wouldn't they?"

He moved toward her, pulling her into his arms. "No," he whispered, bending. "Is this better? I'll hide you, Meg, from any eyes except my own."

She felt his mouth nibble softly at her lips, teasing them into parting.

"You taste of mint," he whispered.

"Spearmint toothpaste," she managed to say.

"Open your mouth," he whispered back. "I like to touch it, inside."

She shivered a little, but she obeyed him. His hands smoothed over her firm breasts, savoring their silky warmth as he toyed with her mouth until she felt her body go taut with desire.

"I want you," he breathed into her mouth. His hands lifted her hips and pressed them to his. "We could lie down on the carpet in here and make love."

She felt his lips move down her throat until his mouth hungrily kissed her breasts.

"David—" she choked "—is downstairs."

"And we're engaged," he whispered. "It's all right if we make love. Even some of the Puritans did when they were engaged."

"Steve," she moaned.

He kissed her slowly, hungrily, moving his mouth over hers until she was mindless with pleasure.

"On second thought," he said unsteadily, lifting her gently into his arms, "the carpet really won't do this time, Meg. I want you on cool, clean sheets."

She looked up into his eyes, her arms linked around his neck. Her blond hair was pinned up. Wisps of it teased her flushed cheeks. His gaze went all over her, lingering on her breasts.

"You want me, don't you?" he asked, his voice deep and soft in the stillness of the room.

"I never stopped," she replied unsteadily. "But, Daphne…!"

"I don't sleep with Daphne," he said as his mouth eased down on hers.

Maybe that was why he wanted Meg, she thought miserably. But none of it made sense, much less his hunger for her. He lost control when he touched her, and she was powerless to stop him.

"Steve, I can't," she groaned as he leaned over her with dark intent.

"Why not?"

"David's just downstairs!" she exclaimed.

He was trying to remember that. But looking at Meg's beautiful nude body made it really difficult. She shamed the most prized sculptures in the world.

"Why did you never tell me that you were with your sister when she died?" he asked softly.

She stiffened. Her face drew up and the memories were there, in her wide, hurt eyes.

He smiled wryly and pulled the cover over her. He sat down beside her, fighting to control his passion. She'd had enough excitement for one night and she was right. This wasn't the time.

"Didn't you think I'd understand?" he persisted.

"You wanted me very much," she began slowly. "But you were so distant from me emotionally, Steve. The one time we came close to being intimate, you acted as if precautions didn't matter at all. And I was young, and shy of you, and very embarrassed about things like sex. I couldn't find the right way to tell you, so I froze up instead. And you blew up and told me to get out of your life."

"I'd waited a month to touch you like that," he reminded her. "I went overboard, I know. But you obsessed me." He smiled with self-contempt. "You still do, haven't you noticed? I touch you and I lose control. That hasn't changed."

"You don't like losing control."

He shook his head. "Not even with you, little one."

She reached up and touched his chin, his mouth. "I lose control when you touch me," she reminded him.

"You can afford to now. Your dancing won't come between us anymore."

"Don't sound like that. Don't be so cynical, Steve," she pleaded, her wide eyes searching his. "You're coming up with all sorts of reasons why I want to marry you, but none of them has anything to do with the real one."

"And what is the real one? My money? My body?" he added with a cold smile.

"You can't believe that I might really care about

you, can you?'' she asked sadly. ''It's too much emotion.''

''The only emotion that interests me is the emotion I feel when I've got you under me.''

She colored. ''That's sex.''

''That's what we've got,'' he agreed. ''That's all we've got, when you remove all the frills and excuses. And it will probably be enough, Meg. You can find a way to fill your time here in Wichita and spend my money, and I'll come home every night panting to get into bed with you. What else do we need?''

He sounded so bitter. She didn't know how to reach him. He was avoiding the issue because he couldn't find a way to face it.

''You said you wanted a child,'' she reminded him.

''I meant it.'' He frowned slightly, remembering what David had told him. ''Did you mean it, Meg?''

''Oh, yes,'' she said gently. She smiled. ''I like children.''

''I've never had much to do with them,'' he confessed. ''But I suppose people learn to be parents.'' He slowly pulled the cover away from her body and looked down at her with curious, quiet eyes. ''I didn't think about anything that first time. Certainly not about making you pregnant.'' He touched her stomach hesitantly, tracing a pattern on it while she lay breathlessly looking up at him. ''Meg, how would it be if we made love,'' he said slowly, meeting her eyes, ''and we both thought about making a baby together while we did it?''

She felt her heartbeat racing. She stared at him with vulnerable eyes, her feelings so apparent that she could see his heartbeat increase.

"That would be…very exciting," she whispered huskily. "Wouldn't it?"

He drew her hand slowly to his body and let her feel the sudden, violent effect of the words. His breath stilled in his throat.

"Damn your brother," he said unsteadily. "I want to strip off my clothes and pull you under me, right here, right now!"

She reached up, tugging his face down. He kissed her with slow anguish, a rough moan echoing into her mouth. His hand explored her, touched and tested her body until he made it tremble. She whimpered and he clenched his teeth while he tried to fight it.

"We can't." She wept.

"I know. Oh, God, I know!" He brought her up to him and held her roughly, crushing her against him so that the silky fabric of his suit made a faint abrasion against her softness. "Meg, I need you so!"

"I need you, too," she murmured, shaken by the violence of her hunger for him. "So much!"

"Do you want to risk it?" he whispered at her ear. "It would have to be quick, Meg. No long loving, no tenderness." Then he groaned and cursed under his breath as he realized what he was offering her. "No!" he said violently. "Oh, God, no, not like that. Not ever again!"

He forced himself to let go of her. His grip on her arms was bruising as he lifted away from her and then suddenly let her go and turned away. He was shaking, Meg saw, astonished.

"I'm going to get out of here and let you dress," he said with his back to her. "I'm sorry, Meg." He turned around, slowly, and looked down at her. "I want lovemaking," he said quietly, "not raw sex.

And we need to think about this. If you're not already pregnant, we need to think very carefully about making you that way.''

She smiled gently. He sounded different. He even looked different. "I don't need to think about it," she said softly. "But if you do, you can have all the time in the world.''

Color ran along his cheekbones. He looked at her with eyes that made a meal of her. Finally he closed them, shivering, and turned away from her.

"I'll see you downstairs," he said in a faintly choked tone. He went out without looking back and closed the door firmly.

Meg saw something in his face before he left the room. It was enough to erase every terror the night had held and give her the first real hope she'd had of a happy future with him.

Chapter 10

But if Meg had expected that look in Steve's eyes to change anything, she was mistaken. He'd had time to get himself together again, and he was distant while he drank coffee with Meg and David downstairs. She walked him to the door when he insisted scant minutes later that he had to leave. David discreetly took the coffee things into the kitchen, to give them a little privacy.

"When this is over," he told Meg, "you're going to marry me, as quickly as I can arrange a ceremony."

"All right, Steven," she replied.

He toyed with a strand of her blond hair, not meeting her eyes. "Daphne isn't who you think," he said. "I can't say more than that. But a lot of people aren't what you think they are." He lifted his eyes to hers. "I'll tell you all of it, as soon as I can."

It was an erasing of doubts and fears. A masquerade, and almost time to whip off the masks. She searched his silver eyes quietly. "I care for you very much," she said simply. "I'm tired of fighting it, Steven. I'll be happy with what you can give me."

His jaw clenched. "I don't deserve that."

She smiled impishly. "Probably not, but it's true, just the same." She moved closer and reached up to kiss him very tenderly. "I'm sorry David wouldn't go away so that we could make love," she whispered. "Because I want to, very, very much."

"So do I, little one," he said tautly. "It gets harder and harder to stay away from you."

"But not hard enough to make you give up Daphne?" she probed delicately, and watched him close up.

"Give it time."

She shrugged. "What else can I do?" she asked miserably. She sighed and leaned closer, so that his mouth was against her forehead. "I love you," she said.

He held her with mixed emotions. She didn't quite trust him, but he hoped she was telling the truth about her feelings. He was in too deep to back out now. "I'll see you tomorrow. Lang had better be on his way to the moon," he added irritably.

"Don't hurt him," she said softly. "He really did save me."

"I know what he did," he muttered, and it was in his eyes when he lifted his head. "Maybe they'll give him to Ahmed as a going-away gift."

"Ahmed isn't going away, is he? I thought he was based in Washington, D.C."

Steve started to speak, but decided against telling her what he'd been about to say. "You'll understand everything in a day or two. Just a few loose ends to wrap up, now that Lang's precipitated things. Don't worry. You're all right now.''

''Whenever I'm with you, I'm all right.''

''Are you?'' he asked dryly. ''I wonder.''

She drew back and smiled up at him. ''Good night, Steven.''

He stuck his hands into his pockets with a long sigh. ''Under different circumstances, it would have been a hell of a night,'' he remarked. He studied her long and hard. ''You're lovely, Meg, and much more than just physically pretty. I don't know why I ever let you go.''

''You didn't feel safe with me. You still don't, do you?''

''You were a career ballerina,'' he reminded her.

''I was an idiot,'' she replied. ''I didn't know you at all, Steven. I was young and silly and I never looked below the surface to see what things and people really were. You were afraid of involvement. Maybe I was, too. I ran for safety.''

''You weren't the only one.'' His eyes narrowed. ''But I get homicidal when you're threatened,'' he said quietly. ''And you get hysterical when I am,'' he added. ''Don't you think it's a little late for either of us to worry about getting involved now?''

She smiled ruefully. ''We're involved already.''

''To the back teeth,'' he agreed. He drew in a long breath. ''In more ways than one,'' he added with a quick glance at her belly.

She laughed. ''I was so afraid of it four years ago,'' she said softly. ''And now, I go to bed and dream about it.''

His hands clenched in his pockets. He searched her

eyes closely. "It would really mean the loss of any hope of a career, even if your ankle heals finally," he said. "How could you take a child with you to New York while you rehearse and dance? How could you hope to raise it by long distance?"

"I thought I might teach ballet, here in Wichita," she began slowly. "It's something I know very well, and there are two other retired ballerinas in town who worked with me when I was younger. I could get a loan from the bank and find a vacant studio."

Lights blazed in his eyes. "Meg!" he groaned softly. He bent and kissed her, his mouth slow and tender.

She was stunned. Why, he didn't mind! When he drew back, the radiance in his face stopped her heart.

"I could help you look for a studio," he said, his voice deep and hesitant. "As for the financing, I could stake you at a lower interest than you could get from the bank. The rest of it would be your project."

"Oh, Steven!"

He began to smile. He lifted her by the waist and held her close. "Wouldn't you pine for the Broadway stage?"

"Not if I can work at something I love and still live with you," she said simply. "I never dreamed you'd accept it."

His eyes blazed into hers. "Didn't you?"

Her arms looped around his neck and she put her mouth softly over his, kissing him with growing hunger.

He tried to draw back and her arms contracted.

"Kiss me," she whispered huskily, and opened her mouth.

He made a sound that echoed in the quiet hall and

she felt his tongue probing quickly, deeply, into the darkest reaches of her mouth while her body throbbed with sudden passion.

There was a ringing sound somewhere in the background that Steve and Meg were much too involved to hear.

A minute later there was a discreet cough behind them. Steve drew back and looked blindly over Meg's shoulder, his mouth swollen, his tall body faintly tremulous.

"That was Lang," David said with barely contained amusement. "He said to tell you that there's a surveillance camera in the hall and the other agents are discussing film rights."

Steve dropped Meg to her feet. He glared around at the ceiling. "Damn you, Lang!"

Meg leaned against Steve, laughing. "He's incorrigible. One day we'll hear that someone has suspended him over a pond of piranhas at the end of a burning rope."

"Please, give them some more ideas," Steve pleaded, glancing up again.

"Do you really think there are any they haven't already entertained? They're highly trained after all, right, Lang?" Meg called with a wicked grin.

Steve muttered something, dropped a quick kiss on Meg's lips and left the house.

The office was buzzing with excitement the next morning, all about the wild chase and the capture of enemy agents. Daphne had told half the people in the building, apparently, because Steve got wry grins everywhere he went.

Ahmed came in late in the morning, surrounded by

his bodyguards. He looked a little pale and drawn, but he was smiling, at least.

Daphne started to say something to him, abruptly thought better of it and left him in Steve's office. The door closed softly behind her.

"Meg is all right?" Ahmed asked quietly.

"She's fine. And none the wiser for it," Steve replied heavily. He leaned back in his desk chair and propped his immaculate black boots up on the desk. "But I'm going to have a lot to say to Lang's superiors about the way he protected her. With any luck, they'll send him to Alaska to bug polar bears."

Ahmed smiled slowly. "I understand there was something of a stir among the surveillance people last evening. Something about man-eating fish and burning hemp…"

"Never mind," Steve said quickly. "What's the latest about the coup in your country?"

Ahmed sat down in the leather chair across from the desk and crossed one elegant leg over the other. His bearing was regal, like the tilt of his proud head and the arrogant sparkle in his black eyes.

"Ah, my friend, that is a story indeed," he said pleasantly. "To shorten it somewhat, the assassins captured last night by your government's agents were the weak link in a chain. We will learn much from them." Ahmed looked very hard when his eyes met Steve's.

Steve felt chills go down his spine. Ahmed had been his friend for a long time, but there were depths to the man that made him uneasy. He might not be a Moslem, but Ahmed was every inch an Arab. His thirst for vengeance knew no bounds when it was aroused.

"When do you leave for home?"

Ahmed spread his hands. "Today, if it can be arranged. The sooner the better, you understand." His black eyes narrowed. "I would not willingly have put you and Meg and David at risk. I hope you know this, and understand that it was not my doing."

"Of course I do."

"Meg...you have not told her?" he added carefully.

"I thought it best not to," Steve said. "The less she knows the safer she is. For now, at least."

Ahmed smiled. "I agree. She is unique, our Meg. If she did not belong to you, my friend, I could lose my heart very easily to that one."

"You're invited to the wedding," Steve replied.

"You honor me, and I would enjoy the occasion. But the risk of returning to your country so soon after this unfortunate attempt at an overthrow is too great."

"I understand."

"I wish you well, Steve. Thank you for all that you have done for my people—and for myself. I look forward to future projects such as this one. With your help, my country will move into the twentieth century and lessen the chance of invasion from outside forces."

"Watch your back, will you?" Steve asked. "Even with the culprits in custody, you can't be too careful."

"I realize this." Ahmed got to his feet, resplendent in his gray business suit. He smiled at Steve as they shook hands. "Take care of yourself, as well, and give my best to your brother and the so beautiful Meg."

"She'll be sorry that she didn't have the opportunity to say goodbye to you," Steve told him.

"We will meet again, my friend," he said with certainty.

Steven walked him to the outer office, where a slender, dark-haired girl was glaring at the Arab from behind a propped-up shorthand tablet with information that she was copying into the computer. She quickly averted her eyes.

Daphne motioned to Steve and pointed at the telephone.

"I'll have to go. Have a safe trip. I'll be in touch when we get a little further along in the assembly."

"Yes."

Steve shook hands again and went back into his office to take the telephone call.

Daphne hesitated, hoping to provide a buffer between the angry look in Ahmed's eyes and the intent look in Brianna's, but Steve hung up the telephone and buzzed her. She grimaced as she finally went to see what he wanted.

Ahmed stood over the young woman, his liquid black eyes narrowed as he glared at her. "You have had too little discipline," he said flatly. "You have no breeding and no manners and you also have the disposition of a harpy eagle."

She glared back at him. "Weren't you just leaving, sir?" she asked pointedly.

"Indeed I was. It will be pleasant to get back to my own country where women know their place!"

She got out of her chair and walked around the desk. Her pretty figure was draped in a silky dark blue suit and white blouse that emphasized her creamy complexion and huge blue eyes. She got down on her knees and began to salaam him, to the howling amusement of the other women in the typing pool.

"How dare you!" Ahmed demanded scathingly.

Brianna looked up at him with limpid eyes. "But, sir, isn't this the kind of subservience you demand from your countrywomen?" she asked pleasantly. "I would hate to offend you any more than I already have. Oh, look at that, a nasty bug has landed on your perfectly polished shoe! Allow me to save you, sir!"

She grabbed a heavy magazine from the rack beside her desk and slammed it down on his shoe with all her might.

He raged in Arabic and two other unintelligible languages, his face ruddy with bad temper, his eyes snapping with it.

Daphne came running. "Brianna, no!" she cried hoarsely.

Ahmed was all but vibrating. He didn't back down an inch. Daphne motioned furiously behind her until Brianna finally got the hint and took off, making a dash for the ladies' rest room.

"In my country..." he began, his finger pointing toward Brianna's retreating figure.

"Yes, I know, but she's insignificant," Daphne reminded him. "A mere fly speck in the fabric of your life. Honestly she is."

"She behaves like a savage!" he raged.

Daphne bit her tongue almost through. She smiled tightly. "You'll miss your flight."

He breathed deliberately until some of the high color left his cheekbones, until he was able to unclench the taut fists at his side. He looked down at Daphne angrily. "She will be punished." It was a statement, not a question.

"Oh, yes, of course, she will," Daphne swore, with

her fingers tightly crossed behind her back. "You can count on that, sir."

Ahmed began to relax a little. He pursed his lips. "A month in solitary confinement. Bread and water only. Yes. That would take some of the spirit out of her." His dark eyes narrowed thoughtfully. "It would be a tragedy, however, to break such a beautiful wild spirit. Do you not think so?"

"Indeed," Daphne agreed quickly.

He nodded, as if savoring the thought. "Your country has such odd people in it, *mademoiselle*," he said absently. "Secret agents with quirks, secretaries with uncontrollable tempers…"

"It's a very interesting country."

He shrugged. "Puzzling," he corrected. He glanced at her. "This one," he nodded toward the door where Brianna had gone. "She is married?"

"No," Daphne said. "She has a young brother in a coma. He's in a nursing home. She has no family."

His dark brows drew together. "No one at all?"

She shook her head. "Just Tad," she replied.

"How old is this…Tad?"

"Ten," Daphne said sadly. "There was an automobile accident, you see. Their parents were killed and Tad was terribly injured. They don't think he'll ever recover, but Brianna goes every day to sit by his bed and talk to him. She won't give up on him."

His face changed. "A woman of compassion and loyalty and spirit. A pearl of great price indeed."

Daphne heard the buzzer and went to answer it, leaving Ahmed to rejoin Steve.

Steve put the Arab on a plane—a chartered plane owned by Ahmed's government—later that morning, with Daphne and two taciturn American agents at his side.

"Have a safe trip," Steve said.

"How can I help it?" Ahmed muttered, glancing at the number of armed guards in his country's uniform gathered at the walkway to the plane. "Many thanks for your help," he added to the agents, and Daphne, who was standing close to the tall blond agent.

"It was our pleasure. Anytime," Wayne replied.

Lang grinned at him. "Just give us a day's notice and we'll cover you like tar paper, sir," he replied.

Steve glared at him. "And watch your every move on hidden cameras," he added icily.

"What can I tell you?" Lang sighed, lifting his hands and letting them fall. "I *am* a spy, after all. I get paid to spy on people. It's what I do." He looked somber as he faced Ahmed. "You'd just be amazed at the things you see on a hidden camera, sir. Like last night, for instance..."

Steve moved toward him threateningly.

Lang grinned. "Actually," he clarified, "I meant this rich guy we were watching who likes to play video games and when he wins, he takes off all his clothes and pours Jell-O over himself."

"So help me!" Steve began.

Lang threw up both hands. "I'll reform. I really will. I'm going to ask that little brunette out and see if she'd like to take me on," he added. "She's dishy, isn't she? I hear she likes to throw things at foreign men. Good thing I'm domestic."

Ahmed looked at Lang with kindling anger, and Steve saw problems ahead. "Better get aboard," Steve told the Arab. "Keep in touch."

Ahmed seemed to realize where he was and to whom he was speaking. He shrugged, as if he'd experienced a minor temporary aberration. "Of course. *Au revoir,* my friend."

He waved and turned to go into the plane, with his entourage at a respectful distance, watching his back.

"Regal, isn't he?" Lang said with reluctant admiration. "I'm sorry to see him go." He grinned at Steve. "Now that this is all over, are you sure you're going to marry that girl of yours? I do like her temper."

"So do I," Steve replied. "Yes, I'm going to marry her. And the next time you point a camera in my general direction, it had better have a lens cap on."

"Yes, sir," Lang said, chuckling. "You'll be glad to know that as of now you are officially unobserved. But if you'd like the results of our straw poll last night, we think you'd give Valentino a run for his money." He threw up a hand and walked away. Wayne followed him a minute later, leaving a sighing Daphne behind with Steve.

"Are you really going to marry Wayne?" Steve asked as they walked back toward the airport entrance.

"The minute we can arrange a ceremony. How about you and Meg?"

"I've got a lot of explaining to do," he replied dryly. "But I think she'll understand. I hope she will, at least."

"She's a sweet woman, Steve. You're very lucky."

"Don't I know it," he mused.

* * *

He left Daphne at the office and gave himself the

rest of the day off. First on the agenda was to tell Meg the truth.

She was sprawled on the couch going over projection figures the bank had given her when she went to inquire about starting up her own business. Steve came in the old way, through the back door without knocking, and stood over her with relief written all over him.

"It's over," he told her. "Ahmed's on a plane home and the secret agents have gone to root out enemy spies somewhere else. We're free."

She put down her figures and smiled up at him. "So?"

"So," he replied, dropping down beside her, "now that it's over and we're unbugged, I can tell you that Daphne is engaged to that blond agent who hangs out with Lang."

"What?"

"She was the unofficial liaison between us. She had to go where we did."

"But you said...!"

"I wasn't allowed to tell you what was going on," he told her. "Now that Ahmed's out of danger, there's no more risk."

She frowned. "I thought they were after you."

"Only as a way to get to Ahmed." He got up and poured brandy into a snifter and handed it to her.

"Do I need a drink?" she asked.

"You may."

"Why?"

He smiled down at her. "Ahmed isn't a cabinet minister. He's the sovereign of his country. To put it more succinctly...he's a king."

Chapter 11

Meg took a good swallow of the brandy and coughed a little. "That explains a lot," she told him finally. "He did have a more regal bearing than you'd expect in a political flunky. He's out of danger, then?"

"Yes. The overthrow attempt didn't go down. The agency thought he was safer here until it was dealt with. Ahmed's government is friendly to ours and we're fortunate to have access to his strategic location when there are problems in the Middle East. The government is anxious to accommodate him. That's why they supported the company when we decided to sell him our newest jet fighter. It's also why he got top priority protection here when his life was in danger."

"I still can't quite believe it."

"You have to keep his identity to yourself, however," he told her warningly. "Because he'll be back to have another look at his purchase when we've got it closer to completion. His life may depend on secrecy. Even in this country, there are nationals from his kingdom with grudges."

"Poor Ahmed." She frowned. "He must not enjoy being guarded all the time." Another thought came to her. "He's a king, which means that he has to marry a princess or something, doesn't it? He can't just marry for love, can he?"

"I don't know," he said. His silver eyes searched hers. "I'm glad that I got to choose my own wife," he added huskily. "Now that I've waited four years for her, I don't intend waiting any longer."

"You sound very impulsive."

"I'll show you impulsive." He pulled her to her feet and bundled her out the door. Several hours later, the blood tests were complete, the paperwork was underway and the wedding was scheduled for the end of the week.

"You aren't slipping through my fingers again," he chuckled when they walked arm in arm into his own house. "My mother will be delighted. We'll have to phone her tonight. By the way," he added, "I've found three possibilities for your studio. I thought you might like to go and look them over tomorrow."

"I'd love to!" She reached up and hugged him warmly, feeling as if she'd just come home. She closed her eyes with a sigh as they stood together in the deserted house. Steve's housekeeper had long since left a note about cold cuts and gone home. "Am I staying for supper?" Meg murmured.

He turned her to him. "You're staying for good," he said quietly. "Tonight and every night for the rest of your life."

She hesitated. "But, David will expect me..."

He bent and began to kiss her, softly at first, and then with building intensity so that, after a few minutes, she didn't remember her brother's name. But they agreed that one lapse before marriage was enough. And while Meg slept in his arms that night, sleeping was all they did together. They had the rest of their lives for intimacy, he reminded her.

Early the next morning, Steve took Meg around to the studio prospects he'd found for her. She settled on one in a good location with ample parking, not too many blocks from his office.

"Now," she said, smiling as she looked around, "all I have to do is convince the bank that I'm a good credit risk."

He glowered at her. "I've already told you that I'll stake you."

"I know, and I appreciate it," she said, reaching up to kiss him as they stood in the spacious emptiness of the former warehouse. "But this is something I need to do on my own." She hesitated. "Do you understand?"

"Oh, yes," he said with a slow smile. "You sound just like me at your age."

She laughed. "Do I, really?"

He stuck his hands into his pockets and looked around. "You'll need a lot of paint."

"That, and a little equipment, and some employees who'll be willing to work for nothing until I establish a clientele," she added. "Not to mention an advertising budget." She clenched her teeth. Was she biting off more than she could chew?"

"Start with just yourself," he advised. "Less overhead. See if you can time-share with someone who needs a studio at night. Perhaps a karate master. Put up some posters around town in key business windows, such as day-care centers.'' He grinned at her astonishment. ''Didn't I ever tell you that I'm more an idea man than an executive? Who do you think calls the shots on our advertising campaign and trims off fat from work stations?''

''You're amazing!'' she exclaimed.

''I'm cheap,'' he corrected. ''I know how to do a lot for a little.''

''How about printing?''

''We use a large concern a block away from here. Since they deal in big jobs, they don't cost as much as a small printer would.''

She was grinning from ear to ear. She could see it all taking shape. ''The only thing is, how will I teach when I can barely walk?'' she asked, hesitating.

''Listen, honey, by the time you get your financing, your carpentry done and your advertising out, that ankle will be up to a lot more than you think.''

''Truly?''

He smiled at her worried expression. ''Really and truly. Now let's get to it. We've got a wedding to go to.''

She wondered if she could hold any more happiness. It seemed impossible.

They were married at a small justice of the peace's office, with David and Daphne and Wayne for witnesses. Brianna waited outside with a camera to take pictures.

''I forgot to hire a photographer!'' Steve groaned when they exited the office. He was wearing a blue business suit, and a beaming Meg was in a street-length white suit with a hat and veil, carrying a bouquet of lily of the valley.

"That's all right," Brianna told him. "I used to help our dad in the darkroom. He said I was a natural." She said it a little sadly, because she missed her parents, but not in any self-pitying way. "Stand together and smile, now."

They started to, just as a huge black limousine roared up and a tall, dark man leaped from the back seat.

"Am I in time?" Lang asked hurriedly, righting his tie and smoothing back his unruly hair. "I just flew in from Langley, Virginia, for the occasion!"

"Lang!" Meg exclaimed, breaking into a smile.

"The very same, partner," he chuckled. "How about a big kiss?"

Steve stepped closer to his new wife, with a protective arm around her. "Try it," he said.

Lang lifted both eyebrows. "You want me to kiss you, too? *Yeeech!*"

"I do not!" Steve roared.

"That's a fine way to treat a man who flew hundreds of miles to be at your wedding. My gosh, I even brought a present!"

Steve cocked his head and stared at Lang. "A present? What kind of a present?"

"Something you'll both treasure."

He reached into his coat pocket and took out a packet of photographs.

Steve took the photographs and held them as gingerly as if they'd been live snakes. He opened the envelope and peeked in. But the risqué photos he expected weren't there. Instead, they were photos of

Meg, from all sorts of camera angles; Meg smiling, Meg laughing, Meg looking reflective.

"Well, what are they?" Meg asked. "Let me see!"

Steve closed up the package and glanced at Lang with a wry smile. "Thanks."

Lang shrugged. "It was the least I could do." He hesitated. "Uh, there's this, too."

He handed Steve a videotape and followed it with a wicked grin. "From the hall camera…?"

Steve eyed him with growing suspicion. "Just how many copies of this did you make?"

"Only one," Lang swore, hand on his heart. "That one. And there are no negatives."

"Lang, you're a good man," Meg told him with conviction.

"Of course I am." He turned to Brianna, still grinning. "Well, hello, hello. How about lunch? I'll take you to this great little seafood joint down the street and buy you a shrimp!"

"A shrimp?" Brianna asked, hesitating.

Lang pulled out the change in his pocket and counted it. "Two shrimps!" he announced.

Brianna smiled, her blue eyes twinkling. "I'd love to," she said. "I really would. But there's someone I have to go and see. Perhaps some other time."

Lang managed to look fatally wounded. "I see. It's because I can only afford two shrimps, isn't it? Suppose," he added, leaning down toward her with a twinkle in his eyes, "I offered to wash plates after and bought you a whole platter of shrimp?" He wiggled his eyebrows.

She laughed. "It wouldn't do any good. But I do appreciate the sentiment." He was very nice, she thought, a little sad under that clownish exterior, too.

But she had so many problems, and her stubborn mind would keep winging back to a tall man with a mustache.... It wouldn't be fair to lead Lang on when she had nothing to offer him.

"Ah, well," Lang murmured. "Just my luck to be so handsome and debonair that I intimidate women."

"That's true," Meg told him. "You're just devastating, Lang. But someday, some nice girl will carry you off to her castle and feed you rum cakes and ice cream."

"Sadist," he grumbled. "Go ahead, torment me!"

"We have to go," Steve said. "Thank you all for coming. We both appreciate it."

"Don't mention it," David chuckled, bending to kiss his sister. "Where are you going on your honeymoon?"

"Nowhere," Meg said. "We're going to wall ourselves up in Steven's house and stay there until the food all goes moldy in the refrigerator. And after that," she said smugly, "I've got a business to get underway!"

"Now see what you've done," David groaned. "My own sister, a career woman!"

"I always say," Steve mused, smiling down at his wife, "if you can't beat 'em, join 'em."

"That's just what I say," Meg replied. She took her hand in his, feeling very newly married and adoringly glancing at the wedding ring on her left hand.

When they got home, Steve lifted her gently in his arms and started up the staircase to the master bedroom. She was a little nervous, and so was he. But when he kissed her, the faint embarrassment was gone forever.

His open mouth probed hers, the intimacy of the kiss making her weak with desire. He was moving, walking, and all the time, his mouth was on hers, gentling her, seducing her.

She didn't come out of the fog of pleasure until he laid her gently on the bed and undressed her. Then he started taking off his own clothes. The sight of that big, hair-roughened body coming slowly into view froze her in a half-reclining position on the bed. He was the most incredibly sexy man she'd ever seen. Their first time, she hadn't been able to look at him because there had been such urgency. But now there was all the time in the world, and her eyes fed on him.

He smiled gently as he sat down beside her, his eyes turbulent and full of desire as he leaned over her. "I know," he said softly. "It wasn't like this before. But we have plenty of time to learn about each other now, Meg. A lifetime."

He bent slowly and put his mouth gently to hers. In the long, lazy moments that followed, he taught her how, watching the expressions chase across her shocked face as he made her touch him. He smiled with taut indulgence until she'd completed the task he set for her, and then he held her hands to him and talked to her, coaxed her into relaxing, into accepting the reality of him.

"It isn't so frightening now that you know what to expect, is it?" he asked, his voice deep and tender as he began to gently ease her out of the last flimsy garments that separated skin from skin.

When he had, he raised and looked at her, his body visibly trembling as he studied the rounded, exquisite flush of her perfect body, her silky skin.

His hand went out and tenderly traced her firm breasts, enjoying their immediate response to his touch, her trembling, her audible pleasure.

"You're beautiful, Meg," he whispered when his exploring hand trespassed in a new way. Despite their former intimacy, the touch shocked her. She caught his wrist and gasped. "No, little one," he coaxed, bending to kiss her wide eyes shut. "Don't be embarrassed or afraid of this. It's part of the way we're going to make love to each other. Relax, Meg. Try to put away all those inhibitions, will you? You're my wife. We're married. And believe me, this is perfectly permissible now."

"I know," she whispered back. "I'll try."

His mouth brushed over her eyes, her cheeks, down her face to her throat, her collarbone, onto the silken softness of her breasts while he discovered her.

His mouth on her breasts made her shiver. The faint suction he made was as exciting as the way he began to touch her, making little waves of pleasure ripple up her spine. She forgot to be nervous and her body responded to him, lifting to meet his touch. Her eyes opened, because she wanted to see if it was affecting him, too.

It was. His face was taut. His eyes were narrow and glittery as he looked down at her, and she could feel the tension in his powerful body as it curved against hers on the cool sheets.

He nodded. His eyes searched hers and his touch became softer, slower, more thorough. She made a quick, shocked sound, and his hand snaked under her neck to grasp a handful of hair at her nape and arch her face up so that he could see every soft, flushed inch of it.

"You...mustn't...watch!" she gasped as a hot, red mist wavered her surprised eyes.

"I'm going to," he replied. "Oh, yes, Meg, I'm going to watch you. I'm going to take you right up to the moon. This is going to be our first real night of love. Here and now, Meg. Now, now, now..."

The deep, slow chant was like waves breaking, the same waves that were slamming with pleasure into her body. She held on for dear life and her voice sobbed, caught, as the pleasure grew with each touch, each hot whisper.

He was moving. He was over her, against her. The pleasure was like an avalanche, gaining, gaining, rolling down, pressing down on her, pressing against her, pressing...into...her!

She felt the fierce throb of it, felt the slow invasion, felt the tension suddenly snap into a stinging, white-hot pleasure so unbearably sweet that it made her cry out.

His hands were on her wrists, pinning her, his body above her, demanding, pushing, invading. She heard his harsh breath, his sudden exclamation, the hoarse cry of pleasure that knotted him above her. As he shouted his fulfillment, she fell helplessly from the height to which he'd taken her, fell into a thousand diamond-splintered fragments, each more incredibly hot and sweet than the one before...

He cried out with the pleasure of it, his eyes wide open, his face taut with the strain. "Oh, God...!"

He sank over her, helpless in that last shudder, and she cradled him, one with him, part of him, in a unity that was even greater than the first one they'd ever shared.

She touched his face hesitantly. "Oh, Steven," she

whispered, the joy of belonging to him in her eyes, her voice, her face.

He smiled through the most delicious exhaustion he'd ever felt, trying to catch is breath. "Oh, Meg," he replied, laughing softly.

She flushed, burying her face in his throat. "It wasn't...quite like that before."

"You were a virgin before," he whispered, smiling. He rolled over onto his back, bringing her along with him so that she could pillow her cheek on his broad, damp chest. "Are you all right?"

"I'm happy," she replied. "And a little tired."

"I wonder why."

She laughed at the droll tone and burrowed closer. "I love you so much, Steven," she said huskily. "More than my life."

"Do you?" His arms tightened. "I love you, too, my darling." He stroked her hair gently, feeling for the moment as if he had the world in his arms. "I should never have let you go. But I felt something for you so strong that it unnerved me." His arms grew suddenly bruising. "Meg, I couldn't bear to lose you," he said roughly, letting all the secret fears loose. "I couldn't go on living. It was hell without you, those four years. I did wild things trying to fill up the emptiness you left in me, but nothing worked." He drew in a long breath, while she listened with rapt fascination. "I...couldn't let you go again, no matter what I had to do to keep you."

"Oh, Steve, you won't have to!" She kissed him softly, brushed his closed eyes with her lips, clinging fiercely to him as she felt the depth of his love for her and was humbled by it. "I'll never want to go, don't you see? I didn't think you loved me four years ago. I ran because I didn't think I could hold you. I was so young, and I had an irrational fear of intimacy because my sister died having a baby. But I'm not that frightened girl anymore. I'll stay with you, and I'll fight any other woman to the edge of death to keep you!'' she whispered fiercely, clinging to him.

He laughed softly. They were so much alike. ''Yes, I feel the same way.'' He touched her forehead with his lips, relaxing a little as he realized that she felt exactly as he did. ''Ironic, isn't it? We were desperately in love and afraid to believe that something so overwhelming could last. But it did. It has.''

''Yes. I never thought I'd be enough for you,'' she whispered.

''Idiot. No one else would ever be enough.''

She lifted her eyes to his and smiled. ''Are we safe, now?''

''Yes. Oh, yes.''

She flattened her hand over his chest. ''And you won't grind your teeth in the night thinking that I'm plotting ways to run?''

He shook his head. ''You're going to be a responsible businesswoman. How can you run from utility bills and state taxes?''

She smiled at the jibe. ''Good point.''

He closed his eyes, drinking in her nearness, her warm softness. ''I never dreamed of so much happiness.''

''Neither did I. I can hardly believe we're really married.'' Her breath released in a soft sigh. ''I really did love dancing, Steven. But dancing was only a poor second in my life. You came first even then. You always will.''

He felt a surge of love for her that bordered on

madness. He rolled her over onto her back and bent
to kiss her with aching tenderness.

"I'd die for you," he said unsteadily. His eyes
blazed with what he felt, all of it in his eyes, his face.
"I hated the world because you wanted to be a ballerina more than you wanted me!"

"I lied," she whispered. "I never wanted anything
more than I wanted you."

His eyes closed on a wave of emotion and she
reached up, kissing him softly, comfortingly. Tears
filled her eyes, because she understood then for the
first time his fear of losing her. It humbled her, made
her shake all over. She was frightened at the responsibility of being loved like that.

"I won't ever let you down again," she whispered.
"Not ever! I won't leave you, not even if you throw
me out. This is forever, Steven."

He believed her. He had to. If this wasn't love, it
didn't exist. He gave in at last and put aside his fears.
"As if I could throw you out, when I finally know
what you really feel." He kissed her again, hungrily,
and as the fires kindled in her eyes he began to smile
wickedly. "Perhaps I'm dreaming again..."

She smiled under his hard mouth. "Do you think
so? Let's see."

She pulled him down to her. Long, sweet minutes
later, he was convinced. Although, as he told her afterward, from his point of view, life was going to be
the sweetest kind of dream for the rest of their lives
together; a sentiment that Meg wholeheartedly shared.

Meg opened her ballet school, and it became well-
known and respected, drawing many young prospec-
tive ballerinas. Her ankle healed; not enough to allow

her to dance again, but well enough to allow her to teach. She was happy with Steven and fulfilled in her work. She had it all, she marveled.

The performing ballet slippers of flawless pink satin and pink ribbons rested in an acrylic case on the grand piano in the living room. But in due time, they came out again, to be fastened with the slender, trembling hands of Steven and Meg's firstborn, who danced one day with the American Ballet Company in New York—as a prima ballerina.

* * * * *

A WISH AND A PRINCE
Joan Elliott Pickart

For my daughter, Robin,
my princess waiting for her prince.

Dear Reader,

It's time to curl up in a comfy chair and dust off forgotten memories of when you daydreamed about marrying a handsome prince and becoming his beautiful princess, so you'll be ready to travel on a journey to true love.

Maggie MacAllister has wished for a prince to call her own since she was a little girl. Now, as a mature woman, she believes that she'll never find a *real* prince, a member of a royal family, but yearns for a man of princely charms, who has a romantic and gentle soul.

On the magical night that ends one year and brings in the new one with all its treasures yet to be discovered, Prince Devon Renault, heir to the throne of the Island of Wilshire, enters Maggie's life in a rather startling manner.

And so it begins…the story of Devon and Maggie, of princes and princesses, kings and queens, a fairy tale that becomes real and wondrous, and is waiting for you to share it.

I hope you enjoy reading it as much as I did writing it.

With warmest regards,

Joan Elliott Pickart

Prologue

"I'll marry a prince, Bobby you'll see," four-year-old Maggie MacAllister told her brother as she blew out the candles on her cake. A year ago, her parents had begun reading her bedtime stories that included *Cinderella, Snow White, Sleeping Beauty* and other fantasy-filled tales of kings and queens, princes and princesses. Now her brother told her she wouldn't get her wish because she hadn't kept it a secret.

"Yes, I will," Maggie said, "'cause I want it with my whole heart."

Every year Maggie made the same wish, and it became a humorous family ritual. So, when Maggie blew out twenty-eight candles and wished for a handsome prince to come into her life and sweep her off her feet, the tradition-loving MacAllisters cheered.

But everyone knew that their Maggie would never really find her prince.

Or would she....

Chapter 1

It was a typical New Year's Eve in the Emergency Room of the Ventura Hospital, Maggie MacAllister mused as she plunked one elbow on the desk and cupped her chin in her palm, sighing as she stared into space.

At an hour before midnight it was quiet, the lull before the storm that would keep her and the other nurses, plus the doctors on duty, running at full speed once the partygoers really got into the holiday spirit. So many people would make foolish decisions that would result in them needing medical attention.

Maggie sighed again.

She was feeling a tad blue, she realized, because this was exactly where she'd been one year ago, the year before that and several more, having volunteered to work so that others could attend festivities with their special someone. Nothing had really changed in her life since the last New Year's Eve, a fact that suddenly seemed rather...sad.

Oh, stop it, she admonished herself, straightening in the chair. She was here by choice, having refused three...count them...three invitations from very nice men to be their date on this couple-oriented night. She'd politely refused...three times...because, well, yes, it was admittedly rather silly of her, a romantic notion she'd had for as long as she could remember, but she believed that the kiss at midnight on New Year's Eve should never be shared with a casual date.

No, that kiss that would welcome in the new year belonged only to her soul mate, her forever man, whom she loved with her whole heart, and that wondrous someone loved her in kind. Since there was no such person in her life, here she was again, working in the hospital because she'd raised her hand and volunteered.

Maggie smiled and shook her head.

According to MacAllister nonsense, of course, she thought, laughing softly, that oh-so-elusive someone had to be a prince—an honest-to-goodness member of a royal family.

That was just a long-standing, silly MacAllister joke as far as her family of countless numbers was concerned, Maggie thought. What they didn't know was that she really was waiting for a prince.

Oh, not a real one, not a titled member of royalty, but a man with princely charms, one who was thoughtful, caring, tender and kind, and who believed in old-fashioned romance. A man, she was beginning to gloomily believe, who didn't exist, at least not for her.

Maggie's thoughts were interrupted by the squawk of the two-way radio on the ledge behind the desk.

"Here we go," a woman said, coming up behind Maggie as the announcement of the incoming arrival of an ambulance crackled over the airwaves. "The transmission on that thing is crummy tonight. What did he say?"

"I think he said they have an unconscious man who has apparently been mugged or something, Betty," Maggie said, "but I'm not certain I got it all."

"Whatever," Betty said, picking up the transmitter attached to the radio. "We live to serve." She pressed a button on the small device. "We read you...sort of... You have a head injury? Over."

"Roger," the voice came back. "ETA is ten minutes. Traffic is nuts out here. Over."

"Okay. See you in ten. Over and out," Betty said, then replaced the transmitter. "Want to flip a coin to see... Forget it. We've got company coming through the front door. Oh, good grief, drunk as skunks. Two of them, and they look like they have been in a brawl. I'll grab Dr. Marks, and we'll take these yo-yos into Rooms Two and Three. You wait for the bump on the bean coming in and use Room One. Okay, Maggie?"

"Sure," Maggie said. "Let me know if you need any help before the ambulance arrives."

"Will do," Betty said. "Oh, and happy new year to you, because this is obviously the last chance I'll have to say that."

"Happy new year," Maggie said as Betty hurried to meet the staggering pair of young men crossing the room.

What would this new year bring into her existence? Her man with princely qualities? Her soul mate? Oh, wouldn't that be wonderful? They would meet, fall in love, gaze into each other's eyes, oblivious to the world around them and make plans for their future together, their forever and ever, and...

The wail of a rapidly approaching ambulance jerked Maggie from her whimsical, romantic thoughts, and she rushed to the double doors. The ambulance siren stilled with what Maggie had decided years ago sounded like a dying cow, then the doors opened and a stretcher was pushed through, accompanied by two attendants and followed by a uniformed police officer.

"Room One," Maggie said. "Hi, Bruce. Hi, Chet. Oh, and here's Officer Jenkins joining the party."

The three men greeted Maggie, then proceeded to the first examining room in the hallway. The ambulance attendants shifted the man from the stretcher onto the examining table, mumbled their farewells and hurried off. Officer Jenkins stopped Maggie in the doorway before she could approach the patient.

"I gotta get back out into the jungle, Maggie," the officer said, then chuckled. "This guy wasn't mugged. He was knocked over on a sidewalk by a roller-blader who is convinced he's going to jail for life." He frowned. "The thing is, the guy had no wallet, no identification of any kind on him. Weird. You've got a John Doe, but not because he was ripped off as far as I can tell, and I saw the whole thing happen. Well, whatever. Happy new year."

"Same to you," Maggie said, smiling.

As Officer Jenkins strode away, Maggie went to

the side of the examining table and stared at the John Doe.

"Oh, my," she said, feeling her heart do a funny little two-step.

He was, without a doubt, Maggie thought, as a strange and foreign heat rushed throughout her, the most incredibly handsome man she had ever seen.

He had light brown hair, that was tousled from his tumble, and long, dark lashes fanned against tanned skin on a face that was ruggedly masculine, yet possessed sensuous, oh-so-kissable-appearing lips. He was around thirty years old and...

He had wide shoulders that were clearly defined in an obviously expensive blue sweater, and long, muscular legs that were covered by dusty black, perfectly tailored slacks. The black shoes he wore probably cost more than she made in a week.

He had, apparently, left wherever he'd started out from without his wallet that held the answer to who he was. Maybe he was a wealthy, absentminded genius, or a...

What color were his eyes? Maggie mused on. What would he look like when he smiled and...

"Maggie, for heaven's sake." She shook her head slightly to dispel the eerie, sensual mist that had seemed to swirl around her and the man, encasing them in a private cocoon. "Get a grip. Be a nurse."

She lifted her hands, hesitated, then sank her fingers into the man's hair, marveling at its silky thickness as she gently probed, then found, an egg-size bump on the back of his head.

"Nasty," she said. "You are going to have a dickens of a headache when you wake up, John Doe."

Maggie pulled her hands free...slowly...watching

as the thick strands of the man's hair slid through her fingers. With a frown of self-disgust, she proceeded to check the patient's heart with a stethoscope, listening to the steady rhythm echoing in her ears. She took his pulse, then wiped the dirt from his face, her gaze riveted on his handsome features.

"Okay, John Doe, it's time to wake up," she said, patting one of his cheeks. "That's enough snoozing. Come on. Open your eyes. Can you hear me? Say, are you my prince? The one I've been waiting a lifetime for? And now you've been delivered right to me, like a special New Year's Eve present?"

"Fifteen seconds until midnight," a man yelled from the outer area. "And here we go, folks...ten seconds and counting."

A chorus of voices from people Maggie couldn't see began the countdown until the big moment. Then a shout went up and honking horns outside the building could be heard along with firecrackers.

Before she even realized she was moving, Maggie bent over and kissed the unconscious man, discovering that his lips were, indeed, every bit as soft and kissable as they appeared.

"Happy new year, my prince," she whispered.

Devon Renault opened his eyes halfway and looked at the nurse who had called herself Maggie. She had delicate and beautiful features, big brown eyes and a gorgeous tumble of wavy, auburn hair that fell to her shoulders.

His lips still tingled from the kiss she'd given him, and he hoped she didn't decide to check his heart again because it was pounding wildly in his chest.

Devon quickly closed his eyes.

"Mr. Doe," Maggie said, striving for a strictly business tone of voice, "wake up."

Not yet, Devon thought. He'd actually come back to earth during the ride in the ambulance, but had continued to pretend he was dead to the world.

He had been frantically searching his mind, through the pounding pain in his head, for a passable explanation of why he had no identification with him without revealing his true identity. He definitely did *not* want any publicity that might result from his ridiculous collision with the kid wearing the rollerblades.

But now? Devon thought. Maggie, this exquisite Maggie, had not only kissed him...and what a kiss it had been...but had revealed the fact that she had been waiting a lifetime for a member of royalty, a prince.

And he was a prince!

This was fate, karma. It had been written in the stars, or some such thing, that he would meet lovely Maggie. All he had to do was open his eyes, say hello, then tell her who he was. Unbelievable.

"Can you hear me?" Maggie said, patting Devon's cheek again.

Devon executed a moan that he immediately decided was a bit overdone, then slowly opened his eyes to gaze into the gorgeous brown eyes of Maggie.

"Hello," he said quietly.

She couldn't breathe, Maggie thought, then managed to take a sharp, much-needed breath. His eyes...oh, his eyes were the color of smoke, gray as a fog on a sultry night, and framed in those long, dark lashes. And his voice? Rich and deep, befitting a man who was at least six feet tall, as he was.

"Well," Maggie said, then cleared her throat as she heard the shaky quality of her voice. "Yes. Well,

I'm glad that you're back among us. I imagine that you have an awful headache. That's because you have a lump the size of an egg on your head. Yes, you do. Which would result in a headache, you see, and…I'm babbling. I'm sorry. Do you…do you know who you are?''

''I certainly do,'' he said.

And then he smiled.

And Maggie's heart seemed to skip a beat, then her knees began to tremble as she stared at that devastating smile that revealed straight white teeth and caused his gray eyes to sparkle, actually sparkle.

''I am Prince Devon Renault,'' he said, ''of the Island of Wilshire.''

''Oh, that's absolutely perfect,'' Maggie said dreamily, then blinked in the next instant and her eyes widened. ''You poor man, you're delusional. You must have suffered more damage than originally thought from the blow to your head. I'm going to go call for a neurosurgeon to come take a look at you. Please don't move. I'll be back just as quickly as I can.''

As Maggie turned and started toward the door, Devon raised up on one elbow, squinting his eyes as increased pain shot through his head.

''Wait,'' he said. ''Maggie, please, wait a minute. Don't go.''

Maggie stopped so suddenly she teetered on her feet, her back to Devon. She turned slowly to face him.

''How do you know my name?'' she said.

''I—I heard you talking to yourself,'' Devon said, then eased back down onto the table, his gaze still riveted on Maggie. ''You said your name out loud.

You kissed me, too, but we can discuss that part later. But you also said that you've been waiting a lifetime for a prince and…and I'm here. I am. I'm Prince Devon Renault, heir to the throne of the Island of Wilshire."

"Of course, you are," Maggie said, nodding. "That's fine. We'll go with that…for now. You just stay quiet and still, and I'll get a specialist in here to determine why you believe you are…" She raised one finger. "Back in a flash."

"You don't believe me," Devon said, then pressed the heels of his hands to his throbbing temples. "I should have seen that coming, but I have such a rotten headache and… Damn, you don't believe me. I can prove that I'm telling the truth by…" His voice trailed off. "Never mind. Cancel that. I have to think this through."

"Good idea," Maggie said. "Stay put."

As Maggie hurried from the room, Devon closed his eyes and struggled to concentrate despite the excruciating pain in his head.

Think, Renault, he ordered himself. If he blew this, he'd never forgive himself. He had to handle this exactly right, because it was important, so very important, not just a coincidence that didn't mean anything.

Maggie had been waiting for a prince, *and he was that prince.*

All he had to do was call the hotel where he was staying, tell the bodyguards…who were no doubt mad as hell because he'd disappeared on them for the first time ever…where he was and to get over here as fast as they could.

Devon's bodyguards were big, burly, identical-twin brothers named Homer and Henry. They were thirty-five years old and had followed in the career footsteps of their father, Harry, who was head of security at the palace on the Island of Wilshire. Assigned to protect Devon whenever he left the island, the pair had even accompanied him to London while he attended college.

Those two burly guys could provide the proof of his true identity. They would bring his passport and a whole stack of legal papers that would clearly state that he was Prince Devon Renault. Yes, that's exactly what he would do and...

No, that was *not* what he was going to do.

Devon dragged both hands down his face, then dropped his arms heavily onto the paper-covered table.

If he proved to Maggie that he was really a prince, then he'd be in the same situation with her that he'd been in with every woman he'd ever met since he'd been old enough to be meeting women.

He would be unable to know for certain if Maggie viewed him as simply a man, or if she saw, first, the wealth, power, the mystique of being in close proximity to a member of a royal family.

But he didn't want to tarnish this fated meeting by lying to Maggie, either.

Man, oh, man, this was complicated.

Think, Renault.

What he wanted, needed, more than he could even put into words in his own beleaguered mind, was for Maggie to accept him, get to know him, in *her* world, not in his with all the trappings of royalty.

So, okay, he'd just...back off a bit from the prince thing. He wouldn't lie exactly, he'd just hedge a tad, dim it down, reintroduce himself as Devon Renault...the man.

Good. That was a dandy plan.

He hoped.

Maggie dropped the telephone receiver at the nurses's station back into place, then pressed her hands to her flushed cheeks.

She was so mortified. Maggie wished she had a magic wand that she could wave and make herself disappear...poof...never to be seen or heard from again.

Devon Renault...no, no, she had to get this right, she thought, rolling her eyes heavenward. *Prince* Devon Renault of the Island of...somewhere or another, remembered that she had kissed him!

This was terrible. Just awful. What if Devon told another member of the staff that she had... Forget that. Who would believe such a statement coming from a man who announced he was a prince?

But, oh, dear heaven, *he* knew and *she* knew that she had kissed him at midnight to welcome in the new year. And *he* knew and *she* knew that she'd revealed her nonsensical, romantic secret of wishing for, waiting for, a man of princely charms.

This was definitely the most embarrassing moment of her entire twenty-eight years on this earth.

"Okay, Maggie, I'm reporting as summoned," a deep voice said.

Maggie jerked and dropped her hands from her face. "What?"

"Me," the man said. "Dr. Franklin? Neurosurgeon extraordinarie? Who'd rather be at a swinging party than on call tonight? You paged me?"

"I did?" Maggie said, then shook her head slightly. "Yes, I did do that, didn't I? And here you are. Happy new year."

Dr. Franklin frowned. "Are you all right? You're acting rather...weird."

"I'm fine," she said, producing a phony smile. "Fit as a fiddle. No problem. Now then, there's a man in Room One who was plowed over by a roller-blader and now thinks he's a prince. Anyway, I thought you should have a look at him in case his head injury is worse than we think because, I mean, my stars, the man believes he's an honest-to-goodness prince, for mercy's sake. So! You just trot right into that examining room and take a look at his bump on the bean. Okeydoke?"

Dr. Franklin nodded slowly. "Maybe you should take a break. Drink a can of soda and bring up your sugar level. Do something, Maggie, because you really sound like a nutcase."

Maggie's shoulders slumped. "Sorry. I'm getting a grip. Right now."

She glanced around. "The waiting room is getting full. See? I'm needed elsewhere. 'Bye."

"Very weird," the doctor muttered, then started toward the first room.

During the next fifteen minutes, Maggie treated a broken nose, sent a woman in labor to the maternity floor and assisted a doctor with the suturing of a cut hand that belonged to a drunken man who had brought in the new year by punching a telephone pole.

And at every opportunity she glanced toward Room One, waiting for Dr. Franklin to reappear. When the doctor finally came out, writing on a chart as he strolled toward the nurses's station, Maggie hurried to his side.

"Hi," she said, smiling brightly. "So! Devon. Mr. Renault. The…prince. Did he have any-thing…interesting to say?"

"Nope," Dr. Franklin said, plunking the chart on the counter. "He didn't even announce that he was a prince, or a king or an alien from outer space."

"He didn't?" Maggie said, frowning.

"He's Devon Renault, age thirty, in excellent phys-ical shape," the doctor went on, "who has a killer headache without having had one thing to drink. He said he didn't own a wallet, which was a bit strange, but…I thought he should be admitted for the night because he has a slight concussion, but he refused. End of story."

"Oh."

Dr. Franklin patted Maggie on the shoulder. "I think you've been working too hard, Maggie. You seem a bit…scattered, shall we say? Well, I'm going back to the doctors's lounge. Page me if you need me again."

Maggie sighed as she watched the doctor walk away.

She didn't know why Devon Renault had changed his story already. But she hadn't imagined how she'd been suffused with a foreign heat and felt the flutter-ing of her heart when her lips had touched his.

"I've had enough of this nonsense," she said, spin-ning around.

If Devon could change his mind about being a prince, then she could do an about-face regarding the ridiculous sensual impact the man had on her. She'd march into that examining room and realize that he was just a man, nothing more, nothing special.

Maggie squared her shoulders, lifted her chin and made a beeline for the first room in the hallway. When she entered it, she stopped dead in her tracks, telling herself that she was not, positively not, registering a bleak sense of disappointment.

Devon Renault was gone.

Chapter 2

Maggie covered her mouth to stifle the third yawn that had crept up on her during the shift-change meeting the next morning. One of the doctors who was coming on duty chuckled as he looked at her.

"Did you have a rough night, Maggie?" he said. "Hey, give us a break. You know nothing much goes on around here on New Year's Eve."

A groan erupted from those who had been operating at full speed through the entire night.

"Okay, okay," the doctor said, laughing. "I get the point. It was a tough one. Well, you people are about to escape from this madness. Go home and get some sleep and happy new year to you all."

Maggie slipped on her coat, waved goodbye to everyone, and started toward the front doors, visions of her comfy bed materializing in her mind, temporarily pushing aside the image of Devon Renault that had haunted her through the long hours of the busy night.

Once she got some much-needed sleep, Maggie told herself as she crossed the waiting room, this lingering nonsense about Devon would be at an end.

"Maggie," a deep voice said.

Maggie stopped and spun around, finding herself staring at a tall, green potted plant near the corner of the waiting room.

That plant, she thought with an edge of hysteria, had just spoken her name. Oh, good grief, she had to get some sleep. Now.

A gasp escaped from her lips as a man suddenly appeared from behind the plant.

"Devon," she said, her eyes widening. "What are you doing here? Is your head worse? Have you come back to have someone check you over again?"

Devon crossed the room to stand in front of Maggie. He was still wearing the same dusty clothes and now had a morning beard darkening his rugged jaw.

"I never left," Devon said, looking directly into Maggie's eyes. "I settled in behind that plant, and no one noticed me."

"But why?" Maggie said, frowning.

"Because it was the only way I could be certain that I'd see you again," he said, dragging one hand through his tousled hair. "I had no idea when you'd be scheduled to work, don't even know your last name and…well, here I am." He smiled. "Good morning."

Maggie was so stunned that when she opened her mouth to reply, she realized she was at a loss for words, and snapped her mouth closed. She shook her head slightly and tried again.

"You sat in that godawful chair all night so that you could see me when I got off duty?" she said incredulously. "That's…unbelievable. Flattering, I guess, but… How's your head?"

"Not bad," Devon said. "It's sort of like having a toothache in my brain." He paused. "I hope you don't think I'm stalking you, or something grim like that. I just couldn't handle the thought of never seeing you again." He smiled. "After all, I'm your very own prince, remember? Cinderella was the one to disappear into thin air, not the royal guy."

"Unbelievable," Maggie said, laughing. "You are really something, Devon Renault."

"That's *Prince* Devon Renault, ma'am," he said, grinning at her.

"Oh, yes, of course, let us not forget your royal title. The one you completely forgot you had when Dr. Franklin examined you."

Devon shrugged. "I'm *your* prince, not his."

"This is so silly," Maggie said. "Look, this is way out of character for me, but I'm so tired that nothing is making much sense at the moment. So…would you like to go to the café down the street and have some breakfast with me? I, for one, am starving."

"Breakfast would be great," Devon said, "but I don't have any money."

"It will be my treat."

Devon frowned. "I've never had a woman pay for my meal. That doesn't set well."

"I bet you've never spent the night snuggled up to a potted plant before, either," Maggie said, smiling. "Having me buy you breakfast will be another new experience. What the heck, why not? It's the least I can do for my—" she laughed "—my prince."

"Okay, you're on," Devon said, matching her smile. "But with one condition."

"Oh?"

"That I return the gesture by taking you out to dinner tonight."

"One thing at a time here," Maggie said. "Come on. Say farewell to your buddy the plant. Let's exit stage left from this place and get some food."

The early morning air was chilly, and Devon shoved his hands into his trouser pockets and hunched his shoulders slightly against the cold. They walked in silence for several minutes, then Maggie glanced up at Devon, ignoring the flutter of her heart as she drank in the sight of his handsome, beard-roughened face.

"Seriously, Devon," she said. "Where are you really from?"

"The Island of Wilshire," he said, looking down at her for a moment. "There is such a place, although I doubt that many people have heard of it. It's a small island of about twenty-five thousand people off the European coast. You'll find it on a map if you look hard enough."

"No kidding?" Maggie said, surprise evident in her voice. "I'll be darned. Well, if you were really a prince you'd be on your island doing your princely duties. Right? Right. So, why are you, Devon Renault, ordinary citizen of said Island of Wilshire, in Ventura?"

Devon Renault, ordinary citizen, Devon's mind hummed. Yes! This was going exactly the way he had hoped. Maggie was viewing him as simply a man, and he hadn't had to tell her one single lie. Fantastic.

Not wanting to be hounded by the press during his

stay in America, Devon had convinced the people at the government agencies he contacted, plus the restaurant owners who planned to purchase the Renault-Bardow wine, to not divulge his identity until the wine was shipped in and the publicity packages were released.

"I've been in this country for six months," Devon said, "and Ventura is my last stop. I'm marketing a new and special wine that was developed on the island by my cousin. That's what our economy on Wilshire is made up of…vineyards.

"There is a mountain of paperwork required to satisfy the regulations of your country, and of each state that I've visited, for importing the wine.

"I've convinced four- and five-star restaurants across the United States to add the wine to their inventory, then worked with each on a publicity package that will be released when we're ready. The wine, I must say, has been very well received."

"Congratulations, Devon. You must be very pleased," Maggie said. "Does the wine have an official name? You know, the one the restaurants will put on the wine list they'll hand to the diners?"

"Yep. It's called the Renault-Bardow, with a hyphen," he said. "It's a red wine, very smooth, yet with a slight snappy edge." He laughed. "I sound like a commercial. I described it like that in the publicity packages I helped put together."

"You're a man of many talents," Maggie said, then paused. "So, if Ventura is your last stop you'll be returning to your island soon?"

Devon frowned. "Yes, well… Yes, I suppose that I will be."

"Mmm," Maggie said, knowing she was frowning,

too. She was overreacting again to everything this man said and did, Maggie thought as they entered the café. Sleep. She definitely needed hours and hours of sleep.

They settled opposite each other in a booth and a waitress appeared almost immediately at their table, her bright smile directed toward Devon. Maggie had to clear her throat to get the woman's attention. After the waitress had taken their orders and walked away, Devon ran one hand over his chin.

"I must look like a bum," he said.

Maggie laughed. "More like the morning after a night of partying."

"Some party," he said, gingerly touching the bump on the back of his head. He shrugged, then leaned back and folded his arms over his chest. "First on the agenda, Maggie, is that I don't even know your last name."

"It's MacAllister," she said. "I'm actually Margaret...for my grandmother...Jennifer...for my mother...MacAllister, known to all as Maggie."

"Whoa," Devon said, raising his eyebrows. "*The* MacAllisters I've heard so much about since arriving in Ventura?"

"I won't admit to that," she said, smiling, "until I know what you heard."

"Smart lady," Devon said, matching her smile. "Well, let's see. The MacAllisters are many in number. They have members of superior reputation who are, or were, architects, construction experts, attorneys, doctors, nurses, law enforcement officers, on the list goes.

"The MacAllisters are also known for their volunteer work, devoting their time and money to many charitable organizations. In short, your family are movers and shakers, and are extremely well thought of in this town.''

''Well, in that case, yes, I'm one of *those* Mac-Allisters,'' Maggie said. ''Actually, we're the only MacAllisters in Ventura, so if any one of us suddenly goes nuts and robs a bank, we'll all be painted with the same naughty brush.''

Devon chuckled and Maggie felt a frisson of heat slither down her back, then curl low in her body, causing her to shift slightly in the booth.

''Believe me, I know the feeling,'' he said. ''The Island of Wilshire is very small and we Renaults are under the magnifying glass for sure, along with the Bardows, my cousin's family.''

''Ah, yes, the woes of being a prince,'' Maggie said, laughing.

Devon was saved from replying by the arrival of their food. Maggie had ordered bacon, scrambled eggs and toast, while Devon had chosen waffles with whipped cream and strawberries dribbled over the four-high stack.

The waitress zipped off, returned with a coffeepot to fill their cups, gave Devon another big smile, then bustled away. Maggie and Devon ate in silence for several minutes, taking the edge off their appetites.

''So, tell me about your island,'' Maggie said finally. ''Is it pretty there?''

''It's gorgeous,'' Devon said. ''Very green and lush, with vineyards in all directions as far as the eye can see. The people take great pride in their surroundings and everything is spotlessly clean. Everyone is friendly, honest and open, and there is very little crime…just kids getting into mischief for the most part.''

''It sounds like a little bit of heaven,'' Maggie said, then took another bite of eggs.

''As close as you can get,'' Devon said, nodding. ''When I left to attend college in London it was a big culture shock for me. That was my first experience of being away from the island for anything other than short family trips. It was a real eye-opener, no doubt about it. It's called growing up in a hurry in order to survive.''

''I can imagine,'' Maggie said. ''Are there a lot of you Renaults, like the multitude of MacAllisters?''

''No, my mother died when I was very young and my father never remarried,'' Devon said. No, King Chester Renault had not brought another woman to the palace to be his queen. ''I'm an only child.

''My father's sister married a Bardow and my cousin, Brent, who developed the wine that I'm marketing, is also an only child. Brent is two years older than I am, and the fact that he and I have yet to marry and produce more little Renaults and Bardows is an ongoing nagging subject.

''And that's the full extent of my clan,'' Devon said. ''We're small in number but…'' Powerful. The rulers of Wilshire. ''…but we're…cute.''

Maggie nearly choked on the coffee she'd just sipped as she started to laugh. She patted her chest and shook her head.

''Cute?'' she said. ''Cute is for puppies, kittens and babies. You're…well, you don't need me to tell you that you're a very handsome man, Devon.''

''Not at the moment,'' he said, rubbing his chin

again. "Do you need me to tell you that you're a very beautiful woman, Maggie?"

"I..." Maggie started, then stopped speaking as she met Devon's gaze.

A strange mist seemed to materialize out of nowhere, encircling them, causing the café to disappear into oblivion. With the mist came the heat that swirled within them, thrumming, coiling, growing in intensity with every beat of their racing hearts.

Hazily unaware that he was doing it, Devon lifted one hand and reached across the table to draw his thumb gently over one of Maggie's flushed cheeks, then shifted his thumb toward her lips, closer...closer...

"More coffee, folks?"

Maggie and Devon jerked at the sudden sound of the waitress's voice, and Devon snatched his hand back to his side of the table. A startled squeak escaped from Maggie's throat.

"Sorry if I woke you," the waitress said, frowning. "Want more coffee?"

"Um...Maggie? Coffee?" Devon said, then took a deep, steadying breath.

"What?" Maggie said. "Oh. No. No, thank you. It will keep me awake if I have any more, and I really must get some sleep." She looked at the waitress. "May we have the check, please?"

"Sure thing," the woman said, then slapped a slip of paper onto the table. "You have a happy new year, folks," she added, once again speaking only to Devon.

Devon smiled. "It certainly looks promising. I started the new year by being this lovely lady's long-awaited-for prince."

"No kidding?" the waitress said. "A prince, huh? I was a tree in a school play in the third grade. My acting career was all downhill after that, though. Better luck to you with your prince thing."

"Oh, good grief," Maggie said, snatching up the check. She dropped some bills onto the table for a tip, then slid out of the booth.

Maggie paid the bill at the cash register, rolled her eyes as the woman stationed there gave Devon a dazzling smile, then she and Devon left the café.

"I guess your car is parked back at the hospital," Devon said.

"No, I walk to work," Maggie said, not meeting his gaze. "It's only a few blocks to my apartment."

"You walk even when you're scheduled to work the night shift?"

"It's well lit all the way," she said. "It's very safe."

"I see," Devon said. "Then may I walk you home, Ms. MacAllister?"

"Oh, I don't..."

"Please?"

Maggie sighed in defeat. "Yes, all right, Devon. Why not?"

They walked without speaking for an entire block, each lost in their own thoughts.

"Maggie," Devon said finally, bringing her from her jumbled reverie.

"Hmm?"

"Something...special is happening between us," Devon said quietly. "You know that, don't you? You felt what I did back there in the restaurant?"

"Oh, Devon," Maggie said, pressing one hand to her forehead for a moment. "I'm not certain what this is that's… I'm exhausted and it would be foolish of me to attempt to understand *anything* right now."

"Fair enough," he said, nodding. "Will you have dinner with me tonight?"

Maggie hesitated, then nodded. "Yes, I will. That's what is needed here…a fresh look at the situation after rejuvenating sleep. I'm quite sure we'll discover that we're overreacting to each other due to being physically diminished from lack of rest."

"That sounded very…nursey," Devon said.

"Nursey?" she said with a burst of laughter.

"Whatever," he said. "Well, maybe you're right. Maybe the fact that whenever I look into your fantastic brown eyes I go up in flames, want to make love with you for hours, is simply due to the fact that I'm…how did you put that? Oh, yes, 'physically diminished from lack of rest.'"

Not a chance, sweet Maggie, he thought. What he was feeling was real and honest, rich and earthy. He wanted to kiss and hold Maggie, touch and caress her and, oh, yes, make love to her for hours.

Maggie stopped walking and Devon took two more steps before he realized she wasn't next to him. He turned and went back to stand in front of her, looking at her questioningly.

"What's wrong?" he said.

"For heaven's sake, Devon Renault," Maggie said, none too quietly, "you can't say things like that when you're strolling down the sidewalk. You go up in flames and want to make love with me for hours? You announce that in front of a…" She glanced around. "…a shop that sells clothes for dogs and cats and ferrets? You say it like someone else would comment on the weather?"

"Well, it's true," Devon said, matching her volume as he flung out his arms. "I refuse to lie to you, Maggie. Ever. That you can take all the way to the bank. *I will not lie to you.* I *do* want to make love with you for hours."

"Sounds good to me, honey," a woman said, passing them where they stood on the sidewalk. "If you don't want him, send him over to my place. Maybe your hunk of stuff won't notice that I'm old enough to be his mother."

"That's it," Maggie said, starting off again. "That's all. I refuse to be held responsible for any conversations I take part in with you until I get some sleep. In fact, I don't think I'll speak to you at all until I'm no longer in such a..."

"Physically diminished state," Devon finished for her, falling in step beside her again. "Got it."

"Good," Maggie said, quickening her pace.

Do not say another word, Maggie MacAllister, she ordered herself. Not a peep. She was so...so shaken, so off-kilter, so consumed with desire-evoked heat, that she was liable to open her big mouth and announce to Devon that she wanted to make love with him for hours, too.

And she did. For hours and hours and...

No, no, no, that was insane.

The way her exhausted brain...and body...were reacting to this man, the next thing she knew she'd start actually believing that Devon was a prince.

Her prince.

"That's absurd," she said.

"Shh," Devon said. "You're not supposed to be speaking, remember?"

Maggie laughed, then shook her head. "This is ridiculous. There's my apartment building around the corner, thank heaven. My bed awaits.''

"Oh?" Devon said, raising his eyebrows.

"Forget I said that," Maggie mumbled.

"Got it."

"Good."

The building where Maggie lived was a fairly new structure that was fifteen stories tall with her apartment being on the tenth floor. She and Devon rode up in the elevator in total silence. At Maggie's door, she retrieved her keys from her purse.

"Seven o'clock tonight?" Devon said. "For dinner? We'll go somewhere fancy, special. You don't have to break your vow to not talk to me at the moment. Just nod if that suits you."

"Seven will be fine," Maggie said, smiling up at him. "I'm sorry I was so grumpy, but..." She paused. "I just realized that you may be miles from where you're staying. Do you need to call for a taxi?"

"I'll walk for a while. The chilly air is actually helping my headache," Devon said. "I can catch a cab later if I get tired of hoofing it. I'm staying at the Excalibur Hotel downtown."

"The Excalibur?" Maggie said. "That's the finest hotel in Ventura."

Devon shrugged. "It's all right. Now I'm glad I'm staying there because of the name. I mean, hey, it's perfect for a prince, don't you think?"

"Oh, indeed, it is," Maggie said, unable to curb her smile. "Well, have a pleasant, restful day, Devon, and I hope your headache completely disappears. I'll see you this evening."

Devon didn't turn and start back down the corridor toward the elevator. Maggie didn't turn and insert the key in the lock on the door. They didn't move. They hardly breathed. They just stood there, unable to tear their gaze from each other.

A groan rumbled in Devon's chest and he lifted his hands and framed Maggie's face as he lowered his lips toward hers. Maggie's purse and keys slipped from her fingers unnoticed and landed on the carpeted floor as she raised her arms to encircle Devon's neck.

And then their lips met.

Their lips met in a kiss they had waited an eternity for, having had a teasing preview when Maggie had kissed her prince at midnight to welcome in the new year.

Their lips met in a kiss that caused an explosion of heat to rocket throughout them, consuming them with licking flames of want and need.

It was ecstasy.

It was senses heightened, savoring the taste of strawberries and coffee, feeling the softness of lips that parted to allow tongues to meet, duel and dance.

It was strong hands gently cradling feminine cheeks, and slender fingers sinking into thick, masculine hair.

It was a kiss like none before.

Devon slowly and reluctantly raised his head and took a much needed breath. He dropped his hands from Maggie's face, then reached down to retrieve her purse and keys from the floor. She took them from him, clutching them to her breasts with trembling hands.

"Seven o'clock," Devon said, his voice raspy with passion.

Maggie nodded, unable to speak.

Devon turned and strode down the hallway. The

elevator doors were still open and before he stepped inside, he looked back, his heart thundering as he saw that Maggie hadn't moved. She was still standing by her door, watching him go.

With every ounce of willpower he possessed Devon forced himself to enter the elevator and press the button for the lobby. As the doors swished closed, he splayed one hand on the cool metal, as a last lingering link to Maggie.

Chapter 3

When Devon returned to his hotel suite, he hesitated with dread outside the door, then entered to find Homer and Henry standing in front of him, their arms crossed over broad chests.

They wore the usual dark suits, crisp white shirts with black ties, and had deep frowns on their faces. Years before, Devon had convinced Homer to grow a mustache so he could determine which twin he was speaking to at any given moment.

"Well, hi. Happy new year," Devon said, producing a bright smile. He frowned in the next instant and sighed. "Forget it. You're ticked off. Big-time. Because I snuck out on you and...I'm sorry." Devon shook his head. "No, I'm not. Let's sit down and discuss this in a calm, mature manner, shall we?"

"Mmm," Homer said, narrowing his eyes.

The bodyguards settled onto one of the sofas in the

enormous room. Devon pulled an easy chair in front of them and sat, lacing his fingers on his chest.

"Just listen for a minute, okay?" he said.

"Mmm," Homer said again.

"Do you realize," Devon said, "that I'm thirty years old and whenever I've left the Island of Wilshire I've had—no offense meant here—baby-sitters shadowing every move I've made?

"I have never in my life carried any money on my person, because one of you steps up and pays for whatever I might be purchasing. I haven't held a credit card in my hand, or done anything else remotely—remotely—normal, like an ordinary man might do."

"You *aren't* an ordinary man," Henry said.

"I know, I know," Devon said, nodding. "I don't take my title and responsibilities lightly, believe me." He leaned forward, resting his elbows on his knees and making a steeple of his fingers. "I just wanted a chance to go out…alone, to bring in the new year like anyone else. Can't you understand that?"

"We were just about to call the police to report that you were missing. You could have told us that was what you wanted to do," Homer said.

"Would you have gone along with it?" Devon said.

"No," the pair said in unison.

"I rest my case." Devon stared up at the ceiling for a long moment, then looked at the men again. "Try to put yourselves in my place. Attempt to imagine what it's like to have shadows wherever I go. No privacy. None."

Devon took a deep breath and let it out slowly. "Whenever I dated during those years in London," he went on, "there you were in the background. You paid the bill at restaurants, sat up front in the limo, waited outside the lady's door when I took her home."

Homer and Henry nodded. "That's part of our job, Prince Devon."

"Devon. It's just Devon, while we're in this country, remember?"

"Yes, sir," Henry said. "Devon."

"Thank you," he said. "Where was I?"

"We're standing outside the lady's door while you...do whatever," Henry said.

Devon straightened in the chair and squared his shoulders. "Yes, and it's a pain in the... It's annoying. Well, not this time. Homer, Henry, I've met a woman and I want—I intend—to spend time with her...alone. Really alone. Meaning you two are sitting right there on that sofa while I'm with her."

"Who is she?" Homer said. "We need to run a security check on her."

"You'll do no such thing," Devon said. "Listen to me, please. *Please.* Don't you have a romantic bone in your massive bodies? This woman is very special, and I want a chance to have her get to know me as a man, not *Prince* Devon Renault of the Island of Wilshire. Just a man. It's important to me, means more to me than I can begin to even put into words."

The brothers exchanged glances, then looked at Devon again.

"One week. I'm asking you to give me that week, seven days, to be an ordinary man spending time with a very lovely, rare and beautiful lady," Devon said. "When I'm with her I feel... There's something happening between us that's different from anything I've ever experienced and— One week. Please, guys, have a heart.''

"Do you think you're...you know, falling in love with this woman?'' Henry said, his eyes widening.

"I don't know what this is,'' Devon said, "but I sure as hell want the opportunity to find out.''

"Love,'' Henry said wistfully. "Wouldn't that be something? She could be the Princess of Wilshire, then later the queen, you'd have a slew of babies and we'd be their bodyguards, and... Isn't that awesome, Homer?''

"It's dangerous, that's what it is,'' Homer said. "We can't let him go out alone in this city for a week. Somebody might kidnap him and...''

"Nobody knows who I am,'' Devon said none too quietly. "My identity has been kept under wraps since we arrived in this country, remember? No one will pay the least bit of attention to me.''

"Well,'' Homer said, "somebody paid some kind of attention to you while you were out last night. You look like you've been in a train wreck.''

"It was a fluke, a silly accident. I got knocked down on the sidewalk and... I'm fine, don't worry. Just got a bump on the head. One week, fellas. I'll call my father regularly just as I'm doing now and report on my progress with the restaurant owners here. If he phones me, tell him I'm in the shower, or I'm taking a nap, or whatever. It will work, don't you see? I need this time with my Mag—with this special woman.

"I won't do anything foolish,'' Devon said. "Will you do it? Give me a week to just...just be?''

"You bet,'' Henry said, smiling. "Love. Wouldn't that be something?''

* * *

Maggie stood in front of the mirror on the back of her closet door and cocked her head to one side as she studied her reflection.

She shook her head and watched with approval as her freshly shampooed, wavy hair fell back into place. Her dark brown eyes, she noted, that were a Mac-Allister trademark, were clear and sparkling due to having slept for hours.

Oh, yes, she'd slept, Maggie thought as she left the bedroom, turning off the light as she went. And dreamed about Devon Renault. Sensuous dreams. Dreams of Devon taking her into his strong arms, kissing her over and over, then...

"Don't think about those dreams, Maggie," she told herself, feeling a warm flush stain her cheeks. "Erase them from your mind this very second."

She set her shawl and purse on a chair, then pressed one hand on her stomach.

She was nervous, she thought. No, maybe she was just excited, anticipating an enjoyable evening ahead with a very handsome and charming man.

No, she was definitely nervous, because when she opened the door to Devon, saw him, heard him speak, she would know if she'd overreacted earlier to his blatant masculinity.

The best thing that could happen, she mused, narrowing her eyes, would be that she'd realize that Devon was certainly good-looking but so were other men she dated. The strange spell that seemed to be cast over her and Devon time and again, that misty, sensual spell, had been a product of her tired imagination.

Yes, she mentally rambled on, that's what would

take place when she saw Devon in just a few minutes from now. It had to go that way because if it didn't she was in a heap of trouble. Devon was leaving Ventura very soon, and she'd never see him again. She didn't want to be left behind aching for him, wanting to make love with him, yearning for what might have been but would never be.

A knock sounded at the door and Maggie jerked, then took a steadying breath.

Okay, this was it, she told herself. She was about to be reassured that there was nothing mystical nor extraordinarily rare and special taking place between her and Devon Renault.

Right?

Maggie crossed the room, opened the door, then attempted and failed to smile at Devon.

Wrong.

"Hello, Maggie," Devon said. "You look absolutely beautiful."

Heat rushed throughout Maggie like a raging river as she stared at Devon. He was wearing a perfectly tailored gray suit that did marvelous things for his smoky-gray eyes. His shirt was a shade darker gray and the tie was a gray, white-and-black stripe with matching accent handkerchief in the jacket pocket.

He was so incredibly…gorgeous, Maggie thought dreamily, and her bones were dissolving from the hot flames of desire that were consuming her. She was definitely in trouble.

"Maggie?" Devon said, frowning slightly.

"What? Oh, I'm sorry," she said, stepping back. "Please come in. I just sort of drifted off somewhere for a second there and… Never mind." She closed the door behind him. "You look... How's your head?"

"Fine. Good as new," Devon said, turning to face her. "I have to say it again, Maggie. You're beautiful. That dress is so pretty on you."

The dress she'd chosen for her dinner date with Devon was a soft shade of mint green. The skirt was a swirl of chiffon that came to midcalf, and the top was a camisole with tiny straps and delicate tucks. She wore silver evening sandals and would carry a silver purse and a white shawl with glimmering silver threads woven through it.

"Thank you," she said, no hint of a smile on her face. "I'll probably freeze to death wearing it, but... Well, you know the old saying about vanity thy name is woman, or some such thing, but I refuse to cover it with a bulky coat so I'll just...

"Oh, Devon, this is terrifying. I'm thoroughly rested, not physically diminished from lack of sleep, but I'm so very glad to see you and when I look at you I— Oh, dear."

Devon closed the short distance between them and placed his hands on Maggie's upper arms.

"And I'm very glad to see you, too," he said. "I've been shaved, showered and dressed for two hours, waiting until I could leave the hotel and come here. I think I wore a path in the carpeting by pacing back and forth, glancing at my watch every minute or so.

"Maggie, whatever this is that's happening between us is not one-sided because we both feel it. It's not terrifying. It might very well be something wonderful."

"How can you say that?" she said, stepping back

and forcing him to drop his hands from her arms. "You don't even live here. You'll be leaving Ventura soon."

"One week," Devon said, frowning. "I figure I'll wrap things up on the business side of things in about a week, then be ready to return to Wilshire."

Maggie's eyes widened. "That's it? One week? Seven days? Then…poof…you'll be leaving, be gone forever, never to be seen again?"

"Don't jump ahead in your mind to the part where I leave," Devon said. "Concentrate on the moment. We have seven whole days to be together, Maggie, and this is day one. Yes, I realize we both have work to do apart from each other, but you know what I mean. Seven days. There's no telling what we might discover about this…this attraction between us in that length of time."

"That's what terrifying," Maggie said, throwing out her hands. "I don't think I want to know what this is, because what difference does it make? You're going back to the Island of Wilshire, remember?

"Actually, the more I think about it, a person can't possibly discover—to use your word—enough about another person in seven days to…" She pressed one hand to her forehead. "I'm totally confusing myself."

"Hey, don't get upset. Okay? We have a great evening planned. Let's just go and enjoy ourselves, take this as it comes. I have a taxi waiting downstairs."

Maggie laughed, a slightly hysterical edge to the sound. "The whole time I've been working up to a nervous breakdown here, you've had a cab waiting with the meter running? I'm sorry. I should have postponed my slipping over the edge until later."

"Ah, Maggie," Devon said, smiling. "You are delightful. If I could find that kid on the rollerblades, I'd thank him a million times for plowing into me so that I ended up in the hospital. If it wasn't for him, I never would have met you.''

Devon took Maggie's hands in his and looked directly into her eyes. ''Say that you'll live for the moment we're in. Say that you'll allow our time together to bring us whatever is meant to be. Say you'll follow your heart, not your mind. Say yes to all that, please, Maggie.''

No, no, no, Maggie thought frantically. That would be so foolish. Follow her heart? That would be impossible to do if Devon took it with him when he left. No, no, no.

''Maggie?''

''Yes,'' she said, the word escaping from her lips before she could stop it.

The restaurant where Homer had made their reservation was one of Ventura's finest. When the taxi driver threw his arms around Devon and hugged him after Devon gave him some bills from a money clip he withdrew from his pocket, Maggie looked up at Devon questioningly as they entered the building.

''What was that all about?'' she said.

''It had to do with the way I calculated his tip, I think,'' Devon said, chuckling.

''Are you one of those people who is in a fog about math?'' Maggie said as they approached the hostess.

''Something like that.''

''I'm a whiz at math, but I'll confess that I can't spell worth a darn,'' Maggie said. ''How's that?''

''That's very magnanimous of you, ma'am,''

Devon said. "We'll just hope our children inherit my
ability to spell and your razor-sharp mind for math."

"Good plan," Maggie said. "How many children
would you like us to have?"

"Six," Devon said, then addressed the hostess.
"We have reservations for two in the name of Renault, please."

"Six?" Maggie said. "Six babies?"

"Aren't men something?" the hostess said to Maggie. "You can sure tell they're not the one who's
going to be pregnant for nine months."

"Oh, well, um," Maggie said, "...we were just
being silly, pretending that... It started with the math
and the spelling thing and then... Never mind."

"Well, it's nice to meet a couple planning on having an old-fashioned family with oodles of kiddies,"
the hostess said. "If you'll follow me, please, I'll
show you to your table."

"Thank you very much," Maggie said, rolling her
eyes heavenward.

Babies, she thought as she and Devon trailed after
the hostess. That was part of her dream, of course,
creating beautiful, healthy children with her prince.
Making exquisite love in the magical, private hours
of the night with her soul mate that ultimately resulted
in the tiny miracle that was a part of him, a part of
her.

She knew, just somehow knew, that Devon would
be a wonderful father, the kind that was right in there
doing his share, taking part in everything from changing diapers to teaching his child how to ride a bike.
Oh, yes, their babies would be blessed to have a
daddy like Devon who—

What? Maggie thought, nearly stumbling. Where

had that thought come from? How had that *"their babies"* snuck into her mental ramblings? That was nonsense, for heaven's sake. Well, it was sort of understandable considering the ridiculous conversation they'd had about spelling and math.

Oh, don't overreact again, Maggie MacAllister, she ordered herself. It had been a silly and fun blip on the screen that didn't mean a thing, so just forget it. And if she dreamed tonight about Devon holding a slew of babies in his arms as she gazed at them with a loving smile, she'd never speak to herself again.

Maggie was pulled from her thoughts by a waiter who appeared at their table and handed them menus with no prices on the one she received. A tingle of excitement swept through her as she realized she had never been in such an elegant restaurant, despite the multitude of fancy establishments the MacAllister clan had gathered in for celebrations.

She glanced around the large room, drinking in the sight of the sparkling chandeliers, the waiters in tuxedos scurrying back and forth, the diners who were all dressed in their finery. It was all picture-perfect, so very special.

And so was Devon, she thought, looking over at him where he was concentrating on the selections available for dinner.

She'd told him she would live for the moment they were in and she would, beginning right now. She wouldn't think about the right or wrong of it, she was simply going to enjoy, savor, be part of creating memories that she intended to keep.

Because when Devon left Ventura, that would be all she would have...the memories of the time she had spent with her prince.

No, no, she thought, forcing herself to look at the menu. No gloomy musings. Not tonight. Not on this Cinderella-is-with-her-Prince-Charming night.

"Have you decided what you want, Maggie?" Devon said.

You, she thought, smiling at him. For as long as it lasted, for the measured seven days—and nights— Devon was hers.

"I'm going to try something I've never had before," she said. Like living in a fantasy world for one week of her life, grabbing hold of each precious hour and not letting go. "Pheasant."

Devon nodded. "Sounds good. I think I'll have the same." He chuckled. "I'll have to hold myself back when I go through the wine-tasting ritual, not tell the steward that the upcoming Renault-Bardow will soon be the best wine on their list."

"You've already done business with the owners of this restaurant?" Maggie said.

"Yep, and it took very little convincing to get them to agree to order in a large supply." Devon laughed. "My cousin is going to have to step up production because the response to his wine has been far better than we ever hoped.

"I have one more restaurant to finish business with. They've already placed their order, but it takes about a week to put together the publicity package. Each one is tailored to the establishment, is uniquely right for them and is done at our expense as an incentive for making a sizable order."

"A week," Maggie said quietly.

"Darn it," Devon said. "Forget I said that. I was just chatting about the wine and... We're not going to bring it up again, Maggie—the length of time we have left together. That subject is taboo. Right?''

Maggie forced herself to push aside the chill that had settled around her heart as Devon had spoken of having only one week remaining in his stay in the States.

''Right,'' she said.

''Are you ready to order?'' the waiter said, reappearing at the table. ''Or would you like more time?''

''Oh, yes, we're ready,'' Maggie said, smiling up at the man. ''Time is not to be wasted, not one little tick of it.''

Chapter 4

His dinner, Devon decided as the waiter removed his empty plate, had probably been delicious but he'd been so totally focused on lovely, enchanting Maggie that he hardly remembered eating it, let alone how it might have tasted.

This evening was perfection personified. Sure, he mused, some of that was due to knowing that his bodyguards were not lurking nearby, hovering in the shadows. But that exhilarating fact was a very moot point in why he was having a wonderful time.

Maggie.

It all centered on Maggie.

The waiter took Devon's order for brandy and coffee, then Maggie excused herself to go to the powder room. Devon leaned back in his chair and stared across the table at the now-empty space.

Babies, Devon thought. He and Maggie had been kidding around with the bit about the spelling and math and how their children should inherit the proper abilities from them, the parents, and not get them reversed.

But when Maggie had continued the game and asked him how many children he would like them to have, something had immediately shifted in his mind.

He was suddenly seeing vivid pictures of beautiful Maggie growing big with his child, their miracle, saw the serene expression on her face as she rested her hands on her protruding stomach, saw himself splay his own hand there with awe and reverence to feel his son or daughter move beneath his palm.

As he'd spoken to the hostess, he'd been acutely aware of the warmth that seemed to encircle his heart then totally consume him. Babies. His and Maggie's, created in the night by exquisite lovemaking shared.

Devon narrowed his eyes and stared into space.

Had he ever before been with a woman he could envision being the mother of his children? No.

Had he ever before been with a woman he could envision growing old with? No.

Had he ever before been with a woman he could envision waking up next to each morning for the remainder of his days? No.

But then, never before now had there been beautiful Maggie MacAllister.

Devon leaned forward and folded his forearms on the top of the table.

How would he feel, he mused, if he knew, right now, this very minute, that Maggie wasn't coming back to resume her place across from him? For whatever make-believe reason, she was gone, had walked away and he'd never see her again. How would he feel?

Devon frowned as a chill swept through him and a cold fist tightened in his gut.

Whew, he thought. That was what he would call a very heavy-duty answer to his question. Okay, asked and answered, but what did it mean? Was he falling in love with Maggie MacAllister? Could it really happen this quickly, be love at first sight, per se?

Why not? That's how it had taken place between his mother and father. He'd heard the romantic tale countless times as he was growing up.

His mother had been coming out of a department store in New York City, his father had been going in at the same moment and they'd collided, resulting in his mom's packages falling to the ground.

Expressing his heartfelt apology, Chester had begun to gather the parcels, their gazes had met, their hands touched as they reached for the same bag and…blam…that was it. Love in its purest and most glorious form had been born in that instant.

They'd been married two weeks later, Prince Chester had taken his bride back to the Island of Wilshire, and when he'd inherited the throne, his mother had taken her place proudly by his side as his queen.

His mother had died of cancer years before and Devon knew that his father still missed her, had seen the pain in his father's eyes in unguarded moments when the king sat staring into the flames of the fire in the hearth in the castle, reliving the days when his dear wife had been there with him.

Oh, yes, Devon thought, love could happen that quickly. But how could a man be certain that that was the emotion he was truly feeling?

There was something so whimsical and romantic about the way he and Maggie had met due to her kissing her long-awaited prince at the stroke of midnight that welcomed in the new year.

Was this really fate? Karma? Whatever? Was Maggie truly the woman of his hopes and dreams, his soul mate, or was he being caught up in the make-believe aura that surrounded his being with Maggie? Was he headed for a crushing and devastating fall when reality burst the romantic bubble they were existing in?

How was a man to know if he was really in love?

But what if... Oh, man, what a crummy thought... What if he came to realize that he truly did love Maggie but she didn't love him in return?

"Well, damn," Devon muttered, "this is getting very complicated."

It took two to make a forever.

There it was...bottom line.

It took two people to fall in love at the same time, to make a commitment, to vow to never be parted again. It took two to create the miracle of a baby. It took two to stay together until death separated them in this world.

How would he know if he was in love with Maggie MacAllister?

And even more, how would he know if she was in love with him?

Maggie slid back onto her chair and smiled at Devon.

"Miss me?" she said.

Devon looked at her intently. "Yes. Yes, I did. I stared at that empty chair and knew I wanted you to hurry back, here, where you belong."

"My goodness, Devon," Maggie said, frowning, "you're so serious all of a sudden. You're acting as though...I don't know...as though you thought I

might duck out the door and disappear into the night,
or something.''

"I'm sorry,'' he said, shaking his head slightly.
''My mind went off on tangent while you were gone
and... Maggie, let me ask you a hypothetical question.''

''Okay,'' she said.

''Do you believe in love at first sight?'' Devon
said, leaning toward her.

Before Maggie could reply, the waiter arrived with
their brandy, coffee and a leather folder on a silver
plate, which he slid close to Devon's side of the table.

''Thank you,'' Devon said to the man before he
turned and walked away.

Maggie took a sip of coffee, her mind racing.

Did she believe in love at first sight? she mentally
repeated. She'd never thought about it, never drawn
a conclusion as to whether or not it could actually
happen between two people.

''Maggie?'' Devon said. ''Are you going to answer
my question?''

''I'm thinking,'' she said, then replaced the china
cup in the saucer. ''I said back in my apartment that
I didn't think that a week was long enough for two
people to discover... But then again, I've heard stories about people who meet and know in an instant
that...'' She shrugged. ''I guess...it could happen, but
it would be a very rare occurrence. It's very easy to
confuse love and lust...well, desire. That's a nicer
word.''

''Mmm,'' Devon said, nodding. ''How do you suppose people know when they're really in love?''

''I don't have a clue,'' Maggie said, laughing.

''My parents fell in love at first sight,'' Devon said.

"They were, at the risk of sounding corny, a match made in heaven. My father still misses my mother even though she's been gone for years."

Maggie smiled. "That's nice, very romantic. I'm surrounded by MacAllisters who are deeply in love, but I really don't know how they knew at the time that they'd found their soul mate." She paused. "Devon, why are we having this discussion? I certainly hope it has nothing to do with what you hope to discover about us in the next week."

"Why do you hope that?" he said, frowning.

"Because...I know we're not supposed to dwell on this, but you're forcing the issue...you're leaving Ventura. Your life is on the Island of Wilshire. Mine is here. We're living for the moment, remember? You *must* remember that, Devon, because that's all we have. Seven days of moments to cherish." Maggie lifted her brandy snifter. "A toast. To moments."

Devon hesitated, then raised his glass. "I'm thinking too much, just scrambling my brain, which is probably already a jumbled mess due to my bump on the head." He paused. "So...to moments. *Our* moments, Maggie."

"Yes," she said softly, then took a sip of the smooth, warming brandy. "Mmm."

Devon tasted the brandy and nodded. "Nice."

"But not nearly as good," Maggie said, smiling, "as Renault-Bardow wine, my prince."

"Not even close, my princess," he said, matching her smile.

They looked directly into each other's eyes and their smiles faded. They set the snifters on the table, each cradling the fragile glass gently between their hands.

The brandy's warmth within them was pushed aside by the rush of heated passion that consumed them. Eyes of chocolate-brown and pewter-gray sent and received messages of want and need, of desire so intense it seemed to steal the very breath from their bodies and cause hearts to race in wild tempos.

The mist, the sensual-beyond-belief mist, swirled around them, encasing them in a private cocoon where no one else was granted entry. Time lost meaning.

"Maggie," Devon said finally, his voice raspy.

That's all he said, just her name, and to Maggie it felt like lush velvet caressing her, floating over her with its soft touch, igniting the whispering flames of desire within her even more.

"Oh, Devon," she said, her voice trembling. "I feel so…"

"Would you like me to take this for you now, sir?" the waiter said, suddenly appearing by the table.

"What?" Devon said, then saw the man incline his head toward the leather folder on the silver plate. "Oh. Yes, just give me a second here." He flipped open the folder, then took the money clip from his pocket and peeled off several large bills. "That should do it."

The waiter's eyes widened, then he snapped the folder closed and picked up the plate.

"Thank you very much, sir," he said. "Very much, indeed. Enjoy the remainder of your evening and do come again soon." He hurried away.

"I must have messed up the math again," Devon said, shaking his head. "I was afraid he was going to hug me like the taxi driver did. Shall we go, before he comes back and decides to kiss me on both cheeks, or something?''

''Yes,'' Maggie said, then took a steadying breath. ''Yes, of course, I'm ready to leave. It was a delicious dinner, Devon, and a lovely evening. Thank you.''

Devon came around the table to assist Maggie with her chair, then took the shawl from her hands and draped it across her shoulders, his hands lingering for a moment on her upper arms.

''Thank you for agreeing to come out with me tonight,'' he said. ''I had a good—great—wonderful time.'' He paused. ''This sounds like a dialogue that takes place at someone's door and we're still standing in the middle of the restaurant.''

Maggie laughed softly, then they walked across the room and out the front door of the building.

''Taxi, sir?'' the doorman said.

''No, my driver will…'' Devon said, then glanced quickly at Maggie. ''Yes. A taxi. Thank you.''

''Your driver?'' Maggie said, looking up at Devon questioningly.

Devon shrugged. ''Hey, I'm a prince, remember? I have bodyguards who double as drivers of a limo and take me wherever I wish to go. It's been so long since I've driven a car I've probably forgotten how.''

''I see,'' Maggie said. ''Do I, the princess, get bodyguards and a limo, too?''

''At your beck and call,'' Devon said. ''No doubt about it.''

''Well, fancy that,'' she said. ''Can I pick the color of my limo?''

''Sure,'' Devon said, nodding. ''Just be prepared for the bodyguards to really get on your nerves because they're always there, lurking in the shadows.''

Maggie glanced around, merriment dancing in her eyes. "I don't see any bodyguard types."

"They're very good at lurking," Devon said. "Here's our taxi. I hope this guy doesn't hug me when I pay him enough to buy a house."

"I'll figure out the fare and whisper it in your ear," Maggie said, then slid onto the back seat of the cab.

"Okay," Devon said, settling next to her. He leaned forward for a second to give the man behind the wheel Maggie's address, then moved back again. "I'll owe you one, Maggie. Just speak right up if you need a word spelled correctly all of a sudden."

Their lighthearted mood slowly dissipated and was replaced by silence and a building, nearly palpable tension between them as the taxi driver drove above the speed limit toward Maggie's apartment building.

Slow down, Maggie mentally pleaded. She and Devon may have already had the conversation-at-the-door thing, but they hadn't actually been standing in front of her apartment. Where they would be in just a few minutes. Where she would have to make a very major decision. Where she would either bid Devon a pleasant good-night, or ask him in for coffee and—

Darn it, who set up these social rules, anyway? Maggie thought peevishly. Why was it always up to the woman to decide whether or not the evening would end with "Thanks, chum, see ya" or "Let's make love"? Why was this tremendous responsibility falling squarely on her shoulders alone? This wasn't fair.

Dandy, she thought. She was working herself up to another nervous breakdown. This had never been a big issue in the past because she was a pro at bidding her escort adieu at the door. But tonight? With Devon?

Everything about her...her relationship, per se, with Devon was different from the norm, and had been from the moment she'd kissed him at midnight to welcome in the new year. There was an otherworld quality to what they were sharing.

The attraction between them was like nothing she'd experienced before, was heightened beyond measure in its intensity, causing the heat of desire to thrum within her whenever she looked directly into Devon's incredible eyes, or was the recipient of one of his dazzling smiles, or felt the touch of his hand, or...

And added to the confusing mix was the already-determined length of time they had together, each minute that passed being one less that they would have to share and cherish.

Maggie pulled her shawl more closely around her and stared out the side window of the taxi.

Day one was almost over. The decision as to how it would end was, she knew, hers to make. Oh, what should she do?

What did she *want* to do?

Maggie turned her head to look at Devon and found him gazing directly at her, causing a shiver to course through her.

She wanted to make love with Devon Renault, Maggie thought, unable to tear her gaze from his. She didn't care, it didn't matter, that they'd known each other such a short time. Old rules of conduct did not apply. She might never again meet a man who made her feel so alive, so special and beautiful, so acutely aware of her own femininity compared to his magnificent masculinity.

She was going to make love with Devon and have no regrets that she had shared such an intimate act with him. She'd throw caution to the wind and just...just listen to her heart, not her mind. Yes.

"Here you are, folks," the taxi driver said, coming to a screeching halt in front of Maggie's apartment building. "Safe and sound."

"Math, Maggie," Devon whispered.

"What? Oh." Maggie leaned forward to look at the meter, mentally calculated a reasonable tip, then quietly gave Devon the figure.

"Got it," he said, chuckling as he opened the door. "Promise I won't get hugged?"

"Guaranteed," Maggie said, sliding across the seat and stepping onto the sidewalk.

Devon paid the driver, who smiled, then whizzed off above the speed limit.

"It's getting colder," Devon said. "Let's get you inside before you freeze in your pretty dress."

As they started up the sidewalk leading to the front door, Maggie frowned. Just a minute here, she thought. Devon hadn't seemed to even entertain the idea of having the cab driver wait for him while he said good-night to her at her door.

Was Devon assuming that they would enter her apartment and march right into the bedroom? she thought, her eyes widening. The nerve of that man. That must be what he was thinking, or he would have told the taxi driver that he'd be back in a few minutes. Well, she had news for Mr. Renault, who was rapidly losing his princely charms. She had no intention of...

Oh, good grief, she was muddling her brain to the point that she couldn't think straight. It was perfectly fine for her to decide that she and Devon would make love, but she was in a huff because he had apparently reach the same conclusion? Was this crazy? Well, it certainly didn't make a whole lot of sense, that was for sure.

Maggie had been so deep in thought that she blinked in surprise when she realized that she and Devon had reached her floor and were now walking toward her door. She fumbled in her purse for her key and removed it with a slightly trembling hand.

"I didn't have the taxi driver wait for me," Devon said, "because—"

"There, I did it," Maggie said as she actually poked the key into the slot.

"Because I'm going to walk for a while, then flag down another cab later," Devon said. "I enjoy strolling around in this city, when I don't get run over by a roller-blader, that is."

Maggie's head snapped up and her mouth dropped open. She shook her head slightly, closed her mouth, frowned, then attempted once again to speak.

"You're leaving, Devon?" she said. "Now? Right this minute?"

Devon took a deep breath, let it out slowly, then dragged a restless hand through his hair.

"Maggie, look," he said. "I thought about this during the cab ride. All I managed to do was carry on an argument in my head that just went in circles, making it impossible for me to come to a conclusion that I was comfortable with. Because of that, I think the best thing for me to do is to leave, to end the evening right here at your door."

"But...why?" Maggie said.

"Oh, Maggie, I want you so much, want to make love with you with a burning need like nothing I've ever known before. I could state my case, say we have such a short length of time to be together that we shouldn't waste one second of it and…

"But that doesn't erase the fact that we haven't known each other very long. I know, just know, that you're not the kind of woman who would go to bed with a man so quickly. It's just not who you are. I don't want to pressure you into doing something you'd regret by using the time factor thing and… Understand?"

"So, you're making this decision for both of us?" Maggie said. "Well, that's certainly different, isn't it? Yes, it definitely is."

"It's not what I *want* to do," Devon went on. "It's what I believe I *should* do. So I am. Leaving. Now. Because I don't want to do anything that might make you think I don't respect you or…" He leaned over and dropped a quick kiss on Maggie's lips. "That little kiss is all I can handle, because I'm hanging on by a thread here. Good night, Maggie. Thank you again for an evening that was so special and— What shift do you work tomorrow?"

"I'm on days," Maggie said, a rather bemused expression on her face.

"So, your evening is free?"

"Mmm," she said, nodding.

"Would you like to go out to dinner again with me tomorrow night?"

"What?" she said. "Oh, no, it's my turn. I'll cook for us."

"Hey, that will be great," Devon said. "It's been a long time since I've had a home-cooked meal." He paused. "So. Well. Until tomorrow night, then. What time should I come over?"

"About seven, I guess," Maggie said.

"Got it. Why don't you go on into your apartment and lock the door? I'd like to know you're safely inside before I leave."

Maggie nodded, turned the key in the lock and opened the door. She took one step forward, then stopped in her tracks, shaking her head.

"No," she said, looking at Devon again. "Everything you just said to me was the most romantic, the sweetest, the most prince-charming speech I've ever heard, Devon. I feel very special and important, and very respected and... But I have a voice in this decision, too, and I wish to be heard."

"Oh. Sure. I'm listening."

"I've gone in circles in my mind with the same arguments that you have," Maggie said, her voice not quite steady. "I want to make love with you, just as you want to make love with me.

"The difference between our bottom-line conclusions is that what I *want* is what I believe *should* take place, because we have so little time to be together. But I respect you, too, Devon, and since you're not comfortable with that then... I just think you have the right to know how I feel on the subject and... Good night and thank you again for a lovely—"

Maggie's words were smothered by Devon's mouth capturing hers in searing kiss as he framed her face with his hands. He parted her lips, delving his tongue into the sweet darkness to meet her tongue. He finally raised his head a fraction of an inch to speak close to her lips.

"Are you positive about this?" he said. "Can you promise me you'll have no regrets if I follow you through that doorway and... Maggie?"

"I promise, Devon," she whispered. "A princess wouldn't lie to her prince. And you *are* my prince...for now. Come into my home with me, please, Devon, and we'll close the door on the world and create a wondrous place for just the two of us."

Devon looked deep into Maggie's eyes, his heart nearly bursting. He encircled her shoulders with one arm and they went into the apartment, shutting the door behind them with a quiet click.

Chapter 5

This man, her prince, Maggie thought dreamily, was so beautiful that he took her breath away. The soft glow of the lamp on her nightstand was cascading over him, making his tanned skin appear like burnished gold.

His shoulders were so wide, his legs muscular, his broad chest covered with curly brown hair a shade darker than the thick hair on his head.

And he wanted her. *Her.* His arousal was evidence of his desire for her.

His eyes, those incredible gray eyes of Devon's were smoky with passion all directed toward her as she stood before him naked, allowing him to sweep his gaze over her as she was doing to him.

It felt so natural, so right, to be stripped of outer trimmings, to reveal to Devon who she was as a woman who wanted him with an intensity like nothing she had ever felt before.

"You're exquisite, Maggie," Devon said, his voice husky. "So lovely, and I want you so much."

"I want you, too, my prince Devon," Maggie whispered. "More than I can put into words."

"I *am* your prince," he said, closing the distance between them. "The one you've been waiting a lifetime for, Princess Maggie."

Maggie smiled, then slipped onto the bed, stretching out and raising her arms to welcome Devon into her embrace. He came to her, capturing her mouth with his as he lay beside her, catching his weight on one forearm, his free hand splayed on her flat stomach.

He delved his tongue into her mouth to seek and find her tongue, to duel and dance and stroke, causing frissons of heat to ripple throughout them. He broke the kiss and moved to one of her breasts, taking the sweet bounty gently into his mouth and laving the nipple with his tongue to a tight bud.

Maggie sank her fingers into Devon's hair, urging his mouth more firmly onto her. Her lashes drifted down as she savored the hot, sensual sensations rocketing throughout her like licking flames.

She was on fire, she thought hazily, burning with want and need. Oh, yes, she'd waited a lifetime for this, for him, for Devon, her prince. For now he was hers and the now was all that mattered. Devon.

Devon shifted to her other breast, his breathing ragged, the coiled heat low in his body tightening to the point of pain.

Maggie, his mind hummed. She was giving of herself so freely, so honestly, holding nothing back. Giving of herself to *him*, Devon, the man, not *Prince* Devon of the Island of Wilshire.

He was overwhelmed, not just physically, but emotionally as well, could feel an achy sensation in his throat that spoke of his awe, his wonder, of that knowledge as well as the pure joy of being with this woman. She was his.

Devon raised his head to look directly at Maggie and she lifted her lashes to meet his gaze. His heart thundered as he saw the desire radiating in the deep, brown depths of her eyes.

"I don't want to rush you," he said, hardly recognizing his own raspy voice, "but I—I want you, want to make love to you, join our bodies and... Oh, Maggie."

"Come to me, Devon," she said, a near-sob catching in her throat. "Hurry. Please."

He left her only long enough to take steps to protect her, then returned to her, moving over her and into her with one smooth, powerful thrust.

A soft, feminine sigh of pleasure escaped from Maggie's lips as a masculine groan rumbled in Devon's chest.

The rhythm began, slowly at first, then increasing in tempo with an urgency that engulfed them both.

Maggie matched him beat for beat, clinging to his shoulders, gazing into his eyes as the tension within them built, tightened, swirled and churned and swept them higher, up and away, and over the top of ecstasy in a splash of bright colors and heat.

"Devon!" she gasped.

She was flung into oblivion, tightening her hold on

him to be assured he would stay with her, go to the magical place with her that was theirs, only theirs.

"Maggie, Maggie," Devon said as he shuddered with release. "Oh…my…Maggie."

They hovered there, filling their senses, savoring the moment, etching it indelibly in their minds…and hearts. Then slowly, and very reluctantly, they drifted back, spent, sated, awed.

Devon rolled off of Maggie, then pulled her to his side, tangling his fingers in her hair as she nestled her head on his chest.

Their hearts quieted, their breathing returned to normal, their bodies cooled. He reached down to pull the blankets over them, then settled back to hold her close, as though he'd never again let her go.

"Oh, Devon," Maggie said softly, "I've never felt so…never experienced anything so…" Her voice trailed off and she sighed in frustration as words failed her.

"I know," he said. "I know. There's no way to tell you how… Magic. I guess that's the way to describe what we just shared. Magic. So special. Ours. It was ours, Maggie, yours and mine…together."

"Yes." Maggie paused. "I'm so sleepy."

"Then sleep and I'll hold you right here in my arms," Devon said. "I'm going to leave later and I'll try not to wake you when I go. We both have jobs to tend to in the morning, but I'll be back in the evening for my home-cooked meal. All right?"

"Mmm," Maggie said. "Perfect. But I wish you didn't have to leave." She yawned. "It feels so good, so right, to be nestled close to you like this, giving way to sleep and… Oh, my," She drifted off.

"Yes, so *very* right," Devon said, then kissed her gently on the forehead.

He shifted just enough to be able to see Maggie's face, drinking in the sight of her as she slept.

He was suffused with a warmth that was far different than the heat of desire, was a foreign feeling like nothing he'd ever known, had had just a hint of earlier in the restaurant. Once again it seemed to encircle his heart with a gentle touch, but now it made him feel complete, whole, as though something had been missing and had now, at long last, been found.

Maggie.

Devon's breath caught and tears stung his eyes as he continued to gaze at Maggie as she slept so peacefully close to his side.

This, he thought, was love. As confusing as the whole question of how a man knew if he was in love was suddenly crystal-clear. There was no doubt in his mind, or heart, that he was in love with Maggie MacAllister. Yes, heart, mind, body and soul, he loved her.

Devon swallowed heavily, then eased carefully away from Maggie and sank back against the pillow to stare up at the ceiling.

Now what did he do? he thought with an edge of franticness. Did he declare his love to Maggie? Ask her to marry him and make a home with him on the Island of Wilshire? Tell her she really was his princess because he was, indeed, *Prince* Devon Renault? Tack on the added fact that someday she would be the reigning queen of the island when he became king?

Yeah, right, he thought, dragging both hands down

his face. Why not throw the kitchen sink into the mix since he was going to totally overwhelm Maggie with the truths of the life he was offering her?

Oh, and, Maggie? There will be bodyguards following you wherever you go. You'll have to look your best and behave like royalty whenever you venture out, too, because everyone watches you. No bad hair days allowed.

Forget about being an independent woman because you won't even pay for anything, will have a couple of burly guys who will step up and settle the tab, even carry your packages for you. You probably won't remember how to drive after a while, because you'll be driven in a limo where you wish to go and…

"Hell," Devon said, frowning.

That had been his world from the day he'd been born and even he had grown weary of it, had snuck out on New Year's Eve to sample a slice of freedom. How could he expect Maggie to go with it, accept it with no hesitation or qualms, just step into an existence that was like being under a microscope and enjoy every minute of it?

Damn, Devon thought, what a mess. What a complicated, jumbled mess, that was beginning to appear like a huge, dark mountain that would keep him separated from Maggie.

What in the hell was he going to do?

Calm down, Renault, he ordered himself. He wasn't going to solve anything by giving way to his rising panic.

Devon took a deep breath, let it out slowly, then narrowed his eyes in concentration.

He'd kept the promise he'd made to himself that

he would never lie to Maggie. He'd continued to tell her that he was her prince. Granted, she thought it was a fun, rather silly game they were playing, but his real title, who he really was, popped up in conversation from time to time. Good. Yes, that was good.

What he needed to do was to make more references to being a prince, a member of a royal family, supply Maggie with information she'd believe was part of the joke. That data just might settle somewhere in her subconscious, be there when he finally told her that he was actually Prince Devon, who would someday be king of the Island of Wilshire, and that he wanted her to be the queen by his side until death parted them.

Was that a lousy plan?

He didn't have a clue, but at least he'd be doing something instead of brooding.

The other thing he had to do was to figure out exactly how Maggie felt about *him,* determine how deeply she cared for him, discover if she was maybe, just maybe, in love with him just as he was in love with her.

Oh, okay, Devon thought dryly. No problem. Hell. He'd never been in a serious relationship in his life, due to his wariness regarding why a woman wanted to be with him. He'd kept his emotional distance because he could never ascertain whether a woman chose to be in his company because of his title, or because of who he was as a person, a man.

He was, admittedly, one of the most inexperienced thirty-year-old men on earth when it came to women, understanding them, knowing what made them tick. He was a babe in the woods.

So, he, Dud Devon, was going to know how deeply Maggie MacAllister's feelings for him were? In this lifetime? Hey, Maggie, you don't happen to be in love with me, do you? It would sure help the situation if you were, sweetheart, so could you just tell me how you feel and…

Get a grip, Renault, he thought.

Look, watch, listen. That would be his mantra.

And if he didn't quit thinking, his brain was going to blow a circuit.

Devon rolled up onto his side and gazed at Maggie, making no attempt to curb his smile as he looked at her.

He had to leave, he thought, and he was going to be kind to himself. He would push aside the turmoil in his mind and take with him the image of Maggie and the knowledge, the incredible inner warmth, of the fact that he loved her beyond measure. So be it.

Devon kissed Maggie gently on the forehead, lingered another long moment, then left the bed and dressed. A few minutes later he left the apartment, already counting the hours until he could return…to Maggie.

Devon paced back and forth in the living room in the hotel suite, a portable telephone pressed to one ear. He glanced at his watch for the umpteenth time, then rolled his eyes heavenward.

"That brings you completely up to date, Dad," he said. "I've covered the same stuff we discussed the last time we talked and added the progress of today on the final publicity package to be put together...

"Sure, I understand that you're interested in every detail, but you must be tired of hearing the same old news over and over again... You're not? Oh...

"Homer and Henry?" Devon said, glancing at the bodyguards who were sitting on the sofa. "They're fine... Well, sure, they're doing an excellent job of protecting... They're performing in the manner I've requested, which is perfect..." He looked at his watch again. "So! That wraps it up for tonight. I'll speak to you soon and... Goodbye."

Devon pressed the off button on the telephone and cringed.

"I think I just sort of hung up on the king of the Island of Wilshire," he said. "Not cool. Did I sound natural while I was talking to my father? Homer? Henry? Did I?"

Homer shrugged. "As natural as anyone who is giving someone the bum's rush and trying to get off the phone. You'd just better hope that King Chester is so busy he doesn't take the time to dwell on how that crummy conversation went."

"I had to do that," Devon said, throwing out his arms. "I don't want to be late for dinner at Maggie's. She's making me a home-cooked meal."

"Ah, that's nice," Henry said, smiling. "Really romantic, you know what I mean?"

Homer jumped to his feet. "No, it's not. Devon is allowed to eat in restaurants, but there are rules about consuming food in private homes. We're supposed to go in first and check things out, Henry, be assured that everything is on the up-and-up and..."

"She isn't going to poison me," Devon yelled.

"It's our job to determine that," Homer said, matching his volume. "Sorry. You've got me so jangled with this bit about letting you go off on your own that here I am hollering at the prince. Cripe. I'm fired."

"No, you're not," Devon said. "I really appreciate what you're doing for me. If anything you deserve a bonus, a raise."

"I can live with that," Henry said, nodding. "I'm getting a little bored just sitting around here but, hey, let it not be said that I stood in the way of true love."

"Speaking of love," Devon said. "Have…have either of you ever been in a position where you wanted to determine if a woman loved you? I mean, really loved you?"

"Nope," Homer said.

"Yep," Henry said.

Devon crossed the room to stand in front of Henry.

"And?" Devon said. "How did you do it? Find out how she felt?"

"Easy," Henry said. "She gave me half of her peanut butter sandwich. That is love, no doubt about it." He paused. "We were in the third grade."

"Oh, hell," Devon said, striding toward the door. "I'm out of here. I hope I can get a taxi without waiting. By the way, Homer, your lesson in tipping was definitely lacking something. I want to buy Maggie some flowers on the way. Okay, I'll have the driver wait while I go into a florist shop and… Do I tip extra for that? Forget it. But if one more of those guys hugs me I'm going to flatten him. See ya."

Devon left the suite, slamming the door closed behind him.

Maggie peered in the oven, nodded in satisfaction, then closed the door. She crossed the kitchen to the dining alcove at the end of the room and scrutinized the table that was set for two, complete with candles in chunky wooden holders.

At one point during the day at the hospital, she toyed with the idea of dashing to her parents' house after she got off duty and borrowing some of their good china and crystal glasses.

That, she'd decided, would lead to a multitude of questions from her mother and father as to who was coming to dinner and was worthy of such fancy trimmings.

No, Maggie thought, looking at her own stoneware on the table, she had not been prepared to tell her folks about Devon.

Her mother, Maggie knew, would not approve of her daughter's fatalistic attitude that Devon would be leaving and that was that. Jenny MacAllister would say with conviction that people who were soul mates should be together, make whatever sacrifices were necessary to achieve that goal.

If Maggie and Devon actually fell in love with each other, her mother would declare, then so be it. Maggie had career skills that were needed anywhere and everywhere, so off she should go with her Prince Charming to the Island of Wilshire.

''No,'' Maggie whispered.

How could she do that? Where would she find the courage to leave the only life—world—she had ever known? Live on a tiny island halfway around the world, separated from the loving embrace of the multitude of MacAllisters? She wasn't that brave, no matter what her feelings for Devon might become.

"Speaking of feelings," Maggie said with a disgusted click of her tongue.

She was racing ahead in her mind like a silly adolescent who was fantasying about the yummy football player on the high school team falling head over heels for her, the cheerleader. She was making herself miserable over something that wasn't even a reality. She was *not* in love with Devon Renault, and he was *not* in love with her, for mercy's sake.

So, there she stood like an idiot, reaching the conclusion that she lacked the fortitude to leave Ventura and live on Devon's island, when that thought had never even crossed the man's mind.

"Get it together," she said. "You're really getting cuckoo here, Margaret Jennifer MacAllister, so just cut it out this very second."

A knock sounded at the door and Maggie felt a rush of relief that she had a means by which to escape from her ridiculous thoughts. She was going to cross the room, open the door and smile at a special man whom she cared for very much, but whom she was not—absolutely not—falling in love with.

Fine. That settled that.

Maggie lifted her chin, marched to the door and flung it open.

"Hello, Devon," she said, producing a bright smile. "I..."

Maggie's voice trailed off as she stared at Devon, her heart racing.

Hello, my Devon, she thought hazily. Oh, there he was. He was wearing dark slacks with a blue sweater, which was bizarre, really, because the outfit *she'd* selected for this evening was dark slacks with a blue sweater and they looked like the Bobbsey twins.

And in one of his hands was a bouquet of flowers wrapped in green florist paper. Oh, how romantic. Devon had brought her flowers.

And now he was smiling at her. And his eyes were radiating such warmth, such a clear message of how very glad he was to see her.

And she was a breath away from bursting into tears because...because...

Oh, God, no.

Because...she was in love with Devon Renault.

Chapter 6

"Hello?" Devon said, frowning slightly. "Maggie? May I come in?"

"What?" Maggie said, staring at him with wide eyes. "Oh. Oh, yes, of course, I'm sorry." She stepped back and swept one arm through the air. "So sorry. Yes. Please come in."

When Maggie closed the door behind him, Devon turned to face her, his frown still firmly in place.

"Are you all right?" he said. "You're very pale all of a sudden."

"I am?" she said. "That's because... Yes, that's because I'm hungry. We were so busy in the ER today that I didn't have time to stop for lunch and... Yes, indeedy, I'm a starving person, but dinner is ready to be put on the table so I'll be dandy fine just as soon as I get something to eat and... Are those flowers for me?"

Devon smiled as he extended the bouquet toward

her. Maggie took it and buried her face in the lovely, fragrant blossoms, telling herself she had just bought about three seconds to get her act together.

She was, for the first time in her life, in love and it was a terrible state to be in. Just awful. It was heartbreak guaranteed and she wanted to flop herself on her bed and cry for a week.

Maggie raised her head slowly and produced a small smile.

"Thank you, Devon," she said. *I love you, Devon, and falling love with you is the dumbest thing I've ever done.* "The flowers are beautiful and romantic and... Thank you very much."

"You're welcome." Devon tilted his head back. "Something smells fantastic."

"Our dinner," Maggie said. "You sit down at the table and I'll serve it up."

"I'd be happy to help you."

"No, no," she said, rushing past him toward the kitchen. "You'd just be in my way. I'll have everything on the table in a jiffy. Did you notice that we're dressed the same? Isn't that funny?"

Devon followed Maggie and sat down at the table.

"Our choice of clothes for the evening says that we're on the same wavelength," he said, watching Maggie take a baking pan from the oven. "What else do you think we match up so perfectly about?"

"Well, let's see," Maggie said, as she continued her chores. She put the flowers in a vase and set it on the table. "We've talked about books and found we've read many of the same titles. The leisure time activities we discussed that we enjoy were very similar. We both like babies and puppies and furry kittens. We also place great emphasis on family love and loyalty. How's that?''

"It's a very lengthy and admirable list," Devon said, nodding.

Maggie lit the candles in the holders, snapped off the kitchen and dining alcove lights, then sat down across from Devon.

"Well, here we are," she said, her heart racing as she drank in the sight of Devon in the candlelight. "I...I hope you like pork chops and...and stuff." She paused. "Maybe I should turn on a light. Can you see clearly enough to know what you're eating?"

"No, don't turn on a light," Devon said, looking directly at her. "You're even more lovely than usual in the glow of the candles." He paused. "I hope that didn't sound corny because I sincerely mean it."

"You're a very romantic man," Maggie said softly. "I think that's...well, nice, very nice." She laughed. "But what would one expect but romance to the max from a charming prince?"

"You've got a point there," Devon said, beginning to fill his plate. "And I *am* a prince. My father, King Chester, used to pick a rose from the royal gardens...or the green house in chillier weather...every morning and put it on my mother's breakfast tray when she was still living. He never missed...not one day while they were married. Now *that* is romantic, don't you think?"

"King Chester?" Maggie said, as she put a pork chop on her plate. "Oh, okay. King Chester. Do you and King Chester live in a castle on the Island of Wilshire? I can't remember if you mentioned a castle."

"My father lives in the castle. I could have a wing

to myself because it's enormous, but I choose to live in one of the houses on the grounds. My cousin, Brent, lives in another one. When I become king I'll take up residency in the castle.''

"Does the castle have a dungeon?" Maggie said, then took a bite of potato.

Devon chuckled. "No. The castle is big, but it's decorated...thanks to my mother...in such a way that it's homey, isn't a gloomy, drafty thing that some people imagine castles must be.

"I was allowed to mess up the place with my toys when I was a boy, behave like any kid would. Of course, there are formal rooms that were off limits to me because they're for official functions and what have you, but for the most part it was like anyone else's house, just on a rather larger scale. I...I think you'd like it, Maggie."

"You're making it sound so real, Devon," she said, spooning applesauce onto her plate. "I can picture the castle so clearly. The vineyards, too, are very vivid in my mind. Of course, there really are vineyards, or you wouldn't be here promoting the Renault-Bardow wine.''

"There's really a castle, too, Maggie."

"Oh, yes, well, I suppose that could be true. But your father isn't the King Chester you spoke of."

"Yes," Devon said quietly, "he is. And I'm Prince Devon Renault, heir to the throne."

"Ah," Maggie said, raising one finger. "Gotcha. Where are your bodyguards tonight? Still lurking?"

"I convinced Homer and Henry to allow me one week of freedom so I could be with you. They're twiddling their thumbs back at the hotel, hoping my father doesn't discover what we're doing."

"Homer and Henry?" Maggie said, with a burst of laughter. "Is that the best you can do? Bodyguards should have names like Thug and Lug, or something."

Devon shrugged. "Their father, Harry, is the head of security at the palace. Homer and Henry are twins and I guess Harry thought they made a dynamic trio...you know, Harry, Homer and Henry. I don't know. I never thought about it, I guess. Harry's wife's name is Frank, but is known as Fran."

"What?" Maggie said, nearly choking on a piece of broccoli. "She was legally named Frank?"

"She said her father wanted a boy so... This is a delicious dinner, Maggie. I'm enjoying every bite and I really appreciate the effort you went to cook it at the end of a hard day at work. As a princess you wouldn't have to do that if you didn't feel like having kitchen duty. I share all my meals in the castle with my father because I can't boil water without messing it up."

"That has possibilities," Maggie said. "I wouldn't mind having my plate set in front of me. My mother taught me and my brother how to cook, but it's not my favorite thing to do, by any means."

"Then you won't cook on the Island of Wilshire," Devon said. "There...that's settled."

"I think we should change the subject," Maggie said. "This topic has gone on for so long that it's beginning to feel like reality...which is nuts."

"Pretend for a minute that it's not nuts," Devon said, then took a bite of the tender meat, chewed and swallowed. "Can you see yourself living on Wilshire?"

"How realistic do you want me to get here while I'm pretending?"

"Very realistic," Devon said.

"Oh, dear," Maggie said, shaking her head, "that means I have to confess that I have no sense of adventure. The thought of leaving the only life I've ever known, of being so far away from my family, is overwhelming.

"I realize that's a very immature attitude for a woman my age, but I guess I've always envisioned myself being married and raising my children here in Ventura surrounded by MacAllisters." She frowned. "Definitely immature, but that's the way it is."

"People can change, Maggie," Devon said, then continued to eat.

That was for sure, Maggie thought. She was presently experiencing the biggest *change* imaginable. She was now a woman in love. A woman in love with Devon Renault.

The Island of Wilshire, she mused. It sounded so lovely, so peaceful and inviting. MacAllisters in general loved to travel. They could hop a plane and come visit her on that island, soak up the sunshine and beauty, eat a grape right off the vines and...

Maggie, for heaven's sake, she thought. She was off on another ridiculous mental tangent. Devon was playing "let's pretend," and she was figuring out how to be brave enough to pull up roots and go with him to his paradise and...Enough of this.

"Save some room for dessert," Maggie said. "Well, you don't have to. It's nothing sensational. I just bought some frosted chocolate brownies from the bakery."

"I always have room for chocolate, no matter how much of a meal I've consumed," Devon said, smiling.

"Me, too."

"See?" he said, leaning slightly toward her. "We keep finding more and more things where we are perfectly matched. It's really something."

Except for one very important item, Maggie thought. She was in love with Devon, but he wasn't in love with her. But...but what if he *did* come to love her as she did him? Could she reach deep within herself for the fortitude to leave her family, her life as she knew it, and go with him to the Island of Wilshire?

What was the alternative? Watch the only man she had ever loved, and who loved her in kind, board a plane and disappear into the heavens, leaving her behind to cry in the night because she'd been such an emotional child? *That* was not acceptable.

And this mental journey she was presently on was not acceptable, either, because she was getting completely carried away with this "let's pretend" business.

"Ready for those brownies?" she said.

Devon leaned back in his chair and patted his flat stomach.

"I think I can manage one...or two," he said, smiling. "I hope you weren't planning on having leftovers from this meal, because I polished off everything in sight."

"I'm glad you enjoyed it," Maggie said, getting to her feet. "I guess the old saying about the way to a man's heart is through his stomach is true."

As Maggie moved to the other side of the table to remove Devon's plate, he caught her around the waist, scooted back his chair and plunked her on his lap.

Maggie laughed in delight and encircled his neck with her arms.

"Sir," she said, "we don't allow our diners to fiddle with the waitresses in this establishment."

"I don't plan to fiddle," he said, then gave her a quick kiss. "I have very serious intentions here, ma'am." He outlined Maggie's lips with the tip of his tongue and she shivered from the sensuous foray. "Very serious, very private intentions. Right now, if that meets with your approval."

"But..." Maggie started, then drew a shuddering breath as the heat of desire rushed throughout her. "...what about the chocolate brownies with chocolate frosting?"

"Which do you want more, my Maggie?" he said, looking directly into her eyes.

"You," she whispered. "Oh, yes, Devon, I most definitely want you." *Oh, Devon, I love you so much, so very, very much.*

Forever, Maggie? Devon thought. God, how he loved this woman.

Devon slid one arm beneath Maggie's knees, the other beneath her breasts and got to his feet with her held close to this chest.

"This is so-o-o romantic," Maggie said, with a dreamy sigh. "I'm so glad you inherited romantic tendencies from your...from King Chester, Prince Devon."

Much, much later Maggie and Devon were once again sitting at the kitchen table, consuming the brownies with tall glasses of cold milk. They'd cleaned up from the meal, then settled in to enjoy the postponed dessert.

Maggie took a bite of the rich chocolate brownie, then stared into space with a rather dreamy expression on her face.

The lovemaking she had just shared with Devon had been so beautiful, so perfect. She had savored every ecstasy-filled moment of it, realizing she was, for the first time in her life, making love with the man who had stolen her heart. The depths of the emotions during their joining had reached into infinity.

After lying close to each other and talking lazily about various unimportant topics, they'd showered together, which had resulted in making love once more with warm water cascading over them.

Devon had dressed again in his clothes, while Maggie had pulled on a terry-cloth robe and ran a comb through her wet hair.

Devon reached for his second brownie, then set it on his plate and looked directly at Maggie, who was still gazing into space.

"Maggie?"

"Hmm?" she said, turning her head to meet his gaze. "Do you like the brownies?"

"Sure, they're great, very tasty. Maggie..."

"Well, fill up on them because my cupboards are bare. I need to go grocery shopping and only bought what I needed for our dinner tonight when I stopped at the store after work. Tomorrow evening I'll have to hit the market with a long list in tow."

"Really?" Devon said. "You're going grocery shopping? I've never done that. Could I go with you?"

Maggie's eyes widened. "You've never shopped

for food? What about when you were going to college in London?''

Devon shrugged. "I ate out, and Homer and Henry brought in whatever snacks we might want in the apartment. I couldn't talk my father out of having them actually live with me while I was going to school. Hey, they're very nice guys, but... Anyway, I'd really like to go with you to grocery shop.''

"Well, sure, why not?" Maggie said. "We could stop for a pizza for dinner first, then go for it. Can you be here about six o'clock?''

"Sold. It'll be fun.''

"I think you're going to be a tad disappointed, Devon. Grocery shopping isn't fun, it's a pain in the katush. I'd be more than happy to have your imaginary Homer and Henry do it for me.''

"They will on Wilshire.''

Maggie laughed. "I'm not cooking on the island, remember?''

"Ah, yes," Devon said. "Well, they'll shop for snacks like chocolate brownies with chocolate frosting.''

"Now you're talking," Maggie said, nodding decisively. "They can also buy chips and dip, popcorn, candy bars, the whole nine yards. Then when I'm fat as a piggy, it will be their fault, not mine, because they brought in the goodies, not me. How's that?''

"Works for me," Devon said. "Except I want to be the one to go to the store for you if you crave something weird when you're pregnant with our child. That would be part of my job description as the father-to-be and I intend to do the very best I can as a daddy, starting even before the baby is born.''

"Oh," Maggie said softly. "That's...that's very

sweet and..." She couldn't handle this. Devon was off and running on one of his "let's pretend" scenarios again, and it was cutting her to the quick because she wanted, truly wanted, to have Devon's baby, be his wife, his partner, his soul mate forever. She had to change the subject before she burst into tears. "Want some more milk? Forget it. There isn't any more."

"I have plenty," Devon said. "Maggie...I..."

I love you. With all that I am, with all that I'll ever be, I love you, Devon thought. Should he tell her that? Now?

He'd heard Maggie state loud and clear that she couldn't imagine leaving Ventura, her family, her life as she knew it. Should he declare his love for her now so she had a chance to start getting comfortable with the idea of his loving her, wishing to marry her and take her home to the Island of Wilshire with him?

No, maybe he'd better wait.

He was doing well with the first part of his plan, was dropping references left and right to his being a prince, had even managed to make reference to *King* Chester.

But the other part of the plan wasn't going so hot. He was supposed to be watching, listening, attempting to determine the depth of Maggie's feelings for him, and he hadn't made any progress beyond his already knowing that she cared deeply for him.

Did she love him? Was she in love with him, as he was with her? He didn't have a clue. Should he just open his mouth and ask her? No, first he'd tell her that *he* loved her, then wait to see if she responded with "And I love you, too, Devon."

But, oh, cripe, he thought, as a chill swept through

him, what if she just stared at him like he was out of his mind and didn't say a word after he announced that he was head over heels in love with her. What a totally, jump-off-a-bridge depressing thought.

No, he wasn't going to tell Maggie he loved her. Not tonight. Not on this perfect night. He'd keep watching, listening, hoping for a hint of what she was feeling. But, ah, damn, there was so little time left to accomplish so very, very much.

"Devon?" Maggie said. "You keep saying my name in such a serious voice, but then you…I don't know… Is there something of importance you wanted to tell me?"

"I…I think," Devon said, then cleared his throat, "you have a special knack for selecting the most delicious brownies in the bakery."

"Hear, hear," Maggie said, raising her glass of milk high in the air.

Devon clinked his glass against Maggie's and their mingled laughter danced through the air.

Chapter 7

From the moment that Maggie and Devon entered the enormous, brightly lit grocery store the next evening, Maggie smiled and continued to do so as Devon's eyes widened and he talked nonstop about the wonders spread out before him.

"Incredible," Devon said for the umpteenth time as he scrutinized the bounty on the shelves. "Look at this. Artichoke hearts in a can. I want to try these." He set the can in the rapidly filling cart. "Don't worry, Maggie. I'm paying for all this great stuff. Whoa. Mandarin oranges in a cute little can. Gotta have 'em."

"Devon," Maggie said, laughing, "you're not paying for the groceries that are going into my cupboards and refrigerator."

"Sure I am," he said, leaning over and peering closer at the shelf. "It will be my way of thanking

you for letting me come along tonight. This…
is…incredible.''

"It's hard to believe you've never been in a big
grocery store before,'' Maggie said, pushing the cart
along.

"Nope, never have. I was really missing out on
something very…''

"Incredible,'' Maggie said, her smile firmly in
place. "I must say, Devon, that this is the first time
I've ever had such fun shopping for food. I've been
doing it for so many years that I dread the chore. So
I thank *you* for this evening, too.''

"Well, isn't that perfect?'' he said.

They exchanged warm, matching smiles until Maggie turned into the next aisle and Devon's attention
was caught by the new treasures displayed.

"There must a hundred different kinds of chips and
things in this row, Maggie,'' he said. "Pretzels.
Here's pretzel sticks.'' A bag went into the cart. "Little pretzels.'' Another bag was deposited next to the
first. "Hey, here's pretzels bigger than my hand. Can
you believe that?'' He balanced that bag on top of
the others. "Incredible.''

"Devon,'' Maggie said, bursting into laughter
again. "How many pretzels can one person eat?''

"There are two of us, Maggie,'' he said. "We'll
make short order of these snacks and…'' Devon
stopped talking and frowned. "Listen.''

"To what?''

"They're playing music,'' he said. "I was so busy
collecting goodies I didn't realize that until now.''

"Oh. Well, I suppose they always do,'' Maggie

said, shrugging. "I don't even hear it anymore, I guess. That's an old Elvis Presley song just ending."

"Let's see what they play next," Devon said. "Here it comes. Oh, man, I love this song. 'Could I Have This Dance' then the line ends with for the rest of my life? It's beautiful." He extended his arms to Maggie. "Dance with me, Maggie."

"Here?" she said, looking quickly around. "People don't dance in the middle of the aisle of pretzels and chips, Devon."

"Why not?" he said, smiling at her. "Come on. This is one of my favorite songs."

"Yes," Maggie said, "why not?"

And there, surrounded by pretzels of every shape and size, potato chips, popcorn in various flavors, tortilla chips and a display of dips, Maggie and Devon danced.

He held her close, inhaling the flowery scent of her hair as they waltzed down the aisle, never missing a step, as though they'd been dancing together for many years.

It was magic.

People stopped their shopping and watched them, smiles forming on faces that had been etched with fatigue after a long day of work.

"May I have this dance," Devon whispered to Maggie, "for the rest of my life?"

"All my dances belong to you, Devon," Maggie said softly. "Oh, my, this is the most romantic… I'll never forget this moment, this waltz. Never."

The song ended and the shoppers who had watched the lovely couple dance applauded and cheered. A flush of embarrassment crept up Maggie's cheeks as she glanced around and saw the beaming audience. She buried her face in Devon's shirt for a moment, then stepped out of his arms and smiled up at him.

"Thank you, Prince Devon," she said, dipping her head. "That was wonderful."

Devon bowed deeply. "You're most welcome, Princess Maggie." He glanced to the side. "We landed back to earth next to the meat counter, it would seem. There's a fish staring at me with a weird eyeball." He encircled Maggie's shoulders with one arm. "We'd better go retrieve our cart before someone rips off my pretzels."

As they walked back down the aisle, Devon dropped a quick kiss on the top of Maggie's head.

For the rest of his life, Devon thought, he wanted to dance with his Maggie, make love with his Maggie, wake up each morning next to his Maggie. Oh, how he loved his wondrous Maggie.

She had said that all her dances were his to have. Could that possibly really be true? All of her dances, her smiles, all the years she had left in this world? Did she—please, God—love him as he loved her?

The sense of magic that had surrounded them as they danced did not completely disappear as Maggie and Devon continued their grocery shopping.

It was there, hovering around them, later that night when they made sweet, slow love for hours. It was there as a majestic sunrise streaked across the sky at dawn and they reached eagerly for each other once more.

The magic was there the next evening as they cooked dinner together at Maggie's, watched an old movie on television and munched on various size pretzels.

The next day, which Maggie had off, the magic went with them to the zoo, on a picnic and a canoe ride in the park, then followed them home to swirl around them as they tumbled onto the bed to journey to their private place of ecstasy together.

The magic did not allow them to talk of how quickly the time was passing, of how many, many hours were ticking away toward the moment when Devon would leave Ventura to return to the Island of Wilshire.

In the late afternoon of the sixth day of Devon's stolen week, Homer entered the hotel suite.

"I've got our airplane tickets for tomorrow night, because the day flights had long layovers," he said to Devon, then handed him a newspaper. "The ads you put together with the restaurant owners here in Ventura are in tonight's paper for Renault-Bardow wine. King Chester and Mr. Bardow should be pleased. The advertisements are very classy. I assume the first shipments of wine arrived."

"Yes," Devon said, frowning as he accepted the newspaper from Homer. "I didn't realize you were going to get the plane tickets today."

"We're right on schedule," Homer said. "And if King Chester doesn't find out about this terrible series of days that my brother and I have been a party to, we'll still have our jobs."

"It has *not* been a *terrible* week, Homer," Devon said, flipping through the newspaper. "It's been very... Never mind."

Devon folded back the paper sheets and studied a half-page ad. ''There we are in all our glory. A full-color picture of my father, me, Brent, in our finery, complete with our royal titles in the caption beneath. There's the family crest on the label on the wine and blah, blah, blah.'' He dropped the newspaper onto the floor.

In the next instant Devon lunged to his feet, every muscle in his body tensing.

''What's wrong?'' Homer said.

''Where has my brain been?'' Devon said, flinging out his arms. ''Oh, man, I've been so focused on Maggie, on what we've been sharing and...I can't believe I could be this stupid. I *knew* the ads were coming out in the newspaper today. I knew that, and just went blissfully on my way, enjoying... Hell.''

''You've totally lost me,'' Homer said.

''Homer, I've never lied to Maggie. I've told her right from the beginning that I was a prince, was Prince Devon of the Island of Wilshire. But it was a...a game to her, a fun thing we did...my referring to myself as a prince, calling her my princess. I've been telling her about Wilshire, how beautiful it is there, how friendly, open and real the people are.''

Homer nodded.

''I've been trying,'' Devon rushed on, ''to determine how Maggie really feels about me, but women are so complicated and mysterious that I have no idea if she— I should have sat her down last night, told her I love her, convinced her that I really was the heir to the throne of Wilshire.''

''So, tell her tonight?'' Homer said, raising his eyebrows.

"Yeah, yeah," Devon said, dragging one hand through his hair. "But I have a cold knot in my gut that says things are not going to go well if Maggie sees these ads before I can do that."

Maggie stared at the advertisement in the newspaper with wide eyes, then sank onto the sofa as her trembling legs refused to hold her.

She had just arrived home, was still in her uniform, but had decided to see what movies were playing in town that night. As she turned the pages of the newspaper, her attention had been caught by a full-color advertisement and at that moment the bottom seemed to fall out of her magical world.

A brisk knock sounded at the door, then was repeated a second later. Holding the paper in one hand, Maggie got to her feet, crossed the room and opened the door.

"Oh, no," Devon said, seeing the pages dangling from Maggie's hand. "You've seen the newspaper." He entered the apartment, closed the door, and reached out his hands toward Maggie. "Maggie..."

She took a step backward, her eyes as wide as saucers, the color draining from her face.

"You...you lied to me," Maggie said, her voice shaking. "No, no, wait. Maybe you didn't. But it was just Let's Pretend, a fantasy scenario we played sometimes. But you actually are a prince.... Oh, dear heaven."

"Maggie, please, let's sit down," Devon said. "You've got to give me a chance to explain. Please, my Maggie. There's so much at stake here. Will you listen to me? Please?"

Maggie dropped the newspaper, and it fluttered into a heap on the floor. She sat on the sofa and wrapped her hands around her elbows.

Devon settled next to her, shifting so he could look directly at her. Maggie turned her head slowly to meet his gaze and he nearly groaned aloud when he saw the pallor of her cheeks, the stricken expression on her face.

"I thought…I thought," Maggie said, tears filling her eyes, "that you were a very special man, who had princely charms. A man who was so very romantic."

"I *am* that man, Maggie," Devon said, forcing himself not to touch her. "Nothing has changed."

"Nothing has changed?" she said as two tears slid unnoticed down her cheeks. "How can you say that? You're not a man with princely charms, you're an honest-to-goodness prince, who happens to be charming. Why didn't you tell me the truth?"

"I did!" Devon said. "I've never lied to you, Maggie. But from the very second I saw you, I knew, just somehow knew, that something very important was happening. And it was, Maggie. It was."

Devon took a shuddering breath.

"Never in my entire life have I been viewed, judged, seen, as anything other than a prince. The title was always there, standing in the way, creating a wall between me and someone I might want to get to know. I never knew if a…a…okay, if a woman wanted to be with me because I was a prince or because of who I was as a man. I could never trust the situation I was in, built a protective barrier around myself.

"But then, Maggie? Then there was you. And the

very special and important…something…there was
between us from the very beginning. I made up my
mind that I would not tarnish whatever it was that
was happening by lying to you, and I didn't, not
once.''

''But you knew that I didn't really believe that you
were a prince, Devon,'' Maggie said, a sob catching
in her throat. ''You knew that. So, you *did* lie. I
guess. Sort of. Oh, I can't think straight.''

''Don't think, just listen,'' Devon said. ''Maggie,
ah, my Maggie, you gave me the greatest gift I've
ever had. You accepted me, came to care for me, not
as a prince, but as an ordinary man. Just a man, who
eats pretzels by the dozen and…

''We made love that was so incredibly beautiful it
defies description. We made love as a man and a
woman, two people who desired each other beyond
measure, not as a woman and a prince. Oh, Maggie,
don't you see? What we have together is real. Honest.
True.''

''I…'' Maggie started, then stopped speaking as
fresh tears choked off her words.

This was it, Devon thought frantically. The time
had come. The rest of his life, his entire future happiness, was about to hang in the balance because he
was going to tell Maggie…

''I love you,'' Devon said, his voice husky with
emotion. ''I love you, Maggie MacAllister, with
every breath in my body, every beat of my heart. You
are my soul mate. You are my princess.

''I'm hoping, praying, that you love me, too, because I want to marry you, take you home to Wilshire
with me, spend the rest of my life with you, have you

by my side as my queen when I inherit the throne, and create the miracles that will be our babies with you.''

''You...you love me?'' Maggie whispered. ''You're in love with me, Margaret Jennifer Mac-Allister? Maggie? Me?''

''You,'' Devon said, nodding. ''I know you have qualms about living so far away from your family, from the only life you've ever known, but you could fly back here and visit just as often as you wanted to, and your family could come to the island and...

''Everything I've told you about Wilshire is true. It's so beautiful and peaceful there, the people are fantastic, you'd never have to cook or... There's a hospital on the island if you wanted to work there, but you could just do volunteer hours if you wished or... The bodyguards are a real pain in the tush and I can't do anything about that, but you'd hopefully get used to them in time and...''

''You love me?'' Maggie repeated.

''With all that I am as a man, who just happens to be a prince.''

Maggie pressed her fingertips to her lips and closed her eyes for a long moment, striving for control. She opened her eyes again and more tears filled them as she looked directly into the gray depths of Devon's eyes.

''And I—I love you, Devon,'' she said, sobbing openly. ''You're really my prince that I wished for when I was hardly big enough to blow out the candles on my birthday cake, and we're soul mates, and we'll create such beautiful, chubby and happy babies, and we'll eat pretzels together for the rest of our lives and— Oh!''

Maggie's emotional blither was halted by Devon reaching over, gripping her shoulders, turning her toward him and capturing her mouth in a searing kiss.

A moment later Devon broke the kiss, then slid from the sofa to one knee in front of Maggie. He cradled her hands in both of his and looked directly into the shimmering depths of her brown eyes.

"Will you, Maggie MacAllister," he said, making no attempt to hide the tears in his own eyes, "do me the honor of becoming my wife? I, Prince Devon of the Island of Wilshire, am asking you to marry me, stay by my side, be my partner in life, my princess, then my queen, until death parts us. Will you marry me, Maggie? Please?"

"Only if you agree to negotiate on one very important issue," Maggie said.

"What is it?" Devon said, hardly breathing.

"The business about us having *six* babies," she said. "Oh, yes, Devon, I'll marry you. I love you so much, so very much, my prince."

"Oh, thank God," Devon whispered.

He got to his feet and pulled Maggie up into his embrace. She wrapped her arms tightly around his chest as he encircled her with his arms, holding her close.

They stood there, simply stood there, clinging to each other, allowing the warmth of loving and being loved in kind fill them with the greatest peace and the greatest joy they had ever known.

"Devon," Maggie finally said, tilting her head back to look up at him, "there's one thing I have to confess, something I feel you have the right to know.''

''Yes?''

Maggie smiled, her eyes radiating the message of love and receiving the same message from Devon's eyes.

''Devon,'' she said, ''I really don't like the taste of pretzels.''

Their mingled laughter floated through the air, gathering the magic that was theirs and had been temporarily scattered, bringing it back to them to have and to hold from that day forward.

Epilogue

The announcement in the newspaper of the engagement of Maggie MacAllister to Prince Devon Renault of the Island of Wilshire caused Ventura to buzz with excitement.

Maggie and Devon explained to the MacAllisters that no date had been set for their wedding that would take place on the island as it would take weeks of planning to follow proper royal protocol.

Reporters from newspapers and television networks across the country went to the powers that be, begging to be selected to cover the royal wedding.

Maggie's parents made no effort to hide their tears of joy as they gave her and Devon their heartfelt blessings. Bobby hugged his sister and told her he'd been wrong years and years ago when he'd said she'd never find her prince because she'd spoken her wish aloud.

Once over the startling news that Maggie was to

marry into royalty, every member of the huge MacAllister clan was thrilled that sweet Maggie had found true love and happiness.

King Chester was delighted with his son's announcement. He sat by the fire in the castle and smiled as he envisioned the face of his beloved wife, then told her the glorious news.

The king then informed Devon that he and the Bardows, would travel to America to meet and get to know the bride-to-be and her family before the gala event of the wedding took place on the island.

The MacAllisters began to make plans to welcome the royal family to their city...and into their hearts.

And through it all, Maggie and Devon savored the magic of their love.

* * * * *

ROYALLY PREGNANT
Linda Turner

Dear Reader,

When I was invited to write "Royally Pregnant" for the *Crowned Hearts* anthology, I was thrilled...and hesitant. I'd never written a story about royalty before and wasn't sure how I wanted to go about it. But once I started working on the manuscript, I realized the story line was a modern version of a classic fairy tale and very much like the old romance movies of the 40s. Once I thought of the story that way, it unfolded right before my eyes.

In "Royally Pregnant," Rafe, the hero, is a duke who feels the weight of family responsibility and the need to do the right thing. I could just see William Holden or a young Clark Gable playing the role of Rafe in the movie version, and that made the actual writing of the story fun and easy.

As for the heroine, Serena, I can hear you asking now if I pictured Audrey Hepburn or Claudette Colbert playing her part. Not on your life. If anyone gets to fall in love with a Hollywood leading man, it's not Audrey Hepburn. It's me!

Enjoy!

Linda Turner

Chapter 1

Arranging a last bouquet of roses and baby's breath for that evening's party, Serena Winters smiled, pleased. As the daughter of the gardener, she'd grown up at the royal palace of Montebello, and over the years she'd helped her father decorate the palace ball-room many times. They'd always done an excellent job. Today, however, they'd outdone themselves.

At Queen Gwendolyn's request, they'd filled the ballroom with white roses and poinsettias for the royal family's annual New Year's Eve party, then strung thousands of tiny white twinkle lights from the ceiling. Elegant white-and-gold linen tablecloths covered the tables, and hundreds of candles were just waiting to be lit. Later that evening, when the royal guests swirled around the dance floor in their beautiful designer gowns and tuxedos, the scene would look like something out of a fairy tale.

Just as it had the previous summer when Princess Julia had married Sheik Rashid Kamal.

Her smile fading, Serena immediately tried to push the memory away, but it was too late. Images came rushing back and there was nothing she could do to stop them. Then, as now, she'd helped her father decorate the ballroom, and her involvement should have ended there. But Princess Anna, Julia's younger sister, had encouraged her to attend the reception and even offered to lend her one of her own gowns to wear. Serena hadn't been able to resist. Wearing a dress that cost more than she earned in six months as her father's assistant, she'd gone to the wedding gala and felt like Cinderella at the ball.

And just like Cinderella, she'd lost her heart to Prince Charming.

Rafe.

Just thinking about him brought the sting of tears to her eyes. English cousin to Princesses Julia and Anna and nephew to Queen Gwendolyn, Duke Raphael Harrington had a well-deserved reputation as a heartthrob throughout Europe, and she'd been a pushover where he was concerned. He'd only had to flash that engaging grin of his and smile down at her with his twinkling green eyes, and all her defenses had crumbled. After he took her in his arms for a dance, she hadn't been able to see anyone but him for the rest of the evening.

She'd known who he was, of course. He visited the Montebello side of his mother's family often, and for years, Serena had silently watched him...and dreamed. She shouldn't have. Not only was he royalty, he was far more experienced than she and out of her league. A man like that would never look twice at the gardener's daughter. She knew that, accepted it. Still, she'd found his dark blond good looks, broad shoulders, and tall, athletic build impossible to resist. Against all reason, she'd had a crush on him for as long as she could remember.

Then that one magical summer night when he'd asked her to dance, all her dreams had come true. They'd talked and laughed and danced every dance. And before the night was through, they'd made love. Just that easily, he'd changed her life forever.

"Serena? I thought I'd find you here. We need to talk."

Mentally jerking back from her musings, Serena looked up to see Princess Anna bearing down on her, her usually sparkling brown eyes dark with a look of determination that Serena recognized all too easily. Ever since they'd learned Rafe would be attending the ball that evening, Anna had been pressuring her to go, too.

Lifting her chin stubbornly, Serena said firmly, "There's nothing to talk about, Your Highness. I'm *not* going to the ball."

The princess's eyes flashed at the use of her title—she'd never liked the use of titles between friends—but she was on a mission and she refused to be distracted. "C'mon, Serena, be reasonable. You know Rafe would want to know about the baby."

In a move as old as time, Serena instinctively placed a protective hand over her rounded belly. "No, I don't know that. We had one night together, Anna. One. I sincerely doubt that he even remembers me."

"Don't be ridiculous. Of course he remembers you! He didn't take his eyes off you all evening. Let me talk to him, Serena. He needs to know."

"No!" Panic gripped her at just the thought of Anna discussing her or the baby with him. He would think that she had sent the princess to play on his sympathy, that she wanted something from him, and nothing could have been further from the truth. She might only be the gardener's daughter and the keeper of the royal greenhouse, but she was a proud woman who was used to taking care of herself and her elderly father without anyone's help. She would do the same for her baby.

"You promised me you wouldn't tell him." Her blue-gray eyes, full of entreaty, pleaded with her. "Please, Anna," she said huskily, appealing to her friend Anna, rather than Her Royal Highness Princess Anna, "you're the only one who knows he's the baby's father. You can't tell him. Think of the scandal it would cause. Your parents wouldn't be happy about their nephew having a baby with a commoner, let alone their gardener's daughter. And Rafe wouldn't be pleased, either. It was just a one-night stand to him."

And then there was her father. Tears filled her eyes just at the thought of how disappointed he would be in her. "My father's an old man, Anna. Right now he thinks I lost my heart to an American tourist who was here on summer holiday. If he finds out differently, it'll only hurt him."

And it wouldn't change anything. They both knew that. Even if Rafe pressed her to marry him, it would only be out of a sense of duty. He was a duke, the son of a long line of dukes, and he'd been raised to do the right thing...which was why she was determined that he never find out about the baby. She would only marry for love. Her mother died when she was six, but Serena remembered the incredible love she and her father had shared, and she would settle for nothing less for herself. Rafe didn't love her. So she'd raise her baby alone.

Over the course of the past six months, she and Anna had had this same discussion many times, and the princess understood her decision. She had, however, never pretended to like it. "I just think you're making a mistake," she mumbled. "You and Rafe were so perfect together. I've never seen him so taken with anyone. And you're crazy about him. You know you are. If you'd just talk to him…"

"Anna!"

"All right," she sighed, giving in at Serena's alarmed tone. "I won't say anything. But I still think you're making a mistake."

Anna liked to think she was a woman of her word, but later that evening as she dressed for the ball, she was far from comfortable with the secret she'd promised to keep. Rafe was one of her favorite cousins, and in spite of the difference in her and Serena's circumstances, she loved her like a sister. They'd been friends forever, and she only wanted the best for her. And Rafe was the best. He would make Serena happy—if she'd just let Anna tell him about the baby.

That, however, was out of the question. She didn't break promises, she reminded herself as she stepped into the slinky red dress she'd bought in Paris for the ball. That didn't, however, mean she couldn't do a little meddling behind the scenes. Her dark brown eyes twinkling at the thought, she surveyed herself one last time in the ornate pier mirror that had been in her family longer than anyone could remember, and grinned saucily. She didn't have to tell Rafe about the baby—she just had to give him a nudge in the right direction and he would discover the truth for himself. Then he would realize that he really did love Serena and wanted nothing more than to spend the rest of his life with her.

Humming the opening bars of the old classic, "Young at Heart," she assured herself that fairy tales really could come true—especially when you lived in a palace! Grinning at the thought, she hurried toward the ballroom like a woman on a mission. Now all she had to do was find Rafe.

He wasn't hard to spot, not even in a ballroom full of people. Tall and handsome, with a smile that could melt a female heart at sixty paces, he was, as usual, surrounded by a dozen or more women who were practically standing on their heads to get his attention. If Rafe noticed, he gave no sign of it. Looking past his wannabe lovers, he scanned the guests who crowded the dance floor, and apparently didn't find the person he was looking for. A scowl wrinkling his brow, he appeared to be anything but pleased.

Delighted, Anna couldn't help but hope he was looking for Serena. Smiling, she headed straight for him.

She wasn't there.

Ignoring the short, buxom redhead who took advantage of the surrounding crowd of women to press in close against his side, Rafe searched in vain for the wavy, shoulder-length curls of the slender blonde who had haunted his dreams for the past six months. He thought he saw her once, but then her partner turned her in his arms and he saw that the woman was much older than Serena and not nearly as pretty.

Dammit, where was she? he fumed. He hadn't been able to get her out of his head since his cousin Julia's wedding, and that irritated him no end. The last woman who'd captivated his thoughts so completely turned out to be a money-grubbing little witch who broke his heart, and he'd sworn then that he'd never fall in love again. And he hadn't.

But, damn, Serena had tempted him. She hadn't been anything like the debutantes who hounded him wherever he went, smiling at him so prettily while they plotted and schemed to become his duchess. Introducing herself simply as Serena, all she'd wanted from him was a dance. And when one dance had led to another and they'd eventually escaped to his room for an incredible night of lovemaking, she'd slipped away before dawn the next morning without even leaving him a number where he could reach her. And he'd thought of nothing but her since.

She'd bewitched him—there was no other explanation. He knew it, accepted it, and had looked forward to this night for months so that he could see her again. And she was nowhere to be found. Frustrated, disgusted with himself for caring, he told himself he was acting like a lovesick fool and he wasn't even in love. Still, he couldn't stop himself from looking in vain for her sunlit curls and laughing blue-gray eyes. Where the hell was she?

His gaze still searching the hundreds of guests that crowded into the ballroom, he didn't notice that the women gathered around him had stepped back to make room for Princess Anna until a lilting voice teased, ''Somebody's in a bear of a mood. Poor baby.

What's the matter? Can't you get one of these lovely ladies to kiss you and make you feel better? You must not have used that new mouthwash I told you about.''

It wasn't often that Rafe let a foul mood get the best of him, but when he did, friends and family respectfully gave him some space. Everyone, that is, but Anna. Her brown eyes bold and dancing, she grinned at him and just dared him to scowl at her the way he was at everyone else.

He couldn't, of course. She was his favorite cousin, dammit, and she always knew just what to say to make him laugh. "Brat," he chuckled. "My breath is just fine, thank you very much, though I'm not sure I can say the same about yours. At least I have company. Where's your date?''

"Who said I had one?" she said, arching a delicate brow. "I wanted to play the field tonight.''

If it wouldn't have hurt her feelings, Rafe would have laughed. He didn't doubt that Anna could have had any man in the room with a crook of her finger— she just didn't know it. Growing up within the high walls of the castle, surrounded by a loving family, she'd been protected all her life from the harsh ugliness of the real world. At twenty-four, she was sweet and beautiful and fun—and still as innocent as the day she'd been born. And she didn't have a clue how rare and special that made her.

"Then that means you're free for a dance," he told her, grinning. And to the irritation of the ladies still hoping to catch his eye, he pulled his cousin out onto the dance floor just as the band broke into a lively swing number.

He couldn't have picked a better partner. She was a good dancer and matched him step for step. When the song ended, they were both breathless and laughing. "Come on," Anna suggested, fanning herself, "let's go out into the garden and cool off."

"In a minute," he promised, only to regret it when the music changed again, this time to a love song that had been played at Julia's wedding last summer. Just that easily, Rafe found himself once again searching the crowd for Serena.

"Who is she?"

Caught up in his thoughts, he hardly heard her. Frowning, he jerked his attention back to Anna and found her watching him with narrowed eyes that saw far too much. "What?"

"The woman you're looking for," she replied. "Who is she?"

A proud man, he couldn't tell her or anyone else about Serena and the way he still ached for her six months after a single night of loving. Not after she'd left him before dawn without a backward glance. So he forced a smile and shrugged. "I don't know what you're talking about."

Not fooled, she arched a mocking brow. "Really? I thought you might be looking for the blonde you were so taken with at Julia's wedding."

"What blonde?"

She laughed. "Just because you don't see her doesn't mean she isn't here. Guests wander all over the place. She could be anywhere. You should look around."

"There's no blonde," he said stubbornly. "I was just looking over the crowd. I heard Julia Roberts was coming with Drew tonight."

As far as Rafe knew, his brother, Drew, didn't even know Julia Roberts, but Anna didn't know that. Her eyes wide with surprise, she said, "You're kidding. He didn't say a thing about it! You're not kidding, are you?"

"Of course not," he said innocently. "I wouldn't do a thing like that."

They both knew he would do exactly that, but she obviously couldn't take a chance. "I'd better go find Mother. She'll be thrilled she's coming. She loved her in *Erin Brockovich.*"

Excusing herself, she hurried away, and Rafe found himself separated from his bevy of admirers by the crowd of dancers on the dance floor. Taking advantage of the situation, he slipped outside.

The second the French doors closed behind him, shutting out the sounds of the party, Rafe sighed in relief. The beauties inside wouldn't follow him—not when it was so cool and the dark clouds overhead in the night sky threatened rain—and that was just fine with him. He needed some time to himself.

Alone with his thoughts, the quiet shadows of the extensive palace gardens beckoned him into the night. His mind once again wandering to Serena, he took one of the many meandering garden paths and soon left the party far behind.

When lightning flashed overhead a few minutes later, revealing a woman on her knees digging among the roses at the far end of the garden, Rafe thought his imagination was playing tricks on him. For a split second something about the way she moved reminded him of Serena.

"You're seeing things," he muttered to himself. "If she was here, she certainly wouldn't be working in the garden!"

Then, with a loud crack of thunder, lightning

flashed again, lighting up the night sky. Startled, the mysterious gardener rose unsteadily to her feet and half turned toward him, giving him a clear view of her silhouette. Shocked, Rafe froze in his tracks. It was Serena. And she was pregnant.

Serena, where are you?

Chapter 2

"Serena?"

Trapped, her heart slamming against her ribs, Serena wanted to sink right into the ground. Lonely and depressed, she'd gone to the greenhouse to work in the potting shed, hoping she'd be able to ignore the party in the ballroom. But the music had drifted on the night air, teasing and tantalizing her, and she hadn't been able to resist the lure of it. She'd gone outside and found some measure of peace working with the roses.

She'd never dreamed anyone, least of all Rafe, would leave the ballroom for a walk in the garden on such a stormy night, or she never would have come out there. Mortified, she could just imagine what he thought of her. Dressed in jeans and a tattered sweater that was too small now for her swollen body, her hair tumbling down from the clip she'd used to secure it, and her hands grimy with dirt, she had to look like a pregnant ragamuffin.

Given the chance, she would have run for cover. But he would have only followed her, and where, after all, would she have gone? To her father's cottage? She cringed at the thought, picturing the scene that would play out when her father learned the king's nephew, not an American tourist, was the father of her baby. He was an old man, honest and respectful of his position at the palace, proud of who he was. He would never understand how she could have ever pretended to be anything other than what she was...the gardener's daughter.

Looking back on that night, she didn't understand it, either. She'd never done anything like that in her life. But the minute she slipped into the beautiful gown that Anna had loaned her, she'd felt as though she'd turned into a princess herself. She couldn't tell Rafe who and what she was. If she had, he never would have looked twice at her, let alone danced every dance with her, then spent what was left of the night making love to her. Caught up in the magic of the moment, she'd deceived him, and now she had to pay the price for that.

Standing in front of him, all her secrets exposed, she faced him proudly. "Yes, it's me. How are you, Rafe?"

His heart leaping with joy at the sight of her, Rafe hardly heard her. In the flash of overhead lightning, he saw that her hair was a tumbled mass of curls, a streak of dirt trailed across one cheek, and she looked absolutely gorgeous. Unable to stop himself, he took a step toward her, his only thought to pull her into his arms. It had been so long since he'd touched her, held her.

Then his eyes once again fell to her swollen stomach.

With a silent oath, he clamped down on his emotions. There was something a hell of a lot more important to deal with here than his needs. "You're pregnant," he said flatly. "Why didn't you tell me?"

She hadn't said the child was his, but there was no question in his mind that she was carrying his baby. She'd been a virgin until that night they'd shared together, and he seriously doubted that she'd been with anyone else since. She just wasn't the type to jump from man to man and bed to bed.

"I'm the gardener's daughter. We come from different worlds," she replied. "There's nothing more to say."

"The hell there isn't," he growled. "You're carrying my baby. We have to get married."

He might have descended from royalty, but his autocratic tone was the wrong one to use with Serena. Her father was American born and raised, and she didn't take orders from Duke Raphael Harrington or anyone else.

Her blue-gray eyes reflecting the flash of lightning, she pulled herself up to her full five foot seven inches and stood as proudly as a queen in her tattered clothes. "I don't *have* to *do* anything, especially get married."

"But you're pregnant!"

"So?" she said with a toss of her head. "That's my business and I'm handling it. It has nothing to do with you."

If she'd wanted to rock him back on his heels, she

couldn't have found a better way. Outraged, he sputtered, "That's ridiculous! The baby needs a father...and a name!"

"She already has both," she replied stiffly, and wondered if he knew how easily he'd broken her heart. Six months. It had been six months since the one and only night they'd made love, and not a day had gone by in that time that she hadn't thought of him, dreamed of him, ached for him. While she'd grown bigger and bigger with the child they'd created together, she'd kept the name of her baby's father to herself and steadfastly held on to the fantasy that he would come back to her one day soon because he'd fallen in love with her that night, just as she had with him.

And now, just as she'd dreamed, he was back. And he wanted to marry her. Without a word of caring. Without a single mention of love. Because their baby needed a name.

Tears stung her eyes. She'd known it would be like this—that once he found out about the baby, he would do the right thing, the responsible thing, and insist on marrying her out of a sense of duty to their child. And while she readily agreed that that was the honorable thing to do, she would never agree to such a proposal. She would marry for one reason and one reason only—love.

Standing in front of him in her too small sweater, she lifted her chin. "If it will ease your conscience, you should know that I don't hold you responsible for my condition. I knew what I was doing. Now if you'll excuse me, I have to go inside. It's late, and I'm cold."

Turning her back on him, she hurried through the

gate at the far end of the garden, leaving Rafe staring
after her in growing frustration. Over the course of
the past six months, he'd lost track of the number of
times he'd dreamed of the moment when he would
find her again. And not once had he pictured it like
this. What kind of man did she think he was? He'd
never walked away from a responsibility in his life,
and he sure as hell didn't intend to start now. She was
carrying his baby—*his,* dammit!—and he intended to
be there for both her and the child. As far as he was
concerned, that meant marriage. If she didn't like it,
tough!

Hurt, angry that she thought so little of him, he
was tempted to go after her and to make that clear to
her right then and there. But she was pregnant, dammit, and he couldn't force her to talk to him when
she didn't want to. For tonight, at least, there was
nothing he could do except let the matter go.

Scowling, he headed back to the ballroom, but he
was no longer in a mood to celebrate the new year or
anything else. He was going to be a father. A man
didn't get that kind of news every day of the week.
He should have been thrilled. After all, he'd had a
great relationship with his father and had hoped that
one day, he would have the same with his own child.
But how could he do that if Serena wouldn't have
anything to do with him?

"Rafe? Are you all right? You look like you just
got hit with a brick."

Looking up from his thoughts, he found Anna directly in front of him, frowning up at him in concern.
Normally he wouldn't have shared the most private
details of his life with her or anyone else until he
knew what he was going to do, but he felt as if his

whole world had just turned upside down. The words just popped out. "I just found out I'm going to have a baby."

Whatever response he expected from his cousin, it wasn't the flicker of relief that flashed in her eyes. Stunned, he said, "You knew, didn't you? How…" Then it hit him. "Serena said her father's a gardener. He's the palace gardener, isn't he? She lives right here in the palace. That's why you told me to look around. You knew!"

Anna winced at his accusing tone, but to her credit, she didn't lie. "Her father's Nathan Winters. He's been the royal gardener since before Serena was born. They live in the cottage just beyond the garden gate."

"So you're friends with her. And all this time, you knew she was pregnant with my child. Dammit, Anna, why didn't you tell me?"

"Because it wasn't my story to tell!"

She hadn't meant to raise her voice, but suddenly they were attracting more than a few interested looks, one of which was from her mother, who gave her a disapproving frown. "Well, damn," she muttered, feeling like a two-year-old who'd been caught whispering in church. "Let's go outside," she told Rafe. And not giving him time to argue, she grabbed his arm to pull him through the French doors to the terrace, where they could talk without being overheard by half the blue bloods of Europe.

"You should have told me," he told her stiffly as she turned to face him in the glow of the candles that lit the terrace. "I had a right to know."

"I agree," she retorted. "I've been telling Serena the same thing for months, but she was afraid you'd want to get married—"

"She was right. My child will not be illegitimate. I'll call Father Joseph and set up the ceremony for the day after tomorrow. Mother'll be disappointed that there won't be time to plan a proper wedding, but it can't be helped. Will you help Serena pick out a dress? A woman shouldn't shop for her wedding dress alone."

Anna couldn't believe he was serious, but he had that autocratic, royal look on his face that warned all who dared to cross him that his will would not be thwarted. Rolling her eyes, she didn't know whether to laugh or to cry. Did he really think he could just waltz right in and *order* Serena to marry him?

"Don't let your royal blood go to your head, Your Highness," she said dryly. "This isn't the Dark Ages, in case you hadn't noticed. Women actually have rights."

"I didn't mean—"

"Of course you did. You're a duke. You want what you want, when you want it, come hell or high water. Well, I've got news for you. Serena isn't looking for a husband—she's looking for love. She won't have one without the other."

Frustrated, he swore, "Dammit, Anna, she's in no position to quibble about hearts and flowers. She's pregnant, for God's sake! I can only thank God my father isn't alive to know about this. I can just hear him now. He's probably spinning in his grave."

Anna didn't doubt that. Uncle Niles had raised his children to be responsible citizens and he would not have approved of his oldest son having a baby out of wedlock. But then again, Uncle Niles, himself, had married for love, and he and Aunt Margaret had had a long, wonderful life together before he'd passed away peacefully in his sleep last year. He would want nothing less than that kind of happiness for Rafe.

"He wouldn't be pleased," she agreed. "But you know how important love was to him, Rafe. He would never want you to marry just out of a sense of duty."

"There isn't time for anything else," he said stiffly. "We only had one night together, and now she's pregnant. There was no love involved. I'll admit I was attracted to her—I still am. But it's just physical. That's all it will ever be."

Anyone else might have bought that, but Anna wasn't fooled. She knew her cousin. He wasn't stupid when it came to women, and as much as he enjoyed their company, he'd never lost his head with one and left himself unprotected. He was smarter than that. Then he'd met Serena, and everything had changed.

Anna had heard the gossip—she kept tabs on what was going on with him and the rest of the family— and she knew he hadn't been linked with any of his usual flirts since last summer. And the reason for that was as plain as the nose on his very handsome face. If he wasn't in love, he was certainly smitten, whether he wanted to admit it or not. Otherwise, he never would have brought up the subject of marriage. Oh, he could talk about his scruples and doing the right thing, but he wouldn't even be considering the M word right now if Serena hadn't found a way to touch his heart.

Not, Anna warned herself, that she had any intention of pointing that out to him. If he didn't want to be in love, who was she to tell him that he already was?

"Okay," she said easily, "you're not in love. But Serena needs to be if she's going to agree to marry you. She needs the fairy tale, Rafe. And you have to give it to her.''

In another flash of overhead lightning, he scowled fiercely. ''How the hell am I going to do that? She doesn't want anything to do with me.''

''You'll have to court her. But first you have to get her to trust you,'' she warned. ''She's not an idiot. If you rush in and try to sweep her off her feet now, after you've already pressed her to marry you, she's going to know what you're doing and send you packing. Just spend some time with her and get to know her better. Then, when she lets her guard down, you can charm her into falling in love with you.''

''In three months?''

She had to smile at his skeptical tone. It wasn't going to be nearly as difficult as he thought—Serena was already in love with him—but that was something he didn't need to know. Because while he was trying to seduce her into falling in love with him, he would be losing his heart to her.

''I didn't say it would be easy,'' she told him. ''But think of it this way. You've already got the odds stacked in your favor. She's carrying your baby and she believes in happily ever after. Now all you've got to do is convince her that she can have that with you.''

''I'm just a duke, Anna. Not Prince Charming.''

''She's not looking for a prince,'' she said simply. ''Just someone to love her. You can be that man.''

Chapter 3

Rafe knew Anna was right, but long after the new year rang in and he'd retreated to his room for what was left of the night, he lay in bed and stared at the dark ceiling, trying to come to grips with the sudden, unexpected turn his life had taken. In the privacy of his own thoughts, he was forced to admit that he was thrilled that he'd found Serena again. He hadn't realized just how much he'd missed her until he'd glanced up and seen her at the far end of the garden. At that moment something had constricted in his heart, something he still refused to put a name to.

Love.

Just the mention of the word was enough to give him hives. No, he didn't love her, he told himself fiercely. He couldn't. He wouldn't. His parents might have loved being in love, but just the idea of giving Serena or any other woman that much control over his happiness scared the hell out of him. He wanted nothing to do with it.

That didn't mean, however, that he and Serena couldn't have a good marriage, he reasoned. There was no question that there was a strong physical attraction between them—one look at her after six months, and all he'd wanted to do was to hold her, to kiss her, and to spend the rest of the night making love to her. Then there was the fact that they liked and respected each other. He hadn't forgotten how they'd talked for hours the night they'd met, without ever running out of things to say. That was more than a lot of married couples had going for them. They could make it work.

But Serena wanted love.

He cringed at the idea of seducing her into thinking he would ever allow himself to feel that way about her, but what choice did he have? She was pregnant, and there was no question that the child was his. They would get married as soon as he could talk her into it.

The matter settled, he finally fell asleep, but not for long. Up at dawn and anxious to see Serena again, he had to force himself to wait until after breakfast to go looking for her. Not surprisingly, he found her in the garden with a white-haired gentleman he presumed to be her father.

During the night, the storm had blown itself out and it was a beautiful morning, but the eaves were still dripping and water stood in puddles everywhere. Rafe hardly noticed. All he could see was Serena. Last night, he'd thought she was beautiful in the glare of the lightning flashing overhead, but now, seeing her in the full light of the morning sun, she stole the breath right out of his lungs. Lord, she was lovely! Dressed in jeans and an old flannel shirt that had once, no doubt, been her father's, there was no question that pregnancy agreed with her. Her skin was peaches and cream, her blond hair glistened with gold highlights, and she carried the added weight of the baby with an ease that he couldn't help but admire.

From the garden gate he watched her laugh at something her father said and wondered if she would ever laugh that way with him. Then she looked up and saw him at the gate, and her smile faded. Caught watching her, he didn't apologize, but instead greeted her with a solemn nod. "Good morning. I see the garden weathered the storm all right."

"There was some damage, but not much," she said stiffly. "We were just going to clean up, but we can come back later if you'd like the place to yourself."

"Oh, no, don't leave," he said quickly. "You're not in my way." Inspired by a sudden thought he added, "Actually, I was hoping you—and your father—could give me advice for my mother's gardener. Her roses never look anything like they do here at Montebello. They don't bloom nearly as much, and the leaves are a sickly yellow."

Hodges, his mother's very skilled gardener, would have had a stroke if he'd heard such an out-and-out lie, but Serena had no way of knowing that. Immediately concerned, she stepped toward him with a frown. "It sounds like they're getting too much water."

"And not enough food," her father, Nathan Winters, said gruffly. "Roses need to be fed."

"Pruning helps, too," Serena added. Stepping past her father to a bank of roses near the garden entrance, she pulled pruning sheers from the small bucket of tools she'd brought with her from the potting shed. "The dead blooms need to be cut back," she began, demonstrating.

That was as far as she got. Rafe stepped to her side and suddenly his hand closed over hers where she held the pruning shears. "Like this?"

His husky words washed over her like a warm caress. Lifting her eyes to his, their gazes locked, and suddenly she couldn't seem to catch her breath. Did he know what he did to her? she wondered as her heart somersaulted in her breast. She wanted to believe she wasn't that transparent, but there was something in his eyes, a knowing glint, that sent hot color surging into her cheeks. Oh, yes, she thought shakily. He knew, all right.

And so did her father. His eyesight wasn't what it once had been, and neither was his hearing, but he knew when a man was being friendly with his daughter. And from the frown knitting his bushy brows, Serena knew he didn't like it at all. Thankfully, his disapproval had nothing to do with the fact that she was pregnant or that he suspected Rafe was the father of her baby—he just didn't think she should be too friendly with the royals.

He was old-fashioned and he didn't believe he or Serena should overstep their bounds with their employers. It just wasn't wise. For as long as she could remember, he'd quietly reminded her that she was the gardener's daughter, and forgetting that would only lead to trouble.

She should have listened, Serena silently mused. Maybe then, she wouldn't be in the position she was in now.

But even as she acknowledged the wisdom of that, she felt her unborn daughter kick her softly, and she knew she regretted nothing. Not the wonderful night she'd had with Rafe, and certainly not the baby that was a result of their union. If she could have changed anything, it would have been Rafe's feelings for her. But some things weren't meant to be.

She knew that, accepted it, and couldn't help but wonder what he was doing there. If he thought he could change her mind about getting married, he would soon learn that she could be as stubborn as he.

Aware of her father's presence as he moved away to prune the roses on the far side of the garden, she pulled free of his touch and lifted a delicately arched brow. "It's a soggy morning for a walk in the garden, Your Grace. If you wanted advice about your mother's roses, you should have called the greenhouse. My father would have been happy to help you."

"Maybe your father wasn't the one I wanted to talk to."

"You could have asked for me."

"And missed the chance to see you in person?" he quipped, flashing her a wicked smile. "I don't think so."

Charmed, but not the least bit taken in, she grinned and leaned close so that her father couldn't overhear. "Nice try," she confided, "but it's not going to work. You're not going to flatter me into changing my mind about marrying you."

His green eyes twinkling, he only shrugged. "Okay. I know when I'm beaten. So where's another pair of pruning shears? I'll help you with your work this morning."

She didn't believe for a second that he'd let the matter go that easily, but she couldn't bring herself to send him away. Not when his mere presence made the day brighter and her heart lighter. After all, what would it hurt just this once?

Giving in to temptation, she said, "There's another pair on the workbench in the potting shed. You'll need some gloves, too."

He retrieved the items from the shed himself, and within moments he was working side by side with her. Her heart singing, Serena couldn't remember the last time she'd been so happy. He made her laugh just with a look. And every time his hand innocently brushed hers, every nerve ending in her body tingled. It was wonderful, exhilarating, and given the chance, she would have been content to spend the entire day working with him in the garden.

But her energy level wasn't what it had once been because of the baby, and by midmorning, she was quickly running out of gas. In need of a nap, she hated to leave Rafe, but she had no choice. The doctor had warned her that she needed to rest more, and she wouldn't take any chances with her baby. Not even for Rafe.

Suddenly exhausted, she pulled off her work gloves and forced a weak smile. "I'm sorry to cut this short, but I've got to lie down for a while. The baby—"

In the process of collecting the cuttings they'd pruned, he looked up and frowned when he saw the protective hand she'd placed on her stomach. Suddenly her words registered, and he dropped the cuttings and hurried to her side. "What is it?" he demanded. "Is something wrong with the baby? Are you okay? Dammit, Serena, answer me!"

He looked so alarmed, she would have laughed, but she didn't want to hurt his feelings. "I'm fine, Rafe. Really. It's time for my morning nap."

Surprised, he blinked. "You have to take naps?"

She did laugh then. "Yes, I take naps. I also go to the bathroom every time I turn around. I used to love fish, but now I can't stand the smell of it. Unfortunately, I can't say the same thing about chocolate. I have cravings in the middle of the night." Not the least embarrassed, she confided, "I sleep with a candy bar under my pillow. Isn't that awful?"

Rafe chuckled and knew then why he had been looking for her in the eyes of every woman he'd met over the past six months. There was a naturalness about her, an unpretentiousness, that was a rare thing in his world. And he'd forgotten how easily she could make him laugh. Given the chance, he would have swept her up into his arms and carried her home, but he hadn't missed the fact that her father was hovering nearby, keeping a watchful eye. So he kept his hands to himself and had to be content with just enjoying the sight of her. Someday soon, though, he promised himself, he would touch her, kiss her, the way he longed to.

"Aha!" he teased. "So candy's the way to your heart. I'll remember that the next time I come to see you. In the meantime, I believe a nap is in order. C'mon. I'll walk you home."

The cottage she shared with her father was just steps away from the old rock wall at the far end of the garden, and they both knew she needed no help finding her way. But she didn't offer a word of protest as he fell into step beside her. Pleased, Rafe just barely resisted the urge to take her hand. Finally, he was making some progress!

Encouraged, he flirted with the idea of kissing her when they reached her front door but he didn't want to chance rushing her now that she'd finally let down her guard. So he caressed the curve of her cheek instead. "Enjoy your nap," he said huskily when her blue-gray eyes darkened in response to his touch. "I'll see you later."

"Thanks for helping me with the roses," she said softly. "It was very sweet of you."

He wouldn't have described himself as a sweet man, but when she said it, he couldn't seem to stop smiling. He was still wearing a sappy grin on his face when he returned to the garden and came face-to-face with her father. One look at Nathan Winters's hard frown and he knew that the older man had put two and two together and figured out that he was the father of Serena's baby.

"I haven't seen her this happy since Princess Julia's wedding," Nathan said flatly. "You were here for the wedding and you haven't been back since."

Another man might have pretended he didn't know what the old man was talking about, but Rafe could have never faced himself in the mirror if he'd done such a cowardly thing. When a man got a woman pregnant, the least he could do was explain himself to a disapproving father. "I didn't know who she was, Mr. Winters—she didn't tell me. And I never had a clue that she was pregnant."

"So now that you do, what are you going to do about it?"

Impressed, Rafe had to respect him. He was doing the right thing for his daughter by demanding to know his intentions, and he didn't give a damn that in doing so, he was calling the king's nephew on the carpet. Not many men in his position would have done that.

"I asked her to marry me, sir," he replied simply. "She turned me down flat."

"Then you didn't ask in the right way," Nathan retorted, not the least sympathetic. "A woman in her condition needs to feel loved and wanted. I want my daughter to be happy, Your Grace. It's your job to see that she is."

Put that way, there was nothing more Rafe could do except agree. "I'll do my best, sir."

The question was...how?

Chapter 4

Rafe readily admitted that he wasn't a patient man. Now that he'd made up his mind to marry Serena, he wanted to get on with it. He felt as though he'd made some progress with her in the garden earlier—at least she hadn't sent him away!—but things weren't progressing nearly as quickly as he would have liked. He hadn't laid eyes on her since she'd retreated to her cottage for a nap. At this rate, it would be another six months or longer before he could convince her to marry him, and they didn't have that kind of time. The baby was due in three months!

Prowling the confines of the suite he always stayed in whenever he visited his aunt and uncle, he came to a stop at the wide windows that overlooked the garden and found himself staring at the small gardener cottage in the distance where Serena had grown up. He'd promised Anna he wouldn't rush her, but he knew women, dammit! He'd never met one yet that didn't melt at the sight of a few diamonds.

That was, he knew, a jaded outlook, but the truth hurt. He'd had his share of women, and every single one of them had been interested in only two things...his money and his title. They all wanted to be his duchess, dripping in the family jewels. He wanted to believe Serena was different, but he'd been burned too many times to be that naive.

Not that it mattered, he told himself. Regardless of whether she was like all the rest or not, he was still going to marry her and give his child his name and legitimacy. Still, he needed to know just what kind of woman he was marrying—which was another reason to send her something that matched the sparkle in her eye. Not only would it advance his courting of her, it would tell him just what kind of woman he would be spending the rest of his life with.

The decision made, he pulled out his cell phone and punched in the home number of Thomas Reynolds, the king's jeweler in Montebello. It was New Year's day, but that wouldn't be a problem. Rafe had been a good customer over the years, and Thomas had told him more than once to call him whenever he needed anything. Today, he needed a favor, and he could trust Thomas to handle the matter discreetly.

"I'm sorry to bother you on a holiday," he said after greeting the older man when he came on the line, "but I need your help."

"I'm at your disposal, Your Grace," Thomas replied. "What can I do for you?"

"I need a bracelet for a very special lady. I know your shop's closed for the holiday, but—"

"You'd like it delivered today," the jeweler finished for him with a chuckle. "I'll take care of the matter immediately. I have just the piece in mind—a three-carat-diamond bracelet."

Pleased, Rafe could just imagine Serena's face when she opened the gift. "That'll be perfect. Have it delivered to Serena Winters at the palace gardener's cottage."

Serena was in the kitchen, peeling potatoes for the stew she was making for dinner, when there was a knock at the front door of the cottage. Surprised, she frowned as she wiped her hands on a kitchen towel and stepped into the living room. Who on earth would be dropping by at this time of day? All her friends were tied up with family for the holiday, and her father was meeting some of his buddies at the Red Dragon Pub in the village after dinner. Who...?

Rafe.

Her heart immediately supplied the answer, and try though she might, she couldn't hold back a smile at just the thought of him. The time she'd spent with him in the garden that morning had been wonderful, and she would have liked nothing more than to see him again. But she couldn't. It wouldn't be wise. He might have appeared to have accepted her refusal to marry him, but she knew better. He was proud of his name, proud of his family heritage, and it was important to him that his child be legitimate. He wouldn't give up. He'd keep proposing until he caught her at a weak moment and she gave him the answer he wanted.

Her smile faded at the thought. She didn't intend to let that happen, she vowed grimly. She couldn't marry a man who didn't love her. And she'd tell him that right now.

The words already forming on her tongue, she jerked open the door, only to blink at the red-headed, freckled delivery boy standing on the front stoop. He worked for the king's jeweler and often delivered surprise gifts to the queen and princesses. "Oh, hello, Jacob. What are you doing here? Did you lose your way to the palace?"

Grinning, he held out a small, elegantly wrapped box. "Oh, no, Miss Serena. This one's for you."

"For me? Are you sure?"

"Oh, yes, ma'am. Mr. Reynolds told me to make sure I delivered it personally to you today." And before Serena could even think to object, he took her hand and closed her fingers around the small box.

Stunned, she looked at it as if it held a snake. "There must be some mistake. It's New Year's Day! Mr. Reynolds's shop is closed today!"

"Someone very special must have asked him to open up," the teenager said with a sly grin. "Aren't you going to open it? I bet it's the sapphire earrings Mr. Reynolds got in just last week. He thought the king would want them for Queen Gwendolyn—they match her eyes—but somebody must have beat him to the punch."

Serena sincerely doubted that Thomas Reynolds would have sold anything he suspected the king would be interested in, but she knew whatever was in the box had to be valuable—Mr. Reynolds didn't deal in anything but the best. And that meant the gift had to be from Rafe. Aside from the fact that only someone with money could have afforded something from the jeweler's shop, no one else but a royal would have been able to persuade him to open on a holiday.

Had the circumstances been different, Serena would have been thrilled at the thought of receiving a present from the man she loved. But he didn't love her, and she could only wonder what his motive was.

"Aren't you going to open it?" Jacob asked with a disappointed frown. "Mr. Reynolds will want to know if you liked it."

Serena suspected Jacob himself was the one who wanted to know that, but she kept that comment to herself and reluctantly reached for the beautifully tied bow with fingers that weren't quite steady. What had he sent her? She was afraid to think.

Later, she never remembered unwrapping the package. One second she was fingering the bow and the next she was staring down at a delicate gold bracelet studded with diamonds that sparkled like fire in the late-afternoon sun. Stunned, she could do nothing but gasp. "Oh, my!"

"Wow!" Jacob exclaimed.

Serena had to agree. It was the most beautiful bracelet she'd ever seen in her life. And just the sight of it infuriated her.

She didn't make a sound, but something in her expression must have given her away. Confused, Jacob eyed her warily. "Is something wrong, Miss Serena? You don't look very happy."

"I'm not," she said flatly.

"Why? You don't like diamonds?"

Torn, her emotions in a whirl, Serena would have laughed if she hadn't felt like crying. Yes, she liked diamonds! What woman didn't? She was sure she only had to slip the bracelet on her wrist to feel like a princess, and that was the problem. She was the gardener's daughter. She spent her days working in mulch and manure, and there were times when her hands looked positively atrocious. She needed a diamond bracelet about as much as the queen needed a spading fork.

That didn't mean she wouldn't have taken it in a heartbeat if circumstances had been different. It was beautiful. But it was also the kind of gift a man sent the woman he loved. And Rafe didn't love her.

Hurt pierced her heart, but her pride wouldn't let her give in to the tears that stung her eyes. Jacob was discreet, but word would soon get out that she was receiving expensive gifts from an unknown man who was, no doubt, the father of her baby, and she wouldn't have the gossips saying that he'd reduced her to tears. So she squared her shoulders and faced him without a tear in her eye.

"It isn't a question of liking diamonds," she said stiffly. "Please tell Mr. Reynolds to give my regrets to the sender. This is something I can't accept." And with no more explanation than that, she placed the lid back on the box and shoved it back into the boy's hands. Before he could so much as open his mouth in protest, she shut the door in his face.

Dumbfounded, Jacob just stood there. Mr. Reynolds wasn't going to be pleased.

Impatiently waiting to hear how Serena reacted to the bracelet, Rafe found himself pacing the confines of his suite and brought himself up short. Dammit, what was he doing? He couldn't remember the last time he'd worried so much about what a woman thought. This wasn't like him. He didn't—

The phone rang, and he snatched it up, knowing immediately that it was Thomas, calling to report on how well the bracelet had been received. "Well? What did she say? I bet she cried, didn't she?"

"Not exactly, Your Grace," the jeweler replied solemnly. "She sent it back."

Stunned, he nearly dropped the phone. "What! Why?"

"She didn't say. She just refused to accept it. I'm so sorry, Your Grace. I feel like this is my fault. Obviously, the bracelet wasn't to her liking. I'll send something else—"

"No!" Too late, Rafe realized he never should have sent her such an expensive gift to begin with. Why had he even come up with the brilliant idea to test her? He already knew Serena wasn't like the other women he'd been involved with over the years— that's why he'd enjoyed her company so much. She wasn't greedy or ambitious and didn't care two cents about his title or money. She'd never asked him for anything, even when she'd discovered she was pregnant with his child, and he could only imagine how insulted she'd felt when she'd opened the package and discovered he'd sent her a bracelet that cost more than her and her father's yearly salaries combined. She'd no doubt thought he was trying to bribe her into marrying him, and she'd been exactly right. If she'd taken the bait, he still would have married her, but she would have proven herself to be just like all the rest.

He'd hurt her, and he wanted to kick himself for that. He didn't love her—he didn't love any woman!—but he liked her, dammit, and the last thing he wanted to do was to lose her now that he'd found her again.

"No, don't send her anything else, Thomas," he said gruffly. "I'll handle this. Just bill me for your trouble."

Not giving the older man time to argue, he hung up, then immediately punched in the number to the gardener's cottage. Serena answered the phone, just as he'd hoped, and he got right to the point. "Serena, this is Rafe. I'm so sorry—"

"I have nothing to say to you," she said coldly. "Please leave me alone."

Lightning quick, she hung up, and a split second later the dial tone buzzed mockingly in his ear. Frustrated, he knew he had no one to blame but himself. If he'd just taken Anna's advice and given Serena the time she needed to get used to the fact that he was back in her life, this would have never happened. But had he listened? Hell, no! Like an idiot, he'd thought that he knew what was best. He knew women.

Yeah, right, he thought cynically. Well, he might know most women, but he didn't know Serena. How could he? They'd spent one night together—one, for heaven's sake!—and instead of trying to rush her into a lifetime commitment, he should have done just as Anna suggested and given her some time to get to know him again and trust him.

It isn't too late to make it up to her, a voice in his head pointed out. But how? He certainly couldn't send her any more jewelry. Or flowers, he added ruefully. She already had a gardenful of roses. She didn't need any more.

Frustrated and feeling like a sixteen-year-old who didn't know how to impress the first girl who'd caught his eye, he reached for the phone. There was only one person who could help him.

"Anna?" he said as soon as she came on the line. "I need your help."

Chapter 5

Dinner, such as it was, was ready. Taking a dried-out pot roast from the oven, Serena found herself fighting tears. Ever since she'd sent Jacob packing with that ridiculously gorgeous bracelet Rafe had sent her, she hadn't been able to concentrate on what she was doing. She'd set the oven too high and not only dried out the roast, but burned the rolls she'd made to go with it. And it was all Rafe's fault!

She should have called him and told him what she thought of him, she fumed as she transferred the roast to a platter. Maybe then she would have been able to cook dinner without crying every time she turned around.

Lost in her musings, she never noticed that her father had been watching her for some time as she moved around their small kitchen. A fierce frown knitting his bushy white brows, he eyed the food she was dishing up at the stove and asked gruffly, "Are you feeling all right?"

"I'm fine," she sniffed, turning away so he wouldn't see the tears flooding her eyes. "Why?"

"No reason," he said quickly. "You just seem a little tired."

"My back is hurting," she said simply, pressing a hand to the small of her back. "It has been all afternoon."

"You should have laid down and left supper to me," her father scolded. "Go put your feet up. I'll take care of this."

He didn't have to tell her twice. Grimacing at the sorry excuse for a meal she'd made, she said huskily, "I'm sorry about dinner, Dad. I just couldn't seem to concentrate."

"Don't worry about it," he said with a quick grin and a wave of his hand. "If you think you can't concentrate now, wait until the baby comes. There'll be days when you'll be lucky if you can remember your own name."

Just thinking about her baby brought a smile to Serena's face. "I won't care, Dad. She'll be worth it."

She wasn't even born yet, but Serena could already imagine her baby's first smile, first tooth, first Christmas, first date. Since her mother had died so young, she'd missed so many of those special times with her. That wasn't to say she hadn't had a wonderful relationship with her father—she had—but there were just times when a girl needed her mother. She planned to be there for those times with her daughter.

Hugging the thought to her heart, Serena moved into the living room and had just eased herself down into her favorite chair when there was a sudden knock at the door. Surprised, she stiffened, swearing softly under her breath. If that was Jacob, back with that darn bracelet...

Springing from her chair at the thought, she told her father, "I'll get it."

Annoyed, she thought she knew exactly what she was going to say. Then she jerked open the door. "Rafe!"

He was the last person she'd expected to turn up on her doorstep. After she'd rejected his gift, she'd really thought she might not ever see him again. "What are you doing here? If this is about the bracelet—"

"Don't worry, it's not," he assured her. "That was a mistake. If you can forgive me, I'd like to take you to dinner."

"No!" She didn't hesitate, though she'd have given anything to say yes. But she'd fought tears all afternoon because of him, and she did have some pride. The last thing she wanted to do was to spend time with him. Besides, her back still hurt and she really needed to lie down.

"We were just about to sit down to dinner," she told him coolly. "I'd ask you to stay, but I'm not much of a cook and I overcooked the pot roast. I'm sure you wouldn't like it."

She'd never treated anyone so rudely in her life, but Rafe didn't so much as flinch. Instead, he turned his attention to her father, who had stepped into the kitchen doorway at the sound of his voice. "Good evening, sir," he said quietly. "Serena was just telling me that dinner didn't turn out very well, so I thought I'd take her out. If that's okay with you," he added quickly.

Serena couldn't believe his audacity. Did he actually think her father would side with him against her? She was his daughter, for heaven's sake. "Of course it's not okay," she retorted. "I already told you we were just about to eat…"

"I think you should go," her father cut in quietly. "You said yourself, dinner's not very good. You need to eat right for the baby."

Serena couldn't have been more surprised if he'd told her to stand on her head. "Dad!"

"Don't look at me like that," he chided, humor twinkling in his gray eyes. "I'm only thinking of you. You haven't eaten anyone's cooking besides mine or your own for months. Dinner out will be a nice change for you."

Serena couldn't believe he was serious, but in spite of the smile that tugged at his lips, there was no doubting that he meant every word. Outnumbered and more than a little frustrated, she gave in. "All right, I'll go. But you're wasting your time," she warned Rafe before heading to her room to change into something more appropriate than jeans and an oversize T-shirt. "This isn't going to change anything."

If Rafe was bothered by her less than gracious attitude, he gave no sign of it as he helped her into his car a few moments later and headed to the village. Acting as if there was nothing the slightest unusual about the gardener's daughter and the king's nephew going out on what could only be described as a date, he talked easily about the weather, politics, and an upcoming trip to the States. Much to Serena's irritation, he only smiled when she responded in mono-syllables.

She knew she was being a baby, but she was determined to not enjoy herself. Then they arrived at the Glass Swan, one of the village's nicest restaurant, and Serena was stunned to find it completely empty. Normally, it was packed to the brim for both lunch and dinner.

Turning to Rafe in confusion when Louis, the owner, showed them to a cozy table positioned in front of the fireplace, she frowned. "Where is everyone?" But even as she asked, she knew. "You bought out the entire restaurant, didn't you?"

To his credit, Rafe didn't lie. "It's not what you think—I wasn't flaunting my money again and trying to buy you. I just wanted to spend some time with you in private, away from the palace and your father's house."

Crossing her arms over her breast, she just looked at him. "Why?"

"So I could apologize," he said simply. "I'd be more than willing to do it in front of the whole town if that's what you want, but I thought it would be better this way. Obviously, I overstepped my bounds again. If you don't want to be alone with me, just say the word and Louis will be happy to open the place back up."

Put that way, Serena felt like a heel. He had hurt her feelings and insulted her, but she knew he hadn't done it intentionally. He wasn't that kind of man. The women in his world just expected to be bought by him, and he obliged them. At least he realized now that she was different and he was trying to make amends.

"No, you don't have to do that," she said huskily. "This will be fine."

Relieved, he grinned boyishly. "I was hoping you would say that. Louis let most of the staff off tonight, and I'd have to wait tables if he opened the place back up."

Serena could just see Duke Raphael Harrington waiting tables, and the image made her lips twitch. His parents had done a fine job of making sure that he was raised with his feet on the ground, but he was still descended from kings, and it showed in every line of his body. He would make a lousy waiter.

"Somehow, I don't think you'd be very good at taking orders," she said with a chuckle. "Maybe we'd better keep things the way they are."

Pleased, he pulled out her chair for her. "My sentiments exactly. Louis, Miss Winters and I will be having dinner alone tonight. Don't bother bringing us a menu. We'll let you order for us."

Rafe had been eating at Louis's since he was a child, and he knew from past experience that the restaurant owner never forgot the likes and dislikes of his customers. He could trust him to see that he and Serena were well taken care of.

"Thank you, Your Grace," the older man replied with a smile. "Your appetizer will be right out." And not asking either of them what they wanted to drink, he served Serena spring water and Rafe white wine before quietly slipping away to the kitchen.

Left alone in the dining room with nothing but the crackling fire for company and an Italian love song playing softly in the background, the setting couldn't have been more romantic. Serena, however, was far from at ease. She couldn't quite look Rafe in the eye and her fingers were restless as she settled her napkin in her lap and absently played with her silverware.

Rafe hadn't meant to touch her, but he couldn't stand seeing her so tense. Impulsively, he reached across the table and took her hand. "I'm sorry," he said huskily, shattering the silence that had fallen between them. "When I sent the bracelet, I never meant to hurt you. I just wanted to give you something pretty. Can you forgive me?"

A wise woman would have at least given the matter some thought before answering, but Serena hated being at odds with him. For an answer, her fingers curled around his. "I'm not marrying you, though," she said, just so there wouldn't be any misunderstandings. "So if that's what this is all about..."

"It isn't," he assured her. "This is just an evening out with a friend, okay? No strings attached."

She could have told him that there were already more than strings between them—their baby would be born in three months—but he was right. She was the one who had set the rules—there were no strings between them just because they were having a baby together. So why couldn't they go out and enjoy each other's company? Wasn't that what she wanted if she couldn't have his love?

Yes! she told herself fiercely, and tried to believe it. But there was a longing in her heart when she teased, "Okay, friend. So what have you been doing with yourself lately? I heard you were thinking about joining a monastery."

"You've been reading the tabloids again."

Her blue-gray eyes twinkling, she didn't deny it. "Guilty as charged. If I remember correctly, you were going to take a vow of poverty and help the poor in

Calcutta. So was this before or after you paid Louis
for renting out the entire restaurant?''

"Cute, Ms. Winters," he drawled.

Grinning, she tossed her head. ''Thank you. I like
to think so. Speaking of cute, that Playboy bunny you
were caught with at Buckingham Palace was very
pretty.''

In the process of reaching for his wine, Rafe nearly
knocked over his glass. ''Dammit, Serena, I can't believe you read that garbage! I wasn't even in the
country that night.''

"I know," she chuckled. ''Anna told me you were
in New York. I just wanted to push your buttons.''

He laughed, and just that easily, the clock turned
backward. The calendar read January first, but it felt
like summer. They laughed and talked as if the past
six months had never happened, and when Louis
served them a dinner that was fit for a king, neither
of them could have said what they ate.

It was wonderful and exhilarating and scary, and
Serena loved it. She had missed him *so* much, and
even though she knew he didn't love her, she didn't
want the evening to end. Not yet. Not when this might
be all she would ever have of him.

Though Louis never looked at his watch or even
hinted at the growing lateness of the hour, they were
both aware of the passage of time. Reluctantly, they
brought the evening to a close and thanked Louis for
a wonderful meal.

Her heart pounding in her chest, Serena didn't say
a word during the drive back to the palace. It was a
clear night, full of stars, and a crescent moon smiled
down on them from a velvet sky, just as it had last
summer. Staring out the passenger window of his

Mercedes, Serena couldn't help but wonder what she would do if he tried to take up where they'd left off six months ago. Would she let him kiss her? Hold her? Make love to her?

"Serena? Hey, where'd you go?"

Grinning, he snapped his fingers in front of her face, jolting her out of her fantasy. With a quick blink, she realized that he'd pulled up in front of the gardener's cottage and had been watching her for quite some time. And she had a face like an open book.

Mortified, she could just imagine what he thought. "Rafe—"

Smiling gently at her, he reached out and trailed a finger down her hot cheek. "Go in and go to bed, sweetheart," he said huskily. "No explanations are necessary."

With no warning, he leaned over and pressed a kiss to her cheek, then got out of the car to open her door for her. Her cheek still tingling moments later when she wished him good night and slipped into her father's cottage, she told herself that she was thankful he hadn't pushed for anything more intimate. And she almost believed it...until she went to bed and dreamed of him.

Chapter 6

Sure that he was making some progress with Serena, Rafe should have slept like a baby after he returned to his suite, but she was all he could see whenever he closed his eyes. Her smile, the dancing laughter in her eyes when she'd teased him about the headlines he made in the tabloids, the softness of her hand as his fingers closed around hers. She consumed his thoughts in a way no woman ever had, and for the life of him, he didn't know why. He was doing the right thing—he was trying to find a way to convince her to marry him—so why was she dominating his every waking and sleeping thought? Why couldn't he get her out of his head?

The answer evaded him all through the night, and by dawn, he was still wide-awake. Wincing at the first bright rays of the sun that streamed through his bedroom window and hit him in the face, he groaned. Coffee. He needed coffee, and lots of it.

Normally, he would have showered and shaved before heading for the breakfast room, but the rest of the family wasn't up yet, and he would have the place to himself. So taking time only to drag on jeans and a shirt and splash some water on his face, he went looking for something to jump-start his tired brain.

He didn't have to glance in the mirror to know that he looked as if he'd been out all night. He didn't care...until he walked into the breakfast room and found his mother already there, enjoying the morning paper and a croissant with her coffee. "Mother! What are you doing here?"

"I could ask the same of you," she retorted. Dressed in winter-white slacks and a blue sweater that matched the color of her eyes, her makeup freshly applied and her strawberry-blond hair elegantly arranged in a simple French twist, Duchess Margaret Harrington took in her son's appearance in a single glance and saw far more than he wanted her to. "It looks like you had a rough night. What's the matter? Couldn't sleep?"

He shrugged. "I had a lot on my mind."

"Oh," she said innocently. "I thought you might be anxious to get home. Elizabeth DuPree must be quite lonely without you."

Rafe grimaced at that. The daughter of his banker, Elizabeth had been chasing him for the past two months in spite of his best attempts to discourage her. "If she is, it's her own fault," he retorted. "I've told her repeatedly that I'm not interested in getting involved with anyone right now, but she wouldn't listen. I guess she'll get the message when she hears I'm staying in Montebello for a while."

To her credit, Margaret wasn't all that surprised.

She'd heard about his dinner with Serena last night…and the quiet speculation that was whispering around the palace. It didn't take a genius to put two and two together. Serena was pregnant, and Rafe had visited Montebello six months ago for Julia's wedding. He'd been acting restless ever since.

Another woman might have been disappointed— no mother wanted to see her son trapped by a scheming hussy who didn't know how to protect herself. But that in no way described Serena. During her visits to Montebello over the years, Margaret had watched Serena grow from a motherless girl to a self-assured, beautiful young woman any mother would be proud to have her son involved with. She liked her…and could have danced a jig at the idea of having a grandchild. She'd begun to think she never would. She just wished Niles had lived long enough to hold Rafe's baby in his arms. He would have been thrilled.

At the thought of her deceased husband, tears threatened to well in her eyes—dear Lord, how she missed him!—but she sniffed and brought herself up short. Niles was gone, and she had to remember that the important thing to consider was Rafe's happiness. How did he feel about becoming a father? Did he want this child? Did he want Serena? What was he going to do about it if he didn't?

Questions without answers swirled in her head, and although she cringed at the idea of being an interfering mother, she realized she couldn't just ignore the situation. After all, there was a baby involved. That wasn't going to go away.

Motioning to the chair across from her, she said quietly, "Sit down, son, and tell me why you're really staying. We both know it has nothing to do with Elizabeth DuPree. It's Serena Winters, isn't it? And the baby.''

Rafe blinked. He didn't know why he was surprised that she knew. She wasn't and never had been one of those mothers that hovered over her children and tried to control their lives. Still, she had always known what he and his brother and sister were up to, regardless of how discreet they were, and he'd never figured out how.

Pouring himself a cup of coffee from the buffet, he joined her at the table, his frown baffled as he openly studied her. "How do you know this stuff? Are you psychic, or what?"

Her blue eyes twinkling, she laughed gaily. "Not hardly, dear. I'm just a mother. Parents know these kinds of things. When your baby is born, you'll understand.''

Just that easily, she brought the conversation back to the subject at hand. Sobering, Rafe said quietly, "Maybe. If I get the chance to raise my child.''

"Is that what you want?"

Over the course of the past two nights, while he lay awake, staring at the ceiling and struggling with his thoughts, he'd lost track of the number of times he'd asked himself that question. And the answer was always the same. "I want to do the right thing, Mother. The honorable thing. I want my baby to not only have my name, but to have the security of knowing that her parents are married and committed to her happiness and well-being.''

"And what about your happiness?" his mother said shrewdly. "And Serena's? Do you think the two of you can make a child happy if you're not happy yourselves?''

Taken aback, he growled, "What are you saying? *Don't* marry her? Dammit, Mother, she's pregnant with my baby! I thought you would want me to do the right thing."

"I do," she replied. "There are all sorts of ways you can do the right thing for your child. You can set up a trust, share custody, even build Serena a house on the estate so that you can be intimately involved in the baby's life. But if you're really serious about marrying her, you need to know that I can't support a marriage that isn't based on love. If you don't love the girl, leave her alone."

Of all the things he'd expected his mother to say when she found out about Serena's pregnancy, this wasn't even on the list. "I don't understand you. You and Dad raised me to—"

"Be a responsible, honorable man," she cut in, reaching across the table to squeeze his hand. "And you are, sweetheart. You're everything your father and I wanted you to be. You wouldn't even consider marrying Serena if you weren't. But the one thing above all others that Niles and I wanted for you and Drew and Vanessa was the kind of marriage we had. You'll never come close to having that if you marry a woman you don't love."

"But she's pregnant, Mother."

"I know, dear. But the baby's not due for a few more months. You don't have to rush into this. Give yourself some time."

No one wanted the type of marriage his parents had had more than he did, but he felt as though time was slipping through his fingers and there didn't seem to be anything he could do about it. "I'll try," he told her. "But I'm not making any promises."

And that was what worried Margaret. Long after the rest of the family had joined them for a leisurely breakfast, she couldn't put their conversation out of her mind. She knew her son. He was a traditionalist—and as stubborn as she. Even though he'd agreed to think about what she'd said, she knew she hadn't changed his mind. He was going to marry Serena, and there was nothing she could do about it.

Except talk to Serena.

Margaret knew she should have rejected the idea immediately. Rafe was a grown man and had the right to make decisions about his own life. He wouldn't appreciate any interference.

But then, again, she was his mother. And mothers had certain rights.

Serena was in the middle of cleaning out the refrigerator when there was a knock at the front door. Stiffening, she swore softly. She didn't want to see anyone. Not after the day she'd had. Not only had she dreamed of Rafe all night, but thoughts of him had dogged her every step all morning long. Then, just when she'd finally gotten him out of her head by throwing herself into housework, Anna had called and she'd let it slip that Rafe had asked her to marry him. What a mistake! Anna had called her every half hour since, urging her to accept Rafe's proposal.

And now she was knocking at her door! It had to be her. Rafe wouldn't... Would he?

Horrified at the thought, she looked down at herself and wanted to sink right through the floor. She had on her grungiest clothes, she'd never even looked at her makeup today, and her hair was tied back in a ponytail with a piece of string, for heaven's sake!

Over the years there'd been any number of times
when Anna had seen her looking worse—she
wouldn't blink twice at the sight of her dirty clothes
and face. But Rafe...she didn't want him to see her
like this. And there was no time to change. Even as
she hesitated, there was another knock at the door.

Her stomach twisting in knots, she almost didn't
answer it. But if her visitor really was Rafe, she
couldn't deny herself the chance to see him again.
She could invite him in, then rush upstairs to change.
It wouldn't take a minute. She'd washed her best maternity outfit last night. She'd comb out her hair, spritz
on some perfume...

Her thoughts jumping to the shoes she would wear,
it was several long seconds after she pulled open the
door before she realized that her visitor wasn't Rafe,
but his mother. Horror took on a whole new defini-
tion. She couldn't have looked worse if she'd tried.
"Your Grace! What are you doing here?"

That was hardly a socially correct greeting, but the
words popped out before Serena could stop them.
Mortified, she slapped her hand over her mouth, but
it was too late. "Oh, God, I'm sorry! I shouldn't have
said that. Please, come in." Opening the door wider,
she stepped back to allow her into the small but comfortable front parlor. "Can I get you something? Tea?
Coffee?"

She was chattering like a ninny, but there didn't
seem to be anything she could do about it. Thankfully, Rafe's mother seemed to understand. Smiling,
she teased, "I'm not an ogre, dear. I'm not here to
bite your head off. I just thought it was time we
talked, if that's all right with you."

Just that easily, Serena knew she knew about the

baby, and her heart sank. Slipping into her father's favorite easy chair as Rafe's mother sank down onto the couch, she said stiffly, "I don't mean to be rude, Your Grace, but if you've come to try to talk me into marrying Rafe, you're wasting your time. I've already told him no. I have no intention of changing my mind."

Far from being offended, the duchess merely lifted a brow in inquiry. "Why? Because you don't love him?"

"No. Because he doesn't love me."

She offered no other explanation than that—she didn't need to. She told Margaret everything she needed to know with those few simple words, and in the process, she had no idea how she reassured her. Not only did Serena have a head on her shoulders, she had principles. And from what Margaret had been able to see, those were rare commodities in the women her son usually found himself involved with.

Relieved, she felt as if a huge load had been lifted from her shoulders. She didn't have to worry that Serena was some money-hungry little wannabe duchess who'd taken one look at Rafe and set a trap for him. Even though Margaret didn't doubt that the girl really wanted to marry him, it wasn't because she wanted to better her lot in life. It was because she loved him. It was right there in her eyes for anyone to see.

Anyone that is, Margaret thought wryly, but her son. From what he'd said, he didn't have a clue that Serena loved him. If he had, he would have let down his guard and looked at her in a completely different light.

"And you're holding out for love," Margaret said with an understanding smile. "I was hoping you would say that. I did the same thing, and I never regretted it. Without love, you might as well be alone.''

Serena felt the same way, but she'd never expected Rafe's mother to agree with her. "You don't mind about the baby? That we're not married?"

"Of course I do," she answered honestly. "You're carrying my first grandchild, dear, and naturally, I want everything perfect for the baby. But we don't, unfortunately, live in a perfect world. Regardless of what happens between you and Rafe, I'll still be crazy about the baby. My main concern right now is Rafe. I only want for him what his father and I had—a love that goes soul deep. That's what will get you through good times and bad, not a marriage license.''

Studying Serena shrewdly, she added, "I think the two of you can have that kind of love. You've already admitted you love him.''

"Oh, I do," she said huskily, wiping at the tears that welled in her eyes. "When he asked—" Breaking off abruptly, she wryly corrected herself. "Make that *told* me we had to get married, all I wanted to do was say yes and throw myself into his arms. But I couldn't. I need him to love *me*, to want to be with me and spend the rest of his life with me, whether there's a baby or not.''

"And he will," Margaret assured her. "You just have to stand strong and give him time to fall in love with you. Trust me, it'll be worth the wait. Love always is.''

Serena didn't doubt that. Although her memories of her mother were vague, she only had to hear her father talk about her mother to see the love he'd had for her. Then there was the great love the king and queen shared. Growing up on the grounds of the palace, watching them together, she'd wanted what they and her parents had had. Love. She would settle for nothing less.

Chapter 7

I missed you yesterday. Meet me at the beach at two.

Reading the note that had been slipped under his door while he was out riding, Rafe lifted a dark brow. Well, well, he thought with a grin. Wasn't this a pleasant surprise? He'd taken his mother's advice yesterday and given himself some time to think by steering clear of Serena all day. And she'd missed him. He'd have to send his mother flowers for unknowingly suggesting he play hard to get. It had worked!

She had missed him. It had to take a lot for her to admit that, and he could have kissed her for it. Because he'd missed her, too. So much so that when he'd found himself wandering out on the terrace to see if he could catch a glimpse of her in the garden, he retreated to his room so he wouldn't be tempted to go looking for her.

And now she wanted to see him.

Pleased, his thoughts already jumping ahead to

their meeting, he glanced at his watch, only to swear softly. It was only just now eleven. He had to wait three full hours before he could see her, touch her, and, he hoped, kiss her. Frustrated, he tore off his shirt and strode into the bathroom for a shower. It was going to be a long three hours.

The pounding of her heart drowned out by the roar of the waves, Serena walked along the palace's private beach and just barely resisted the urge to look at her watch. She was early, but she hadn't been able to stay away. Yesterday had been interminable, and it was all Rafe's fault. She hadn't seen him all day, and it had been the longest day of her life. She'd missed him, missed his smile, the sound of his voice, the touch of his hand.

That should have worried her. He would leave by the end of the week and return to his home in England, and once again, she would have to find a way to live without him. Knowing that, accepting it, she still couldn't hold back the smile that curled the edges of her mouth. She would see him soon. Nothing else mattered.

Lifting her face to the cool sea breeze, she buried her hands deep in the pockets of her jacket. Then she heard his step behind her and she whirled, her eyes bright with anticipation and love.

"I got your note."

It was a simple greeting, and hardly anything that should have caused the surprise that flared in his eyes. "What?"

"I got your note," she repeated, her smile fading when he frowned at her. "The one you slipped under my front door this morning. Is there a problem?"

For an answer, he just started to laugh. "You didn't happen to bring it with you, did you?"

In her pocket, her fingers curled around the note that hadn't been out of her possession since she'd found it. Without a word, she held it out to him.

Rafe didn't need to read it to know what it said. Reaching into the pocket of his own jacket, he pulled out a folded piece of stationery that was identical to her own. Arching a brow, he grinned at her. "Look familiar?"

"That's my note!"

"No, that's *my* note," he corrected her. "Someone slipped it under my door while I was out riding earlier. Shall I read it to you?" Not waiting for her to answer, he unfolded the note and read, "'I missed you yesterday. Meet me at the beach at two.'" When he saw her eyes widen in surprise, he said, "Why do I have a feeling yours said the same thing?"

"How…oh, my God!" she said, horrified, putting two and two together. "Anna!"

"Exactly," he said dryly. "Apparently, she's playing matchmaker."

"Oh, Rafe, I'm so sorry! I had no idea. I can't believe she did this. I'll talk to her—"

"So will I. I need to thank her."

Caught up in her mortification, she hardly heard him. Then his words registered, and she glanced up, startled. "What? Why?"

"I wish I'd thought of it," he said simply.

Just that easily, he made her heart sing. And suddenly, she couldn't stop smiling. "Me, too."

"We could stay, since we're here. If you don't have anything else planned," he added quickly. "It's a beautiful day."

Yes! she wanted to cry. She wanted to stay, wanted to be with him more than she wanted her next breath, but her pride wouldn't let her appear too eager. "I can spare a few minutes, I suppose."

"Good. Because I brought you something."

Once, she would have been thrilled that he'd thought to bring her anything. But all she could think of was the last time he'd given her a gift. Her smile fading, she stepped back. "No! I don't want anything!"

The pain in her wounded eyes struck Rafe in the heart, and he knew he had no one to blame but himself. Cursing himself, wanting, needing to touch her, he had to content himself with holding out the candy bar he'd brought her. "It's just chocolate, sweetheart," he said huskily. "I remembered how you craved it."

He'd only meant to reassure her. Instead, tears flooded her eyes. Bewildered, he frowned. "What is it? What did I say? I didn't mean to hurt you!"

"I know," she sniffed, wiping at the tears that spilled over her lashes to trail down her cheeks. "I just didn't expect you to remember."

"I remember everything," he murmured huskily. "Everything."

When he reached for her, she never thought to object. Suddenly, she was in his arms, his mouth hot and hungry on hers, and nothing had ever seemed so right. This was what she had dreamed of, longed for, ached for every night since last summer, when he'd made love to her and changed her world. And she wanted it to last forever.

Marry him and it can.

Kissing him back with all her heart, Serena des-

perately wanted to believe that. He cared for her—
she could feel it in his touch, taste it in his kiss. A
lot of people had a lot less than that, she reasoned.
They could find a way to be happy if she'd just give
them a chance.

But even as she considered it, she knew she had to
hold on to the dream of him loving her. Because without love, they had nothing.

But it still hurt. Dear God, how it hurt. Fighting
tears, she choked, "Rafe, no. I can't."

"It's all right, sweetheart," he murmured, soothing
her with gentle kisses. "Everything's okay. Please
don't cry. I didn't mean to upset you."

"I know," she sniffed, burying her face against his
chest. "I'm sorry. I'm just so emotional right now. I
overreact to everything."

"No, you don't," he growled, tightening his arms
around her to hold her closer. "I'm the one who
screwed up. I shouldn't have sent you that bracelet. I
won't do anything like that again. So can we relax
and just enjoy the beach? I promise I won't pull any
diamonds out of my pocket. Okay?"

When he cupped her face in his hands and smiled
down at her so contritely, alarm bells clanged wildly
in her head and she knew she should have made some
excuse to leave. But she loved being with him, and
now that he really seemed to understand how she felt
about the bracelet, she couldn't bring herself to walk
away from him. Not yet. Not when he was so close
and they were all alone, with nothing but the wind
and the waves to keep them company.

"Okay," she said with a smile as he took her hand
and linked his fingers with hers. "I think I can manage that."

Pleased, he carried her hand to his lips for a lingering kiss. "Good. Then you're mine for the next two hours. Let's walk."

For now, there was nothing Serena wanted more. Feeling like she was walking on air, she fell into step beside him.

The newest nightspot in town was loud and smoky and jammed. Up on the small stage, a live band pounded out the latest Rod Stewart hit, while at the bar, bartenders hustled to keep up with the demand for fresh drinks. And everywhere Rafe looked, men hit on women, and the women returned the favor.

Normally, Rafe would have been in the thick of the crowd and enjoying every minute of it. Not tonight. All he could think of was Serena and the hours they'd had together on the beach.

"Hey," his brother, Drew, said, nudging him. "The blonde in the blue dress at the end of the bar's really giving you the eye."

Not the least bit interested, he drawled, "You mean the one who looks like she can't add two plus two? No thanks."

Surprised, Drew arched a brow at him. "What's going on with you? I've never seen you so disinterested in a woman in your life. Are you sick? You should have said something—"

In midsentence, Drew abruptly swallowed what he was going to say next as comprehension hit him right between the eyes. "Wait a minute. I know what this is about. Serena—the gardener's daughter."

"I don't know what you're talking about."

Delighted, his brother grinned. "The hell you don't. Did you think I wouldn't find out you rented the Glass Swan just for her the other night? The whole village is talking about it. And who can blame them? That's not like you. You usually keep your affairs more private.''

''There's no affair!''

''No? That's not what it sounds like to me. I'd say you're falling for the lady.''

''Don't be ridiculous. I'm not—''

''What?'' he cut in teasingly. ''Hooked? I wouldn't be too sure about that if I were you. A man doesn't rent an entire restaurant for a woman unless he's crazy about her.''

''My personal life is none of your business.''

Far from intimidated by his snooty tone, Drew only laughed. ''If you didn't want me sticking my nose into your business, you shouldn't have had a little brother. So why aren't you with the lady tonight?''

Much to his irritation, Rafe had to admit that was a good question. Why wasn't he with her? He'd never felt closer to her than when they were together at the beach, and he knew she'd felt the same way. All he'd wanted to do was sweep her up into his arms and carry her off to church to get married. Which was why he'd decided to go out with his brother tonight…so he wouldn't be tempted.

But wasn't that what he wanted? Instead of taking his time, as his mother had advised, and not rushing into anything he might regret, he knew he had to do the honorable thing and convince Serena to marry him. And he couldn't do that if he kept his distance.

''You're right,'' he told Drew, making a snap decision. ''What am I doing here with you when I could be with her?''

Startled, Drew took a step after him when he

headed for the nearest exit. "Hey, wait! We're in your car. How'm I going to get back home?"

"Tell the blonde at the bar you're an earl," he tossed over his shoulder with a grin. "I'm sure she'll be delighted to give you a ride anywhere you want to go."

Shooting through the back entrance of the palace gates, Rafe couldn't help smiling as he made his way to the gardener's cottage. His thoughts on Serena, he didn't realize how late it was until he pulled up in front of the cottage and saw that the place was bathed in darkness. Surprised, he glanced at his watch and swore softly under his breath. It hadn't seemed late when he'd left Drew, but it was going on eleven, and Serena had probably been in bed for some time.

She needs her rest, a voice murmured in his ear. *You can talk to her tomorrow.*

Another man might have left in disappointment, but he was a duke, dammit! He didn't often deny himself anything. He wanted to see Serena, and by God, that's what he was going to do. If he was going to persuade her to marry him, he had to take advantage of every opportunity, and there was no time like the present. But first he had to set the scene.

Smiling at the idea forming in his head, he reached for his cell phone and called local information. A few seconds later he had Angelo Talerico on the line. "I know it's late, Angelo, and you've probably shut down for the night, but I could really use your help. Could you send a driver to the gardener's cottage at the palace? There's a lady there I'd like to impress."

"Serena," Angelo said with a chuckle.

Surprised, Rafe lifted a brow. "You know her?"

"She took my mother roses from the palace gardens when she was in the hospital," he said simply. "She's a good girl. Everybody knows Serena."

Which meant everyone knew she was pregnant. Montebello wasn't all that big. And by now, after renting the restaurant for her last night, everyone had, no doubt, guessed that he was the father of her baby, he thought grimly. And that only gave him one more reason to pressure her into marrying him. He didn't want people talking about her or his baby.

"So you'll send someone to the cottage?" he asked Angelo. "I'd like to surprise her."

"Peter will be right there," he assured him. "Give him ten minutes."

It was more like fifteen minutes than ten when Peter, Angelo's oldest driver, arrived. Sitting atop one of the horse-drawn carriages Angelo rented out to tourists, he spoke to the horse as if she were an old and dear friend. "C'mon, Daisy, you can make it, old girl. I know it's late and you want to go back to the barn, but we've got to surprise a pretty lady. That'a girl. I thought that would do it. We can't keep a lady waiting."

Making no attempt to hide his smile, Rafe greeted Peter with a nod. "Thanks for coming out tonight, man. I owe you one."

They both knew Peter would be well compensated, but all the older man said was, "It looks like everyone's gone to bed, Your Grace. I can come back tomorrow night, if you'd rather do this then."

Rafe considered the suggestion for all of two seconds, then shook his head. "Thanks, Peter, but I'd rather do it tonight. A woman likes to be surprised, so I don't think she'll mind me waking her up. Wait here. I'll be right back.''

Leaving him at the gate, he approached the cottage on silent feet and stared at the darkened windows with a frown. How was he supposed to wake Serena up without waking her father up, too? he wondered. Then he remembered that she'd told him on the night they'd met six months ago that her bedroom windows overlooked a rose garden. At the time, he hadn't realized she was talking about the royal garden right there in the palace.

Moving around to the side of the small two-story cottage, he gazed up at the only windows that overlooked the garden. They had to be Serena's. "You better hope you heard her correctly," he muttered as he reached down and grabbed some pebbles from the walkway. "Otherwise, you're going to have to deal with Nathan, and he's not going to be thrilled at the idea of his daughter receiving visitors in the middle of the night."

Knowing that, he was still willing to risk her father's wrath to see her. Taking a chance, he tossed the pebbles at her window.

Chapter 8

Her head buried beneath her pillow, Serena heard the light tapping at her window and frowned sleepily. It sounded as though it was raining, but it couldn't be. She'd listened to the weather before she'd gone to bed, just as she did every night, and there'd been no forecast of rain for the rest of the week. Her imagination had to be playing tricks on her.

Telling herself to go back to sleep, she settled into a more comfortable position and yawned tiredly. Then she heard it again...the sound of something hitting the window, and this time, she could tell it wasn't rain. So what the heck was it? Barely able to open her eyes, she groaned and crawled out of bed, knowing she wouldn't be able to sleep until she got up to investigate.

Not bothering to turn on a light, she stumbled over to the window and half expected to see a storm brewing outside, in spite of the forecast. After all, Montebello was an island, and unexpected storms blew up all the time.

But when she glanced outside, she immediately spied the cause of her sleeplessness, and it wasn't a storm. It was Rafe, and he was standing right below her window, throwing pebbles up at her.

A surprised smile blossomed on her lips. How had he known she needed to see him just once before the day ended? Throwing open the sash, she leaned out the window and called softly, "Did you lose your way, Your Grace? The palace is the other way."

"I've come to take you for a ride," he replied in a voice as hushed as hers, and turned to motion to the horse and buggy and driver who waited just beyond the cottage's picket fence. "It's the only way to see the harbor."

Entranced, Serena would have fallen in love with him at that moment if she hadn't already been crazy about him. She'd grown up on Montebello. All her life, she'd watched the tourists take a slow, romantic carriage ride along the harbor, and envied them. But gardener's daughters couldn't afford the fare for such a frivolous outing, and even if she could have come up with the money, there'd been no man she'd cared to share the experience with. Except Rafe. And until that night at Julia's wedding when she'd bumped into him in all her borrowed finery, he hadn't known she was alive.

Suddenly feeling as if her heart had wings, she smiled and had no idea how beautiful she looked in the moonlight. "I'll be right down. Give me a second to get dressed."

Ducking back inside, she shut the window and hurriedly switched on a light. It was cold out—she needed something warm to wear—and she refused to even consider why it had to be pretty. It just did. And she had just the thing. Pleased, she rushed to her closet for the emerald sweater and maternity jeans her father had given her for Christmas.

Two minutes later, when she slipped outside and found Rafe waiting for her on the front stoop, she told herself she was breathless because she'd thrown on her clothes in a rush. But she knew the frantic pounding of her heart had nothing to do with the speed with which she'd dressed and everything to do with Rafe. He just looked so wonderful in the moonlight.

"Hi," she said shyly.

"Hi." Taking her hand, he smiled into her eyes. "Ready?"

When he stood so close and looked at her like that, she was ready for anything. Nodding, she squeezed his hand and let him lead her to the carriage.

And just that easily, the night turned magical.

Dazed, Serena stepped into the carriage and sank down onto the cushioned seat. Rafe's arm slipped around her shoulders to pull her close against his side. A split second later the driver, seated high up on his seat at the back of the carriage, clicked his tongue and called softly to Daisy to take them on a spin around the harbor. Nodding her head as if she understood every word, the mare snorted and headed back to the village at a slow, leisurely pace.

If this is a dream, Serena told herself, I never want to wake up. Hidden from the driver's view by the small canopied roof that protected the occupants from the weather, they seemed totally alone in the world. They spoke in soft whispers and touched and laughed together and were aware of nothing but each other. And when the harbor came into view, they never even noticed until the driver stopped at the village fountain so the horse could get a drink.

Serena would have been content to stay right where she was, with Rafe's arm around her shoulder, holding her close, but he had other ideas. "C'mon," he murmured, "let's go for a walk."

"Now? But what about our ride?"

"Peter'll wait for us. Won't you, Peter?" he called up to the driver as he helped her from the carriage. "We're going to take a stroll up to the overlook. You don't mind, do you? We won't be gone long."

His smile understanding, the older man said, "Take your time, Your Grace. Daisy isn't as young as she used to be. She'll welcome the rest."

"I'll buy her an extra bale of hay for the late hour," Rafe promised with a grin. "We'll be right back."

They had both seen the harbor overlook more times than either of them could remember, but as Rafe tucked her arm in his and urged her up the stairs to the high point where wives had waited for their seafaring husbands for centuries, anyone would have thought he was a kid rushing to beat his friends to the top for the first time. He didn't give her a chance to so much as catch her breath at the halfway point before he started up the last flight.

Panting, her side aching, she gasped, "Are we going to a fire or what? What's the hurry?"

"This," he growled, and pulled her into his arms. The second his mouth covered hers, they were both transported back to the day at the beach and the quiet intimacy they found there. He kissed her hungrily, tenderly, with a sweet need that brought tears to her eyes, and suddenly Serena's breathlessness had nothing to do with rushing her up the stairs and everything to do with Rafe. She loved him so much! With every touch, every kiss, she could feel them growing closer, and she knew he felt it, too. And it was wonderful. With a murmur, she melted against him, wanting, needing more.

Just that easily, she destroyed him. His mind blurred, his common sense flew right out of his head, and all he could think of was that he never wanted to let her go again. Tearing his mouth from hers, he kissed his way down the side of her neck and growled, ''Marry me, Serena. You know it's the right thing to do. We're having a baby together. We need to be married.''

The second the words were out of his mouth, he knew he'd made a mistake. Serena stiffened, then, before he could stop her, stepped free of his touch. In the glare of the harbor lights below, her face was pale, her eyes stricken. ''No,'' she said stiffly. ''I won't marry you because of the baby.'' The matter settled, she wrapped her arms around herself and turned away. ''I'd like to go home now. I'm cold.''

Silently cursing, Rafe wanted to kick himself. Dammit, he never should have pushed her. Anna had warned him, but all he'd been able to think of was how much he wanted her in his arms, his bed, his life. The words had just slipped out, and now he couldn't take them back. He didn't even try. Without a word, he escorted her to the carriage.

The ride back to her father's cottage was very different from the one to the harbor. This time, Serena sat as far away from him as she could manage without falling out of the carriage, and he made no move to put his arm around her. He didn't dare. Sitting side by side, they stared straight ahead and didn't say a single word all the way back to the palace.

Serena didn't sleep the rest of the night. She couldn't. Every time she closed her eyes, she heard Rafe say over and over again, "Marry me... We're having a baby together... We need to be married."

Just thinking about it twisted a knife in her heart. After the incredibly romantic afternoon they'd shared, she'd foolishly thought he was falling in love with her. So much for fairy tales and happily-ever-afters. He didn't love her. He just wanted to make sure that the baby wasn't illegitimate.

She should have been furious. At the very least, she was entitled to more than a little outrage. He'd deliberately set her up—there was no question of that. He'd set a seductive scene with the intimate carriage ride, the soft touches and hot glances under a romantic starry sky, and then he'd surprised her with another marriage proposal. And she'd very nearly fallen for it. If they'd had a few more moments alone together at the overlook, if he hadn't rushed the proposal but taken the time to kiss her once more, she would have been hard-pressed to resist him.

And it was that, more than anything, that kept her up the rest of the night. What if he tried it again? How would she ever be able to tell him no when all she wanted was for him to hold her again, to kiss her, and to promise her they could spend the rest of their lives together?

She had to get out of there.

With the rising of the morning sun, she knew she

had no choice. She had to leave. Now, while she still could. Because if she didn't, he would wear her down and it would only be a matter of time before she gave him the answer he wanted.

But where would she go? And how? She had some money set aside for when the baby was born, but it wasn't nearly enough to support the two of them for an extended time. She had to have help, and even though she knew her father would do what he could for her, his resources were limited. Anna, however, knew people all over the world. Surely, she knew someone who was in need of a gardener who would give her shelter until she had the baby and was ready to go back to work.

Hurriedly throwing on the same outfit she'd worn last night when she'd rushed downstairs to meet Rafe, she impatiently waited until her father's old mantel clock struck seven before hurrying out of the cottage to the palace stables. It was a cold morning, but for as long as Serena could remember, Anna invariably started her day with a ride whenever she could. Serena was counting that this day was no different.

Bundled in a wool jacket that had once been her father's, Serena rushed into the stables like a woman possessed and was sure she'd missed her when she found the place deserted. Disappointed and feeling as if she was going to shatter at any second, she sank down into a pile of hay in the empty stall of Anna's favorite mount, Napoleon. Then she heard her friend conversing with her horse as if he could understand every word as they slowly made their way toward Napoleon's stall.

"You should have known better than to try and take that fence," she scolded. "If Mother had seen me take that tumble, you'd be on your way to the glue factory right now, and I'd be confined to my room—Serena! What are you doing here? Are you okay?"

Dragging herself up from the hay she'd dropped into, Serena forced a crooked smile. "I should be asking you the same thing. It sounds like you took quite a fall."

"It was nothing," she said with a grimace, sweeping back the fall of dark curls that had tumbled in her face. "What are you doing here this early? I thought you'd be in the greenhouse."

Serena hadn't meant to cry, but suddenly tears were welling in her eyes. "I need your help. I have to leave."

Horrified, Anna rushed forward to console her. "Why? What's happened?"

"He just won't let go of this idea of getting married." Wiping away her tears, she told her about yesterday and how vulnerable she'd become to his kisses. "I have to get out of here, Anna, before I do something stupid. And I don't know where to go."

"But don't you think you should at least talk to Rafe? Maybe he really is falling in love with you."

"Then why didn't he mention it?"

Anna didn't have an answer for that. "I still think you should talk to him, but if you want to leave, you know I'll help you. You can go to the ski lodge. No one's using it right now, and Rafe will never think to look for you there." Handing Napoleon over to a groom, she told her, "C'mon. I'll go call Leonardo right now and let him know you're coming. He'll take good care of you."

Serena didn't doubt that he would. From what

she'd heard, the caretaker had been with the family as long as her father had and would do anything the family asked of him. Touched by her friend's generosity, she hugged her. "Thank you," she choked. "You don't know what this means to me. I didn't sleep all night. I'm just so afraid Rafe's going to catch me in a weak moment. You won't tell Rafe, will you? I know how much you want the two of us to get together."

To her credit, Anna didn't lie. "I think you belong together, but that isn't my place to decide," she replied honestly. "Right now, my only concern is you and the baby. Go pack your things while I call the lodge. Then I'll take you to the airport."

If there was one thing Serena knew about Anna, it was that she had her welfare at heart and would never deliberately do anything to hurt her. Satisfied that she could trust her, she sighed in relief. "Thanks. You don't know what this means to me. I'll be ready in ten minutes." Turning away, she hurried to the cottage to pack.

Chapter 9

Serena had never been to the lodge, but she'd seen
pictures, and they didn't do it justice. Located high
in the Italian Alps, but only a couple of miles from
an excellent hospital, it had been owned by the Se-
bastianis for generations and was absolutely beautiful.
Serena took one look at it and knew why Anna and
the rest of the family loved coming there.

"You like it, *signorina?*" Leonardo asked with a
kind smile as he fetched her luggage from the taxi
that had brought her from the village's small airport.
"You'll be happy here."

If she hadn't already been missing Rafe so, Serena
would have agreed with him. After all, how could
anyone not love the place? Nestled among fir and pine
trees that were thick with snow, the old log-and-rock
lodge fairly oozed charm with its diamond-paned
windows, steep-gabled roof, and arched doors. Smoke
rose from the rock chimneys, and with no effort what-

soever, Serena could picture herself curled in front of the fire…with Rafe.

"*Signorina?* Are you all right? Why do you look so sad?"

Caught up in her musings, Serena jerked back to awareness to find Leonardo watching her, his weathered face lined with concern. *Don't!* she wanted to cry. *Please don't show me any sympathy.* But he was only being kind, and she couldn't be rude. "It's nothing," she said with a weak smile. "I'm just tired. It's been a long day."

"And a long trip," he added. "Please, come inside. I have dinner on the stove. You will eat, then rest. For the bambino, yes?"

At the mention of her baby, Serena felt her heart lift. He was right. She would eat and rest and do whatever was necessary for her baby. That was, after all, the reason she'd made the trip to Italy. It was a mother's responsibility to give her child the best life she could, and she couldn't do that if she married a man she didn't love. If she'd just remember that, she would find a way to get through the next few weeks and months until the baby was born.

"Yes," she replied. "For the *bambina.*"

"Ah, a girl," he laughed. "Every man wants a son…until he has a daughter." Loaded down with luggage, he motioned her ahead of him through the front door of the lodge, chattering all the while. "Did Princess Anna tell you about my Angela? My granddaughter? She's two, and such a beauty. And headstrong! Goodness, that child has a mind of her own!"

Clearly crazy about his granddaughter, he rambled fondly on as he carried Serena's luggage up to her room, and Serena was thankful for his presence and the conversation. She didn't want to be alone with her thoughts.

It was growing late, however, and Leonardo eventually had to retire to the small cottage he lived in behind the main house. Staying long enough to make sure she was settled in and comfortable, he served her a steaming bowl of stew, then wished her good night and slipped out the back door.

In the silence left behind by his leavetaking, the fire crackled merrily, but Serena took little comfort from it. She'd managed to push back thoughts of Rafe all day, but she was tired, her defenses down. When loneliness crept in and tugged at her heartstrings, she couldn't stop herself from thinking of him. She'd done the right thing by leaving—there was no question of that. She just hadn't expected to miss him so much. Tears gathered in her eyes, and this time, she didn't try to blink them away. What did it matter? There was no one there to see.

Rafe knew he should have called first before showing up unannounced at Serena's door, but after the way he'd blown things last night, he was afraid she'd hang up on him if he called. Hopefully, she wouldn't be quite so quick to slam the door in his face. He had given her most of the day to get over her hurt—now if she'd just give him a few moments to apologize, maybe they could find a way to get past all this. If she didn't, he had no one to blame but himself.

He thought he was braced for anything...until her father opened the door at his knock and announced, "She's not here."

Disappointed, he said, "Would you ask her to call me when she gets in—"

"She won't be coming back, Your Grace," Nathan Winters cut in smoothly. "She's moved out."

Rafe took the news like a blow to the heart. "What do you mean *moved out?* Where? She's pregnant! She's got no business being alone."

"I agree. But she felt like she couldn't stay here any longer."

He didn't say, *Because of you,* but Rafe heard the words nonetheless. And he knew the old man was right. He'd pushed her to this, and the knowledge knotted in his gut like a fist. "Where is she?" he asked quietly. "I need to speak to her, to apologize."

For a moment he thought he saw sympathy in Nathan's eyes, but then, with a blink, it was gone. Standing proudly in the doorway, he met Rafe's gaze head-on and said, "I can't tell you that, Your Grace. She asked me not to."

If he'd been a petty man, Rafe could have gotten him fired for that, and they both knew it. But how could he do something so hateful to a man who was only protecting his daughter? If their circumstances had been reversed, Rafe would have done the same thing. And for what it was worth, he needed her father to know that.

"I know this won't change anything," he told him, "but I understand, and I don't blame you. This is my fault. I asked her to marry me again. It's the right thing to do, but I guess she wasn't ready to hear that."

"Have you ever stopped to think that maybe she did hear you but what you're asking isn't the right thing for her?"

Caught off guard, Rafe blinked. "What?"

"Marriage might be right for you, but obviously it's not for Serena," he replied. "I'm not saying that's what I want for her, but this isn't about me. It's *her* life, not mine. Like it or not, she's doing what's right for her. Do you love her enough to let her do that? Even if that means letting her walk away from you because it's best for her? If you don't, you've got no business asking her to spend the rest of her life with you.''

Shaken by the questions Nathan threw at him like darts, Rafe told himself that his need to marry Serena had nothing to do with love. He cared about her and his baby. That was enough.

Yeah, right! a voice in his head drawled. *Why don't you admit why you're really worried? Sure, you care about her and the baby, but not knowing where she is is tearing you apart because you're afraid you've lost her. You think she's not going to come back after the baby is born and you'll never see her again.*

No! he almost roared. She wouldn't do that. Would she?

Suddenly afraid, he said hoarsely, ''I want Serena to be happy—with me. We're having a baby. We need to be together. But you don't have to worry. I won't ask you again where she is. I wouldn't ask you to betray her confidence. I'll find her some other way.''

He meant every word—unfortunately, he didn't have a clue where to begin looking for her. But he knew someone who did. Anna. Turning sharply, he returned to the palace.

''No.''

Stunned, Rafe couldn't believe he'd heard her correctly. ''What do you mean…*no?* She's your friend and she's six months' pregnant! There's no way you let her leave Montebello without finding out where she was going. Hell,'' he added in disgust, ''you probably helped her leave.''

She didn't deny it and that was a dead giveaway, but she didn't waste her breath making excuses neither one of them would believe. Instead, she lounged comfortably on the couch in the library and never took her eyes from the book she was reading. ''I have nothing to say to you, Rafe. Go away.''

''Dammit, Anna, I have to talk to her! I don't want to lose her—''

Her head snapped up at that. ''Why?''

''Don't even think about going there,'' he growled. ''I went through this with her father—I won't with you. I'm not in love with her!''

''Then you have nothing to say to her,'' she retorted, deliberately returning her attention to her book. ''In case you hadn't noticed, you've already lost her.''

He swore royally, using a few choice phrases that Anna had never heard anyone use in quite that way before. ''Congratulations,'' she said dryly. ''You have quite a way with words. So does this author. Now if you'll excuse me...''

His lips twitching in spite of his frustration, Rafe couldn't help but be impressed. She didn't do it often, but when she looked down her nose like a queen dismissing a subject, she did it damn well. ''Nice try,'' he told her, ''but I'm not going anywhere. Not until I know where Serena's gone.'' And giving action to his words, he pushed her feet to the side of the chaise longue she reclined on and sat down next to her. His eyes fixed unblinkingly on her, he just sat there, staring.

''Damn you, Rafe, stop it! I promised her I wouldn't tell you!''

''Then I guess you'll have to break your promise.''

''I will not! Serena—''

Before she could say another word, the phone beside her chair rang. With a sigh of relief, Anna snatched it up. Any distraction to get him off her back. ''Hello?''

''Anna? Thank God! I was afraid you wouldn't be home and I didn't know what to do!''

At the sound of Serena's panic-stricken voice, Anna stiffened in alarm. ''What's wrong? Are you okay?''

''No!'' she sobbed. ''I think I'm going into labor!''

''What?! You can't be! It's too soon.''

Dragging in a shaky breath, Serena swallowed more tears. ''I know,'' she said thickly. ''But I've been having contractions for the last hour and they only seem to be getting worse. Can you come? I don't know what to do, and I don't want to be alone.''

Worried sick, Anna didn't hesitate. ''Of course. But it's going to take me a while to get there. You can't wait that long to see a doctor. Have Leonardo take you to the hospital. I'll be there as soon as I can.''

Her mind already jumping to how she was going to get to Italy as quickly as possible, Anna had completely forgotten Rafe's presence…until she hung up and turned to find him blocking her path. She had only to take one look at the jut of his jaw to know that he had not only guessed that the call was from Serena, but that he was determined not to let her go anywhere without him.

Swearing silently, she warned, ''Don't even think

about going with me, Rafe. She doesn't want to see you."

"I don't care," he retorted. "She's in trouble, isn't she? What's wrong? Dammit, Anna, tell me! It's the baby, isn't it?"

She shouldn't have told him. She'd given Serena her word. But when she'd made that promise, she'd never dreamed that Serena would go into labor months before the baby was due.

Afraid for her, she nodded. "Yes. She's having contractions. She's afraid the baby's coming and she's scared to death. I can't let her go through this alone."

"Neither can I," he said grimly. "I'm going with you. She's at the lodge, isn't she?"

Since he'd heard her mention Leonardo, there was no point in denying it. He, as she, had been going to the lodge with the rest of the family all his life and was well acquainted with Leonardo. "Yes, but she doesn't want to see you."

"We'll take my jet," he continued as if she hadn't spoken. "C'mon. I'll call the airport from the car and have the jet gassed up. It'll be ready when we get there."

Turning sharply on his heel, he strode out, leaving Anna staring after him in frustration. Damn him, she didn't have time to argue with him, and he knew it. Promising herself she was going to give him a serious piece of her mind on the way to Italy, she was left with no choice but to follow.

Chapter 10

He'd learned to fly when he was eighteen, and he loved it. But as Rafe took off from Montebello and raced toward Italy, he cursed the jet because it seemed as though it was barely moving. Serena needed him and he wasn't there for her. If something happened to her or the baby, he'd never forgive himself.

"She's going to be okay," Anna said quietly beside him. "She has to be."

He wanted to believe her, but he'd never been so worried in his life. Or felt so helpless. He didn't know a thing about pregnant women or babies. Even if he got to her in time, how could he help her?

"I feel like a heel," he said, staring unseeingly at the horizon in the distance. "I pushed her too hard, and she bolted. You told me to give her some time, but all I could think of was that we were running out of time. I wanted us to be married by the time the baby was born, and now that seems so unimportant."

"You couldn't have known this was going to happen, Rafe. No one could. Don't beat yourself up."

"But she's pregnant," he argued. "I should have realized the stress wouldn't be good for her. If anything happens, I wouldn't blame her if she never spoke to me again."

"Don't talk like that," Anna scolded. "Nothing's going to happen. Leonardo took her to the hospital as soon as we hung up. She's in good hands."

Rafe wanted to believe her, but he couldn't remember the last time he'd been so scared. With his father's death, there'd been no emergency—he'd died peacefully in his sleep, so there'd been no time to worry, only to grieve. This was much more frightening. Women died in childbirth. Granted, with modern medicine, that didn't happen nearly as often as it once had, but there was still a danger...for both Serena and the baby. And there wasn't a damn thing he could do to help either one of them.

"I hope so," he said gruffly. "Because if something happens to her or the baby, I don't know how I'm going to stand it. I'll spend the rest of my life blaming myself."

Anna was feeling more than a little guilty herself. She should have insisted that Serena talk to her doctor to make sure it was all right for her to travel at this time in her pregnancy. But she hadn't even thought of that.

"I'm not exactly proud of myself, either," she admitted huskily. "I should have tried harder to talk her into staying. But she seemed so determined to go, and I was afraid she'd leave anyway if I didn't do something. So I arranged for her to go to the lodge. I thought she'd be safer there. It never entered my head that she'd be a long way from home if something happened.''

Using her own words to comfort her, Rafe said, ''You couldn't have known this was going to happen.''

No, she couldn't have, she silently agreed. That didn't make her feel any less guilty...or make the waiting any easier. Even though she knew Rafe was flying as fast as he dared, she just wished they'd hurry up and get there. Every second lost was one in which Serena could be losing the baby.

Lying in her hospital bed, Serena fought back tears. It had been touch and go for a while, but the doctors had finally managed to stop her labor. The baby, thank God, was all right, but the doctors had scolded her for not taking better care of herself. They'd advised her to avoid stress as much as possible until the baby was born and to rest more. Just to make sure she did, they'd insisted she stay the night in the hospital.

She knew it was for the best, but all she wanted to do was to go home. Not to the lodge, but to her small bedroom under the eaves of her father's cottage in Montebello. She hadn't even been gone an entire day, and she was already so homesick, she could have cried.

But tears wouldn't do either her or the baby any good, she reminded herself. She had to relax, to rest, and to somehow find a way to forget about Rafe. She didn't kid herself into thinking it was going to be easy. Not when he haunted every waking and sleeping moment. And it would only get worse when the baby came. Every time she looked at the sweet, wonderful baby they had created together, she would be reminded of him.

He doesn't love you, a voice in her head reminded her. *He isn't worth all this pain.*

She knew that, but it didn't change a thing. She'd never felt so alone in her life.

Lost in her misery, she didn't even hear the soft tap at the closed door to her private room. Anna poked her head inside the door and grinned at her. "Is this where they lock up the mothers-to-be? I've got a file in my purse. Want me to break you out?"

"Anna!" Thrilled that she'd come, Serena hugged her fiercely when she stepped over to the bed. "How did you get here so fast? I was just lying here thinking how lonely I was—"

Whatever she was going to say next was lost when she looked past Anna and saw Rafe standing in the doorway. Stiffening, she pulled back to give Anna an accusing look. "You told him where I was!"

"I had to. He was there when you called."

"I don't care. You didn't have to bring him with you—"

"She didn't," Rafe growled, stepping farther into the room. "*I* brought *her.* We came in my jet."

"Then you can just turn around and fly back home again," she told him flatly. "I don't want you here."

Rafe hadn't expected her to welcome him with open arms, but her words hurt nonetheless. And that irritated him. He'd spent the past few hours worried sick about her and had pushed his jet to a speed that no sane man would have dared, and this was the thanks he got? He didn't think so!

"I'm sorry you feel that way," he retorted coolly. "But just for the record, that's my baby you're carrying, and I'm not going anywhere. If you don't like it, too bad."

Her eyes narrowed at that. "Don't think you can waltz in here and throw your title around, Your Grace. I doubt that my doctor will be impressed. He specifically ordered me to avoid all stress for the duration of my pregnancy, and in case you haven't noticed, you're stressing me out!"

That was an understatement. She looked as if she wanted to skin him alive, and if circumstances had been different, Rafe would have laughed. But that really would have sent her over the edge, and that was the last thing he wanted to do.

"Look," he said with a sigh, "I didn't come here to upset you. I just needed to see for myself that you and the baby were all right. If you'd just let me take care of you..."

"Why? So you can catch me in a weak moment and convince me to marry you? No, thanks." Dismissing him, she deliberately turned to Anna. "Would you call my doctor for me and talk him into releasing me? I need you to call Leonardo, too, and arrange for him to drive me to a hotel. Obviously, I won't be staying at the lodge—I can't trust your cousin to leave me alone now that he knows where I am."

"Dammit, Serena!"

Ignoring him, she added, "I have enough money for a week or so at an inexpensive hotel. After that, I'll have to call my father. I hate to ask him to dip into his savings, but I'll pay him back as soon as the baby's born and I can go back to work."

"Don't be ridiculous," Rafe growled. "There's no need for you to ask your father for money—or for you to work, for that matter. You know I'll take care of you and the baby.''

"Thank you, but that's not necessary," she replied with a toss of her head. "We don't need your help. I'm perfectly capable of taking care of myself and my baby.''

"Really? Then why do you need to borrow money from your father, Miss Independence? Why are you even in the hospital to begin with?''

Listening to the two of them go at each other, Anna had had enough. "Stop it!" she cried. "Stop it right this minute!''

Caught up in their own frustration, Rafe and Serena both blinked in surprise. That was all Anna needed to get a word in edgewise. "Will you two listen to yourselves? You sound like you hate each other's guts!''

"It's not me, it's her! She won't listen to reason.''

"No, I won't listen to all this dribble about responsibility! Maybe that's why dukes get married, but that's not a good enough reason for this gardener's daughter. Tell him, Anna—''

"Knock it off!" she snapped. "I mean it!" she said when they both sputtered in protest. "This has gone on long enough. Why are you doing this? Do you even know? No, don't answer that," she said quickly before they could start up again. "Anyone with eyes can see you're in love with each other.''

"We are not!''

"Oh, yes, you are," she told Rafe. "And don't tell me I don't know what I'm talking about just because I've never been in love. I've been around plenty of people who have, and you've got all the symptoms. The second you thought Serena was in trouble, you came running to her rescue.''

"Because I was concerned!"

"Because you love her," she corrected. "And she loves you. But will you admit it to each other? Hell, no! You're both so afraid of getting hurt that that's exactly what's going to happen if you're not careful."

She'd wanted to get their attention and she finally had, but they both remained stubbornly silent and that just frustrated her all over again. "I could just shake you both. Don't you realize you have something most people would give their eyeteeth for and you're throwing it away? Love means taking a chance, having the faith to know that if you fall, the other person will be there to catch you. But all you can think of is you don't want to get hurt. Well, who does? That doesn't mean you can go through life avoiding hurt. If you do, you might as well go home and lock yourself in your rooms. You're not living."

She'd hoped to generate some response from them, to shake them up and open their eyes, but if she'd touched a cord in either one of them, there was no sign of it. They wouldn't even look at each other. And that hurt. They loved each other so much, but if they refused to admit it to each other, she could talk until she was blue in the face, and it wouldn't change a thing.

"I've been trying to get you two back together since last summer," she said quietly, defeated. "Obviously it's not working, so from now on, I'm going to mind my own business. If you'd rather be alone and miserable than happy and together, have a good time. I'm out of here." And without another word, she turned and walked out.

Chapter 11

The door swished shut behind her, leaving a silence that was as deep as the grave. Dutifully chastised, Rafe knew he was the one Anna was most disgusted with and he couldn't say he blamed her. She was right. He'd acted like an idiot, refusing to face how he really felt because he was afraid of getting hurt. He'd told himself he was only protecting himself, but in the end, he'd nearly lost the only person in the world that meant everything to him. Serena.

He loved her.

The wonder of it hit him like a bolt of lightning and nearly knocked him out of his shoes. How had she stolen his heart? When? He couldn't even say; he just knew that it seemed as though he'd felt this way from the first moment he'd met her. And he'd stupidly wanted to believe it was just lust.

What a jackass he was. He was thirty-four years old, for God's sake, and he'd dated his share of women over the years. He knew what lust was, and what he felt for Serena went a hell of a lot deeper than that. It seemed as though he'd been looking for her his entire life and he hadn't even known it.

He had to tell her.

But when his eyes met hers, baring his soul wasn't nearly as easy as he'd thought it would be. Doubts crept in. There was no question in his mind or heart that he loved her and wanted to spend the rest of his life with her. But what if Anna was wrong and Serena didn't feel the same way he did? What if Serena'd really meant it when she'd said she didn't want to marry him?

Love means taking a chance, having the faith to know that if you fall, the other person will be there to catch you.

Anna's words rang in his ears, encouraging him. Still, he couldn't help but hesitate. Did he have that much faith in Serena? Could he trust her to be there for him if he let down his guard and opened his heart to her? There was only one way to find out.

Stepping away from the door, he approached her hospital bed cautiously, not wanting to upset her but unable to keep his distance when he told her how he felt about her. "She's right," he said quietly. "I was afraid to admit how I felt about you. For the past six months, ever since I woke up the morning after Julia's wedding and found you gone, I couldn't get you out of my head. Everywhere I went, I found myself looking for you."

"Rafe, I was always right there at the palace."

"I know that now, but at the time, I didn't know anything about you except that your name was Serena. When I couldn't find you, I told myself I didn't care. But I couldn't wait for Aunt Gwen and Uncle Marcus's New Year's Eve party because I was hoping you'd be there. I looked all over the palace for you that night. Then, when I stepped outside, there you were, waiting for me right there in the garden.''

"I was restless," she admitted huskily. "Anna told me you were coming for the party, and I wanted to see you, but I couldn't. I knew you would propose once you found out I was pregnant, and I didn't want that."

"And like a fool, that's exactly what I did," he said with a grimace. "I didn't want to lose you again, so I used the baby as an excuse. Even when your father told me you'd left Montebello, I refused to look too closely at my own feelings. Then I was with Anna when you called and told her you were having contractions."

Blinking back tears, she dropped a protective hand to her belly. "I was so scared. She's so much a part of my life already, and she's not even here yet. I didn't know what I would do if I lost her."

Needing to touch her, he covered her hand with his and felt his heart turn over when his daughter kicked in what seemed to be approval. "I know, honey. I felt the same way about you and the baby. Why do you think I insisted on flying Anna over here? I had to see for myself that you were okay. Because I love you."

There. He'd said it, and he couldn't help but wonder why he'd been afraid of those three little words for so long. Telling Serena how he felt about her was as natural as breathing.

"I love you," he said again, and knew that if she gave him a chance, a day wouldn't go by from now on that he wouldn't tell her how he felt about her. "I love you and I want to spend the rest of my life with you…as your husband."

"Oh, Rafe…"

She didn't say she loved him, too, but he saw emotion flash in her eyes and wanted to take her in his arms. But he couldn't. Not yet. Not until he was sure she understood why he was asking her to marry him. Taking both her hands in his, he said huskily, "This has nothing to do with the baby. Even if you weren't pregnant, I'd still want to marry you. I know," he said before she could say anything, "talk's cheap and I might be saying this just so you'll marry me. I'm not, but there's no way for me to prove I love you. You're going to just have to take me on faith."

Could she do that? Serena wondered as her eyes searched his. Could she believe this sudden declaration of love? Her common sense said no. It was just too convenient. The only reason he was bringing up love now was because he couldn't find any other way to convince her to marry him.

But even as her head was telling her to not be taken in, her heart was reading his eyes. And the steady, glowing love she saw there was all the proof she needed to convince her that he was telling the truth. A man didn't look at a woman like that if he didn't mean it. Especially Rafe. She'd never known a man with more honest eyes. He couldn't fake something he didn't really feel.

He loved her!

The wonder of it filled her like the warm rays of the sun after weeks of rain. For years she'd watched him from a distance whenever he'd visited his aunt and uncle and cousins at the palace, and she'd never ceased to be fascinated by him. But it wasn't until she'd met him the night of Princess Julia's wedding that she'd fallen in love with him. Even then, she'd thought her love for him was doomed. After all, he was a duke and she a gardener's daughter. How could they possibly have a future together?

Oh, ye of little faith, she thought ruefully. All this time, Anna had encouraged her to take a chance, to believe in happily ever after. She should have listened. Because life really could be a fairy tale if you just believed.

Love for her very own Prince Charming filling her heart with joy, she reached for him. "I love you, too," she said huskily. "So much it hurts sometimes. That's why I kept turning down your proposal. I couldn't marry you if you didn't love me as much as I loved you."

"Thank God you did," he said with a smile, wrapping his arms around her to cradle her close. "You were driving me crazy, but you did the right thing. If you hadn't forced me to look at my feelings, I would have married you without knowing that I loved you and we both would have been miserable."

Leaning down, he kissed her hungrily, and they both knew it was better than anything to be found in a fairy tale. And when he finally let her up for air, they were both smiling. "When are you going to marry me?" he growled.

"When you put a ring on my finger," she said with a grin, holding up her left hand. "Size six, yellow gold."

"I'll get right on it," he promised. And after giving her one more scorching kiss, he reluctantly released her and called for the one person who had been there for both of them all along. "Anna? Get back in here—I need your help. I need to buy a ring. Today!"

* * * * *

Next month meet the rest of the
royal family of Montebello in
ROMANCING THE CROWN,
brand-new, twelve-book continuing series!
The glamour and excitement begins with
THE MAN WHO WOULD BE KING,
by Linda Turner.
Available in January, 2002
from Silhouette Intimate Moments.

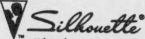

When California's most talked about dynasty is
threatened, only family, privilege and the power
of love can protect them!

THE COLTONS

Coming in December 2001

THE HOUSEKEEPER'S DAUGHTER

by

Laurie Paige

Mighty Navy SEAL Drake Colton could handle the most
dangerous military mission. But when the woman
carrying his child closed her heart to him, Drake was
puzzled. He was used to getting what he wanted—and
Maya Ramirez would not be the exception!

Available at your favorite retail outlet.

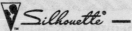

AT TWILIGHT...

they awaken with a growing hunger and need. Yet the yearning isn't always for blood, but rather a true joining....

Born in Twilight
"Beyond Twilight"

Don't miss these wonderful, stirring stories from *USA Today* bestselling author

MAGGIE SHAYNE's

WINGS IN THE NIGHT

series, coming to your local stores February 2002.

Available at your favorite retail outlet.

Silhouette®

Where love comes alive™